THE RAINBOW PLAYER

DAVID KERBY-KENDALL

Whiteley Publishing

Published by Whiteley Publishing Ltd
www.whiteleypublishing.com
First paperback edition (published as 'The Last Taboo') 2014
Second paperback edition (published as 'Sammy')2016
Third paperback edition 2017
ISBN 978-1-908586-87-2
Author's photograph by MAD Photography
Cover design by Adam Lewis

For my Nan, G. Caroline Kendall
(who was a shoulder to lean on, lender of money when I was a teenager
and my soul-mate)

ACKNOWLEDGEMENT

I would like to thank: HT for her knowledge of all things literary (and the coffees), Sam Hiller for his knowledge of all things football (and the coffees), Adam Lewis for his knowledge of all things graphic, Matt Nieman-Sims, Professor Mark Whiteley for his constant help together with his unceasing belief in my writing ability and Emily Whiteley for all her help and dealing with my unending emails and changes of mind.

DECISIONS (PROLOGUE)

I think they should introduce a school exam in 'Making Decisions'.

Then again, I'm not entirely sure.

Or maybe one in 'Saying the Right Thing at the Right Time'.

Perhaps invent a Time Machine that could take you back to just before those moments when you've opened your mouth and inserted two Doc Martens. We could call it the T.A.R.D.I.S. Time and Relative Dickhead-Inspired Statements.

I've always wanted to be the sort of person for whom the god of 'the right thing to say' was in perpetual attendance. Unfortunately, this has not always been the case. I'm thirty-one and still effortlessly making the same verbal Chernobyls as I was twenty years ago.

You know, those times when you're in a crowded bar in London and the music's so loud you can hear it in Reykjavik and it's got a bass line that measures 6.8 on the Richter Scale. You're talking to someone you've never met before and they've said something twice already and you've said 'sorry?' twice already and, because it's apparently less embarrassing to make a complete arse of yourself than to say 'sorry' again, this is what happens:

"Yeah, I'm going through a pretty bad time at the moment. I went bankrupt last month, my wife's left me and taken the kids with her and I'm living in a cardboard box outside Tesco."

"That's great. Cool. I think that warrants another beer!"

They say you never know the true value of a moment until it becomes a memory. I don't think that's true. I *know* that what I say next will inform the rest of my life. I wish I could say it was less than momentous, but I can't, because it is.

Maybe, if time wasn't linear, we could live different lives based on different decisions that we've made and, much later, see which one we liked the best.

Because, now I have *this* decision to make, and, in thirty years' time, I might say 'wow, what a great road my life has taken; full of hedgerows and no traffic jams and on and on into a perpetual sunset'; or I might say 'umm, interesting cul-de-sac'.

This should be an enchanted moment, but it's too important to be so. Maybe enchanted in thirty years when I look back with the reconfigured reality of nostalgia.

I know my heart has made the decision already and it's now gallivanting around my body, cheering my brain on. But my brain has seized; unable to form a sentence from letters and words it suddenly doesn't recognise. It's like sending a text; you don't know how the other person will feel about it because saying it out loud is so different from writing it down.

So, as I stand here in this fairground, looking at a little girl wearing her candy-floss as a wig and her mother trying to decide whether to be annoyed or laugh hysterically, I understand how thin the divide is between life's priorities: love and hate, right and wrong, scrambled eggs on toast or boiled eggs with soldiers. And I want to hug and hate the world for giving us these endless possibilities.

And, as I look into the eyes of the person I must give the answer to - an answer without hesitation, for then it would not be an answer - I search for the fifteen year-old inside me, so that he can push me toward what I already know I want to do.

Fifteen year-olds don't think, they just say. There is no analysis. There is a decision, be it right or wrong. When do we start making rules for ourselves, over-analysing, contorting the situation to talk ourselves in or out of it? What makes it happen? Our changing relationships with our parents? The putting away of childish things? Losing our virginity?

All I know is that I must conjure my teenage self, so that I can remember how he felt, how he flew...

1

I lost my virginity at a bus stop. Bit of a disaster really. Bus came before I did.

It was extraordinarily bad luck. Normally it would have been ten minutes late and, at fifteen, that's enough time to do it twice and smoke an after-shag fag.

On this one particular occasion, however, my awkward and generally inept attempt at becoming an instant Lothario was thwarted by the local bus timetable, for once, not appearing under 'Fiction'.

I could see the bus cresting the hill, its rather dirty and depressing mauve making very little difference to a drab and purgatorial November morning sky. It's strange, but I began to feel rather sorry for it. Weird that I should have emotional feelings for a bus whilst losing my virginity, but I couldn't help wondering how it felt about itself now, as opposed to its first day in service; leaving the garage, a sparkling sunset purple; new seats, pristine floors and stairs. It must have been so proud. And now, crawling and misfiring toward the end of its useful life.

At the same time that I was psychologically evaluating the bus, I was also trying to work out how long it would take before it reached the bus-stop; and, most importantly, whether I could finish before it got there. Though, to be honest, we'd only been going for a minute and I could quite easily have finished at least twice in that time. I guesstimated about fifteen seconds and, of course, now that I needed to finish, I couldn't. I was using my left arm to lean against the inner wall of the shelter and each panic-inducing thud of my new Timex watch brought the realisation that my sex-life was not going to begin with a vast display of fireworks and a John Williams movie score bringing things to a climax. Literally.

Katie (who'd been here several times before and was a connoisseur of the local bus shelters) couldn't actually see the bus but appeared to either have eyes in the back of her head or some sort of public transport claircogniscence. They could have used her as the forerunner of the satellite system. Perhaps she just heard the poor thing coughing its way down the hill, but within two and a half nanoseconds, she had pushed me out of her and pulled up her pants with one hand whilst using the other to retrieve the piece of chewing gum she had thoughtfully stuck on the glass before we began.

Consequently, when the bus began to arrive at the stop, it was greeted with the sight of a seemingly innocent schoolgirl standing next to a somewhat dishevelled and manic schoolboy with his erect penis flag-poling out of his flies, saluting the early morning traffic.

I dived behind Katie.

"Don't move," I said.

"Why?"

"Because my… 'thing' is still out."

"Well, put it away then."

"What do you think I'm trying to do?"

The bus doors opened.

"You getting on love?" intoned the driver, with the smug self-satisfaction of being on time for once.

"Yeah… just a sec."

"OK, done," I said.

Katie popped a large bubble in response. What it was supposed to convey, I have no idea. Nonchalance, I imagine.

We got on the bus. She immediately sat with her two best friends and began chatting to them as though nothing had happened. In her defence, I suppose, not a great deal *had* happened, but she could, at least, have looked a little pleased… or flustered… or something. But, no. There they sat; Alison Rombart, Nicole Kenwood and Katie Turnpike, combined IQ of a small hair-grip, slagging off anyone they hadn't already slagged off that week and discussing last night's episode of Coronation Street with almost biblical reverence.

I slid my satchel in front of my crotch (tight, black school trousers not the most useful things to hide an erection) and walked down the bus in as normal a manner as I could muster. Though, to everyone else, I probably looked like Bambi on ecstasy.

"Sam, mate, your team were shit last night."

'Oh God', I remember thinking; keep walking, but think of something witty to say back.

"Yeah, Nige. Yeah, they were."

Excellent. Brilliant comeback. Wilde at his best.

Luckily, Nige turned back to Robbo and continued discussing either football, masturbation or girls. These were the only things they ever discussed. Unfortunately they were the only things they ever discussed with girls as well, leaving them, unsurprisingly, with experience of only football and masturbation.

I found an empty seat at the back, sat down and exhaled for the first time in five minutes.

So I finally had time to reflect on the magnanimous event that had just taken place and the obvious fact that magnanimous wasn't the best adjective to describe it.

I hadn't wanted it to be like this. This was what happened to other boys. Even though I was only fifteen (a baby, for goodness sake; a baby with too many hormones), I knew this was cheap and meaningless. I'd hoped that love may have entered into it in some capacity. I'd almost tried to convince myself that I was in love with Katie. I'd bought her a bottle of wine to say thank you. To say thank you for sex. The thought behind it was nice, I suppose, which was more than could be said for the wine, which should have had a label on it saying; *It took 125 cats to fill this bottle.*

I'd had one previous sexual 'experience' (with someone other than myself that is). Her name was Georgina Simmons. Georgina was in my year and generally considered to be really classy because she didn't smoke and none of her family had ever been to prison.

Like me, Georgina was a virgin and had stated that that was how it would remain even if she came back to my house. However, she did say that I could see her naked and we could study each other. I was a little worried that I was going to have to write an essay about it afterwards, but I liked Georgina; she was blonde and pretty and smiled a lot.

I'd tried to be romantic beforehand. I'd bought her some chips (from *Joe's Fish Plaice* – Deptford's answer to *The Ritz*) and held her hand as we walked across the park.

I'd almost decided against it when we got to my bedroom. Suddenly this wild anticipation became child-like embarrassment. But then I realised that the current embarrassment would be hugely exacerbated if I were to change my mind now.

I opened the door to my room; a child's room, yet to take on the banality and prissiness of an adult's. I had, of course, made sure that the Thomas the Tank Engine duvet cover that still adorned my bed when the posh Stone and Mocha one was in the wash, was nowhere to be seen and I'd removed the week-old dirty socks that patterned the carpet. These were now back in my sock drawer, mingled with the clean ones. We sat tentatively on the edge of the bed and discussed the posters on my wall for fifteen minutes. Finally I rediscovered the word 'courage', leaned in toward her and we kissed. I began to undo the top button of her blouse. After five minutes, I gave up and she undid it for me. We took off our tops. I stared at her bra. She recognised my look of complete helplessness and took it off herself. Then she popped the button on the side of her skirt and it fell balletically to the ground. I undid the buttons of my fly, shimmied my jeans down to my knees and begin to extract my left foot, never once taking my eyes off her, desperate that the moment would be lost and she would change her mind. Unfortunately this caused me to lose my balance. I vainly attempted to grab the edge of my desk, executed a perfect double axel, smacked my head on the wall, nutting the poster of Michael Jackson squarely in the testicles, finally lost my grip on the table and reality and fell rather unceremoniously to the floor, leaving me with a red face, a pounding forehead and an Action Man up my arse.

"Are you OK?" she asked.

"Fine," I replied, as though I'd intended to be in this position from the outset, "I thought you'd like a comedy trailer before the main film. Er, would you like to…" I said, gesturing toward the bed in the manner of a supermarket assistant showing you where the eggs are.

"Oh, yes, thank you," she said.

We lay on the bed and I wondered if this could be real. Also, what the hell I was supposed to do now? But, just as I was about to suggest we get dressed again and help each other with our algebra homework, eureka, she seized the day. Carpe Diem! Or Carpe Testiculum in this case. Several seconds later, when I thought things couldn't get much better, she grabbed my penis and I realised they could. As she rubbed her delicate fist up and down, I tried to think of chemistry exams or The Antiques Roadshow so that it wouldn't be over quicker than it takes a Ferrari to get from 0 to 60. After a short while, I realised I should try to return the compliment but, due to her lack of a penis, I had no idea what I was supposed to be doing. I fumbled as professionally as I could for a while but hadn't a clue how to find the appropriate spot. They should produce an Ordnance Survey Map of the vagina. After a brief period of my hand movements resembling someone rewiring a plug, I elicited a small moan from her, which made me think I was at least in the right area. Now I could stop concentrating so hard and remember that she had been playing with my penis for the last two minutes, seemingly to no avail as I hadn't even murmured 'oh that's nice'. So I tried to make up for it by letting out a sexy noise, which actually came out sounding like a cross between a Red Indian battle cry and a vacuum cleaner starting up.

At this point I also remembered the need for romantic, ambient background music; so I rolled over to the CD player and hit 'play'. I suppose the Spice Girls singing *Spice Up Your Life* in no-part harmony was appropriate to what we were doing, but, unfortunately, it wasn't appropriate to the atmosphere I wanted to create. As soon as the song started, she took her hand away and said:

"That was lovely. Thank you."

And that was it really, until the underwhelming bonk in the freezing cold at a vandalised bus-stop with Katie Turnpike.

Now, I wouldn't say Katie was easy. Everybody else would, but I've always tried to see the good side of people wherever possible. It's not that she's been around the houses a few times; more like she's been round the entire estate, the Community Centre and most of Southern England. If she suddenly sprouted handlebars and a saddle, nobody would bat an eyelid.

So, I hadn't seen a sexual heaven as we did it. What I'd actually seen was some graffiti saying *Mike is a poofter*. But, so what, I thought, it would be better the next time. I would make sure I loved the person and that there wasn't a compilation album bought for me by my grandparents in the CD player.

Anyway, this is what I told myself as I sat on the bus.

Gradually, I faded out of my daydream and back into reality. I glanced around. Nobody was looking at me. This made me sad and relieved at the same time. Relieved because I didn't want people to laugh at me (who does?) and sad because I had, after all, just 'done it' and I wanted my prowess to be acknowledged. Except, it wasn't prowess was it, really? I suppose if you use the analogy of an ocean liner sailing on a long journey toward its exotic destination, mine would have hit an iceberg and sunk just after leaving dock.

I stared out of the window for a while, checked my satchel, re-read my homework and looked at the seat in front. Someone had written *Rob likes it up the arse*. I must introduce him to Mike, I thought.

The rest of the day continued in a bit of an anti-climactic blur. Double geography ceded to break time which was followed by physics, a meandering and thoughtful lunch, then French, home economics and maths. I didn't see Katie at all. At one point I thought I would go and find her, just to reassure myself that it wasn't the worst sex she'd ever had; but she wasn't in her usual place. Probably off doing double 'soap opera studies' or whatever she did.

Anyway, that's how I lost my virginity.

2

I was a dichotomy as a child. Later to be wrapped in an enigma and finally to be tied rather clumsily in a ribbon of anathema.

I read.

People didn't read at my school. Reading was on a par with macro-economics and rape. (Quite which they considered the worst, I'm not sure). Books were considered unnecessary and way behind the fun to be had from letting the headmaster's tyres down or setting fire to frogs. There was an innocence to it, of course. I'm not sure the frogs saw it that way, but there were no knives or guns; just a lot of charred Gallic cuisine; the smell of which became quite common to the headmaster as he waited, yet again, for the breakdown company to tow him home.

I loved books. No, 'loved' doesn't cover it. Worshipped books. I still do.

I used to hang around the second hand bookstall in the Saturday Street Market, touching each one, especially the hardbacks. I had my own little ritual. I removed the jacket – even at fifteen I considered them to be gaudy, over-commercialised and not a real part of the book – and ran my fingers over the cover; all over; twice. I liked the textured ones best; possibly because I thought it gave them more literary weight but probably because I used to like the feel of the knobbly bits against my fingertips. Then I would pick them up and carefully, almost reverentially, sniff the pages. The older the smell, the better. Why this was so, I don't know. Maybe to grasp some tenuous connection with those who had turned these same pages before me.

When I found something I really wanted, I would look, doe-eyed, at Old Thomas, who ran the stall, with an expression that said 'you know I'm the only fifteen year-old who doesn't come up to your stall with the singular intention of tipping up the trestle tables and creating as much literary carnage as possible and that I really love books but have no money and with my floppy dark-brown fringe and large brown eyes, I couldn't be cuter if I was a puppy cavorting in a sea of toilet paper... and I know the word 'carnage'... and 'cavorting'... although I'm not too sure of the meaning of the latter, but... there you are, 'latter' as well'.

You see, if I'd been standing there in a tailcoat and an Eton bow-tie, the situation would have been very different. But I wasn't. For two reasons. One: I didn't go to Eton, I went to the Banton Avenue State Comprehensive and Two: Eton isn't in Deptford. Instead I was wearing trackie bottoms, trainers and a Taddersham football shirt. More council house than Charterhouse.

But Old Thomas was no idiot. In fact, he was more intelligent than a lot of South East London put together. He knew I was genuine. He also knew I was genuinely penniless and the only way I could repay him was to take him a cup of tea occasionally. Unfortunately it was a good half mile from my house to the market so it was usually cold when I got there; and my mum complained for days afterwards that her cups were going missing. However, he always seemed very grateful for the gesture and, especially in the middle of winter, I was worried about him catching something and wanted to make sure he kept warm... well, mildly tepid. Eventually my grandparents heard about this, mostly from my mum who had to come to the second-hand crockery stall every month to replace the cups and gave me a thermos flask and a supply of different flavoured teabags. Earl Grey was his favourite. I did try Elderflower and Camomile once. Old Thomas suppressed a grimace, smiled at me and told me that it was very kind of me to attempt to broaden his tea-drinking horizons but would I never bring this flavour again as he had no immediate plans to become a vegan or a lesbian.

On this particular occasion I was clutching *Tutankhamen's Treasure* like my life depended on it.

"We're doing Egyptopoly for GCSE," I said.

"*Ology*," Old Thomas replied.

"What?"

"*Egyptology*. Egyptopoly sounds like an ancient board game. 'I'd like to buy two pyramids to put on Cairo High Street, please. Go straight to the Valley of the Kings, go directly to the Valley of the Kings, do not pass the Sphinx, do not collect two hundred Qurush'."

I laughed uproariously. Mainly because I hadn't got the slightest idea what he was talking about. But I knew he liked me and I liked him; and I think some social graces must be built in even at such a young age. And I wanted the book.

"Now, let me work this out," he said, "a cup of tea in the cafe costs 75p; there are three cups in a thermos, so that's £2.25 and that book costs £9. So that's four flasks of tea you owe me."

"I'll bring the first one next week," I said, grinning, "and... thank you."

"That's alright, my son," he said.

As always, the phrase rooted me to the spot. Old Thomas is the only person to have ever called me 'my son' and it never ceased to stop me from functioning. I don't know why this was. I stood there looking at the ground, looking at him and I was filled with a fleeting sense of comfort; and sometimes I wanted to cry and at others, I wanted to hug Old Thomas. 'But I'm too old', I would think, 'and he's just Old Thomas, the bookseller'. But still...

I asked him once if he had any children.

"No," he said.

"Do you have any family at all?"

"No."

"I'm sorry."

"Don't be sorry, my son," he said, "I don't need them."

"Why?"

"Because people don't have to have a label for you to love them."

"Oh."

"And even if they have labels, if they don't treat you properly, it doesn't mean that you *have* to love them."

"Right," I said.

Of course, later I understood what he was trying to tell me but, at the time, 'label' just meant something you sewed into your football kit.

"Thank you," I said, again.

"It's my pleasure. You'd better hurry or you'll be late for football practice."

"Yes," I said. "Bye. See you next week. Hope you sell lots of books."

"Hope you score lots of goals."

I hugged Tutankhamen's and my, treasure, to my chest as I headed for the bus stop.

3

Deptford Cross Community Sports Centre was a hideous, ramshackle pile that looked as if it had originally been designed by a drunken, medieval architect whose plans were found, six hundred years later, by an origami expert. It was an archaic, ugly mound of concrete and steel with outside playing areas that would have made a great backdrop for a film about post-apocalyptic Britain.

I ran in through the entrance gate to *Football Pitch 3*, which tended to confuse most people as there were only two of them. I threw down my bag and joined my team-mates for what promised to be the usual dreary five-a-side knockabout.

"Ten minutes late, Hatchington," said Nibbsy, our coach and about as much use as a handbrake on a canoe.

"Were you, Sir? Wow, I must be really late then."

The rest of the boys stifled giggles.

"I mean, YOU'RE ten minutes late, boy!"

"Yes, Sir, held up buying a book."

By now the boys had reached the 'shaking shoulders, please can I be anywhere but here' stage.

"Don't screw around with me, you little prick."

"I wouldn't want to, Sir. And I don't have a little prick."

"You think you're really something, don't you, Hatchington? Got a lot of people telling you what a fantastic footballer you are; how one day you'll play for a Premiership club. Let it go to your head, haven't you, boy? Think you can be a fucking Gary Lineker without even trying. Well, I'm telling you, you can't. I've seen ten year-olds with twice your talent. You're a lazy, egotistical little wanker, Hatchington. Oh, you'll get a trial… for Leighton Orient or Scunthorpe and they'll drop you like a hot stone. You'll end up a fat, middle-aged has been that never was."

"You mean like you, Sir."

The giggling stopped and was replaced by a sense of nervous anticipation. I had overstepped the mark. In the past Nibbsy had been known to throw a piece of scaffolding at one of his pupils. He stared at me for about ten seconds, put down the ball he was holding and swaggered toward me. He stuck his face as close to mine as he could get (basically, my chin, if he stood on tip-toe) and said:

"I had trials for Arsenal, you little piece of shit."

"I know, Sir."

"And the only reason I didn't get on the full-time books was that I was-"

"Five foot, three. I know, Sir."

The malice and hatred in those eyes could have deflected a meteor from its course. I could feel the red-hot fury, the bitterness and murderous intent; not aimed purely at me but at the world in general, for the crushing burden dealt him by his fifteen minutes of near-fame happening so early in his life.

I was scared. I was very scared.

Eventually, after what seemed like an hour, he took his eyes off me and began to turn away and I started to breathe a massive sigh of relief; a sigh that lasted exactly 1.37 seconds, which was the time it took him to swing round and bring his knee into my testicles with a crunch that could be heard in Scotland.

I fell to the ground, almost blacking out as I did so. I don't remember the pain. When pain is beyond a certain level, I think the brain obliterates the memory. It's like, you can understand the death of one person but not the deaths of a hundred thousand. It's too much to take in. It's the same with pain. There's a twinge, an ache, a pain, a pain that makes you cry and then nothing. I imagine childbirth must be like this.

The boys didn't do anything. I don't blame them. They couldn't exactly beat the teacher up and they couldn't do anything for me except fan or massage my balls, neither of which is high on the agenda of most fifteen year-old boys.

It was funny but, as I lay there in something beyond agony, I felt sorry for Nibbsy. The man had just tried to destroy any chance I had of being a father, but I still wished him no harm. He *had* had trials for Arsenal and Newcastle, but ended up playing for York City and Shrewsbury Town and retiring when he was thirty-three, spending the next twenty years coaching in faithless institutions like this one. But it wasn't fair that he should take out his anger on us; and that is the only reason I had answered him back.

I don't know how long I lay on the ground. When the shock finally cleared and the tears began, I tried to hide them, but it's difficult when your hands are clamped firmly between your legs.

After a while I was dimly aware of Nibbsy standing a few yards away shouting 'get up and play, you fucking pansy'. But I couldn't; I just couldn't move. I would willingly have stayed in that position for years until the pain went away. And, probably because I hadn't done what he'd instructed me too, Nibbsy began to move toward me again with one obvious intention.

"Don't touch him, Sir."

"You what, boy?"

"I said don't touch him, Sir, or I'll report you for what you've just done."

This was Davey; a boy I'd barely spoken to before. He was taking a big risk. Nibbsy was virtually untouchable.

Davey had spoken very calmly. So calmly in fact that it had the desired effect of forcing Nibbsy into thinking before acting for once and he very slowly returned to his chair on the touchline.

Five minutes later I was able to stand up and limp back to my team-mates.

"Davey, er... thanks. I mean, really, thanks."

"That's alright. If I hadn't spoken to him, I would have had to hit him."

I think he would. Davey was six feet tall and, at the age of fifteen, built like a rower. He spent a lot of time in the gym; but only to keep fit and healthy.

"Are you ok?"

"Yeah," I said, "I think so."

"Then let's show him how to really play football."

I could have hugged Davey, but again, at fifteen, this is tantamount to fanning your mate's testicles.

"You're on," I said.

So we did, Davey and me. We played like this was Wembley and we were England's two centre forwards. Nibbsy was running up and down the touchline shouting orders:

"Red team, play a holding game. Yellows, try to get the ball off them!"

We were red, but we weren't holding; we were flying. I won the ball on the right wing, dinked past the defender, chipped the ball to Davey who turned, span on the ball and played it just in front of me as I steamed in and crashed the ball into the top left-hand corner of the net.

Straight after the whistle we stole the ball back. Davey lobbed it to me from the left wing this time; I stood on the ball, dummied to pass it to Gareth, making their defender go one way, then tore past him, looked up for one hundredth of a second and sent an inch-perfect pass to Davey, who took it first time and cracked it past their keeper.

It continued for the next ten minutes. Nibbsy yelling instructions to hold it up and us ignoring him and slamming that ball into the back of the net like there was no opposition, like we had golden boots. It was as if I wasn't connected to the earth, to thought, to the drudgery of life; but I was beyond it all, with Davey, flying somewhere, unstoppable; and, up to that point in my life, I don't think I'd ever been happier.

Of course, it couldn't last and ten minutes and six goals later, Nibbsy finally lost his temper, grabbed the ball and shouted, "I told yer to play a holding game, yer show-off little bastards. Now piss off home and let me work with the real footballers."

Davey and I trooped off the pitch and began to collect our belongings.

"Did you really buy a book?" he said.

"Er…"

I didn't know what to say. I mean, in Deptford, you simply didn't admit to buying books, let alone an historical one. It would have been easier to say you had gonorrhoea.

"Er… yes."

I waited for the inevitable brainless surge of sarcasm.

"What's it called?"

"*Tutankhamen's Treasure*; we're doing *Egyptology* this term."

Oh hell, I was going red. I was actually blushing in front of another boy.

"Did you know that he married his half-sister and she had two still-born sons by him?"

"Er, no… no I didn't."

"Well, enjoy reading it. I've got to run. You go to Banton Avenue, don't you?"

"Yes."

"I'm at Blaisworth Road Comp."

"Right."

"What time do you get out, normally?"

"Around four."

"Fancy a kick-around in the park after school on Wednesday?"

"Er, yeah. Yeah, that'd be great."

"OK. Meet you by the main gates."

"Will do. See you then."

"Bye."

As I was putting my old trainers back on and getting over the shock of a fellow fifteen year-old not only knowing who King Tut was but also details of his life, I looked up to find two guys standing in front of me, wearing suits that, in Deptford, singled them out as either drug dealers or pimps.

"Hello, young man."

"Er, hi."

"We've just been watching you."

Or paedophiles.

"Oh."

"We think you have a lot of potential."

As what, a rent boy?

22

"Oh."

"I'm Michael Cantry and this is Clive Ingles. We're youth team scouts for Flitcham and we were wondering whether you would be interested in coming along for a trial?"

Before I could blurt out several 'YES's, Nibbsy stomped over.

"You blokes want anything?"

"We were just having a word with… I'm sorry, I've forgotten your name."

"Sam Hatchington."

"Sam. We wanted to know if he would be interested in"-

"Well, he wouldn't. He's my star player and I'm not having him poached by some talentless pipsqueak boys' club run by a couple of suits that know fuck all about football."

"My card."

Michael Cantry
Chief Youth Team Scout
Flitcham F C

I think Nibbsy crapped himself right there. I couldn't smell it, but I'm pretty sure he did.

"Now," said Mr Cantry, "if you would get back to your… er, coaching, I wish to speak to Sam alone for a minute. Oh and by the way, in the future I suggest that you refrain from beating up your star player and side lining him for scoring four goals in as many minutes. Rather a waste of his talent, wouldn't you say?"

I didn't think that Nibbsy could shrink beneath five feet three, but apparently he could. As he meandered, speechless, away from us, he looked rather like an overweight twelve year-old boy. Even with burning testicles that were probably going to have to drop for a second time, a small amount of pity for him crossed my brain. It was a very small amount and it crossed very quickly.

So I gave my name and address to the Chief Youth Team Scout at Flitcham and my life was changed. Not immediately of course, for, as is usual with me, I don't register change until long after it's happened. But, I rode home that afternoon on a bus that wasn't really real, back to my home that wasn't real either, or maybe had just been redecorated. Whichever, it wasn't quite the same as when I left it that morning.

4

"Mum, mum, I've got a trial with Flitcham!"

"Are they any good?"

"Yeah, they're in the Premiership!"

"Well, that's nice then."

"Where's dad, I need to tell him!"

"Don't bother your father, the horse-racing is on."

Unfortunately, my rational head had temporarily deserted me and left my 'excited, hug the world' head in charge and I raced into the lounge.

"Dad, I've got a trial for Flitcham!"

I've never quite experienced a silence like it. He didn't even look up.

"Dad... I've..."

Ever so slowly, I backed out of the room.

My mum was in the kitchen, where I'd left her.

"He didn't even look at me."

"Well, what do you expect; the telly's on."

"But this is important."

"Is it? As important as his racing?"

"Yes. More important."

"What's important to your father is important to your father."

"But that doesn't make any sense."

"Don't question me, Samuel. Now, get out of my kitchen while I'm cleaning and leave your football kit on the landing outside your door. And don't go traipsing up the stairs in those horrible trainers."

"But they're the only trainers I've got."

"Then buy some new ones."

"I don't have any money."

"Well, maybe your new employers at Flitcham will give you some. Stop bothering me."

I took off my battered trainers and trudged up the stairs to my room.

I wasn't angry. I wasn't even upset. I was… indifferent. And, thinking about it, it's *so* wrong that a fifteen year-old boy should be indifferent about anything.

I sat on my bed and stared vacantly at my Action Man, thinking three things. How unbelievably excited I was to have a trial with Flitcham, why weren't my mum and dad excited for me and why did I still have an Action Man?

I don't know how long this mental battle continued for. Time became unimportant; indeed, ceased to exist. Half of my mind ran around like a young child, (I was fifteen, why shouldn't it?) waving flags and shouting to the world that I had the chance to be a professional footballer. The other half sat down, wearing trousers with an elasticated waistband and comfortable slippers and told the first half to shut the hell up because nobody other than me actually cared. For a while it was stalemate; a mind game of two halves, as the football commentators would have it.

Then something happened inside me. A little switch clicked over from the 'I care so much' setting to 'I don't care anymore'.

Not about the trial. No, I still cared about that. The 'excited, flag-waving' half of my mind had won. Unfortunately, at a price. The price being, that I didn't care what my parents thought any more. The little switch had taught me that, no matter how much I longed for something to happen – in this case to control my mum and dad's reactions to my happiness – if it was impossible to accomplish, you simply had to let it go. I remember Old Thomas saying to me, 'some mornings I get out of bed, open the bedroom curtains and it's pouring with rain. And, do you know what I do? I let it'.

In one month I had grown up so much. I had lost my virginity, I had got a trial with Flitcham and I had lost the need for my parents.

The third of these things made me very sad. The first didn't make me much happier, but at least I could improve on it as I got older.

I still loved my parents, then. Partly because this was something I felt duty bound to do; and partly because I loved them.

I can't remember my father's running days; they ended before I was born. He knew Mary Peters back in the seventies; used to go drinking with David Bedford. Giants of their day. Mary Peters won a gold medal in the 1972 Olympics and my dad used to talk to her. I had a book about it. I bought it from Old Thomas. It had all the famous athletes from that period. I bought it to see if I could find my dad's name in it. I couldn't; but, at the time, it enabled me to get to know him more.

When I was twelve we had a 'show and tell' at school (America, of course, had started the idea and, like all things American, made it sound like it was the most fun you could ever have). Ours was the British version called 'bring something crap in'. We had to take in an item that summed up one of our parents. I took the book. When it was my turn, I marched up to the front of the class, held up the book and said:

"My dad ran with these people."

The teacher, Miss Forbes, said:

"Can you show us his photo in the book?"

"Er, no, he's not in there."

"Is there a paragraph about him?"

"No."

"Is his name mentioned at all?"

"No."

"Well, never mind. Pass the book round."

I did. It went down quite well until it got to Gazza Ramsey.

"So, your old man ran with Mary Peters?"

"Well, not *with* Mary P"-

"Miss, Miss! Hatch's dad ran in the women's team. Hey, Hatch, did he wear a wig and tights?!"

By now the moron corner of the room were in hysterics.

"Miss, Miss, Hatch's dad invented drag-racing!"

If it had been aimed at anybody else, I would have laughed; but it wasn't, it was aimed at my dad.

"Alright Rammo, so what does *your* dad do?"

"He's a bin-man, mate, like yours."

Against that I had no argument. My dad *was* a bin-man. He had quit running at twenty-one. He had no money (you weren't paid in those days) and wanted to be like the rest of his mates. 'Don't stand out'. That was my dad's motto, or would have been if he could have been bothered to think of one. He ran for England in the 1974 Commonwealth Games when he was eighteen and twice for Britain in the 800 and 1500 metres in international meets. He was a good runner.

My mum was studying to be a nurse when she met my dad. As a young woman, she was no slouch. Gran and Gramps were desperate for her to have a career. They met when they were nineteen and, for a year, they were something of a celebrity couple in their street. My dad, the runner and my mum, the would-be nurse. But then, my dad gave up on life and my mum quit her studying to massage his empathy and to make sure he was comfortable in his wallowing for the rest of his life.

There's a line in a poem that I love by Dylan Thomas:

26

Rage against the dying of the light.

My dad didn't so much rage against it as ask my mum to shut the curtains.

He got up at 4.30 every morning and went off emptying people's dustbins; collecting people's refuse; discarding the populace's unwanted paraphernalia. He was a bin-man.

Finding a small, unexpected burst of energy, I jumped off my bed and decided to phone my grandparents, making a mental note to put my Action Man in a dark corner of the wardrobe.

They never made an Action Woman, did they? I mean, Ken's got Barbie, but Action Man has just got a tank, a rifle and a grenade. Poor guy must have never stopped masturbating.

As I left my room my dad was going into the bathroom - the 2.30 at Ascot must have finished - and I temporarily forgot my indifference.

"Dad, did you hear me earlier? I've got trials with Flitcham."

There followed the longest pause in the history of pauses. It made *War and Peace* look like a pamphlet. Finally, he pushed open the toilet door and said:

"Have you."

The door closed and, with it, any form of reconciliation. Not that there was much to reconcile.

I think I would have preferred it if he had said 'Only Flitcham? Why couldn't you have got trials with Arsenal'? But he didn't. He was my rain and I would let him.

I went downstairs, picked up the receiver and dialled Gran's number.

She picked up on the first ring as usual. There was only one phone in the house but they'd had an extension cable fitted to it several years ago and she took it with her wherever she went in the bungalow. Thinking about it, she probably invented the world's first mobile phone. A little cumbersome, admittedly, and rather limited in range, but still mobile. She could have patented it; called it the Gran-phone; the g-phone; a dyslexic iPhone.

"The Kenning residence."

Honestly, it was a council bungalow in a particularly dodgy area of Deptford.

"Gran, it's me."

"Hello, love. How's the footie?"

'Footie'? I ask you! Not the sort of word every Gran would use; but mine liked to consider herself 'down with the street kids'. She went into raptures once when she told me she'd heard a great song on Radio 2 called *I Would Do Anything For Love* by a band called *Meat Ball*. I love her.

"Footie's going great. That's why I called."

I was just about to dispense my wonderful news and receive the sort of adulation only grandparents can give and an invitation to tea and cream scones if I 'got my arse round there in the next half an hour', when my dad drove the final nail into my once euphoric coffin and bellowed from the bathroom:

"Muriel, he's on the bloody phone again"!

My mum, omnipresent as ever, aspirated in front of me, removed the receiver from my hands, placed it back on its cradle and said, rather matter-of-factly:

"Now, you know very well your father doesn't like you using the phone."

"But I was ringing Gran to tell her"-

"The reason is irrelevant, Samuel."

"It's relevant that Gran and Gramps should know that I've-"

And I was cut off again by another bombastic outburst from the toilet.

"What's relevant is who pays the bloody bill!"

I think there must be a textbook given to parents who have no imagination, when they first conceive, called *One Hundred And One Mind-Numbing Stock Phrases To Say To Your Children To Really Piss Them Off.*

Silence ensued from the toilet. Two sentences in a week must have tired him out. He probably didn't have the strength to wipe his arse.

I ran the mile to my grandparent's house and I did, indeed, get tea and cream scones and my Gran lavished praise on me, showed me her new Pilates video and asked me if I liked *I Should Be So Lucky* by *Kylie Synagogue.*

Even Gramps came in from the greenhouse to congratulate me. Gramps doesn't say much but, unlike my father, he's not being ignorant, he just speaks when there's something relevant to say. He told me that Flitcham were a very old team with a fantastic history and that I'd done extremely well to get a trial with them and that he was very proud. He then did something which I remember to this day. He turned to my Gran and said:

"Do you mind washing up, Doris, I'm going to take our Sam into the garden."

"You go ahead, Herbert, I'll sort this lot out."

My grandparents were so polite. I never once heard them argue. They would occasionally rib each other, but always in jest. They were genuinely in love. I once asked Gran if Gramps ever did anything that annoyed her. She said, "Oh yes, but he does far more good things than bad and the bad ones are just things I wouldn't do personally, which doesn't necessarily make them bad."

"Thank you, dear. Come on, lad."

Gramps took me out into the garden - oh, I forgot to mention; you had to be the Pope to be allowed out there - and showed me where he was planting the cabbages and sprouting broccoli and the plans he had for another cucumber frame. Then he turned to me, put his hand on my shoulder and said:

"Sammy, you're a bright kid. Not overly bright and by no means academic (thanks for the honesty, Gramps) but you've got intelligence and a good head on your shoulders. You've got a great future ahead of you. Always a good place to have a future, I feel."

We laughed.

"What I'm saying is, don't throw it away, like your mother did. She had a lot going for her too. Then she married that unsociable slob and gave up her life. Stupid to stop living at twenty-one."

This was strong stuff. It was the first time I'd ever heard Gramps speak badly of anyone.

"He can be nice to her sometimes."

"It's praiseworthy of you to try to defend him, but the man's behaviour is subhuman. You're a very, very good football player. Keep working at it. Keep loving the game. Keep reading. Don't let him, or anybody else for that matter, dampen your enthusiasm and stop you doing what you want to do."

The next spring, I ate the cabbages that he'd planted; even the sprouting broccoli, which I have never really liked but still eat even now, because it reminds me of the day I was promoted to Pope and given permission from someone older than my father that it was alright to ignore him.

5

Davey and I met up on the Wednesday after school.

I'd played 'knockabout' with lots of friends before. It was always good for a laugh. If there were a few of you it could be quite fun. Two-a-side, two and a half-a-side, rotating goalies, dog poo for goal-posts. But with one friend, it was usually boring. You passed it to him, he passed it back and so on ad infinitum, or teatime; whichever was the sooner. Oh, you could bend it, chip it, lob it, do a few tricks; back-flip the ball and catch it on the back of your neck. Rarely worked though; no one was there to see it and it didn't matter if you failed. Basically, after five minutes, it became hopelessly boring.

But with Davey it was different. We didn't talk much. We didn't shout encouragement - 'on my 'ead, mate' - or point and laugh if the other one accidentally slipped or miss-kicked. We had, right from the beginning I suppose, an understanding. We would put our bags down a little way apart and sometimes I would defend and he would attack and sometimes it would be the other way round, but neither of us suggested we change; it just happened. Occasionally we would suddenly take off and run the entire length of the park; passing, heading, one-two-ing, back-heeling, changing sides; charging about in this mad, physical dance with improvised moves borrowed from the back catalogues of Beckenbauer, Eusebio, Charlton and Barishnikov. *Soccer Ballet* we could have called it. A bit like Rudolf Nureyev, only with smaller balls.

The first time, it must have lasted for over an hour. At the end we both arrived back at our bags, which miraculously were still there and collapsed on the ground. We'd run the entire length of the park and back, twice, without stopping. We were exhausted, but elated; gasping from a need for oxygen and an endorphin-fuelled feeling of amazing accomplishment. Like reaching the top of Everest, only lower.

We opened our cans of Coke and took two hefty glugs (solace is in the first mouthful of Coca-Cola). Then the grass caressed our backs for a time that could have been five minutes or two hours. It's funny, isn't it; normally you need to know a friend for ages before not feeling an embarrassed urge to make small-talk. Silences are the litmus test of a friendship. I remember Davey once saying to me: "Small-talk is what it says it is. Small."

It was as the horizon began to claim the sun that we finally spoke.

"I've got a trial for Flitcham."

"That's great, Sam. Well done."

"I wasn't going to say coz it sounds like I'm boasting."

"Well, you're not. You're just telling me."

"Yeah."

"So, when is the trial?"

"A week on Saturday. We're all being taken on a tour of the stadium before going to the training ground."

"Are your parents coming to support you?"

"Probably not."

"I'll come, then."

"Oh. Thanks."

When I arrived home, my dinner resembled a sacrificial offering and my mum got a bit dramatic and asked me where I'd been for so long.

"Out with Davey, Mum. Playing footie in the park."

"Who's Davey?"

"Friend."

"Well, don't disturb your father, there's a Western on."

I don't know why she bothered warning me. It was a bit like saying to somebody, 'here's a hand grenade; if you want to live, don't take the pin out'.

So I sat in the kitchen and ate my sausages or chops, or whatever they had been earlier in the day. I didn't even ask for gravy. After all, it was my fault that my dinner resembled an exhibit at the Tate Modern.

Mum announced she was going to watch the end of the Western.

"Why?" I said, "You don't even like Westerns."

"No, but your father does."

"Why do *you* have to watch it, then?"

"Why do all your sentences start with 'why', Samuel?"

"Why can't he watch something *you* like for a change," I said, instantly forgetting what she'd just accused me of.

"Your father puts food on the table and clothes on our backs."

"No, he doesn't. *You* put food on the table and clothes on our backs. You work as many hours as he does *and* you look after the house. He's finished work by lunchtime and half the time they're on strike anyway, which makes no difference because for most of the day he just sits on his ar-"

"Language, Samuel. I will *not* have that word said in my kitchen."

"What word?"

"Arse."

"Um, mother," I said, grinning through a mouthful of charcoal, "how could you say such a word in front of your young son. Wash your mouth out immediately with this concentrated washing up liquid."

She actually laughed.

"You cheeky little so-and-so!"

For a moment I thought she was going to hug me. But, instead, she went into the lounge and watched the end of the Western.

Thursday and Friday happened. Those details that I do remember are somewhat murky. I know we had double chemistry because Martin Jenson set light to Craig Levitt's pubes with a Bunsen burner. I know that, on one of the days, Ja, Tommy and myself went down the town centre and had a McDonalds. We had just enough money between the three of us for a cheeseburger and a medium Coke. So we carefully cut the burger into thirds and spent the next twenty minutes nibbling them so delicately, you'd think we were extras in *Brideshead Revisited*.

I know that Friday evening happened because I was in bed by 9.30. My mum was so shocked she actually spoke during the *X-Files* and invoked the half-hearted wrath of my dad. Obviously Scully had failed to believe in telepathy for the twentieth time that episode and my father had been insipidly annoyed to have missed Gillian Anderson's withering look at David Duchovny.

I lay on my bed, with Thomas the Tank Engine pulled up to my neck and willed myself to sleep; which is pointless. You'd just as well will yourself to win a Nobel Peace Prize. If it's not going to happen, it's not going to happen. I tried counting sheep; I tried counting how often I'd stared at Angela Romilly's breasts. I counted how many times the clouds covered the tiny thread of moonlight that slipped through the gap in the top of my curtains and spot-lighted three of the books on my bookshelf; *The Famous Five go off to Camp*, *To Kill a Mocking Bird* and *The Life of Julius Caesar*. I think I must have drifted off at some point because I have a muddled memory of Anne cooking breakfast for the whole of the Roman Senate whilst Julian and Dick fought the Gauls, Atticus took Timmy for a walk and George took an instant liking to Scout – probably recognising another future lesbian in the making.

7.30 was announced by my alarm clock making its usual noise - like a frog vomiting. I hit snooze, burrowed under the duvet and pretended it was 3 a.m.

I don't do mornings. I never have done. God, I've always wished I could, though. I wanted to be like the people in those ads on TV - *'Good morning, San Francisco! It's 7 a.m. and it's a beautiful day'*. It's inspiring. It makes you want to live; really live! Unfortunately, *'Good morning, Deptford, it's 7.30, it's pissing down and there's been another gang murder on the High Street'* doesn't quite make you want to grab life by the bollocks and swing it round your head. Seriously, if I could have showered, run out into the golden morning sunshine, got the Trolley into the Bay Area and quaffed down Eggs Benedict and an entire carton of orange juice, I'd have been out of that bed like a shot. But, instead, I made myself into a foetus again and tried to metaphorically crawl back into the womb.

This temporary reverie lasted exactly two and a half minutes. My alarm clock vomited again and my mum banged on the door with the same decibels as the Greeks invading Troy.

"Samuel, it is 7.30!"

"I know," came a voice from somewhere under Thomas the Tank Engine's funnel.

I heard the door handle turn, then footsteps, then my duvet was hauled off me.

"Mum! You can't just walk in my room. I could have been…"

"Could have been what?"

"Sleeping."

"You were; that's why I came in."

Deptford's Trojan Horse turned and galloped out of the room, shouting over her shoulder:

"If you're quick, there'll be some bacon butties left over."

I was quick. I had the world's fastest shower. You didn't really have a choice. The shower was the best thing about the house. It was a power shower with the accent on the word 'power'. As soon as you turned it on, you had to grab hold of the towel rail, otherwise you ended up in the toilet.

Then I threw on my 501's, my best trainers and a white T-shirt that was a little too small but made my pecs and biceps look massive by comparison and ran downstairs.

Depositing half a bottle of ketchup on my buttie, I made one final attempt to cajole my parents into coming to see me.

"What're you doing this morning, mum?"

"Your dad and I are going out."

"Dad's going out? On a Saturday? Are we due a plague of locusts or something?"

"Don't be cheeky. Your father's taking me to the garden centre. He needs his antirrhinums."

She made him sound like a drug addict. 'Yeah, I do the antirrhinums, but I've got it under control'.

"It's just that it's my trial with Flitcham and guests are allowed to watch and… well, it would be really nice if you could come."

"Well, we can't."

And that was that.

So I grabbed my sports bag, swept my fringe out of my eyes, opened the card that had just been delivered for me - 'Hope it goes well, Sammy; lots of love, Gran and Gramps' - put it on the telephone table and left without saying goodbye, slamming the front door behind me deliberately loudly; like a Trojan invasion.

The first of the two buses that I needed to reach Flitcham was arriving at the stop just as I got there. I leapt on and took a seat near the central doors. I was never an 'upstairs deck' teenager. Most of the kids who went up there thought they were cool. Frankly, even back then, I thought they were just twats. If you had to conform to what the brainless majority imagined as cool, then there was simply no way you *were* cool.

At Putney I changed buses. It was only a short journey to what could, if I did well, be the beginning of something too huge to contemplate. I had tried to switch off just how much this meant to me. I had attempted to convince myself that this was just an ordinary day of training and the worst that could happen would be Nibbsy cuffing me round the ear and telling me to play worse or something. But the closer I got, the more this became impossible. I could fail; I could have an off day and that would be it; they wouldn't want to see me again. Could you fail in one session? Did you get another chance? Would they see me again next year?

Just before my brain gave in and curled up under its own Thomas the Tank Engine duvet cover, I stopped thinking. Staring out of the window became infinitely more preferable and I took to watching the incessant drizzle lethargically, almost apologetically, skimming the glass. I hate drizzle; it's pathetic. I love rain, though. Rain has definition, drizzle has nothing. Drizzle is like people who say 'wouldn't it be great to do the Inca Trail one day' and rain is the people who do it.

I opened my bag, took out the card I'd placed there last night and read the words I'd already read twenty times the previous evening:

'This is the start. It is not the end or the middle. It is the beginning of a journey during which you can get off at any time you wish. But I think you should continue to the very end. Lots of luck for your big day, my son. Thomas, the Bookseller'.

I put the card back in the envelope and ignored the drizzle.

When I arrived at the front gates of Catteridge Road (Flitcham's ground), there were three other boys already there. I nodded to each of them and then we all individually found something extremely interesting to stare at in the mid-distance. This ritual was repeated a further six times as other new boys arrived. Finally we were saved from this macho, squirming embarrassment by Michael Cantry and Clive Ingles arriving, smiling enthusiastically, ready to take us wordless wannabes around this famous stadium.

It's difficult to appreciate anything when the world's entire butterfly population has migrated to your stomach, but the first of the two things that stood out for me was walking out onto the pitch. The *Pitch*. This was where it happened. This was where the culmination of all that effort, all that training, finally became a reality. This grass; this huge expanse of grass. That so much emotion, so much happiness, sorrow, elation, skill, dying for your team-mates, should happen on this rectangle of lawn.

The other thing was the home dressing room. Two thoughts flashed through my head. The fact that players who appeared on my TV screen, on millions of TV screens, actually *sat here,* was beyond comprehension. And the history. Now, Flitcham have never been one of the greats, but they've always been 'up there'. Some of the best players in the history of football sat here, wearing shorts that looked like two scout tents stitched together.

I think we were all a little bit in awe.

Michael and Clive kept up a running commentary throughout, then announced that the coach was ready to take us the short distance to the training ground.

We got on, feeling like reluctant VIPs (is there such a thing?). After all, a coach just for us kids?

I sat next to a boy called Jake. He was a year older than me, nearly seventeen and lived in Highgate in North London. Highgate is very upmarket. There's a coffee bar every second building. You get a free glass of champagne on entering the area.

Jake was a nice guy. We actually managed a conversation of sorts; mostly along the lines of: 'What team do you play for?' 'Where do you live?' 'Yeah, the changing room was smaller than I thought it would be, too'.

Our arrival at the training ground heralded the disappearance of some of the butterflies. It wasn't quite so mind-numbing. It felt more like a park where we'd all played 'knockabout', albeit a park where your ball wasn't likely to be stolen by a bulldog or a six year-old gang member.

"OK, guys," said Michael, "all the over-sixteens come with me; we've got some exciting form-filling to do. Under-sixteens, you're lucky, your parents have already done this. Changing rooms are over there; get into your kit and start warming up."

So my parents had filled in some forms for me. Parental consent. More realistically, my mum had filled in the forms, then had to remind my dad who I was, before showing him which end of the pen to hold to sign his name.

For a few fleeting seconds as we emerged from the changing block, I thought that the garden centre thing may have been a ruse after all and they'd both be sitting there in the visitor's area but, after a cursory glance that way, I realised there was more chance of the 'Famous Five' being there, drinking ginger beer and planning on how they could use their pre-pubescent charms to wangle some eggs and milk out of the local farmer's wife. (Didn't these adults ever think there was something wrong about four un-chaperoned kids and a dog gallivanting around the countryside, so near the point of starvation that they had to beg for eggs and milk?).

Someone who *was* sitting there, though, was Davey. I saw him, waved and ran over.

"About time," he said, "I've been here so long my balls have frozen."

"Sorry," I said, "tour of the stadium took longer than expected."

"What was it like?"

"Bit jaw-dropping really."

"Go in the changing rooms?"

"Yeah."

"Smaller than you thought?"

"Yeah."

"So much history, though."

"Too much to take in, really."

"Pitch?"

"Yeah."

"And?"

"Don't think I have the words."

"You will do; just not now. Hey, I think the trainer wants you."

I turned to see a guy who looked like a trainer gathering all the boys around him. Football coaches always look the same; a sort of halfway house between a used car salesman and a ballet master.

"Better go. Look, you don't have to…"

"I know I don't."

"Keep your balls warm, then."

The trainer's name was Grant. He was terrific. Put us all at our ease. Told us he wasn't expecting an Alan Shearer, just for us to enjoy ourselves, not to be nervous, but to give it all we had. He also told a boy called Sean, who'd won the 'arsehole' award by wearing a Liverpool shirt to a trial for Flitcham, that there was a ritual sacrifice at the end of the session and that he was to be the victim because of his taste in shirts. The rest of us laughed but I think Sean actually believed him for a few seconds.

We didn't really do much. Just some basic ball-control skills, some dribbling around cones and a few one-twos before shooting at their reserve goalie. Then we had a five-a-side for half an hour. Occasionally I glanced over at Davey, but he was just sitting there. I think his testicles must have completely iced over. I gave it everything. I wanted to be noticed but I didn't want to show off, so I played the same sort of game that I'd played when Michael and Clive watched me at Deptford Cross, hoping that, by replicating it, I'd show consistency as well as flair.

After we'd showered and changed, we were told that some of us would be asked back next week for the second round and some of us wouldn't, but not to be discouraged as we may be brought back to try out again the future. We were taken into the office individually. I was seventh.

"Hi, Sam."

"Hi, Mr Cantry."

"Please, Michael."

"Erm, Michael."

"Well, you certainly played as well as you did when we saw you last. Great control;

dazzling running at the defence."

"Thanks."

"We won't, however, be inviting you back next week."

"Oh…? Well, thank you anyway. I'll, er, be going then."

I couldn't work out what to do with my hands, couldn't find the strength to raise my head up. I tripped on the chair leg as I got up and had just reached the door when Michael said:

"We're not inviting you back to trial next week because we've seen all we need to see. We'd like to offer you a place in the Youth Team squad."

It was like all the fifteen Christmases that I'd had rolled into one. I hadn't got to rip the wrapping paper off, but I didn't need to because I knew what the present was; and it was something I'd wanted all my life.

"Thank you. Thank you," I said, trying not to jump up and down.

Michael shook my hand.

"We'll be in touch early next week," he said.

I left the office and forced myself to behave like an adult. 'This is the beginning', I said to myself, 'it's time to be a grown up'.

I said goodbye to the guys and raced over to Davey.

We looked at each other. He resembled a drowned rat; a drowned, frozen rat. Although he was wearing a huge old army trenchcoat and a scarf that would have made Tom Baker's Dr Who jealous, the freezing rain had plastered his jet-black hair to his forehead and he was trying and failing, not to shake.

"You look awful," I said, thereby putting an end to any possible career in the diplomatic service.

"Thanks."

I looked at him again. He'd come all this way and sat here in the cold, just to support me.

"Well, don't just stand there, take me to a cafe and buy me a hot chocolate. My balls are currently doing their best to reverse climatic change."

I laughed and we found a cafe where I bought us hot chocolates.

The best part about a hot chocolate is the anticipation and the first sip. That unexpected mix of chocolate and heat slips down your throat, delivering so much pleasure, you think you might pass out. But, like everything, it can't last. The second sip isn't as good and by halfway down the mug, you're thoroughly sick of it. And, when you've drunk two-thirds of it, it's cold anyway.

Davey took two hefty gulps and tried to stop shaking.

"You should have cupped your balls in your hands to keep them warm," I said.

"Um," he said, "and what would that have looked like, exactly? Guy sits on a bench watching other guys in shorts playing football with his hands down his trousers."

"Yeah, suppose you've got a point."

"You were good, Sam. Your goal was a bit lucky but, otherwise, you were the best player

37

out there."

"Wow, thanks."

We paused again. Easy pause; like Pinter, only real.

"So, what did they say?"

"I'm in. I'm on the Youth books. I'm training every week from... I don't know. Soon."

"They didn't even need to see you for the second week?"

"No. They asked six back next week, but Jake and I have been accepted straight away."

"Congratulations. That's brilliant."

"Yes."

"Aren't you pleased, Sam?"

"Yeah. Yeah, I am."

"Well, forgive my lack of astuteness, but I find that difficult to believe at the moment. I mean, I'm not expecting you to put on clown shoes and cartwheel around the room, but you could smile about it."

I smiled.

"Was that a smile or is your hot chocolate repeating on you?"

I laughed.

"That's better."

"I just wish you were playing too."

"Well, I'm not, because you're better than me and you deserve to be out there."

"I'm not better than you."

"Don't say that because you feel you have to."

"I'm not. I think you're a really good player."

"I am. But I'm not a really *really* good player, which is why you're training with Flitcham and I'm thinking of a hundred and one ways of disposing of Nibbsy's body after I've suffocated him with one of his own jockstraps."

We laughed and ignored the last third of our hot chocolates.

"Oh, before I forget," said Davey, searching in his duffel bag and taking out a weather-beaten book, "Read this, it's brilliant."

Scoop by Evelyn Waugh.

"OK," I said, "thanks."

Half an hour later we left the cafe and braved the arctic drizzle to search for a bus that would take us home.

A few yards down the road, a hugely optimistic ice-cream man had parked his van in a small layby.

I have *ice cream OCD*. I can't walk past a shop or van without buying one.

"I really fancy an ice cream," I said.

Davey stopped and stared at me for a while, as if I had antennae coming out of my head.

"Well, I do."

I was an inch shorter and two months younger than Davey but I began to feel like he was the headmaster and I was an unruly eleven year-old who was late handing his homework in.

"I just… like ice cream," I said, more to the pavement than to him.

When I looked up, he was smiling.

"You knob-jockey, Hatchington. Come on, I'll buy you an ice cream. What do you want?"

"Er, just a cornet, please."

"Two cornets, please."

"Erm… I have to have raspberry sauce on it."

"Pardon?"

"I have to have raspberry sauce on it."

"You are joking?"

"No," I said, finding temporary comfort in the pavement again.

"Two cornets, please. One plain and one with raspberry sauce for my girlfriend, Samantha, here."

I laughed and he laughed and the ice cream man laughed and for a few seconds, it wasn't freezing anymore. And then it was again; and the ice cream was nice, but we had to eat them quickly before the freezing drizzle diluted them.

When we got off the bus in Deptford, we began heading in opposite directions.

"Well done," Davey said, as he began backing away. "See you around soon."

"Davey," I shouted, as he started to turn.

"Yes?"

"Thanks. Thanks for coming."

"Wouldn't have missed it."

"We still up for a knockabout on Wednesday?"

"You bet, Samantha," he said.

"Fuck you," I said.

6

I sat my GCSE's later that year.

Well, 'sit' doesn't really describe it properly. 'Mope', 'flounce', 'walk nervously up and down desperately trying to remember the date of the battle of Agincourt and other trivia that would subsequently be of bugger all use to me', sums it up a little better.

I'm not intellectual. Never have been, never will be. You see, only people who aren't intellectual say 'never have been, never will be'. They're only two rungs up the academic ladder from people who say 'at the end of the day'.

I took six and I got six. An 'A' in English Language, a 'B' in English Lit and 'C's in everything else, including the battle of Agincourt.

My mum told me I'd done very well, Gran and Gramps took me to the beach for the day, Old Thomas gave me a forty year-old copy of *The Complete Works of Oscar Wilde* and I basked in a summer of freedom, no money and that funny, quivery feeling you get in your stomach when you realise that life is bigger than you thought; that there will be some very scary challenges ahead, but that, with the right attitude, you can get to the end and have a lot of fun along the way.

There was also the minor problem of my future.

Flitcham were saying some really nice things about me but had yet to come forward with a really nice contract for me to sign. I was still, very much, a youth player. You can, if you're some type of superstar-in-the-making, make it into the seniors at sixteen, but normally, you spend up to two years in the youth squad and then a decision is made on whether or not to keep you. In the meantime, I wanted to take 'A' levels but wasn't sure if I was good enough.

I mentioned this to a few people. Actually, I mentioned this to most of the world, who didn't seem particularly interested, being more involved with famine in Africa and the Poles melting, I suppose.

Gran suggested I get a job in a bank. 'Banking's just right for you, Sammy; it's for people who aren't bright enough for university but who would get bored stacking shelves.'

Thanks, Gran. Ever the ego-booster.

Inevitably, I spoke to Old Thomas about it. The weather was warmer and I didn't need to bring him tea anymore. I'd taken to dropping in at his stall on my way back from Flitcham and helping out for a while. He seemed very grateful, though I realise now that he was just being kind; it wasn't exactly like the first day of the Selfridges sale. He told me that he normally sold ten books every Saturday; nine from the Agatha Christie end and one from the Non-fiction/Shakespeare/Dickens end. In Deptford, an Agatha Christie reader is an intellectual.

I told him about my predicament.

"What do you want to do?" he said.

"Either play for Flitcham professionally or stay on and take my 'A' levels."

"And Flitcham have stupidly not taken you on yet?"

"No."

"So we are left with a conundrum."

"A what?"

"A conundrum."

"I can't work out what that is."

Old Thomas smiled and said:

"What we need to ascertain are, which subjects you will be studying for 'A' level. English, certainly, but what else?"

We discussed it for an hour, during which eight people stopped to ask if we had Mills and Boon. When the final one ambled up, Old Thomas said:

"I'm terribly sorry but the god of literature became so vehement that he caused a massive conflagration and all the Mills and Boons on the planet were sacrificially burnt. Unfortunately, the multitude of cerebrally-stunted housewives who read this excreta, were too busy watching reality TV to bother pissing on the fire to extinguish it."

"What?"

"I don't have any."

I nearly wet myself. I had to turn my back and pretend to be sorting through some books, otherwise I'd have lost it completely.

"That was rather terrible of me, wasn't it?"

"That was hilarious. I can't believe you said 'pissing'!"

"I'm not a saint, Sam, I'm a bookseller. A bookseller in the wrong place at the wrong time. I'm like herpes; you hope it will go away but it probably won't so you just get used to it."

"So, English, History and Sports Science," I said.

"I think that's an excellent choice. You're good at them and you like doing them. And, most importantly, you don't want to end up stacking shelves. I will not allow you to do that."

"Thanks. I mean, really, thanks."

"That's alright, my son. Now, make yourself useful and put these books in the Classical section in alphabetical order, would you."

"I thought you said you wouldn't allow me to stack shelves."

Old Thomas laughed, gave me five pounds and told me I wasn't stacking shelves, I was arranging classical literature on horizontal strips of mahogany.

Later, I asked to speak to both my parents about my future.

They were in the lounge. The football results were on. I watched for the Taddersham score and then announced in a voice that was as close to Old Thomas' as I could get:

"I wish to speak with you both. It's important."

"Your dad's watching the football programme and why are you speaking like Little Lord Fauntleroy?"

"I'm not. And dad doesn't even like football. It's about what I'm going to do now I've done my GCSEs."

"Now is not the time, Samuel."

"When will be the time?"

"When your dad's not busy."

"Dad's never busy. And the TV never goes off, so *when will be the time?*"

He was there, my dad, five feet away from us, but we had to talk about him because his communication channels had been closed off in 1979, four years before I was born.

"I want to stay on and take my 'A' levels."

"I'll talk to your father."

"No, mum, *I* want to talk to him; man to man. I know it means you both have to pay out more for me, but I'll get a part-time job."

"Samuel, not now."

Then I did it. I stood in front of the television, feeling like a first-time singer at a stadium concert.

"I want to take my A levels. Can I... please?"

It was like a dragon that had been asleep for a hundred years and hadn't wanted to be woken up.

"You'll get a job and bring some money into this house."

"I don't want to get a job... yet. I got the grades in my GSCEs to be able to take my 'A's. Only four of us in my school got them."

"I don't care how many people got them. You'll get a job. Never did me any harm."

"Didn't it?"

I had no idea he could move so fast. Some long-hidden remnant of his athletics training, I suppose; but when the onyx ashtray smacked into my head and gouged out a small chunk of skin just above my eye, it was the shock rather than the pain that affected me most.

I nearly fell, but in the few seconds that the wallpaper swung across my vision and the entire room appeared to be circling at mach 3, I still had the strength to galvanise myself so that he wouldn't know he had hurt me.

"Clive, for God's sake!"

"I'm OK, mum," I said, though anyone could see I wasn't.

"Let me dress that for you. Oh my God, that'll need a stitch. Clive, he was just asking. You shouldn't have stood in front of the telly."

I stared at him for several seconds. He didn't look at me, but he knew what I was doing. Then I turned and walked out of the room.

I didn't go to the hospital, even though mum insisted. In the end she gave up and went to cook his dinner. I didn't go out that night either. I lay on my bed for a while. The pain was horrible and I wanted to cry; but I couldn't. I think I buried the emotion so far down it couldn't reach the surface. After a while, I began to read *Tutankhamen's Treasure*. Davey was right; he did have two still-born children by his half-sister.

It transpired that Gran and Gramps talked my parents into letting me go to Sixth-form College. Some financial deal took place. I've never found out exactly what it was. I know they paid for my books and offered some sort of weekly allowance. He probably took it too, the tight-fisted…

7

I went to Langton Sixth-form College, Deptford's equivalent of Oxford University and my life began to change.

I would train most mornings at Flitcham and then study in the afternoon.

It was then that I started to shed lots of my old friends. I didn't mean to. It was just that I hardly ever saw them and the ties that had held us together at school were no longer there. We couldn't bitch about the same teachers, hide somebody's gym kit and copy each other's homework.

I still hung out with Ja and Tommy occasionally and, although we fought to keep that bond between us, I think we realised that adult friendships would supersede us. And we were, of course, right. Ja got his first girlfriend and, like a lot of guys who discover girls for the first time, gave up on the rest of his mates completely. Tommy and I continued to meet at McDonalds for a few weeks but both of us eventually realised that it was impossible to keep burning this rather unhealthy flame of school-life.

What makes us drift apart, I wonder? What happens in that split second when you know the friendship will end? Do you both feel it at the same time? Do you outgrow each other, as people say? You're both growing, so you must grow in different directions; at different speeds. But I like people who aren't like me so why would I stop wanting to have them as friends? Or is that people *do* stop growing; stop trying; know that they won't, can't, don't want to succeed any further than they have?

I don't know. I didn't stop liking Ja or Tommy. On an emotional level, nothing changed; but on a practical level, I had gone, moved on, grown, something…

Now I had a new group of friends. A different group; more adult, more sure of themselves. Friends who hugged each other; friends who shared each other's drinks and tasted each other's food.

I'd always wanted to hug my friends - male or female - but, of course, up until the age of sixteen, this would have made me a mummy's boy in the eyes of my peers.

There were two types of physical contact at my school. Violence (with other boys) and sex (with girls). If you had a girlfriend, you didn't even hug *her*. You held hands to prove you were together and you shagged. With mates, you didn't even high-five or shake hands. You certainly didn't sit next to each other on the bus. You sat on opposite sides, three seats away and shouted your conversation; then got really annoyed when other people got on and ruined your line of sight.

I asked Old Thomas why none of my friends ever hugged; why none of the adults on my estate seemed to hug. He said:

"Because they're scared. They think that showing emotion is a sign of weakness and that others will take advantage of that. They won't do anything that is different from the accepted norm. They stay in the shadows, desperate to not be noticed."

"But surely people want to be hugged?" I said.

"Of course they do; but they're afraid of rejection, of ridicule; and, if you're a boy, of being called gay."

"But hugging isn't sex." I said.

"Depends how you do it," said Old Thomas, grinning. "As you get a little older you'll find yourself changing your friends, becoming a young adult; and then you'll be able to hug, because it will now *be* the norm; because your new friends won't be scared of being themselves."

As always, he was right.

I didn't know anyone at Langton, but, during the lunch hour on our first day, I ended up sitting on a patch of sun-dried grass, rather grandly called the 'College Green' (I suppose it was almost green and it was in the college, but it was also the dimensions of a king-size duvet cover) talking to Rachel, Susie, Tommy (New Tommy as opposed to McDonalds Tommy), Seb and Tara. They were all from Greenwich; next door to Deptford, but in the same way that Concord would be next to a paper aeroplane. They weren't Oxbridge standard, but they *were* academic.

We'd just had a very elongated English class and were discussing what we were currently reading. I remember Rachel had just started *To Kill a Mocking Bird* which was great as I could join in with that conversation. I asked Seb what he was reading.

"*Krapp's Last Tape* by Kafka."

Well, frankly, he'd just as well have spoken to me in Swahili. All I could think of was that it was the story of a video of someone taking their final poo, written by an Eastern European car.

"Any good?" I asked, speculatively.

"Oh well, you know Kafka."

God, yes; nought to sixty in two and a half minutes and can't make it up anything steeper than a one in ten.

I mean, *obviously* I didn't say that. I just nodded, rested my head on my hand and stared into the mid-distance. A bit like 'The Thinker', only with no thought behind it.

"What are you reading, Sam?"

"... Erm, sorry, what?"

"What are you reading at the moment," Susie repeated.

"Oh, *The Complete Works of Oscar Wilde*."

"Oh, lovely," she said and there general nods and murmurs of agreement.

"What's your favourite of his stuff?" asked New Tommy.

"Oh, definitely the letter he wrote to Lord Alfred Douglas when he was in jail; *De Profundis*."

That'll impress, I thought.

Unfortunately I had pronounced it *Dee Proffendis*.

New Tommy said, "Yes, it's brilliant, isn't it. He was given one sheet of paper every day to write on and then it was taken away, but he hardly ever repeats himself... Erm, not sure if you actually know, Sam, but it's pronounced *Day Profundis*. *Dee Proffendis* sounds like an Anglo-Greek hairdresser."

Everyone laughed.

I felt my fists curl before I could stop them, felt my heartbeat hit rocket-launch pace and my whole body tense so much I would have made the cast of an Australian soap opera look animated.

Then, as suddenly as it had begun, this habitual knee-jerk mindlessness give way to thought. I realised that they weren't laughing at *me*; they were laughing at the *situation* and at New Tommy's joke. They *were* more educated than I was; they *were* from a class above me. But these weren't insults to me, they were just facts. It didn't make me an inferior person, it just made me not know how to pronounce *De Profundis*. And now I knew. So I joined in the laughter and, when it had died down, I said:

"I am to Latin what Dostoevsky was to comedy."

Everyone laughed again.

Thank goodness Old Thomas had suggested I read *Crime and Punishment*.

After that first lunch hour, the six of us became a bit of an item. Other friends from college joined us sometimes. There were parties, picnics, trips to the cinema, lazy Sunday afternoons spent traipsing around Camden Market, buying sculptured leather-bound notebooks and jade necklaces (the Maori friendship stone) and getting drunk in the pub by the Lock. Still can't remember its name.

This became my life and I loved it. College became my home. My friends became my family. My 'constants', as Old Thomas put it.

I even loved the studying. I would sit, rapt with attention, just revelling in where I was, what I was doing; making frantic notes, making lazy notes; gawping over New Tommy's shoulder when the teacher said something über-complicated or used a word I didn't know. When New Tommy cottoned on to this he would, bless him, surreptitiously write down the meaning on his notepad and slide it toward me. Then he would push back the loose blond curl that invariably hung over his right eye and smile. I'd hurriedly read what he'd written and smile back when I'd understood. This was our secret code.

I remember a picnic we went on toward the end of our first year. It was sunny, gloriously so and hot. Not stifling, just comfortably warm enough to sunbathe, with an occasional visiting breeze that tingled and soothed our senses at the same time.

We'd driven down to somewhere in Kent in Susie's old Mini. Six of us and a department store of picnic food in a car that held three people and a bucket, as long as you all stopped breathing and threw the bucket out of the window.

I sat in the back, next to Seb, with Rachel sitting half on me and half on him, her head thrust forward due to the lack of height in the car and her feet turned outwards in some surreal ballet position. She looked like an Egyptian hieroglyphic. Tara was scrunched up at the other end, partially on Seb but mostly in the ashtray. New Tommy sat in regal splendour in the front and, of course, Susie was driving.

I say driving.

Susie is five feet one inch, has a blonde bob and the face of an angel. A bit like a shorter, non-curly version of New Tommy. She smiles nearly all the time and touches your arm or your leg when she's talking to you, whilst playing with the beads she always wears round her neck. She's invariably nice to people, even those she doesn't like. She's kind and a natural born peacemaker.

Until she gets behind the wheel of a car.

Then she turns into Dick Dastardly from *The Wacky Races*.

She doesn't actually have a pointy black moustache but, if she had, she'd be constantly curling it. She drives like, wherever she's going, she should have been there five minutes ago. She treats every road as a motorway, even a dirt track. Anything below fourth gear is for sissies.

"Everyone ready?" she said, slamming her door so hard the boot flew open. "Bugger, hang on a sec."

She got out and slammed the boot shut, making her door slip off its lower hinge. It was an old car.

"Right, everybody ready now?"

"Er, pretty much so," said New Tommy, turning to the rest of us. "You all took a Valium with breakfast, I take it? I've got some in my pocket if it gets really hairy."

"Oh, do shut up, Thomas," Susie said.

"How many, Tom?" Seb asked.

"About thirty."

"Stop it," Susie said.

"Each."

"Fuck off! There's nothing wrong with my driving. At least we'll get there quickly."

I said, "Yes, Suse, but travelling with you is a bit like the transporter in Star Trek. You get there quickly, but sometimes in several pieces."

"I hate all of you; you know that, don't you."

"Yes," we chorused and Susie crunched the car into first and allowed the clutch to bite for one thousandth of a second before taking an inch of tread off the tyres in the three seconds it took her to travel the length of her street.

A twenty-five year old Mini, driven by a lunatic and with a suspension that felt like it was held together by two paper clips and an elastic band, is not the smoothest ride. Seb's and my thighs were so close together, they seemed to be engaged in some permanent fandango. Rachel was bouncing up and down on both of us and the easy intimacy of this situation suddenly registered in my jeans. She had edged slightly toward my crotch and to the side where my cock had decided to dress itself. (I hate that saying – 'which side do you dress?' Why don't they just say 'which side does your penis hang, mate, or does it just do its own thing like most guys'? And anyway, nowadays it doesn't really matter. Back in the old days, when underpants could double as a parachute, I suppose it was necessary but, unless your schlong is eight inches flaccid, it's rather irrelevant now. And, if it was eight inches long, believe me, I'd want to show it off).

Anyway, back to the car and Rachel's rather delicate left buttock using my penis as a trampoline. Now, you have to remember that I'd only had sex once. I had a total sex life of one minute and fifteen seconds. It's not a lot. Bromide is not high on the shopping list of seventeen year old boys, nor are evening classes in self-control. Within five seconds it was so definitely set to magnetic north, you could have used it as a compass. I prayed hard (if you'll pardon the expression) that Rachel wouldn't notice. Unfortunately, it was so impeccably placed that it would have been rather like poking someone in the eye and hoping they wouldn't notice. Rachel was beautifully diplomatic and, to her credit, didn't say anything. To her detriment, she didn't move either. I think she was enjoying the attention, especially when I glanced down and saw that Seb was also doing a pretty good impression of a compass, though a little more north-north-east.

Fortunately, five minutes later, I was saved from a possible... no, probable, embarrassing outpouring, shall we say, by New Tommy announcing he was desperate for a piss and the god of service stations arranging that one should be located half a mile ahead of us. When we got back to the car, I made sure the arrangements were pointing the other way.

We parked by an orchard somewhere near Sevenoaks, stretched our contorted limbs and, after unpacking enough food to feed Norway, began to amble through the apple trees. Well, not *through* them, obviously; around them.

There's something about an English summer's day that I think must be the origin of the word 'perfection'. Maybe it's because they're so rare, we over-emphasise their beauty. I wonder if other countries feel that way. 'You can't beat a Hungarian summer's day'. 'A French summer's day - parfait'. Perhaps, wherever you are, the feel of the sun on your skin, the scent of flowers, the smell of newly-mown grass, the sheer escapitude (I know that's not a word, but it's how I felt) from the stress of city life and the knowledge that, despite the best efforts of the twenty-four hour news channels, we are surrounded by such peace and beauty, gives you the most wonderful feeling of contentment and freedom.

I know that's how I felt as the six of us walked at a happy pace, an 'I might have somewhere to go but it doesn't matter what time I get there because life's too short' pace. Occasionally, Seb, New Tommy or myself would lift Susie up and she would pick apples from the lower branches for the journey home.

After a while, Tara said, "Suse, I thought orchards were private. Should we really be picking apples?"

"They are dear, but this one belongs to my grandparents."

"Wow, really?" Was the general consensus.

"So, Suse, are your grandparents rich?" Asked New Tommy.

"-Ish."

"Do you think they could buy you a bigger car and some driving lessons?"

New Tommy received an apple in between his thighs for his cheek. Susie was a good aim.

Eventually we found a clearing and set down our, by now, heavy picnic baskets and bags and spread a selection of tartan blankets over the grass. It was like a Scottish clan picnic convention.

The food was unwrapped and plated to general appreciation and the two bottles of champagne that Rachel had magically produced from the bottom of her cooler won the 'picnic food of the day' competition. There were cheeses I hadn't heard of, meats I had, a pear and stilton salad that I wouldn't have even considered had I been on the point of starvation, humus of every description apart from plain and six different types of bread. Six! When Rachel said "try some focaccia, Sam, it's gorgeous," I must have looked so helpless that all five of them went to tear a piece off for me. My own contribution had been sausage rolls, pork pies, a mixed salad I'd got from the salad counter at Sainsbury's that I thought was posh because it had cherry tomatoes in it and some deep-fried camembert and cranberry jelly. This was supposed to be the piéce de resistance. Unfortunately, the piéce was somewhat overshadowed by the resistance as I hadn't checked the box and didn't realise you had to cook it first. My sausage rolls and pork pies were met by smiles from the girls and 'Thank God, junk food, nice one, Sammy' from the boys.

I don't think I'll ever forget that afternoon. The easiness of the conversation; the way one subject slipped into another without you really noticing. The way we moved, things happened, glasses were raised, positions changed, food was eaten, smiles recorded, laughter changed to serious expression, changed to laughter. Points were made, stressed, disagreed with, nodded at. Sarcasm and companionship abounded. How things mattered, but not really. How I loved just being there. I made a discovery that day. Me. As I climbed into this new person I realised that this new way of thinking and moving wasn't as alien as I had imagined and I was filled with passion and excitement at the prospect of my future.

Rachel had asked New Tommy to open the first bottle of champagne, probably because he'd worked as a silver service waiter during the holidays in his dad's restaurant.

"OK," he said, "do you want a fizz or an orgasm?"

"Oh God, orgasm," chorused three dirty-minded sopranos.

"Er, what exactly do you mean?" I asked.

"Well, in polite society, when you open a bottle, you should manipulate the cork in such a subtle manner that it makes a barely audible 'phzz' sound when it comes out. But, as we're not in polite society, apart from Rachel, of course-"

"Fuck off, Tommy."

"Then I propose that you all hold up these delightful crystal champagne flutes that Rachel's parents got free with the last castle they bought and I'll make the cork fly at least a hundred yards and the champs froth more than the climax of a 1970s Swedish porno movie."

"My parents do not own a cast-"

"Yeah, porno movie," Seb and I said together.

"I'd like to point out that my family are not rich, they're just-"

But the rest of the sentence was drowned out by a cork that wouldn't have looked out of place at Cape Canaveral and a rush of champagne that fountained into the air like a low-level liquid firework. We caught as much as we could and, when it had calmed down, New Tommy filled up the rest of our glasses.

"Great orgasm, Tom," Seb said.

"Isn't there a cocktail called an orgasm?" asked Tara.

"I think so," said Susie.

"What's in it?"

"Semen, mostly," said Seb.

"Great champagne, Rach," I said.

"Thank you, Sam, it's-"

"From one of her cellars. One of the five. Tastes to me like the chateau in Normandy, or could it be Toulouse," said New Tommy.

"Oh, bog off, I-"

"Whichever", said Seb, "it's definitely vintage, Rachel. Full-bodied-"

"Just a hint of bitterness-"

"All drowned in a vat of pseudo-liberal angst."

"My family are not rich. We are not posh. We only have five houses, three cars, six horses and a boat."

"Yeah, it's the word 'only' I'm having trouble with," Seb said.

"Look, mummy even goes-"

"And now the word 'mummy'."

"My family are very aware of their roots."

"Then they should get them dyed," I said.

Seb and New Tommy collapsed, Susie giggled uncontrollably, even Tara smiled. Humour was always considered funnier when I said it. Probably because I was the most common of us.

"We were farmers," intoned Rachel, in a voice that was incapable of forming the word 'muckspreading'."

"Darling, you were landowners from Leicestershire," said Susie, mixing diplomacy with the truth; an almost impossible feat.

"I gave up the chance to go to private school."

"Yes, but you *had* the chance." This was Tara. Tara didn't say a great deal but, when she did, it was often bang on the mark.

"Rach, we're only ribbing you because we're jealous," said New Tommy, "you know we don't mean it."

Rachel knew this but still wanted her moment to sulk.

"And I am *not* full-bodied."

She wasn't; although, with all that riding, she did have thighs you could build a suspension bridge on.

"Anyway, Rach," said Seb, "think yourself lucky, you could be like Sam and live in a council house."

"Excuse me," I said, "we got that council house free when we bought six champagne flutes."

Even Rachel laughed this time.

"Do you have an indoor toilet, Sam?" asked New Tommy.

"Depends whether we can be bothered to bring the bucket in from the yard."

"And electricity?"

"What?"

New Tommy picked up the salt cellar and pretended it was a microphone.

"Hello, I'm interviewing Scum Hatchington, a common person. Scum... may I call you Scum? What's it like being poor?"

"Eh up, well, I couldn't reetly say."

"Do you *have* to be northern," said Seb, whose original Manchester accent only appeared when he was drunk or watching sport.

"Well, geezer," I said, "it ain't all bad – just ninety-eight percent of it."

"Describe your typical day. Oh, sorry, the word 'typical' has three syllables in it; perhaps you didn't understand?"

"Three what?"

"*Syllables.* Do you know what they are?"

"Are they stupid spheres?"

"What?" said Tara.

"Silly balls, dear," said Susie, "do keep up."

"Well, I get up around mid-day. We have a newspaper delivered... which we tear up, put in a pan of water and pretend it's porridge. Then it's a quick trip down to the Unemployment Office, spend half me benefits on cheap lager at the 'Burglar and Pickpocket', stagger home, knock the wife around for a while, mix up some sawdust and meths and call it couscous; then it's a few games of gin rummy, watch *Big Brother*, sit round a candle if it's cold, light it if it's really cold, then all six of us sleep on a single mattress."

"Oh my God, that's awful," said Rachel.

"Which bit?"

"Watching *Big Brother*."

"Thank you, ladies and gentlemen," said New Tommy, "that was Scum Hatchington and a day in the life of a common person. Actually Sam, you're not really common... well, just a little bit... well, quite a lot really... actually, I don't think I can speak to you anymore."

The two of us laughed, but I leapt on him anyway and a very silly and childlike play fight ensued. There were a couple of pretend punches but mostly manly tickling, if there is such a thing.

"You'd better watch out," New Tommy said, "or I'll damage that handsome face of yours."

"Not before I've damaged that handsome face of yours first."

"Anyway, you don't tickle, you poke and it really hurts sometimes."

"Wimp."

"Thug."

There then followed a protracted discussion as to who was the sexiest male and female singer of all time.

Seb had plumped for Debbie Harry, which had produced considerable nodding and murmurs of support from New Tommy and myself and comments of "God, that's just *so* predictable," from Rachel and Tara.

"Why do guys like her?" said Rachel, "she's just all hair-dye and pouting."

"She *was* a modern day Monroe," said Seb.

"She was rather beautiful when she was younger, Rach," said Susie, who could have been used as the Middle-East peace envoy at the age of ten, "she can't sing but she's very sexy."

New Tommy was in favour of Kate Bush. "God, the first time I saw her singing *Wuthering Heights* on those re-runs of *Top of the Pops*, I just had to run upstairs, close my bedroom door and-"

"Yes, thank you, Tommy," said Rachel, "we don't need to know."

"And play one of her CDs, was what I was going to say."

"Oh… sorry."

"Which I would obviously use as background music to wank to."

Rachel threw a sausage roll at him.

"Don't waste the sausage rolls, Rach," Seb said, "it's the only food that Sam recognises."

I threw a sausage roll at him.

"Who do you think is the sexiest, Sammy?" said Susie.

I hate being put on the spot. I can never think of my favourite anything. My brain just turns into a neuron version of cotton wool. I don't think I have any favourites. I remember once telling a friend that my favourite song was *Summer of '69* and then meeting that friend again, ten years later and her being astounded that, although I still loved it, it wasn't my favourite. "But, it was always your favourite," she said. "I know, but it's not now." "Why?" "I don't know." "Well, what is?" "Er, I don't really have one." "But you must have." "Why must I?" "Because everyone has." "Well, I don't." "But, everyone has a favourite song for life." "Are we given it at birth?" "No, but it's what defines us." "So, we're never allowed to change anything?" "No." "Well, I used to breastfeed but I don't think I'd like to now." And then she got exasperated and changed the subject.

"Er, Dido," I said, grasping at the first name I could think of. And, anyway, she was attractive in that slightly sultry 'girl next door' way. A sort of cross between one of the alien vixens in Star Trek and Princess Diana.

I benignly accepted approval from everyone, except Tara, who stared at me in that way she had. It was a strange mixture. Friendliness, but also something darkly quizzical that made me feel I'd grown a third ear or that someone had stuck an 'I'm a twat' sticker on my back.

Rachel, Susie and Tara went for Diana Ross, Jennifer Lopez and Suzi Quattro respectively. This produced no response from us boys, apart from Seb who said, "Who's Suzi Quattro?"

Then it was time to vote for the sexiest male singer, at which point Susie and Rachel went into a lather discussing the various possibilities. They were the human equivalent of an old twin-tub with too much washing powder in it. Tara had already stated 'Bob Dylan' which had been met with a wall of incredulous silence. Finally, after what seemed like three days, they dismissed Enrico Iglesias as being 'too beautiful', Damon Albarn as being 'pretty, but in a pre-pubescent way' and Ricky Martin as being just 'too' and settled on Frank Sinatra.

"So, boys, who do you think is the sexiest male singer of all time?" said Susie.

"How should we know," replied Seb, "we're guys."

"What difference does that make?"

"Guys can't judge other guys' looks."

"Why?"

"Because…"

"Yes?"

"Just because."

"Because it might make people think you're gay?"

"No."

There followed a little interlude when no one spoke and no sausage rolls were thrown, then Tara said:

"I always think that its guys who are totally sure of their heterosexuality and who have nothing to prove that can say whether another guy is good-looking or not."

Another pause with no airborne sausage rolls.

"And, anyway, Tommy and Sam think each other are handsome."

"Yes, Tara," said New Tommy, "but we *are* shagging like rabbits in private."

I laughed and threw a sausage roll at him.

"Guys," said Tara, pushing Seb even further into a metaphorical corner, "do *you* think that Seb is good-looking?"

"Yeah," I said, "definitely."

He is. Not quite as much as New Tommy, but Seb has that chiselled look that guys in GQ have, with the obligatory short brown hair. His only drawback then, was that he was a late developer and the last six inches of his six feet two inches had only occurred in the past two years. He needed to flesh out a bit. When he danced he looked like a windmill on Acid.

"You bitch," shouted New Tommy, flinging the final sausage roll at me, "you said I was the only one!"

We all laughed again, only stopping when we realised that 'all' didn't encompass Seb.

Susie, as usual, was first up to the mark. She knelt in front of him and took his hands in hers.

"Seb, darling, we know you're not gay and we're not having a go at you. We're just trying to break down the last remnants of your mid-teenage macho defensiveness. I think Rachel and Tara are gorgeous, but it doesn't make me want to strip naked and have sex with them right here."

"Unfortunately," said New Tommy.

There was a hiatus whilst Seb took all this in. I suppose it was a minor epiphany for him; more of a 'piph' really.

Then he said, "Chris Martin."

"Oh God, that is *so* gay," said Rachel.

"Er, yeah, Rach, that's not helping."

"No, he's a great-looking guy," repeated Seb. "If I was a poo-puncher, I'd do him."

And with that understatement, Seb finally let go of his mid-teenage macho defensiveness.

A while later, Tara opened a pack of cigarettes and, although only she smoked, we all took one. It just felt right. If this had been the 1920s we would all have been smokers. And there was an aura of the Twenties about us. Like those Art Deco posters you see with the flappers and their beaus sitting flawlessly on a perfectly manicured English lawn, relaxing after drinking and Charlestoning the afternoon away. Wrong fashions, right feelings.

And all that sausage roll flinging began to take its toll and, although our spirits remained high, our bodies and minds began to wind down, like a Westminster chime clock in a rarely used room.

Eventually we slept, with the serenity of a post-siren peace. I remember drifting awake for a few seconds with Tara lying on my arm and New Tommy's head on my tummy and, for a fleeting moment, wondering how I came to have such friends and whether this happiness could ever be bettered.

Later, after we had packed up what remained of the food (not very much), Tara took my hand and didn't let go until we reached the car.

8

The summer holidays came and went. My life had become such fun that I didn't really notice them. It was just like normal, only without the lessons.

By some unspoken agreement, Davey and I had outgrown our Wednesday afternoon kick-about. Instead, we went to the gym. The Deptford YMCA. Most of the equipment probably saw action during the Crimea. Still, a dumbbell was a dumbbell. 'Dumb' pretty much summed up most of the people who went there too. Still, it kept them off the streets and out of trouble; or made them stronger, so that when they went back on the streets, they could cause even more trouble.

Some of the guys there were so huge and muscle-bound they could hardly walk. They looked like something out of *Transformers*, only with less personality. I don't know why guys do this. All the women I've asked find it pretty repulsive. Maybe it's an addiction. Better than alcohol or drugs, I suppose. And it shrinks your genitals, apparently. All the blood is too busy being pumped to the over-sized muscles. I mean, there's not much point having the body of an iron man if you've got the cock of an iron filing.

We'd been going for about a month when Davey was approached by one of the trainers and asked if he would be interested in becoming a trainee trainer.

For once, Davey's unreadable exterior had floundered just a little and he looked genuinely surprised.

"Wow, you're going to be a trainee trainer," I said.

"Er, yes."

"That's like a plimsoll."

"What?"

"A plimsoll… A 'trainee trainer'."

"I don't understand."

"Oh God, don't make me explain it in detail. OK, a plimsoll wants to be a trainer when it grows up, so it's a trainee tr-"

"That's the worst joke I've ever heard."

"Well, it is *now* because you took nearly a week to work it out."

Then he forced me down on to a bench and, in a mock-threatening voice, said:

"If you are ever that unfunny in the future, I will never speak to you again. Now, get down and give me forty."

I dropped and did forty press-ups with my nose touching his trainer on each one. After twenty, I couldn't resist any longer:

"Nice plimsolls."

When I'd finished, he said:

"Right, let's work on those abs of yours; grab the Swiss ball and do sixty sit-ups."

"Hang on, you don't start till tomorrow."

"Hatchington, your abs are like an under-set jelly."

"Fuck off, are they, I've got a six-pack."

"Yes, of Babycham."

I grabbed the Swiss ball and did as I was told and later realised, as my stomach muscles squealed at me to stop, that Davey's and my friendship had moved on to a new level. We had always had this link. I'd always known I could trust him, rely on him, tell him anything; and that he could do the same to me. We had an unspoken, unrivalled bond. And now, suddenly, the masculinity of this connection had been joined by something lighter, more playful. And, although any change in a friendship frightens me, I welcomed this new fun, childlike addition and I remembered Old Thomas' comment of 'you can never count anyone as a truly close friend until you can be appallingly rude to them'.

By the end of the session I had sweated enough to irrigate most of the Sahara.

"Come on, Jelly Tummy," said the new trainer extraordinaire, "let's hit the showers."

In the changing rooms, I peeled off my sports vest, shorts, socks and pants. The showers at the YMCA were communal, by which I mean that they didn't have cubicles, as opposed to being used by both sexes.

Three guys had just left, leaving Davey and I to brave the controls alone. There were two temperatures; 'tepid' and 'so cold it's advisable to forget it and stay sweaty for the rest of the day'. We grabbed the two adjoining showers most likely to aspire to the dizzying heights of tepidness.

I was halfway through soaping when I got cramp in my right calf.

"Ow! Ow, ow fuckety ow!"

"What's up?"

"Cramp."

"Where?"

"Right calf."

"OK."

Davey rinsed the shampoo out of his eyes, grabbed hold of my lower leg and straightened it to the point that I thought it would snap.

"Ow!" I repeated, "it's so painful."

"I know, but it'll go in a second. Breathe for me."

I breathed.

"OK, just be careful with it for the next two minutes."

He turned back to the shampoo bottle.

It was at this moment that I looked at Davey, naked in the shower next to me. Guys don't often do this. If they do, it's just a glance to find out if the other bloke's got a bigger penis. It's all about comparisons.

He had the perfect body. He was never tanned but you could see every single muscle. From his broad shoulders the water ran curves round his triceps, cascaded to the small of his back and ran into a delta over his bottom, splashing onto his hams and calves. 'Michelangelo's Davey', I suddenly thought.

I don't know how many seconds I'd been looking for when he suddenly turned to face me.

"You OK?"

"Er… yeah, yeah."

"Cramp not come back?"

"No, it's fine; thanks."

"Good."

Of course, I looked away immediately and thrust my head under the raging dribble emanating from the shower-head. I closed my eyes and began to ponder why I'd just stared at him.

It wasn't for any sexual reason; at least I don't think it was. I hadn't become aroused. I hadn't felt any impulse to leap on him. I just wanted to look at him. What had I felt as I'd done so? Warmth? Fondness? Admiration? I don't know. Perhaps we need some new words to describe feelings and emotions that we don't know exist because someone has yet to arrange a few letters of the alphabet into a recognisable form that explains them. Maybe we should have a new word that encompasses warmth, fondness and admiration. But there isn't one. So I'll invent it.

Tenderlence.

I felt tenderlence.

For a while I was embarrassed by what I'd done. Personal embarrassment. It can be as profound or as minimal as you wish it. It had started out as intense but, because I, alone, could decide on its level, I had reduced it to 'barely noticeable' and then to 'non-existent'. I looked at him when he was fully dressed; what difference was there? He was my friend. That was all.

We dressed and began to walk toward the High Street where we would part for our respective homes.

As we did so, it dawned on me that my friendship with Davey stood alone. He'd never met any of my other friends. He'd never asked; I'd never suggested it. We just did things together; gym, football, conversation. It was at that moment that I realised I knew hardly anything about him; not even his surname.

"What's your surname?"

"Where the hell did *that* come from?"

"I don't know your surname."

"Is it important?"

"Yes."

"OK, it's Hunston."

"Oh."

"Feel better now?"

"I just wanted to know."

"Well, I hope it's changed your life."

"Where do you live?"

"What?"

"Where do you live? I don't know that either."

"Charlotte Street."

"What number?"

"Are you going to start stalking me or something?"

"No."

"Thirty-two."

"Oh."

I suppose it felt rather anti-climactic really. Davey, as usual, was right. What difference had it made? Now I knew his surname and address. Whoopee-doo.

"You must come back to my house sometime."

"I'm not going to marry you, Hatchington."

"No, I mean we only ever meet up in town or at footie."

"Yes."

"There's a party this Thursday with lots of my college friends. Why don't you come?"

"OK."

"Cool. It's at Rachel's castle."

"Castle?"

"Well, not really. We just take the piss because her family's pretty well off. It's a six-bedroom house in Greenwich."

"*That's* a castle."

"I'll text you the address."

We had reached our parting point.

"See you Thursday, then," Davey said.

"Yeah and good luck at the gym tomorrow. Hope your first day goes really well."

"Thanks."

For once, he didn't immediately walk away. We stood, facing each other.

I hugged him.

I didn't know whether I should and I thought he might back away, but he didn't. He hugged me for, maybe, ten seconds.

"Bye," he said and walked off.

9

I arrived at Rachel's with enough lager to guarantee a forty-eight hour hangover. It was nine o'clock and the party was already in full swing. The theme was the 1980s and I, like about eleven other people, had turned up as Adam Ant.

Rachel opened the door dressed as Kim Wilde (Rachel, not the door).

"Wow," I said, "are there a lot of 'Kids in America' here?"

"No, there aren't, 'Prince Charming'," she replied.

"Oh my God, is this going to be the standard of the humour for the night?"

"I hope not," she said. "Anyway, come in and get drunk so we can bear it if it is."

I went through to the kitchen, flipped the top off my first bottle of Grolsch and downed about a third of it.

"Oh my God, you're even more gorgeous with make-up on," said Susie.

"Thank you… I think," I said, my ever-deepening blush emphasised by the white stripe across my face.

"Oh, Rach, I've invited my friend Davey along. Hope you don't mind."

"Really? The famous Davey. Of course I don't mind. Is he cute?"

"Well, yeah, he's very good-looking."

"What does he do?"

"He's a trainer at a gym."

"Oh my God, he's mine," said Susie, emerging from her fourth Tequila Slammer of the evening.

Within half an hour we'd drunk another three drinks each. (It's essential to drink a lot at the beginning of a party, mainly to convince your brain that the facade of confidence you're currently trying to put over, is real).

By eleven-thirty, everyone had settled. Ice had melted, cliques split up, safe enclaves eliminated. Everyone was dancing, chatting, laughing with people they'd never met before. New Tommy was in the music room, sitting on a stool with someone from Bananarama on his lap, rewriting *Beethoven's Love Sonata* on her tonsils; Seb was engaged in a deep political discussion with Simon Le Bon; Rachel was being the perfect hostess, if a little unstable from the combination of borrowing Sigue Sigue Sputnik's eight inch heels and the bucket of Pinot Grigio she'd chucked down her throat; Susie was regaling a group of people she didn't know with some of her love poetry – they seemed to be enjoying it even though every fourth line was 'I'm sorry, I'm so drunk'; Tara was... well, Tara. She didn't get drunk, she got slightly less sober. She'd come as Boy George ('well, he looked like a girl') and, I later realised, had spent most of the evening next to me. We were currently chatting to Margaret Thatcher and Johnny Rotten about whether ghosts existed. And Davey still hadn't arrived.

At midnight I felt the need to not make any more conversation for a while and so Tara, Seb and I went into the drawing room to dance. We were halfway through *Tainted Love* when Rachel lurched into the doorway with my gym partner on her arm and drunkenly announced:

"This is Darcy... I'm so sorry, this is Davey."

Everyone in the room stopped to look. The guys glanced round, then turned back to whatever they were doing, but several female jaws dropped in unison and stayed that way for several seconds.

At that moment, Susie fell into the room.

"Oh my! Sammy, you said he was cute; you didn't say he was *this* cute."

Davey hadn't worn a costume. He was dressed in figure-hugging jeans (most things were figure-hugging on him) and a slim-fit white shirt.

"Gosh, just look at you," slurred Susie. "Can I feel your pecs?" she asked, about a minute after she'd started feeling them.

Davey took it all in good part and didn't even flinch when Susie moved down past his abs and insisted on an in-depth analysis of his thighs.

"Hi," I said.

"Hi."

We hugged.

"You had a drink yet?"

"No."

"Then I insist you come into the kitchen and down two of the cans of Fosters you've brought. You've got a lot of catching up to do."

"OK."

We went into the kitchen, followed by Rachel and Susie who had both suddenly remembered they wanted ice in their drinks; though quite why you needed ice in a Tequila, I really don't know.

Davey duly downed two cans and made heroic efforts to catch up over the next hour by drinking four more.

Two o'clock in the morning found us all outside on the lawn, near the duck pond. (Duck pond - I ask you).

The last I'd seen of New Tommy, he'd been trying to teach the girl from Bananarama how to play the piano. Apparently they had both left the party at around one o'clock. No doubt he was now thrusting his pianissimo with considerable allegro into her cadenza.

Susie had fallen asleep, leaving Rachel, Tara, Davey, myself and a random guy who was dressed as Elvis Costello or someone else with glasses. It was late and the alcohol was attempting to sing my brain to sleep.

We'd ended up lying down together in a slightly surreal line. You know, when they film people from above and the shapes of their bodies spell out a word? Ours was 'CIIIV', a rarely used Latin word meaning 'lots of drunken people lying on a lawn'. Susie was curled up at one end, then we had Rachel, Davey, Tara, myself and Elvis Costello.

It was one of those beautifully still nights. There was a willow tree overhanging the pond, which acted as a makeshift pair of curtains for our open-air communal bedroom. Above us, the sky was that beautiful shade of Indian-blue when autumn still believes its summer. 'This majestical roof fretted with golden fire', as Hamlet, I believe, put it, hung above us, minus golden fire, but suspended by timeless, dimensionless space. I remember feeling so small and yet so a part of everything around me; the other guys, the grass, the tree, the sky; I knew all of these things and they knew me. And, for a while, I realised that there are no strangers, no unexpected situations, no fears, no lonely people. Everything fitted together like a jigsaw puzzle, albeit an enormous one. And, although some people were determined to lose pieces and to bugger everything up, they would never be able to because the jigsaw has been around for so long that the pieces have moulded inseparably together.

Obviously I wasn't the only person thinking this because, when we began to talk again, the conversation reverted to the same subject, but via a slight detour.

It was Rachel who broke the silence.

"You know," she slurred, "we should all go through life with the feeling you have after drinking one pint or smoking half a joint."

"Why's that, Rachel?" Tara said.

"Because... well, because after one pint you're not drunk but you're really happy and relaxed and more likely to get on with people. And you make wonderful plans because suddenly you feel as though you can do anything. So no one gets aggressive because someone else is different to them and they realise that diversity is what makes the world tick".

"Well said!"

"Thank you. Who said that?"

"Elvis did," I said.

"Elvis?"

"Yeah. Sorry, I don't know your name."

"It's Gavin."

"Gavin said it. Gavin Costello."

"Actually, it's Gavin Saunders."

"Oh, sorry."

"Thank you, Gavin Saunders," said Rachel.

"Trouble is," continued Gavin Elvis Costello Saunders, "there's too much patriotism in the world."

"There's nothing wrong with patriotism," Davey said.

"Yes there is; it causes wars."

"Nationalism causes wars."

"Same thing."

"No it's not. Patriotism is the love of one's country; nationalism is the hatred of everyone else's."

"Do you know," said Rachel, resting her arm on Davey's chest, "you're really profound." Rachel didn't take her arm away. In fact, she moved it only so she could stroke his face. "Beautiful... and deep," she said.

I was watching this to see exactly where it would go and was only stopped when Tara rolled on top of me and stuck her tongue down my throat.

It was a good thing I couldn't speak because the comment I would have made was 'bloody hell, Tara, what do you think you're doing'? Instead I kissed her back for a while.

When she'd finished, after one final attempt to pull my top lip away from the rest of my face, I said:

"Wow! That was unexpected."

"Why?"

"Well... it just, sort of, was."

"Sam, I've been giving you the come-on for the last ten weeks."

"Oh? How?"

"Holding your hand, asking you out for coffee, inviting you to the cinema, telling you how much I liked you, mentioning that I was fed up with being single. Subtle things like that."

"Oh."

"So, either I'm rubbish at making my feelings felt or you're just very naïve."

"He's very naïve," said Davey, seconds before Rachel copied Tara and sent her tongue in search of his trachea.

"I didn't realise," I said to Tara, "I just thought we were being friends. I mean, if I'd have known-"

"Shut up and just kiss me."

"Sorry. OK."

We two couples kissed, until I suddenly remembered Elvis Gavin and pulled away.

"Elvis Gavin," I said, "sorry, we're ignoring you."

"He's gone," said Tara, "he went ages ago."

So we continued to kiss under Hamlet's 'majestical roof' until Susie suddenly woke up.

"Oh my God! The world has gone mad. I close my eyes for a few seconds and everybody's pashing."

"You've been asleep for an hour, dear," said Rachel.

"Have I? Well, even so, a lot has obviously happened in a short space of time. Tara and Rachel, you're both hussies."

"How do you know we started it?" said Rachel.

"Because you're both on top."

"Oh, yes, fair enough."

Then Elvis Gavin came out of the house, announced that he was leaving and that everyone else had now gone and it had been a great party and thank you so much for inviting him.

Rachel remembered, a little belatedly, that she was the hostess and showed him to the door.

"Well, I'd better be off as well," I said, "training in... oh God, six hours."

"I'll come with you," Davey said.

Rachel's face radiated disappointment. Tara, as usual, was unreadable but, just as we were leaving, she grabbed my hand and said:

"You have got the message now, Sam?"

"Er, yes, pretty much. I think I'd have had to be dead to have missed it."

"Good," she said.

Our swimming heads protested silently as Davey and I walked into town. When we reached the High Street, he made me jump by suddenly saying:

"Look, I don't want to put on you or anything but, would there be any chance of sleeping on your floor tonight?"

"Yeah, of course. Don't you have your keys?"

"Yes, but they put the chain on at midnight and I won't be able to get in."

"God, that's a bit unfair of your parents."

"Yes."

So we went back to my house and climbed the stairs as silently as we could. We'd just entered my room when I remembered my manners.

"Oh, would you like a coffee?"

"No thanks, I'd just like to sleep."

"OK. Shit."

"What?"

"I don't have a spare duvet."

"Don't worry, I'll sleep on the floor in my jacket."

"No, don't be silly."

"I'll be OK, really."

"No. Look, you sleep in my bed and I'll sleep-"

"No way, you've been kind enough to let me stay-"

"Yes, but you're my guest and-"

"I'm not chucking you out of your bed, so-"

"Well, it's *my* bed so *I'll* decide who... this is getting ridiculous, isn't it."

"Yes."

"Shall we just stop being so polite?"

"Good idea."

"OK, you're sleeping on the roof. Here's a spare T-shirt. Now, get out the window and start climbing."

Davey took the T-shirt, opened the window and began to climb out. I grabbed him round the waist and hauled him back just as his second leg was about to disappear.

"I'm joking, you idiot."

"So am I," he said.

"Right, we'll both sleep on the floor under my single duvet and pretend we're not adults yet."

"We're *not* adults yet."

"Well, that's OK, then."

We had one pillow each and lay on the rug with the duvet barely covering us. I must have fallen asleep within seconds because I don't remember saying goodnight or even one of our famous pauses. I woke up once, at 6.30, desperate for the toilet. As always, I was foetal and I realised that Davey must sleep that way too as I could feel his breathing against my shoulder and our legs had become so intertwined it was almost impossible to extricate mine without waking him. When I finally succeeded and began to tip-toe toward the bathroom, Davey said:

"Be quick, I'm desperate too."

When we were both back in our makeshift bed, I said:

"You OK?"

"Yes. You?"

"Yes. You got enough duvet?"

"Yes, thank you."

"Good. Night."

"Night."

The next thing I knew it was 8.30 and my frog was vomiting.

"What the fuck is that noise?!"

"It's my alarm clock. It's a frog. It croaks."

"Doesn't sound like it's croaking to me; sounds like it's throwing up."

"Er, yes, it does that."

"You wake up to that every morning?"

"Yes."

"Sam."

"Yes?"

"Get a new alarm clock."

I yawned, tried to stretch and realised we'd woken up in exactly the same positions as before.

"How do you feel?"

It was a question I hadn't yet entertained. Of course, as soon as I thought about it, the consequences of drinking the Atlantic Ocean in lager smacked me between the eyes.

"I feel shit."

"Very descriptive."

"How do *you* feel?"

"Bit of a headache."

"Bit of a headache?!"

"Yes."

"What are you, a machine?!"

"No, just more of a man than you."

"Bollocks," I said, not helping my cause by hitting him over the head with my pillow like a ten year old girl.

"I'm going to take a shower," I said, removing myself from the manic etch-a-sketch of our legs and throwing him a spare towel. "Have one after me and then we'll go and get some breakfast."

"Great, thanks. Can I borrow a T-shirt?"

"Yeah, of course," I said, diving into my T-shirt draw and lobbing one at him.

"Thanks. Er, could I borrow one *without* Mickey Mouse on the front."

"Shit."

After we'd both showered and dressed, we took our respective hangovers down to the kitchen.

My mum had just put a plate of bacon and eggs on the table. Is there anything more welcome, tastier and more comforting after a night of excessive drinking than a large plate of bacon and eggs?

No.

"Er, Mum, this is Davey. He stayed last night coz he couldn't get home. Davey, this is my mum."

"It's a pleasure to meet you, Mrs Hatchington."

"And you too, Davey. What a charming young man your friend is, Sam," she said, as though Davey had suddenly disappeared and couldn't hear her.

"Davey can have my breakfast. I'll just have a slice of toast."

"Nonsense, Davey can have this one and I'll cook another one for you."

"Oh, thanks."

For the next fifteen minutes Davey kept up a conversation with my mum, politely enquiring about why she gave up nursing, had she enjoyed it and what were her interests now? She was enchanted by him, patting her hair on numerous occasions and cooking him extra fried bread.

Then, like an arctic blast through a smashed window, my father walked into the kitchen.

We hadn't spoken in several months. My mum said it was causing an unbearable atmosphere in the house. I said that, as far as he was concerned, it was no different to how it had always been. Of course, now I had no choice; I had to break our unspoken, mutual vow of silence.

"Er, dad, this is my friend, Davey. Davey, this is my father."

Davey immediately stood up and held out his hand.

"Pleased to meet you, Mr Hatchington."

My 'father' turned to Davey, looked at his outstretched hand, turned back to my mum, said 'three eggs this morning' and walked into the lounge.

Davey was wonderful. He didn't seem fazed (though I later found out that he was) but just sat down and said to my mum, "that was a terrific breakfast, Mrs Hatchington, thank you very much."

I'd never seen my mum quite so embarrassed. She re-arranged a t-towel, put some bread she'd already toasted back in to the toaster and said:

"I'm so sorry about that, Davey. He's… having a bad morning."

"He's having a bad life," I said.

"Samuel, please."

And there I left it so as not to embarrass her any further.

She backed out of the kitchen in an almost subservient manner and followed 'him' in to the lounge.

"Er, Davey, I'm sorry mate; I'll explain when we've left the house. Let's grab our stuff and get off."

As we walked past the lounge, we heard a snippet of conversation.

"Clive, that was too much. He's a very nice, polite young man. You completely ignored him."

"He's a friend of *his*, so I have no compulsion to speak to him."

Davey said, "aren't you a bit shocked by that?"

"The only thing that shocks me," I said, "is that he knows the word 'compulsion'."

I described the behaviour of the person who created a void where my father should have been as we zigzagged through a particularly busy town centre. I'd mentioned some of his antics before, but only in private. As a child loyalty usually overrode the desire to tell the truth about my parents.

When I'd finished, Davey said:

"I'm so sorry, Sam. Are you OK?"

"Yes," I said.

"Really?"

"Yes. Totally. I don't like him. I certainly don't love him. If he moved out tomorrow, I would celebrate."

Davey looked sideways at me for a while and decided I was not overflowing with fake 'head-in-a-bucketness', but that I actually meant it.

"OK," he said, "but any time you need to talk about it…"

"Thanks. What are you parents like?" I said.

"Oh, you know…"

"No, that's why I asked."

"They're, er, pretty normal."

"Do you talk to them?"

"Often."

"That's good."

We marched on in silence till we reached the bus stop that Davey needed.

"OK," I said, "try not to kill Nibbsy."

"I'm not going there anymore."

"Oh? How come?"

"I've been taken on by Craytown FC."

"No. No way!!"

"Way."

"Davey, that's just brilliant. I mean, they're semi pro."

"Yes."

"When did you find out?"

"Monday."

"Why didn't you say anything?"

"It didn't come up in conversation."

"Of course it didn't; because I'm not physic, you dick."

"Well, you know now."

"Mate, I'm so chuffed. I really am."

"Thank you."

"Look, what are you doing on Saturday afternoon?"

"Nothing much. Why?"

"Meet me by the library; there's someone I want you to meet at the Saturday market."

"OK."

I told him again how pleased I was. I got the idea that people didn't tell him these things very often because, after the initial 'Davey' look, a mixture of mild embarrassment and neutrality, the smile he boxed and gave to me traced the merging paths of innocence and beauty.

Then he went to Craytown and I went to Flitcham.

10

I enjoyed the routine of changing into my kit and indulging in football banter with the guys; mostly at Pete, who was a devout Preston North End fan and, therefore the butt of all jokes. "Hey Pete, hear about the Preston fan who rang up the ground and said 'what time does the match start'? And they said, 'what time can you get here'?!" We all got on well, without any close ties developing. Jake, from Highgate, was my best mate there, but even he was just a mate, not a friend. We didn't socialise outside work.

We'd warmed up and spent a short time practising free kicks when Michael Cantry suddenly appeared by my side, coincidentally just as the ball was passed to me. He took it off my toes, flipped it onto his head and then volleyed it about thirty yards, skimming the crossbar of the goal.

We applauded. It was, after all, pretty good footballing skill.

"Sam, can I have a word with you, please?"

"Er, yeah; yeah, of course."

He'd said it too nonchalantly. If someone says something as if it's the least important sentence in the world, it means it's the *most* important.

My brain began doing its suicidal juggling act as we left the field. It tossed three hundred reasons why Michael wanted to speak to me into the air and, naturally, dropped all of them. The only one that remained in my mind was that he was going to fire me because I hadn't seen him coming up behind to tackle me. It was some sort of test that you had and I'd failed it. Of course, there was the other option; he was going to fire me because I hadn't made the grade.

In his office I dropped into the firing squad chair. Michael crossed his legs and knitted his fingers together.

"We've been watching your progress closely, Sam."

"Thank you," I said, in the absence of anything more intelligent coming into my head.

"When you started, you had raw talent. A large amount of raw talent... That's a compliment, by the way."

"Thank you," I said, falling back on the only two words in the English language I appeared to be able to remember.

"You developed slowly. It was difficult, sometimes, to get you out of old habits. You have a considerable amount of stubbornness in your character but, more importantly, a huge appetite and enthusiasm to learn."

Don't say 'thank you' again, I thought to myself.

"Thank you," I said.

"What we tried to do was take that terrific talent and blend it with an analytical attitude to the game; to improve your already considerable skills, but give you more foresight and maturity. Everything you did when you first came here was spontaneous, so we had to ground you..."

Then my brain did that thing that brains do when the situation becomes too stressful/boring/overwhelming to handle and went off into a parallel universe where everything is made of spray cream and the sun never stops shining.

I have no idea what he said for the next ten seconds/five minutes/two weeks. I came round on the helpful word, 'so'...

"So, taking all this into account, we would be delighted if you would join us as a full-time Flitcham player."

There was a pause when several works of art were painted, a couple of volcanoes erupted and a new African state was created and then my brain slammed back into my head and I jolted so violently I nearly fell off the chair.

"Fuck...! No, no, not fuck. Sorry. Shit... No, not shit either."

Michael laughed.

"Can I translate that last sentence as 'yes'?"

"Yes. Yes you can. Thank you. Thank you. I..."

"Can't quite believe it?"

"Yes. I'm just amazed."

"I pretty much worked that out!"

We laughed and I remembered at the last second that it was appropriate to shake hands and not hug your new employer.

At that moment the Flitcham manager walked in, a smile enveloping his face. He had a brief chat with me, telling me how pleased he was to have me on the books and saying what a great asset I was going to be to the team. Then I left the office, somehow. I know my legs had nothing to do with it. I trained for another hour, then showered, said goodbye to the guys and, as I walked out the gates, had this strange feeling that I wasn't actually inhabiting my body at that moment; like I was watching me from a distance. A new TV drama about a boy whose dream comes true and you excuse the corny ending because the story was actually quite good.

11

By the time the bus lurched to a halt outside the library in Deptford High Street, my 'I have to tell somebody now' gland had gone into hyper drive.

I wasn't seeing the gang until Monday; Gran and Gramps had gone to Southend 'for some culture, Sam' (good luck, Gran); It wouldn't have been fair to tell Davey yet, not on the day he'd started at Craytown and, obviously, the only other person I really wanted to tell was Old Thomas, but I was about to take Davey to meet him. I could have told my mum, I suppose. She would have been pleased, deep down; but deep down had been anaesthetised so it could never reach the surface.

So I told my brain to calm down (a bit like King Canute giving orders to a tsunami) and affected a look of nonchalance and just another day at the office.

I had plenty of time to practice as Davey was half an hour late.

Eventually I saw him get off his bus and walk toward me through the crowds; a bit like a Greek God on his day off.

"Sam, I'm really sorry I'm late, I just couldn't get away."

"That's OK, gave me time to think."

"I wasn't *that* late."

"Shut up. So, how was Craytown?"

"Oh, you know, lots of shops closing down, couple of dodgy gangs on street corners, general feeling of economic uncertainty."

"Right. No real change then."

"Yes, indeed. Sorry, did you want to hear about the football?"

"No, I was just interested in the local economy. Of course I want to know about the football, you idiot!"

"It was good."

"That's it?"

"Well, yes."

"Nobody else enter the 'Verbosity of the Week' contest; it's already been won."

"OK, I played well. We did some training, no more than your basic Nibbsy stuff. Then we had a couple of five-a-sides and then they told me I was playing centre forward for the reserves next Wednesday."

"Davey, that's fantastic!"

"Well, it's just the reserves."

"Doesn't matter. You've been picked. I'm really pleased, mate, you deserve it."

"So, how was Flitcham?"

"Oh, you know, alfresco dining in the fake French cafes-"

"Yes, I think we've already done that bit and it was only mildly amusing the first time."

"Well, it was *you* that was being only mildly amusing."

"Very grown-up comeback."

"Bog off."

"Umm."

"It was fine. Played well in the practice match. Didn't score though."

"And?"

"And?"

"Your other news?"

"Well, I… how do you *know* these things?"

"You look like a seven year old when you're excited about something."

"Do I?"

"Yes."

"Specifically seven?"

"Specifically."

"Flitcham have taken me on full time."

Davey turned to me and, in the two seconds before he hugged me, I saw in his face pride and love and absolute happiness for me.

I think this was the first time that I had realised how we so rarely acknowledge happiness. It's only many years afterwards, in the full bloom of an exaggerated memory, that we create a temporary utopia of that particular time. But I *was* happy at that moment. I didn't have to brag about my happiness; if I had done, it wouldn't have been real. There was – OK, there's a cliché coming up, but it's the only way I can describe it – a glow inside me. I can't tell you all of its components. Love was one of them, minor self-confidence at my achievement, friendship; but mostly, I think the comparison of how things had been so bad and what an utter relief it was that they now weren't. I know some people think that it's wrong to be happy when so many others aren't, but happiness is comparative. A homeless person would be happy if they found a tent to sleep in; the richest man in the world would be happy if he suddenly realised he was no longer grieving for the death of a loved one. It wasn't that I felt I didn't deserve happiness, I simply felt that I didn't deserve to be *un*happy.

Eventually, Davey said:

"You weren't going to tell me because you didn't want to dampen my excitement at being taken on by Craytown, were you?"

"Er, that's about right."

"Well, thank you. But, you know, you really must tell me these things. This isn't a competition. You were always going to be the professional, I was always going to be the semi-pro. I'm happy about being taken on by Craytown, you're happy about Flitcham. Tell me stuff, Sam. Tell me everything, OK?"

"OK. Sorry."

"And don't apologise."

"Sorry."

And, having received one of my Davey statements, as I called them, we fell in line, pace matching pace, toward the open-air market. I don't know what Davey was thinking but, as I sank down into the comfortable bubble-wrap of my thoughts, it was as if all the other people on the crowded pavement weren't there. Like when you get so used to the motion of a train, you only notice it when it stops. The people *were* there, of course, but they existed in a slightly altered reality. You've seen films where the leading actor is walking down the street and the camera fades everyone else into a haze so you just see him? Well, it was like that.

We had almost arrived at Lazy Deborah's before I actually acknowledged my surroundings and realised I was about to introduce Davey to Old Thomas.

Lazy Deborah ran the first stall. She was about a hundred and fifty stone and sold domestic cleaning products that had mostly fallen off the back of a lorry, which had probably fallen off the back of a larger lorry. She was lovely, but could never be bothered to get out of the steel-reinforced chair she sat in. 'Elp yerself, darlin', I know what stock I've got', was her usual mantra.

"Hi, Deborah," I said.

"'Ello, Gorgeous and who's this hunk?"

"This is Davey. Davey, Deborah."

"Nice to meet you, Deborah," said Davey, who didn't even need to open his mouth to make women melt.

"D'ya know, Davey, if I were a couple of hundredweight lighter, twenty years younger and didn't have a face like a bag o' chisels, I'd *so* go for you."

"Thank you and you're a very lovely lady," said Davey, a cross between a U.N. peace envoy and the Great Gatsby.

"Oh, go on and charm the pants of someone else. You two must have women falling at your feet. Have you got girlfriends?"

"Er, well, we're not quite sure," I said.

"Tell me, 'ow can yer be not quite sure?"

"Well, it's in the very early stages. You know, we're still having talks about talks."

"Well, stop talking and get shagging, that's my advice. And I've got a special offer on *Vim* this week. Tell yer mum."

"I didn't think they made *Vim* anymore, Debs."

"They don't. That's why it's a special offer."

We moved on until we reached Lynda, whose stall was next to Old Thomas.

"Hi, Lynda. How's business?"

"Hello, my love. Fair to middling."

Lynda sold second hand china crockery. She was fifty-two, had thrown a drunken, abusive husband out when she was twenty-five and brought up three kids single-handedly whilst holding down a full-time job. She'd never claimed a state benefit in her life and had got a 2:1 in Art History from the Open University three years ago. I liked Lynda. Not only because she was a strong, positive woman but also because she kept Old Thomas company. Although they were mostly nice people, the other stall-holders, like Deborah, were hardly conversation bedfellows for him.

"Thomas has just popped for a tea. He'll be back in a sec."

"Thanks, Lynda."

I turned to find Davey already perusing a hardback on New York Art Deco. I peered over his shoulder.

"I love this era," Davey said, flicking through photographs of the Empire State building, Radio City and the Chrysler building, "I wish I'd lived back then. It was like everything was new. New architecture, new fashions, new outlook on life."

"A perfect description of the period," said Old Thomas, who had returned from the cafe with a steaming plastic beaker of tea which he promptly poured into the china teacup that Lynda had given him. "My parents were young then and they told me it was the most marvellous era. For the first time there was real freedom of expression; in politics, morality, love, ambition and, as you said, architecture and fashion. There was a structure to Art Decoratif, but also an absolute creative freedom."

"And that freedom began to trickle down to the people who had never experienced it before?" said Davey.

"Exactly," said Old Thomas, "Art Deco was universal."

We continued to look at the photographs, commenting occasionally on repeated themes or a lesser-known building we'd never heard of, until I realised that I hadn't actually introduced everyone.

"Oh, sorry. This is Davey; Davey, this is…"

And I realised that I'd never called Old Thomas by his name and, indeed, had no idea what his surname was.

"Er, Mr Thomas."

"'Mr Thomas?!'" said Old Thomas, "I sound like a dodgy children's cartoon character."

"I was trying to improve my formal skills and didn't know-"

"My surname. For the record, it's Hetherington; and don't try to improve your formal skills, they're fine as they are. Please call me Thomas," he said to Davey.

"It's a pleasure to meet you, Thomas," said Davey, playing the adult even more and so consigning me to the role of shoe-scuffing adolescent, "Sam has told me a great deal about you. I think it's amazing that you run a proper book stall in Deptford."

"Thank you," said Old Thomas, "it's rather like selling hamburgers at a radical vegetarian convention. Sam has told me much about you too, Davey. I must say it's wonderful to find two young men that can't be pigeon-holed."

"How do you mean, Thomas?" asked Davey.

"I mean, Davey, that you and Sam have your own personalities, your own characteristics; that you refuse to be led by regimented factions whose call to arms is to be as narrow-minded about their outlook on life as is humanly possibly; whose contentment in their own smallness is to find others who will imitate them. You refuse to conform either to the football set or to the book set. You're not the sort of young men who will laugh at opera to cover your own ignorance of it; you will ask questions and experience things and, if you decide you don't like something, you will have come to that conclusion through a knowledge of it and not through ignorance and an assumed stance of superiority. The fact that you both love and are very talented at football is only part of you, not your entire life, as is your love of books. Your stereotypical football fan will hate books because he's scared of not understanding them. These people should be locked in a library and not allowed to watch another match until they have read ten novels. And your stereotypical bookworm will hate football because, to him, academia is the only thing that is worth existing for. These people should be made to wear an anorak with 'I'm a tit, please kick me hard in the testicles' emblazoned on it."

I'd never seen Davey laugh so hard before. I laughed too, of course, but I was used to Old Thomas' rhetoric and already knew how clever he was at emphasising a point by throwing humour into it. I don't think Davey and I had understood everything that he said but we certainly got the general gist and, when I looked at Davey, I saw how mesmerised he was.

"Basically, there are two categories of human being. Those who define their character by the things they like and those who define their character by the things they hate. Whenever you meet one of the latter, ignore them completely; or better still, Taser the bastards."

"Sir... sorry, Thomas, I can understand why Sam spends every Saturday afternoon here."

"Well," Old Thomas replied, "you are welcome to join us whenever you wish, Davey."

The next three hours seemed to melt into a fraction of that time. I'd worried about whether they would hit it off. It's easy when it's just the two of you, but when two different facets of your life come together, you're suddenly faced with a social situation which actually needs thinking about. My, admittedly, minor fears were totally unfounded. Within a short time we were all chatting as if we'd been meeting like this for years. I'd like to think it was me subtly manipulating the conversation to make it easier for the other two, but it wasn't. A – because I'm rubbish at it and B – because they just hit it off straight away. In fact, they did most of the talking. I was pleased; Davey was my best friend and I loved him and Old Thomas was my... I had no label to give him at that point, but I loved him too. Indeed, it wasn't until six o'clock and the other stallholders began to pack up, that I really noticed the time and also realised that I hadn't told Old Thomas about Flitcham. Davey, as usual, was one jump ahead.

"Sam, you haven't told Thomas your news."

"No, I completely forgot."

"What news is this?"

"I've been taken on by Flitcham, full time."

Thomas paused for a moment; then a smile that would have ended any war in the world encompassed his face.

"That is wonderful news," he said, "absolutely wonderful."

"And Davey has been taken on by F.C. Craytown."

"Davey, I'm so pleased. Congratulations."

"Thank you."

"Look, boys, would you mind getting me a cup of tea whilst I begin to pack up."

When we arrived back, there were two books waiting for us on his table. One was the book about New York Art Deco, which he gave to Davey. Inside the inscription said:

'To Davey. F.C. Craytown are richer for having you in their team. Congratulations. Thomas.

The other was an old copy of *The Call of the Wild*. Inside it said:

'To my son,

On the day his hugely successful football career began.

I am so very proud of you.

Thomas.

After I'd read this, I looked across to the opposite page and my eye caught the words *first edition*.

"But this is a... it's a..."

That's as far as I got.

I don't know where tears come from. I know, physically, it's from the eyes but, emotionally, it's from somewhere much lower. The feet, possibly, or maybe it's subterranean. All I know is that I was only aware of them cascading up my body when they reached my stomach. I told them, in no uncertain terms, to stop when they got to my chest; but tears are stubborn and will do as they wish; and so they continued, until the flood barriers that I had mentally built in my eyes proved useless and Old Thomas put his arms round me and told me I must cry for as long as I needed to. Then I felt Davey's hands on my shoulders and I gave up the battle to stop. After all, if I couldn't cry in front of the two most important people in my life, who could I cry in front of?

Later, as we began our goodbyes, Davey said:

"It was a pleasure to meet you, sir."

"The pleasure was mine, Davey," said Old Thomas, "and do come and visit again."

"I will. Definitely."

"Bye," I said, "and thank you so much."

"Goodbye, my son and well done again. See you next week."

"Yep," I said and, grinning, held up my book and waved to him.

"Look, what are you doing tonight?"

"Nothing planned."

"Let's get drunk."

"OK."

"Why don't I come back to your place? I can meet your parents and then we can go up to the Porterhouse Arms and drink way too much Guinness."

"Er, no Sam."

"OK, lager, then."

"No, it's not the drink."

"Well, what then?"

"You can't come back to my house."

"Oh? Why?"

"It's not a good time."

"Why isn't it a good time?"

"I can't explain."

"Why?"

"It's complicated."

"But, why is it-"

"Sam, please, no more whys."

"OK."

This time a different silence ensued.

"Look, let's both go home, grab a shower and meet up at Porterhouse at eight."

"OK," I said. "There's my bus. I'm going to run for it."

On the journey home, Davey's words did a little folk dance around my head. What was so wrong, I thought, that he couldn't take his best friend home?

By the time I let myself in the front door, I couldn't work out if I was worried or a bit angry that he'd refused to give me an explanation, so I decided to do what all teenagers do when faced with a difficult situation; the wrong thing.

Mum was in the lounge with 'him', no doubt watching something inane on the TV.

I didn't go in. 'He' barely left the room. It was his domain and so no longer a part of my home. My home consisted of the kitchen and my bedroom. We didn't have cable but fortunately Gran and Gramps had bought me a second-hand portable TV which got all five channels as long as you pointed the aerial exactly at the edge of the bookcase, draped a pair of underpants over it at a forty-five degree angle to the table, there was a prevailing force two breeze from the jet stream passing by and no volcanic activity north of the Equator.

Channel Five was a bit hit and miss, but that was just the programmes.

I showered, put on my 'going out' jeans and a black shirt, stuffed a twenty pound note in my pocket and ran out the front door.

The bus that I boarded wouldn't take me to the Porterhouse but it *would* drop me somewhere near Davey's street. It was just after seven. I had plenty of time to get there and reach the pub by eight.

The only problem was that I didn't know what I was going to do when I got there. I couldn't go into his house. He'd made it quite clear that there was something wrong. I couldn't stand outside because I would look as though I was checking the place out with a view to robbing it and I couldn't sit on the wall and wait for him to come out because I wasn't eleven any more.

I formulated several plans of action. None of which made any sense.

Eventually I decided I would walk down his street, pass his house, nonchalantly glance through the lounge window (no doubt whilst simultaneously walking into a post box) and then get a another bus to the pub.

Quite what this was going to accomplish, I wasn't sure.

I was worried. Worried because Davey was always so calm, so seemingly in control of any situation; and the Davey that had looked Nibbsy in the eye (which would have warranted him kneeling down) and not even flinching, was not the Davey who said 'no, you can't come round to my house'. I was afraid for him and afraid for me because this was the first time that the serenity of our friendship had been challenged. And when something is perfect, the tiniest flaw becomes over-emphasised.

I reached the top of his street and looked down the two lines of impressive Edwardian houses. If this had been a movie I would have been the hero returning, triumphant from the battle and the soundtrack would have consisted of thundering percussion, trumpets and horns. But it wasn't. Instead it was just me, with Sister Sledge on my CD player, looking like a twat trying to be a warrior.

Head down, eyes registering every imperfection in the pavement, I walked along the street toward number thirty-two. Occasionally I would look up and glance at a number on a door, almost hoping that I'd already walked past it.

When I reached 28, I stopped, decided that the best plan of action was no plan of action which, conveniently, fitted with the fact that this was actually the case and walked ten yards to the front of number 32.

The sign above the door of a double-fronted house, said:

'*The Mountsorrel Home For Children*'

Several ice-ages later I snapped out of the shock.

Maybe it was just an old sign that his parents had kept when they bought the house. Maybe it wasn't.

Only one way to find out.

I rang the door buzzer. A lovely maternal voice said 'hello'?

"Er, hello, I've come to see Davey."

"OK, my dear, come in."

She buzzed me through.

Inside was a little reception area. Seated there was a lady in her late fifties with a friendly smile and the sort of hair that's so perfectly permed, you wonder if she sleeps standing up.

"Davey should be on his way down soon," she said.

"Thank you," I said.

"Off anywhere nice?"

"Not really. Both of us got taken on by football teams today and we're going to have a little..."

"Ah, here he is," she said.

Davey stopped on the stairs, adjusted an expression of disbelief that had flitted across his face for one millionth of a second, descended the rest of the stairs and said:

"Bye Emily, I'll be back before midnight."

"Er, nice to meet you," I said to the perfectly coiffed Emily.

"And you too, my dear; have a good night."

I'd always loved our silences before. They were happy, peaceful silences. Silence because words were simply not necessary.

This one was different. Words were absolutely necessary, but would not come. Davey's mute button was jammed and I daren't say anything for fear of the words being all wrong. I wanted Old Thomas there; he would know what to do.

The unwanted silence seemed to quadruple real time. From walking to the bus stop to opening the door of the Porterhouse made eternity seem like a TV commercial.

I suppose it was a testament to our friendship that we functioned at all and, indeed, still went to the pub.

I ordered two pints of Guinness. When I turned round, Davey was sitting at a table by the window. I took the drinks over and sat opposite him. He picked his up, took a baby-sip and stared at the passing traffic.

I drew the pattern in the carpet with my foot for a while, tried to peel the front off a beermat, picked up my pint, didn't drink anything, put it down again and then removed an invisible piece of fluff from my jeans.

"You're angry with me, aren't you?"

"No."

"But you asked me not to come round and I did."

"I'm not angry."

"Why didn't you tell me you lived in a home?"

"I've never told anyone."

"Why?"

"Because I don't want anyone to feel sorry for me and… because, if you don't vocalise something, you can pretend it's not real."

"But you said you talked to your parents."

"I do. They were killed in a car crash when I was one. If they're in Heaven and can hear me, then that's great. If they're not, it makes me feel better anyway."

"Didn't you have any family?"

"One uncle. He had an alcohol problem."

"So, they wouldn't let him take you."

"No."

"I shouldn't be making you talk about this."

"There's not much to tell. I was fostered until I was three by a family who were told they couldn't have kids."

"And?"

"And then they had a kid."

"Oh."

"And I was suddenly surplus to emotional requirements."

"They dumped you?"

"That's one way of putting it. So I was put in care and have stayed there ever since. I have to move out when I'm eighteen, of course."

For a few seconds my brain sought profundity. Then I realised that it was simpler to be simple.

"Davey…"

"Yes?"

"I'm sorry."

"Don't be. I was never abused. I never went hungry. I went to a good school."

"You went to Blaisworth Road Comp."

"OK, good point. I was schooled then. I was lucky, it could have been a lot worse."

"It could have been a lot better."

"No-"

"Yes! You suffered. The fact that other people suffered worse than you doesn't diminish your own suffering," I said, quoting Old Thomas and, for once, feeling like the grown up. "I suppose there must be one person in the world who is in the worst state, but does that mean that everyone else hasn't suffered?"

I paused to get over the shock of my sudden and unexpected entry into the realms of philosophy.

"You didn't have your parents. That's not fair."

"I have them in my head."

"But if you've had a bad day or something is worrying you, you can't go home and talk to them about it."

"It doesn't matter."

"But it does. If something goes wrong for me, I can go to my parents and…"

I stopped, because what I was about to say was as far from the truth as it was possible to get. However, this wasn't about me, so I ploughed on –

"And tell them," I stuttered.

"Sam, no offence, but if I had the choice between the imagined memories of my father and the reality of yours, I'd take the memories any time."

"Yeah, you're right, but I still think you're really brave to have managed without a family. I think that's what makes you like you are."

"What am I like?"

"Private and independent."

"Possibly. If you don't get attached to people, you can't lose them."

"But you're attached to me."

"Yes."

"Well, let me tell you something."

"What's that?"

"You will never, *ever* lose me."

Two seventeen and a half year old boys are not supposed to be in this position. This is a situation that demands the maturity and knowledge of adults. But, there we sat, innocent of these experiences and yet, maybe because of this, more able to deal with them. There were no need for platitudes, for stock phrases, for repetitions of lines we'd heard in a movie. We just looked at each other for a very long time without embarrassment. I knew that I would die for him and him for me.

After a while he looked at his pint and said:

"I'm sorry, Sam, but I don't actually want this."

"Me neither."

"Do you know what I'd really like just now?"

"No."

"An ice cream."

We abandoned our pints to the slop bucket and sought the nearest cafe.

"Two cornets, please," I said, "one with raspberry sauce."

"Actually, make that both with raspberry sauce."

"You do know I will never let you forget this," I said.

"Yes," he said.

12

People speak of sea-changes and I suppose that would describe the next six months of my life.

But, like all popular clichés, its over-use and constant exaggeration tends to dilute the intensity of its meaning.

Why does everything have to be exaggerated nowadays? Nothing is 'good' anymore; everything has to be 'awesome'. No one goes to see a film and says 'yeah, it was ok; some of the dialogue was a bit contrived but the performances and guerrilla-style direction made up for it'. No, it's either 'total shit, man' or 'like, way out phenomenal'. Everyone exaggerates. Exaggeration is acceptable lying. Take eggs for example. When I was a small kid they were small, medium and large. Now they're medium, large and very large. They're not. You're lying. Stop it.

So, my sea-change was more of an Adriatic than a Pacific but, that said, pretty way out phenomenal, man!

The Monday following Davey's revelation and my becoming a professional footballer, I went into college to deliver two messages; both of which I knew would upset me.

The meeting with Mr Geraghty, my course tutor, was the easiest. I told him my news, thanked him for believing in me and accepted his congratulations and a warm handshake. Telling the guys was always going to be more difficult. We were a team, inside and outside college. They were my friends, the general bedrock of my fast-growing self and the flag I flew to prove that I had escaped from what I could have become.

They were incredibly pleased for me. Actually, I don't think 'pleased' covered it. 'Elated' may have fallen short of the mark. Their reaction mirrored my own as, after the initial congratulations, the real-life dawning of the fact that we wouldn't see each other every day, kicked in.

"Oh Sammy, but we won't see you."

"Of course we'll see him, Rachel, darling" Susie chirped, "We are the Famous Five. Er, no, hang on…"

"And this year's Nobel Prize for arithmetic goes to-"

"Shut up, Sebastian, you know I'm not very good at math."

"Maths, dear, this isn't New York."

"Maths. We are the Infamous Six."

New Tommy said "One for six and six for-"

The bell rang.

"Six for double Classics… five for double Classics. Oh God, mate, don't ever lose touch, will you."

"Don't be ridiculous, you idiot," I said, "I am Scum Hatchington, Superfriend."

Rachel said, "Circumstances often change in a friendship. That's the acid test of how deep that friendship is. We'll adjust. We'll see less of Sam in class and more of him socially."

"Look, I love you guys," I said.

I need to learn not to say these things. Love makes people cry; or, at least, its articulation does. Even Seb was welling up as we all hugged.

"When do we see you next?" Susie asked.

"Friday," I said, "drinks at the Caldecott?"

"Then roller-disco on Sunday afternoon," said Susie.

Seb feigned disgust.

"God, Suse, can you think of anything camper?"

"Yes I can," she said, "so watch out."

"You guys go in; I'll join you in a sec." Tara had spoken for the first time.

So, as four of the Infamous Six took their seats for an hour and a half of Aristotle, she looked me up and down.

"Two things," she said, "one is that I am very proud of you; two is 'are we or aren't we'?"

"We are," I said.

"Then when do we see each other alone to prove that fact?"

"Er, Wednesday? Pick you up about eight?"

She kissed me on the cheek and went in to deepen her acquaintanceship with Aristotle.

So began my relationship with the mysterious Tara. I was still not sure I knew any more about her several months later.

On the Wednesday I took her to a Thai restaurant in Soho, which was great for her as she loves Thai food, but a minor disaster for me as anything spicy turns my stomach into a gastric Vesuvius. Consequently, my second day of training was curtailed somewhat by me needing to be in permanent close proximity to a bathroom.

Two more dates followed: one to see The Phantom of the Opera in the West End (they crashed a chandelier onto the stage; I mean, just how like way out phenomenal is that!) and the other for coffee and cake on the South Bank. It was on this occasion that Tara subtly slipped the fact that her parents had taken her little sister to Venice for the week into the conversation.

My heart did a little flip. Not so much of excitement as from the memory of bus-stops, Katie Turnpike and the curse of disastrous sexual encounters.

I needn't have worried. She asked me if I would like a bath. I said I was from a council house and wasn't due one for another two months. She smiled (Tara's version of hysterical laughter) and added the word 'together' to the question.

"Er, yes," I said, "that would be lovely."

"That would be lovely," she mimicked.

I looked on as she began to run the bath.

"Would you like some essential oils?" she asked.

"Are they essential?" I replied.

She upended in a little bottle of lavender oil into the bath until it was so pungent I thought I was living inside a plug-in air freshener.

We lay at either end of the bath with our legs forming parentheses around each other.

She had a rubber duck. That's not cockney-rhyming slang. She actually had a rubber duck. It was called Peter.

"Why is it called Peter?" I asked.

"Because it looks like a Peter."

"What do Peters look like?"

"My rubber duck."

I'm not entirely sure a lot of Peters would be happy with that comparison.

Later we made love; something she'd obviously done often and something that, as we know, I hadn't.

This first time was the only occasion with Tara that I called it 'making love'. The rest I would always refer to as 'having sex'.

The only time I was really close to her was when we lay together in bed before sex, when I was inside her and just after, usually me, had finished.

Afterwards we would rarely speak; just roll apart and sleep that way. There was no waking up in the spoon position. I couldn't get close to her physically in the same way I couldn't reach her mentally. Her character book was tightly closed. Mine was wide open: tattered covers, broken spine and some pages missing, but there for all to read.

If she hadn't been my girlfriend, I don't think we'd have even been close. Friends, yes, but never in each other's top ten.

The roller disco that Sunday spurned another relationship.

Tara had told the rest of the gang about us and I, of course, had told Davey.

Rachel, not to be outdone, put her skates on (literally), downed four double vodka and cranberry juices in half an hour, skated up to Davey, via a barstool, seven people, two wall decorations and one actual wall and said:

"I'm drunk, you're beautiful. Let's go out."

Davey said, "Rachel, you would have been an inspiration to Austen."

"Oh my God, you're a man and you've actually *heard* of Jane Austen. I think I've died and gone to Heaven."

She kissed him to tremendous applause from all those she hadn't flattened and then apologised for the voracity in which she'd asked him out and said that she wasn't usually this forward.

Davey told her it was fine and, anyway, he was very fond of cranberry juice.

And, as New Tommy had officially announced that he and the girl from Bananarama were now an item, that just left Seb and Susie. But, much as we wished that they would do a 'Ross and Rachel', it never happened. "I love him," Susie said, "but he's my friend. He's very pretty and has a perfect penis – I saw it when we were changing on the beach – but I only admire it aesthetically."

Our social lives fell into a routine. Tuesdays and Saturdays were reserved for the Infamous Six, now the Magnificent Seven, Wednesdays and Sundays were for partners and Friday was for Davey and myself, though as alcohol was out of the question as he had a match the next day, we would usually see a film, go to an exhibition or simply have a coffee in the National Theatre cafe and exercise our pretentious muscles.

Training was quite a shock to begin with. I'd always been fit and had made the transition from Nibbsy's medieval techniques to the Flitcham Youth team with absolutely no problem. But this was different. This was intense and scary and exhilarating and pressurised and exciting and spasmodically social and simply wonderful.

With Nibbsy, you went into a training session with a heavy heart, mismatched kit and one eye permanently on the clock. You hung around for ages either trying to look cool or bored; then there would be some passing practice, a few free kicks and one-two's, followed by a five-a-side with such epically low energy levels, anybody seeing it would imagine they were watching the action replays.

The Youth team was a major step up. This was proper training run by people who coached with verve and knowledge and actually cared. Every morning we'd start with a warm up (Nibbsy's views on warm-ups were that they were 'for ballet girls and poofs'). Then we trained without the ball; flexibility and cardio; lots of shuttle runs and the thing I hated at first but gradually came to love, interval training. Sprint for a minute, walk for thirty seconds, ad infinitum. Well, not infinitum, obviously, but around the time your legs rather pointedly told the rest of you it could hold itself up. And all this before we even began working on skills and tactics.

But, although this was far in advance of anything I'd experienced before and, although I adapted very quickly, we were still being closeted from reality. We knew we had to try to do well but we were still allowed to fail. It wasn't real. It was, I imagine, what public school is like; a safe world within an unsafe world.

So, although I was still legally a short time away from adulthood, I had to learn to become a football adult.

The game became the majority of my waking existence and, as a consequence, my life took on a stricter regime. It was a bit like being in the army, I suppose; dedicated training, dietary and lifestyle regulations. Just with a training ground rather than a parade ground. And less khaki.

Training was usually Monday to Friday, 10am to 1pm. Doesn't sound a lot, I know, but I was expending more energy in those three hours than most people would in a month, apart from professional athletes and Paris Hilton's hairdresser.

What's more, I loved it. Working with a partner; throw and head, throw and kick; working in formation; how to defend a free kick, a corner; how to attack them; pass and move; keeping your shape. It was often new, all of a standard I'd never known before, but one I could not wait to emulate. I was exhilarated; part of a whole; a marvellous, integrated, creative ball-busting whole. I was a very, very lucky nearly eighteen year-old boy.

I'd always been happiest as an attacking midfielder, playing just behind the forwards. Holding the ball up wasn't my style and passing backwards was for rugby players.

Fortunately, Flitcham also decided this was my best position and so nurtured me in this role.

My dribbling and short game skills were pretty well-developed already. I could do step-overs till the cows came home (usually with great exaggeration – a bit like *Lord of the Dance*) and I could shoot.

It was my long game that needed the work. I had to get more vision, they told me. So I would spend hours passing the ball (I'd like to say with pin-point precision, but it was more like car-park-point precision at first) until I actually began to land it in the same town that I was aiming it at.

Within three weeks I was picked for the Reserves and within two months I was permanently installed playing just behind our two strikers.

I made new friends at the club. However, although I occasionally went to a party that one of them threw, the vast majority of my social life was taken up with Davey, Tara and the gang.

Of course, my Saturdays with Old Thomas became hugely disrupted. Three months in to my new career however, I brilliantly managed to tear all my intercostal muscles and was side lined for a month on a cocktail of Tramadol and Valium which took away the pain and also my ability to remember things, like my name and where I lived. Inside my head felt a re-enactment of the 1960s. The upside to my injury was that we could resume our lazy, idyllic market days. It felt so good to slip back into being the slightly promising child again, rather than the fledgling grown-up, straining against the walls of the demands and expectations of adulthood.

When I did resume training Thomas suggested that, if it was alright with me, we should try to find an hour a week to meet for coffee. So I was elevated to the status of a coffee-bar equal. I love coffee bars. As I walk through the door I feel like I'm space-slipping into another Universe where micro Big Bangs happen on a daily basis; the nucleus of everything new. Picasso expounding to Dali about surrealism, Gore Vidal hunched forward in intense discussion with Norman Mailer, people writing, composing, contemplating, contentedly window-gazing through a curtain of rain. We would put the world to rights, he and I, over half-cold mochas and biscotti. He would tell me stories of his life. I asked him if he told them so that I could learn lessons from them. "No," he said, "Unless you see something that fires your imagination, in which case, do with it as you will." We did what families and friends did, which was appropriate in both cases.

My parents found out about my change of life, inadvertently, through my grandparents. I had told Gran and Gramps shortly after their return from the Costa Del Southend. Gran immediately switched allegiance from Liverpool (who she supported because she 'likes their outfits and quite fancied the young man who plays in goal') to Flitcham and both of them took me out for a slap up meal at *Wendy's* and bought me a silver tankard with:

Our Star Player, Congratulations, Love from Gran and Gramps

engraved on it.

I hadn't asked them not to tell my parents, but I think they may have guessed as it was two months later that my mum collared me as I came in one night and said:

"Sam, why didn't you tell me you were playing for Flitcham?"

"Well, it's the reserves at the moment, mum."

"But you should have told me."

"I didn't want 'him' to know."

"But he'd be so proud."

"No he wouldn't."

"But-"

"Mum, he wouldn't give a shit."

"Sam!"

"Sorry."

She started to cry. So I put my arms round her because I understood why she was crying. Not so much because I hadn't told her my good news, but more because of this un-crossable chasm that now existed between myself and 'him'; the fact that her family was broken, permanently. And, although I loved her and was upset for her, a part of me wasn't able to feel completely sorry for her because she could have stopped him; she could have told him what all of us thought. I suppose, because not only didn't she leave him, her acceptance of his inhuman behaviour meant that she had chosen him over me.

"Come on, mum, I'll tell you all about it."

In the kitchen, I made us a pot of tea and told her all the details. She made me promise to update her on everything in the future. I said I would.

"He must love you deep down," she said.

"I don't care," I said.

"Perhaps if I could persuade him to come to a match?"

"It's the word 'persuade' that renders that thought completely insignificant," I said.

"Perhaps you could make one last attempt?"

"How many times do you want him to kick me?"

She looked at the floor.

"I'm very proud of you, Sam," she said, in a voice made almost inaudible by emotion and contained love.

"I love you, mum," I said and went upstairs to my room.

13

It was two weeks before my eighteenth birthday. The time was one o'clock in the afternoon and I was spending my usual decade in the shower after training when Nick, one of my fellow reserves, popped his head round the door and said:

"Sam, boss is outside; wants to see you."

"Thanks, Nick," I said, turning off the comforting Niagara and towelling down as quickly as I could. Throwing on my jeans, T-shirt and Converses and leaving my floppy, public school fringe to do its own thing (which was mainly to look floppy and public school-like), I bid a monosyllabic farewell to the guys and hightailed it to the front of the building where the manager of Flitcham FC was stubbing out his 78ᵗʰ cigarette of the day.

"Hey, boss," I said, "How are you?"

"Very well, thank you, Sammy (he was the first in the game to call me Sammy; being young and having floppy hair makes people put a 'y' on the end of your name); and you?"

"Great, thank you."

"Still enjoying it?"

"Oh, boss, I still have to pinch myself occasionally to believe it is happening. Please excuse the rather tired old phrasing."

He laughed.

"It's excused. Now, Bill and I agree that your form has been excellent in training and, having watched you in the Sunderland game last Wednesday, it's obvious that you have become a major lynchpin for the reserves. You're feeding Tom and Benji brilliantly and, at the same time, giving us an unofficial third striker."

I had been relishing the role I was playing. It was the most creative position on the field. I was virtually free to do whatever I wanted with the ball, which was usually to run at the opposition and draw as many defenders in order to carve out openings for Tom and Benji. I'd also managed to net five goals in twelve games, three of them from long range, the second of which was intended as a cross, but we'll gloss over that.

"Now, you'll know that Steve has torn a hamstring."

"Yes, poor guy and he was really on form."

"Indeed and he will be again. In the meantime we need to replace him."

"Of course."

"Do you know where I'm going with this?"

"Er…"

"You're in the first team against Chelsea this Saturday. Congratulations."

My mouth hung open for so long, I must have looked like a demented goldfish.

"You know, Hatchington, for someone as eloquent as you can sometimes be, you're lost for words on a worryingly regular basis."

He laughed and offered me his hand, which I took with both of mine and pumped for a little longer than was comfortable.

"Thank you, boss, I'm extremely grateful."

"We'll play you in the same position as you have been with the reserves, so that will cushion the move up in level. You'll be training with the first team squad for the rest of the week. I'll see you tomorrow morning."

At school I was always told that, if you add a positive to a negative, you end up with a negative. I think that, in real life, it's down to the individual. My negative was turning my stomach into an abdominal rollercoaster whilst my positive was riding that rollercoaster, shouting and laughing and letting go of the safety bar. That's how we should live life, don't you think? Let go of the safety bar.

For the second time in my life I skipped an entire bus journey. As we trundled through South London's nonchalant traffic, my brain created its own painting of my future. It would hurriedly draw one story in pencil, then rub it out and begin again, before picking up the brush and lavishing oil on the canvas. Sometimes the picture would take me into my thirties, sometimes only to the end of this Saturday's game. Whichever way, I ended up scoring a wonder-goal and receiving the adulation of my fellow players and the fans.

I kept my promise to my mum when I got home.

"Mum, I'm in the first team this Saturday and you're the first person I've told."

"Oh my goodness, the first team! Oh Sam, I'm so… so…"

"Mortified?"

"No!"

"Bored?"

"No, stop it!"

"Pleased would do!"

"No, pleased isn't enough. My son is a premiership footballer. I'm going to tell all the neighbours. But first, I'm going to ring your grandparents."

"OK, mum."

She rushed off in a frenzy of motion, dropping the receiver and dialling the wrong number before she finally got through to Gran and Gramps.

In my room I rang Davey.

"Davey, I'm in the first team this Saturday."

"Sam, that is fantastic."

"Thank you."

"Porterhouse. 7.30 tonight?"

"I can't drink, mate, I'm training with the first team tomorrow."

"I know that, schmuck; I do play a little football."

"Sorry."

"Just half a lemonade and two straws."

"And no ice."

"Definitely no ice. And Sam..."

"Yes?"

"There are no words that can express how proud I am of you".

Then I rang Thomas. As always he managed to mix calmness and tranquillity with congratulations that would rival an acceptance speech at the Oscars.

I asked him if he was free for coffee the following evening. He'd said yes before I'd finished the sentence.

"Oh and have a nice time with Davey tonight."

"How did you know I was seeing Davey tonight?"

"I have Extra Sensitive Perspiration. Of *course* you would see Davey tonight. Say hello to him for me."

"I will," I said.

As Susie would say, my evening with Davey was split into three halves. The first was our mutual congratulations to each other. Me, for my inclusion in the first team and him for the hat-trick he'd scored against Tonbridge the previous Saturday. The second half was our general Davey and Sam chit-chat and the third was him calming me down when my rollercoaster went a bit too fast.

"Davey, I... you see, it's... like, two years ago... um... nothing really sort of makes... there's just... God, I don't know how I got here."

"Impressive. An entire Mamet play in one sentence."

I laughed and some of the seismic onset of panic began to recede.

"Are you parallel-parking with reality, Hatchington?"

"Yes, I suppose I am."

"What did you want to be when you were a kid...? When you were a younger kid?"

"A footballer... What do you mean a *younger* kid?!"

"Well, that's what you've become. It's a dream that's morphed into a reality. But, as the rate of morphing is a bit non-specific, it's only just sunk in."

"You remind me of Thomas," I said.

"Good," he said.

I continued to parallel-park the next day in training. I was so intent on doing well that the three hours seemed like thirty minutes.

Afterwards I went shopping, looking for a present for Thomas. It wasn't his birthday, I just felt a sudden impulse to buy him something. I finally settled on a framed print of an A.A. Milne drawing. Eeyore had his bottom to the viewer in a gesture that made boredom look positively uplifting. Pooh Bear and Piglet were sitting in contented silence under a huge oak, an empty jar of honey testament to that contentment.

Later, when we met in our usual coffee bar, Thomas said it was 'National Indulgence Day' and we should consequently eat the gooiest cake in the cafe.

"I've never heard of National Indulgence Day," I said. "When did it start?"

"About five minutes ago. Do you think it will catch on?"

"Definitely," I said, tucking in to a strawberry and white chocolate cheesecake. "You know I shouldn't be eating this."

"Of course you shouldn't. Look at the size of you. I'm surprised they don't stuff you and exhibit you in the Natural History Museum. 'Samosaurus Obeseoraptor'."

"I am Beerus Bellyus," I said, lifting my T-shirt to my chest, "the Roman god of Liver Failure."

"Nice six-pack, mate," said one of a couple of guys on his way out of the cafe.

"Er, thanks," I said, realising that a cafe probably wasn't the best place to show off my abs.

"I know the answer to this already," Thomas said, "but how are you feeling at the moment?"

"I'm feeling like you know I'm feeling."

"Excellent. So, which emotion is nudging ahead? Excitement or terror?"

"It's pretty much neck and neck. I think it may come down to a photo finish."

"Well, if it's any help, I am looking forward immensely to watching you play."

"You're coming to the match? But you hate football!"

"Let's just say I have taken an interest in its future Hall of Fame."

"But what about the stall?"

"Lynda is going to look after it for me."

"I'm really pleased you're coming. Thank you."

"Sam, I've known you for two and a half years now."

"Is it that long?"

"Yes. Look, please tell me to shut up if this sounds too patronising or wankish. Is that a modern 'street' word?"

"Wasn't, but it is now."

"OED. 'Wankish' – to speak as that of a TV chat show host."

"Or a politician not answering a direct question."

"Indeed. Actually, that's more 'lying dressed up in a thin veneer of avoidance'. It's simply a grown up way of saying 'wasn't me, sir, it was Simpkins. I *saw* him do it; *and* he deliberately lost his rugby boots so he wouldn't have to play; *and* his mum works in a supermarket so he's probably a bit common and doesn't shower enough'. They don't change; it's the same attitude, just a slightly more inventive parlance."

I laughed, finished the last of my cheesecake, took a sip of my skinny decaf mocha and looked around this cafe that had come to mean 'Thomas' to me nearly as much as the bookstall. Its exposed brick walls parading the obligatory Vetriano pictures, the faux deco wall-lamps, the doll-size vase of flowers on each oak table.

"So," he said, "stop me if I get too unbearable."

"That would never happen."

"Of course not, I am the Superman of Oratory. But, just in case there's a chunk of kryptonite in this somewhat stale caramel shortcake, let me know."

"OK."

"In the time I've known you, I've watched you change. No, change is the wrong word. Develop. When you first to came to the stall, you had a confidence in *you* but also a confidence in the fact that you didn't know who you were yet. You knew he was there somewhere. He visited your dreams; he made your brain do things that surprised and excited it, occasionally pushed you in directions you'd never imagined moving in. You could have ignored him; it would have been easier. He didn't fit with the stereotypical box-set conventionality. But you didn't. You let him influence you to a greater and greater degree, until finally you realised that he *was* you and the former person was someone else whom your father and domestic limitations had created. What I'm basically saying, in an extraordinarily pompous way, is that you are a positive and giving person who refuses to rest on his laurels (which can be a little uncomfortable, especially if you get a sharp twig in the wrong place) and the success you are currently having is your reward from the Universe and whoever runs it. You are a warm, loving and caring person, Sam and I am very proud of you."

No one had ever spoken to me like this before. Gran and Gramps were often lovely, Davey and I would complement each other; but they were individual things, never reaching a conclusion.

For the first time in my life, I found the right words. They didn't stall on the way to my mouth as they normally would; they poured out; all the right ones, if not necessarily in the right order.

I can't remember exactly what I said, but I know I spoke like a Gatling gun. It's difficult to cram two years of feelings into the remaining dregs of a lukewarm mocha, but I tried.

"Everything I have learned about life that makes sense, I have learned from you."

"I'm sure I've only taught you how to swear in a posh accent."

"No. No! You have taught me everything. You didn't have to. I was just a schoolboy who came to your bookstall, begging for books. You talked to me as an equal. You never patronised me. *You* gave me that confidence. You taught me everything my father should have done, but you were more than that."

"More than a father?"

"Yes, *you* let me find *me*. You were my teacher and my philosopher and… and my father."

The world stalled for a few seconds and neither of us could restart the engine.

Eventually and surprisingly, it was me that found a voice.

"Oh and this is for you. It's a present. Well, obviously it's a present; it's covered in wrapping paper."

Thomas meticulously pulled off the rather Tate Modern Sellotape design (I can't wrap presents) and stared at Eeyore, Pooh and Piglet. It was the only time I ever heard his voice waver.

"It's the nicest present I've ever had," he said, "thank you, my son."

We talked on for another half an hour. Normal stuff. How things were with Tara; how Davey was doing; Old Thomas' trip to a Stately Home book sale where he'd met two friends he hadn't seen for thirty years and now remembered why he hadn't seen them ('God, they were dull; I'd rather have watched creosote peel').

Eventually we had to leave so I could get an early night. We hugged and he wished me all the luck in the world for Saturday ('not that you will need it') and told me where he was sitting for the match.

The following day was the usual training, followed by the first team playing the reserves, who would recreate the style of the team we were playing on Saturday; except this time I wasn't recreating, I was being.

Friday was a light session, a massage and then off to our hotel in preparation for the match.

I was roomed with Joe, the club jester and Steve's usual room-mate.

"Be nice to our new boy, Joe," said one of the guys, as we all retired for the night, "he's going to be great but he's also going to be a bit nervous."

"Don't worry, Kez, I'll look after him."

He did. He sat on the bed with me, rattled off a few jokes and told me exactly how he'd felt the night before his first game.

Joe was twenty, but had been playing first team football for three years. He was a left-sided midfielder and, in training, he'd been practicing incisive through passes to me. We hadn't interacted much on the field. He was usually bantering with the other guys, playing pranks, indulging in the easy chatter of team brotherhood. He had a habit of creeping up behind someone, pulling their trackie bottoms down and running away like a seven year-old kid. He was popular and I was a little in awe of him.

That night, however, he curtailed his playfulness, put his arm round my shoulder and told me not to worry; he would make sure I was fine.

As I lay in bed that night, listening to Joe's breathing across the room (he'd fallen asleep as soon as he'd got into bed), I knew I wouldn't be able to sleep. The bed was unfamiliar, the room was unfamiliar, I was playing my first match in the premiership tomorrow but, most of all, my frog wouldn't be vomiting me awake in the morning.

I tried thinking about having sex with Tara. That didn't stop my mind whirling, it just gave me an erection. At around 4 o'clock I imagined myself having coffee and conversation with Thomas and Davey and this was enough to calm me and allow my brain to press the slumber button.

The next thing I knew was Joe's hand tousling my hair.

"Wake up, sleepyhead, you slept right through our wake-up call."

"Did I? Oh, sorry. Got to sleep really late."

"Not surprising. You OK?"

"Er, yeah."

"Want to use the shower first?"

"No, you go ahead, I'm not a very good 'morning' person."

"No shit, Sherlock."

Joe had a shower whilst I promised myself five minutes of daydreaming which, apparently, turned into fifteen minutes of actual dreaming as I fell into another deep sleep. I dreamt about a giant football that was chasing me down the street. The only problem, apart from the fact that it was about twenty feet in circumference, was that it had a bomb in it. I had two choices. One was to stop it and dismantle the bomb, the other was to keep running. I never found out what happened as, at the point of having to make the decision, I was woken again, this time in a slightly less subtle manner. Joe dragged the bedclothes back, hauled me out of bed, flung me over his shoulder (he was a strong guy; we were about the same size) and fireman's-lifted me to the shower cubicle, where he set me down and pulled my pants down to my ankles.

"Lift! Now the other foot. Right, this is called a towel, this is called shower gel and this is called cold water."

He turned the icy jet on my head.

"Ahhhhh, it's freezing!"

"Then turn the dial to 'hot'. I'm not actually going to soap you down, you lazy sod."

"Oh, sorry, I thought you were the maid service," I said, finding my personality for the first time in twenty-four hours.

Joe laughed.

"Get a move on, Hatchington and we'll go down to breakfast."

I think I reinvented force-feeding. It was the only way I could eat anything. The guys were great; referring to me whenever they could, encouraging me, telling me I was going to play a blinder; but I still felt out of it. They had their private sayings, their practiced easy social intercourse and I wasn't a party to it.

We arrived at the ground at 1 o'clock, had a rub-down, then went out on to the pitch for a pre-match warm up. When I used to watch as a kid, I thought it was all a bit haphazard, but now I knew just how choreographed it was.

Then it was back to the changing room for the final talk from the boss. Again, my memory only holds forth on two things he said. One was to all of us:

"Just do what we've been doing all week in training. Keep the shape at the back, counter quickly on the break. Look after our Sam, but get the ball through to him as quickly as possible."

The other was to me:

"Sammy, enjoy it; it's what you love doing. You're an unknown quantity to them. Use that. Catch them off their guard."

Then we walked the short distance from the changing room to the pitch. There is no tunnel at Catteridge Road so no one could use the rather tacky analogy of it being the birthing canal of my life as a footballer. It's a nice ground; a homely ground. Not exactly Wembley, but not exactly tiny either, especially to a boy about to play his first grown up game.

I could hear the anticipation of the crowd as we met up with the Chelsea team before running out and I waited for nerves to cripple me, for my muscles to lose all connectivity with my brain, for the mere proximity of these iconic footballers to overwhelm me.

But none of this happened.

Instead, some force, some energy, some*thing* took over and I was transported to another plane. Like an actor becoming his role as he makes his entrance, I became a footballer. I stared at the broad shoulders of Andy, in front of me and I did what Thomas had told me to do. I thought forwards.

'Whenever we become nervous, we shrink back into ourselves; we become foetal again and our vision turns inward as we hide from whatever is scaring us', he'd said, just before we left the cafe. 'Don't let this happen. Think forwards out of your forehead and this will make you positive and confident'.

Running out on to that pitch to the swell of twenty-five thousand voices was exhilarating. Truly, truly inspiring. It lifts you up; whirls you around. The noise bounces off every part of the stadium. It's encompassing and fluid yet, at the same time, challenging and provocative.

This crazy, formal greeting seeped into me, charged me with battle-readiness, suffused me with the energy of a million colliding atoms; and still I thought forwards.

Out of my mind went any thoughts of Thomas, Davey, the Gang, Gran and Gramps. I knew where they were sitting but, to look for them now, would be to lose focus; to stop being this temporary soldier and return to being the mocha-loving, book-reading kid from

Deptford.

When the referee blew the whistle and Dimitri passed to Luca who sent a perfect ball to the feet of Joe, who dinked past one of the Chelsea midfielders and passed to me where I'd set off on a charging run toward their penalty area before hurtling over to the right side of the pitch, drawing two of their defenders and flying the ball over to Craig, who cracked the sweetest shot against the crossbar, the world was transformed. The crowd's reaction probably registered on a seismograph and, for the next ten minutes, we continued to surge forward. Joe and I appeared to have some sort of telepathy; he knew where I was going to run, I knew where he wanted me to be. I made four incisive runs in that period; on three occasions getting the ball through to Craig or Stewart in the box. We didn't score, but Chelsea knew they were in a match.

Then, inevitably, we couldn't keep up the pressure. Passes began to go astray (two of mine in particular) and, when Dimitri got in a complete muddle and gave the ball away on the halfway line, they strung fifteen perfect short passes together across the park, cut through our defence who, until that point, had been merely spectators and slid the ball into the bottom right of our net. Gary almost got a hand to it, but we were one down.

The rest of the first half saw us repelling wave after wave of Chelsea attack; sometimes with good defensive skills, sometimes with a small child's clumsiness, stumbling like a new-born giraffe as we hoofed the ball out of our penalty area.

At the half-time whistle we trooped, heads bowed, back to our dressing room.

The boss was as calm as ever.

"You won the first ten minutes," he said, "then you missed a couple of passes and suddenly decided you couldn't play anymore. Maradona used to miss passes occasionally; didn't make him crap; just made him human. It's not all black and white, boys. The difference between us and Chelsea is that, when they make mistakes, they don't panic, because they know that, eventually, they'll play better again. If a pass goes astray, just remind yourselves how good you were in the first ten minutes, how good you *are*. And, Sammy, pretend you're playing for the reserves."

I did and we *did* remember how good we were at the start and, although Chelsea had just about the majority of possession, we played some exciting football and constantly encouraged each other. In the 81st minute, Joe stole the ball on the halfway line, belted ten yards up the left touchline and played it just in front of me. It was also just in front of one of their defenders as their back line were beginning to push up to play the offside trap. I reached the ball first, then my brain ignored the rest of my body and decided to do its own 'Nike' commercial – *Just do it!* And I did. I span on the ball. I actually *span* on the ball in my first senior game. The sheer unexpectedness of this threw their player and I set off at the speed of a very determined footballer for their penalty area, with the Chelsea defence backpedalling like fury. I knew Joe would be there. With the extreme of my peripheral vision, I'd seen him set off after he'd passed to me. I looked up for one hundredth of a second and slid the ball through to him just inside the area. Boy, can Joe shoot. If this had been a cartoon, the ball would have torn through the back of the net, carried on out of the ground and disappeared in to the hemisphere. But it wasn't a cartoon, so it just blasted the back of their net instead.

Up until that day, I'd never heard a noise like it.

It completely filled my ears; it rushed in to all my senses. A massive audible endorphin, if you will.

I ran to Joe and leapt at him. He caught me, kissed me on the cheek, put me down on the ground, then threw himself on top of me. Within seconds, seven more of our team followed suit and I was at the bottom of a thunderous maul and so missed what Joe said to me.

Chelsea came at us like a train for the final nine minutes but we defended in numbers and 1-1 was a fair result; unless, of course, you were a Chelsea fan.

At the final whistle we applauded our fans, shook hands with the somewhat disconsolate Chelsea players (three or four said 'well done, mate') and walked back to the changing rooms where the boss was grinning a welcome.

The debrief was short and sweet. 'Proud of you'; 'did everything I asked'; 'matched them for much of the second half'; 'great goal, Joe'; 'round of applause for our terrific debutant'.

During the communal bath (we only switched to showers in my third year in the team) I was hugged, slapped on the back and ducked under the water.

I'd arranged to meet everyone afterwards at a local restaurant.

As I left the ground, there were still a few diehard fans hanging around. I smiled at a couple as I walked through them and it wasn't until I heard:

"Sam, er, could you… I mean, would you mind signing…"

The realisation that I was no longer a fan, but a player, took me somewhat by surprise.

"Oh, sorry, thought you were waiting for someone."

"We were. You."

"Oh. Well, thanks. I'm er… what's your name?"

"Sheryl. And this is Rob."

"Hi Sheryl, Hi Rob," I said as I tried to work out how I was going to sign my name.

To Sheryl and Rob.
Thanks for being great fans.

Sam H-----n

I gave the 'S' a bit more flourish that was really necessary and just put a straight line between the 'H' and the 'n'. Honestly, you'd think I'd been doing it for years.

I signed about twenty programmes altogether, chatted to everyone, thanked them for their congratulations and watched whilst their body language changed from timidity and humble staccato movements to openness and spatial closeness as they realised that I was just an ordinary guy who couldn't do his shoelaces up until he was seven, put virtually a whole bottle of tomato sauce on his bacon butties and had the musical taste of a pre-pubescent girl from the 1970s.

But I knew how I'd always thought of people I'd seen on the TV or watched on a sports field. How, indeed, I *still* think of them. It's like they're supernatural. Nine feet tall, partially made of gold and bathed in an eternal halo of sunlight. Then you meet them and they're five feet seven, have dandruff on their collar and their flies are undone.

When I entered the restaurant I knew exactly where my group were sitting, mainly due to the fact that they all stood up and applauded me.

I blushed my usual copper-red.

"Sammy, you were amazing," Susie said, "I loved that bit where you did that 'Kirov' thing with the ball."

"Er, Kirov?"

"Yes, when you sort of pirouetted and left that rather creamy Chelsea player looking somewhat nonplussed."

"Susie, darling, no one says creamy anymore," Rachel said, "unless they're in a St. Trinian's movie."

"Well, I do and he was. Sammy, do you think you could-"

"I don't know his number, Susie," I said, pre-empting my angelic little friend's request.

"Oh, shame. I shall have to become a Chelsea fan, then."

We chatted and ate and laughed and drank; and when the waiter found out why we were celebrating, he brought out a cake with one candle on it, to signify my first game and everyone cheered when I blew it out; and Thomas asked whether we minded if he bought us all champagne and nobody minded at all; and Gran and Gramps told me how much I was coming up in the world and weren't my new friends really posh, but not snooty and wasn't Davey such a nice young man and that Thomas was a proper gentleman 'like what gentlemen used to be'; and Thomas promised Gran some Agatha Christies and Gramps, a fifty year-old book on gardening, which elevated him to almost god-like status; and, at the end, everyone hugged me and each other like we did this every week. And I know I sound like a seven year-old but we adults should be allowed to get excited without being patronised or compared to a child, for these moments are the best things in life. They are like the lighting of the Olympic flame, when something so small ignites something so large. This is life. This IS life.

As we left the restaurant, the sudden exhaustion was overwhelming. The extraordinary jet-engined ride of the previous week left my body and I plunged from high energy to an empty tank without bothering to stop in the middle.

The following day Tara had wanted me to herself, to celebrate in private, as she put it. I told her that celebrations would need to be mooted as I needed to rest. So we reached a compromise or, at least, I did; the fleeting expression of annoyance before she agreed giving away her real feelings. I would have a long lie-in, meet her for a pub lunch, then we'd both pick up Davey and the gang and go to the cinema.

When she heard me turn the key in the front door, mum rushed out of the lounge. Her fingers fiddled with her skirt and her face screamed anticipation.

"Sam, how did it go?"

"It went well, mum. Didn't you see the results?"

"No, your father was watching a programme about Hitler."

"Appropriate."

"Well?"

"We drew one-all."

"That's good… isn't it? How did *you* play?"

"I was a bit crap for some of it, but I had two or three good spells. Oh and I got an assist."

"What's that?"

"It's where you lay the ball on for the goal scorer."

"That's *very* good."

"Yes, mum."

"Your father's watching a film later but I'm going to record the highlights programme and watch it early tomorrow morning. I was wondering if you'd like to see it with me?"

"No thanks, mum. I don't need to. I know what happened. I was there."

"Yes. Yes, of course."

Then 'his' voice rang out.

"I'd like that coffee tonight, Muriel."

"Yes, dear, I'm just finding out how the match went."

There was a three second pause, then the lounge door opened and he was standing two feet away from me, the closest he'd been in six months.

It was as if I wasn't there.

"Tonight, Muriel, tonight."

He disappeared back in to his lair. The dragon that was too lazy to breathe fire.

"Er, I'd better just… put the kettle on for your dad's coffee."

"OK, mum."

"Would you like one?"

"No thanks, I'm going to have an early night. I'm pretty tired."

"OK."

We stood, facing each other, in some unmoving dance. There were a thousand things she wanted to say to me and a thousand things I wanted to say to her; but the words were too long buried and so could not bring the dance to life.

"Goodnight, mum."

"Goodnight, Sam… Sam?"

"Yes?"

"I'm very proud."

"Thanks, mum."

The following week I trained with renewed energy. I was a part of things now.

On Wednesday evening, I popped round to see Davey's new bedsit (he'd moved out of the home a few weeks before). It was a rather small room in a rather small house.

"It's small," I said.

"It's bijou," he said.

"No, it's small," I said.

"That's what bijou means," he said.

"No, bijou means 'pretending not to be small'," I said.

"Look, I can lie in bed, turn the TV on, wash my face and cook a meal at the same time."

"You'd need three hands."

"Well, if you're going to be literal, Hatchington."

"It's nice," I said, "I like it."

"No you don't."

"No, you're right, I don't."

"It's all I can afford at the moment. When I've got some more private clients at the gym, I'll get something better."

"Get them quickly," I said.

We ended up having a coffee whilst washing our faces and cooking beans on toast.

I'd arranged to meet Thomas on Saturday at the bookstall. England were playing that weekend so there were no premiership games.

That morning my frog vomited me awake as usual and I opened my eyes to a bright javelin of sunlight parting the top of my curtains. For once I found the energy to leap straight out of bed.

There, on the floor, was *The Complete Works of Oscar Wilde*. 'Must have fallen off the shelf in the night', I thought. It had landed on the carpet open at the page that Thomas had made the inscription. I made sure the pages weren't damaged and put it back on the shelf.

Even the kitchen was off limits on a Saturday morning so I left the house straight after my shower and decided to make Thomas smile and take him a flask of tea, just like the old days.

I bought a thermos and asked Greg, the barista at the cafe, if he would fill it with tea. Then I grabbed a couple of croissants and made my way, in some happy Neverland, to the market.

Lazy Deborah was doing a roaring trade and only had time for a smile. She'd even got out of her chair, which must have involved the use of a passing fork lift truck.

I reached Thomas' stall. Except I didn't. I reached where his stall should have been.

For a moment I was totally confused. It was like going into Trafalgar Square and finding

Nelson's Column wasn't there.

Lynda was just finishing serving a customer.

"Hi Lynda," I said, "Where's Thomas?"

"Oh my love," she said, "he's died."

14

I don't remember the rest of the day.

I think my brain shut down and obliterated the memory.

I know I didn't cry. Couldn't cry. If I had, it would have been at something sad. This was beyond that.

I didn't faint either. I suppose 'catatonic' would best describe me in those lost hours.

Deep down at some sub-primordial level I must have wanted to scream, to shed a rainstorm of tears, to fly at whoever organises this life that we stumble through and vent my fury at their insatiable desire for unfairness.

But all this was trapped, unable to breach the surface of my emotional core; like those poor people who cannot move their facial muscles.

I'm told that I stood and stared into nothingness for ten minutes. It took Lynda and two other people to get me to sit down.

After half an hour and having been unable to illicit even a monosyllabic answer from me, an ambulance was called and I was taken to hospital where I was given a tranquiliser.

Lynda, who knew my family situation, had found Davey's number on my mobile. They'd both spent the night at my bedside and were there when I emerged from my drug-induced sleep.

It took a while for the haze to clear. When it did and I was able to sit up in bed, Lynda said:

"How are you feeling, my love?"

"I'm OK, thank you."

"Do you remember anything?"

"Not really."

"Do you remember why you're here?"

"Thomas has died."

"Yes, my love."

Davey stood up and took a step toward the bed.

"No, Davey, please," I said.

He sat on the bed anyway, his bodyweight tilting the mattress and bringing me ever so slightly closer to him.

"No," I said again, trying to push him away.

But he knew what I was too scared to admit; that to heal we must grieve. And, as his arms began to envelop me and the first tear sprung from my eye, I made one last feeble attempt to stop him. But the strength would not come and I sank into him, holding the back of his neck like it was my last link to the world, hearing my sobs resonate against his chest, feeling my grief erupt through fissures of uncontainable emotion to be absorbed by this glorious friend and, once, feeling a single tear splash from him on to my shoulder.

When Davey gently lowered me back to the pillow, I was overcome by a relief that was, I suppose, akin to what people who lived during the war must have felt at the sound of the All Clear.

Lynda, bless her, fetched us three cups of tea and I was finally able to ask what had happened.

It appeared that Thomas had been sitting in an armchair at home, drinking a cup of Earl Grey and, inevitably, reading a book, when he just peacefully died. Lynda said:

"When I found him I thought he was asleep. He looked really serene and had dropped his book on the floor. I know it's sad, love, but it's the best possible way he could have gone."

"I know," I said, "what was he reading?"

"Something by Oscar Wilde. It was *The Complete Works* that he had dropped."

It wasn't until two weeks later when the funeral was over and a tiny semblance of normality had returned to our lives, that the significance of this actually hit me.

I told Davey about the book I'd found on my bedroom floor the night Thomas had died and, although I recognised the profundity of its meaning, I couldn't actually vocalise it.

"It's an amazing coincidence, isn't it," I said.

"There is no such thing as coincidence," Davey replied.

"No," I said.

I don't understand it. Who does? But I *do* know it was Thomas telling me that he was OK.

"I don't want to bother you with things now," Lynda said, "but Thomas had wanted you to be an executor."

"What's that?"

"It means someone who sorts out the will and all his affairs."

"Oh."

"But you have to be eighteen and that's not for another week and we really need to start now. But don't worry, I'm the other executor so I'll do it and I'll let you know what's happening."

"No," I said, getting out of bed and leaning ever so slightly against Davey, "we'll do it together, but you'll have to sign everything."

"OK, my love, that will please him."

"You said 'will'."

"Yes."

"Present tense."

"Yes. You knew Thomas better than most people. How could someone as wonderful, as full of character and energy as him, die? No, love, he's just finished here and gone back home."

Later, Davey took me home and stayed with me in my room until it was obvious I could barely stay awake. As he was leaving, I said:

"I haven't told Tara."

"Tell her tomorrow," he said.

I did. She told me she would do anything to help, but only after another fleeting look of annoyance that I was beginning to know so well, because she'd been kept in the dark for twenty-four hours and Davey had been the one who'd looked after me.

I also rang Seb, who was the one least likely to make me cry and asked him to pass on the message. This turned out to be a fruitless piece of planning as, within the hour, the rest of the gang had rung me back.

And, of course, I rang Flitcham and explained that my father had died. They were wonderful, telling me to take as much time as I needed, asking me to let them know how I was doing and offering me the team's psychologist should I need him. I was touched.

So Lynda and I set to work. I offered to help her sort out Thomas' house but she said that she'd already done it. She'd also delivered his clothes to the charity shop, as he'd requested and boxed up his personal effects which she'd put in the attic.

On the Thursday we had an appointment with the solicitor for the reading of the will.

We sat in the rather plush waiting room on a sofa that probably cost more than all the furniture in my parent's house put together. Neither of us could find a reason to speak. So we fell into private conversation with our thoughts. I don't know what Lynda's were. I know that mine were along the lines that we shouldn't be dealing with the practicalities of the will, the finances, the funeral arrangements; that some third party should be taking care of it. Surely we had suffered enough without having to be continually reminded of what had happened. How do you choose a coffin? Do you pick the cheap one because it's pointless spending money on something that's going to be lost to sight almost immediately? Or do you choose the expensive one to assuage some guilt because you weren't the best son/mother/friend, or as some medal of respect. But you loved them anyway, so it's an irrelevance; and yet it plays on your mind and adds to the already swirling miasma.

Then I realised that, to leave all this to someone else, would be to bury your head in the Sahara. Thomas wouldn't want someone else to do this, he'd want us to. We were his family and it was our job.

"Ms Moreton and Mr Hatchington?"

"Yes?"

We both jumped in unison before following the secretary through to the office.

Mr Fanshaw of *Fanshaw & Goodall* was what I suppose you would call Old School. Ramrod straight and shirt collar so impeccably starched you could probably have sliced steel with it, he shook our hands and gestured with a curt 'please' toward two enormous leather chairs that, when we sat in them, made both of us look like six year-olds.

He said a few words which were probably in English but mostly sounded like 'hereuntoforthwith' and then opened the will.

It was straightforward. The monetary assets totalled £80,467.39. £10,000 was to go to charity, £10,000 to Lynda, £5000 to Davey (oh, Thomas) and the remainder and Mr Fanshaw peered at me as if assessing whether I was human, before reading, 'to my son, Sam Hatchington'.

"He does go on to explain that you're not his real son, just someone whom he considered to be his son."

"It's the same thing," I said.

"Not in law," he said.

"But it is in humanity," I said, getting the word wrong, but my point across.

Lynda diffused the situation by asking this legal robot what else the will contained.

He barked on for a while and then, with an overflow of disdain, said:

"'And my house is to go to Sam Hatchington, on condition that he moves into it immediately and escapes finally from the oppression of the man who fathered him and then gave up all rights to that status'."

I couldn't move.

"You alright, love?" Lynda asked.

"But… I can't. Not all that money *and* his house."

"It's what Thomas wants."

'Wants', you see; not 'wanted', 'wants'.

"I hope you are happy with these arrangements," Fanshaw said, making no attempt to disguise the sneer in his voice.

"He's very happy, thank-"

"No, Lynda, I'll answer."

I took two steps toward his desk.

"I have just lost the man who became my father. I would give up all the money and the house and everything else I own to have him back."

"Really," he said.

"Yes – mate – *really*."

Lynda forced me back down on the seat.

After we had been dismissed from his legal torture chamber and taken two hefty gulps of the early afternoon Greenwich air, Lynda turned to me:

"Well, what an absolute tosser."

And most of the churning anger in me dissipated.

We went for a coffee and a chat.

"I don't want it all, Lynda," I said, "the house and the money, it's not what I want."

"No, it's what *he* wants."

"Yes," I said, looking at the empty froth in my cup and its cold, melted chocolate tapestry.

"None of this will make sense at the moment, my love. Don't try to analyse it. In a few weeks everything will fall into place but, right now, just let things happen. Only, never forget that Thomas is still looking after you."

The funeral took place on my eighteenth birthday. Neither of us realised when we booked it.

Lynda, Davey, myself and Tara sat in the front row with the gang; a few friends, book acquaintances and the market stall holders behind us.

It was held in the crematorium with a Layman taking the service. Thomas believed in a Higher Entity and the continuation of the soul, but not with any labels attached to it.

I read his favourite poem, *The Soldier*, by Rupert Brooke; Lynda said a few words; a man I'd never met before spoke on behalf of Thomas' professional friends (I hadn't realised he had been so highly thought of; though I should have done) and, with typical Thomas humour, they played someone called Gracie Fields singing *Wish Me Luck As You Wave Me Goodbye* as the coffin disappeared.

Then we went outside to look at the flowers. Mine was a huge bouquet of white carnations, his favourite flower, with a card that read simply:

'*To my father,*
With love from your son'.

Finally, at Thomas' written insistence, we retired to a pub to spend the remaining £467.39.

At 8 o'clock and more tired than I've ever been in my life, we left and Tara and Davey took me home. They wanted to stay but I said that I would be fine and just needed a little time to myself and would see them both the next day. Tara put up a bit of resistance but Davey just told me to ring him whenever I needed to.

Later, I sat on my bed and waited for the torrent to hit. I'd cried briefly a couple of times during the day, but had tried to save it up for when I was alone.

But the tears didn't come. Instead, I got undressed, put the *Complete Works of Oscar Wilde* next to my pillow and descended into sleep.

15

When the vast majority of Thomas' affairs had been dealt with, I resumed training.

The guys were wonderful to me. Looking after me, over-praising everything I did and encouraging me whenever I made a mistake.

I'd missed the previous Saturday's game against Aston Villa (which we'd lost 2-0) and had been given permission by the club to take more leave, thereby missing the home game against Everton. But I'd said no and that I wanted to come back. The two weeks since Thomas died had been a slowly improving journey that was only bearable when I, physically and metaphorically, had my friend's shoulders close at hand but, when I was alone, the world did that thing it does when you're suffering and shrinks to the size of your room, imprisoning you there and temporarily destroying all purpose in life.

The training was an emphatic relief. The frantic physicality helped to clear the sad toxins and reintroduced normality into my life, be it only in short bursts.

Of course, like a caffeine rush, the crash was horrible but, as with any drug, if you know the fix will come the next day, it gets you through.

I bought my mum a present; both because I wanted to and to sweeten the pill that I would be moving out.

She was in the kitchen cooking 'his' dinner when I gave it to her. I'd wrapped it as best I could (which was pretty badly). She dried her hands on her apron and said:

"But, Sam, it's not my birthday for another two months."

"Doesn't matter."

"But, you mustn't-"

"OK, it's a non-birthday present."

She tore open the already torn wrapping paper.

"Well, it's very sweet of you. I'm sure I shall love it whatever-"

And she took the diamond necklace out of its box.

"Oh Sam, it's beautiful. It even looks like a real diamond."

"That's because it *is* a real diamond, mum."

"But… but how can you afford…?"

"You remember Thomas who ran the bookstall?"

"Yes?"

"He died and left me some money."

"Oh? Oh, well, how nice. But why?"

"Because we became great friends and… well, he said that I was the son he never had."

"Well, that was lovely of you to let him think it."

"I didn't let him think it. It's true."

"Pardon?"

"I *was* the son he never had. And he was the father *I've* never had."

"Sam, please, you've had a father for eighteen years."

"Just enjoy your present, mum. Put it on, I want to see you wearing it."

She looked beautiful.

I don't know whether my mum told 'him' what I'd said (I doubt it, to be honest) but, whichever way, he certainly found out that Thursday when the local free newspaper, the *Deptford Gazette*, landed on the doormat.

Across the back page rang out the headline:

TRAGEDY FOR LOCAL FOOTBALL STAR

Local boy and new Flitcham player, Sammy Hatchington, was dealt the cruellest of blows when, just after his debut against Chelsea, his father was found dead at his home. Hatchington, who laid on the goal for Joe Stark in the 1-1 draw, is only just eighteen…

My 'father', like Mark Twain before him, thought that the reports of his death had been greatly exaggerated.

Apparently he initially reached the heady heights of being irritated, which must have sapped his energy. Later, this reaction was replaced by something far worse.

Gran and Gramps had told me about the article. I had popped round for tea and shortbread ('It's got tartan on the tin so it must be good') and also to take them a present I'd been longing to buy them. Their old TV only worked if you hit the top right hand corner every five minutes and, even then, all the programmes looked as though they'd been filmed somewhere near the North Pole in a blizzard.

Gran started kept touching the screen and saying:

"But Sam, it's huge; it's like having a cinema in the lounge, isn't it, Herbert?"

"Look, lad," said Gramps, "this is very kind of you, but are you sure you can afford it?"

I told them about Thomas.

"Ah, that explains the newspaper, Herbert," Gran said and showed me the article.

Gramps put his hand on my shoulder and told me that he understood and Gran made me tea and bacon sandwiches because 'it's comfort food and will help you to feel better'.

"He was a real gentleman," she said, "You don't meet his kind very often."

"No," I said, "you don't."

That Saturday I started on the substitute's bench. There was a short paragraph about my father's death in the programme and, when I walked out to take my seat, twenty-two thousand people stood as one and applauded.

The boss leaned over.

"They're applauding *you*, Sammy. Stand up and wave to them."

I did and was suddenly overwhelmed by the capacity of human beings to genuinely care. I started to cry. The boss hugged me and applauded the fans, then the rest of the team did the same.

After twenty-five minutes we were 2-0 down and the boss decided the 4-4-2 formation we'd switched to wasn't working.

"Start warming up, Sammy," he said and went to tell the rest of the coaching staff that we were going back to 4-3-1-2.

If you're not au fait with football formations: 4 is the number of defenders, 3 is the number in midfield, 1 (me) playing just behind the strikers and, with devastating logic, 2 is the number of strikers.

On the stroke of half-time, Craig pulled a goal back after a one-two between me and Joe on the edge of the penalty area.

I'd told Lynda I was going to play this game for Thomas. She'd said:

"No, love, don't. It'll put too much pressure on you and, if you don't play well, you'll think you've let him down. He'll be there, that's all you need to know."

In the second half, we were all over them.

Joe and I continued to develop our already considerable understanding and, in the sixty-first minute, he scored with a brilliant header from my cross. Then, after seventy-two minutes, Craig was pulled down in the box and got straight up to score from the resulting penalty.

At the final whistle I ran to every side of the pitch and applauded our fans. Joe draped his arm round my shoulder on the way back to the changing room and told me I'd 'played a bloody blinder' and that he was very proud of me.

The debrief was delayed till Monday (as I later found out, in deference to my emotional state before the game); so, after a very quick 'well played, lads' and a bath in which there was no ducking, just a general bonhomie, I dashed over to the Player's Lounge and treated Lynda to wine and canapés.

She told me she thought I'd played wonderfully and she'd thoroughly enjoyed her first football match and could see why Thomas had been so excited.

A couple of glasses of wine later, she said:

"Do you know what, love, I think you should move into Thomas' house next week."

"But it's not mine legally, yet."

"Oh, blow bloody legally, love, it's what Thomas wants, so you have every right to be there."

"OK," I said, "but I'll have to break it gently to my mum."

"Well, you do that and we'll book a van for Wednesday afternoon."

"That soon?"

"You've got to do it, love."

"I know."

"You want to, don't you?"

"God, yes."

"Then Wednesday it is."

"Thanks, Lynda," I said.

When I got home, mum was in the back garden, cutting some roses.

"Mum, are you free tomorrow lunchtime? I want to take you for a meal."

"Thank you, Sam, but I'll be cooking your dad's dinner."

"Well, cook his dinner and then come out with me."

"Don't be silly, I can't leave your dad."

"He's not an invalid."

"He likes a cup of tea about an hour after his dinner."

"Well, he knows where the damn kettle is!"

"Language please, Samuel."

"So, you won't come?"

"No, I can't. I mean, it's very nice of you but why did you want to take me out?"

"I've got something to tell you."

"Oh?"

She had the beginnings of a bunch of roses in her hand and it suddenly struck me that I should be giving *her* roses while I told her that I loved her but could no longer live in her home.

"Mum…"

"Yes? Well, spit it out, Samuel, it can't be that bad."

"I'm moving out. On Wednesday, mum. I'm moving out on Wednesday."

"But, you can't."

"Well…I am."

"But you're eighteen."

"Yes."

"And we're a family."

"No, mum, you and I are a family. And, if I could take you with me, I would. But you wouldn't come because you're the only person left in the house who knows how to put a teabag in a mug."

My mum looked at the ground that was simultaneously swallowing her and tried to come to terms, in a few seconds, with the fact that she was losing her only prison-mate in this suburban open prison that she'd voluntarily walked into over two decades ago.

I told her I was sorry, that I loved her and that I was moving into Thomas' house in Greenwich so I wouldn't be far away.

Maybe to ease the pain she muttered spontaneous comments under her breath as she turned her back on me and walked toward the house. I caught the odd phrase; 'too young', 'doesn't know how to cook', 'don't understand', but I was powerless to heal the wounds as I was the one who had inflicted them.

Later that night, Tara and I went to see a film. I don't remember what it was. I know I didn't enjoy it, mostly because the relief I felt at moving out was temporarily usurped by the guilt of my mother condemned to a life sentence with no parole.

After training on Tuesday, I went home and started to pack which, as we know, involves 10% packing, 60% finding photographs we'd completely forgotten about and T-shirts stuck in the back of the drawer that we haven't seen for five years and 30% sitting on the bed in some dazed recollection of the memories recounted by said photographs and T-shirts.

That night, with everything boxed up, I slept in a room that wasn't mine anymore. Things weren't in the right place and I realised that I had already mentally left.

There had been no word from 'him'. I'd presumed he was either overjoyed or, more likely, couldn't summon the will to comment.

I was wrong on both counts.

Mum had shut herself in her bedroom the next morning. I'd tapped on the door twice but had received a curt 'I'm busy' on both occasions. I realised it was fruitless trying to coax her out, much as I wanted to see her and say goodbye. She would come round in her own time.

It was 11 o'clock. Lynda and I were just loading the final things into the van. I was carrying a box on which I'd written the word *Stuff*; basically, items that didn't fit into any category; on top of which, in isolated splendour, sat my vomiting frog. Lynda was carrying my duvet and my teddy bear, which I'd had a bit of a teenage moment about when she'd noticed it.

"What's his name?"

"Ness."

"Unusual name for a he-bear?"

117

"It's short for Necessities."

"Pardon?"

"Bear Necessities."

She'd looked at me like Mr Bumble looked at Oliver Twist.

"I was eight! That's quite clever for an eight year old."

"Yes, love."

Then his car drew up. Not a flicker of acknowledgement as he got out.

"He's home an hour early," I said.

"Is he indeed?"

"Look, Lynda, I need to say goodbye to my mum, even if she won't come out of her room. I can't just go without... I mean, she's my mum."

"Of course you must, my love. I'll wait out here. Shout if you need me."

"Thanks, Lynda."

I went back inside for, as it would turn out, the last time in my life.

I presumed he'd gone into the lounge. He usually did. This was his routine. A routine for someone for whom life held nothing, because this was his choice; and life will only attempt to coax for so long before it takes its boundless energy to people who smile and welcome it. As Wilde said, 'Consistency is the last refuge of the unimaginative'.

My mum would, of course, be shovelling the last of five spoonfuls of sugar into a mug. Perish the thought that he should wait more than five seconds for his tea.

But mum wasn't in the kitchen.

'She must still be in the bedroom', I thought.

It was with some trepidation that I knocked on the door.

There was no answer.

"Mum, it's me. I'm going now. I want to say goodbye... Mum? Please open the door. I can't leave like this. Look, in a couple of days when I've got things organised, you can come and visit and we'll have a cup of tea."

The downward movement of the handle made me jump and the door opened so slowly I thought I was in one of those old second-rate horror movies. I remember thinking 'there should be creaking and a silhouette of a bat bouncing up and down on a piece of elastic'.

But there wasn't; just my so-called father's face looming in the gap where the door had been.

I tried to look around him, but he moved to cut off my view.

He was so abhorrent to me that I couldn't even look at his face. It was the physical manifestation of the evil underneath.

"Mum, please come out so I can kiss you goodbye."

Nothing.

"Mum, I was going to move out eventually. It's not that I don't love you, or appreciate everything you've done. It's just that..."

I petered out. Like when you start leaving an overly-long message on someone's voicemail that you know won't be listened to.

"Clive, let him in."

"I'm not having him infesting this room."

"Infesting?" I said.

"Clive, please, this is my room too."

The behemoth, for once, did what his wife asked of him; but not before he'd paused for a few seconds; an impenetrable portcullis to his insignificant castle.

Then, machismo proven, he stepped back and I walked into my parent's bedroom; a room I hadn't entered since I was nine years old and would sit in her vanity chair and tell her about the dreams I'd had the night before.

Mum was sitting on the edge of the bed. As I walked in, she looked up at me. I'd imagined, for some reason, that she'd been crying, but I was wrong. Her face was rock-hard. She looked like an eighteenth century spinster schoolmistress about to scold her young pupils.

She almost bit through the sentence:

"You're going, then."

I was very aware of 'him' standing just behind me.

"Mum, this is something I want to do."

"Or is it something that you're being forced to do?"

"Forced? How can I be forced? Who would force me?"

"Well, it's very convenient; that's all I can say."

"What? You think Thomas died just so that I could live in his house? I'm eighteen. I'm not a kid anymore," I said, my guilt beginning to be replaced by a hardening of my stance.

"Really? Well, then maybe you should stop acting like one."

"Oh, come on, that's such a cliché."

"Don't you dare speak to your mother like that."

The voice was low. It virtually growled. The words, laced with latent venom, felt like they had passed through a concrete block before they reached my ears.

But, despite the fear, or maybe *in* spite of the fear, I still would not turn and look at him.

"I'll just leave that to you then," I said.

The tension circled, like the beginnings of a hurricane, stinging the air and burrowing into everything in its path.

"You what?"

"I said, I'll leave it you to speak to my mother like that."

He must have moved toward me because my mum said:

"Clive, please."

"Shut up, Muriel."

"Clive!"

"I said shut up!"

"I think that proves my point." I said, trying to force an edge into my voice.

"You – apologise – right – now – or – I'll-"

"You'll what? Gouge my eye out with an onyx ashtray? Is that what you'll do? Well, maybe I'd welcome that, because at least it would mean that you're acknowledging my existence."

"You ungrateful piece of shit. Your mother slaves for you-"

"What?! How the hell can you-"

"Don't interrupt me! She goes out to work, she cooks, she cleans, so you can hang around with your snobby mates, go to your poncy college, kick a ball about and pretend it's a career. We have worked ourselves into the ground so you could have everything you wanted and how do you repay us? You piss off at the first opportunity to live in some dead bloke's house that you've known for two years. Well, I'll tell you now; you are staying here. You can go and get your stuff and bring it back into this house. You are not going anywhere until you have repaid us in full. Is that clear?"

"I am moving out."

The menace was two inches from my ear.

"You – will – do - what – you – are – told."

I turned very, very slowly and looked directly into his stagnant eyes. His was the face of a mindless tyrant, a small-scale suburban Hitler; a man who clung to the last vestige of any status with his fists; who had shadow-boxed with life for a short while, then climbed out of the ring and allowed negativity to germinate into lethargy and, ultimately, to flower as evil.

I had no idea that you could feel hatred and pity at the same time. The depth of hate I felt at that moment was so alien to me, that I didn't recognise it at first. But it was there, fast-tracking to my brain, dismissing all rational thought. Yet, there were also strands of pity that permeated it. Pity that an eighteen year old could see through this imaginary defence and know that the man was, after all, conscious of the gutter level of self-esteem he'd willingly allowed himself to fall to. It was almost as though I were the elder of the two of us. But this pity could not dilute the temporary storm of hatred that I could see reflecting back at me from his eyes.

'You are eighteen', I told myself, 'you do not have to take this anymore'.

"I'm eighteen," I said, "I can do what I like with my-"

The punch hit me like a bolt on an archery target and I flew backwards across the room.

We'd been standing so close, I didn't think he had the space to swing. But he'd been clever. He'd used the old trick of a swift kick to the shins and, as I contorted with the pain, one small step backward and an upper cut to my jaw.

"Clive!" I heard my mum shout, just before I landed and broke the glass on her mirror-fronted wardrobe.

For a couple of seconds I was too shocked to move, but then the smarting in my jaw mixed with venom. I got up, pushing the pain back with an all-consuming hate, terrified of the fact that I was losing control.

"YOU PATHETIC BRAINLESS MORON," I yelled at him.

"Do NOT speak to your father like-"

"SHUT UP! SHUT UP YOU STUPID WOMAN! WHY THE HELL DO YOU ALWAYS… Why do you always stand up for him, eh? You could have been something. You could have been a nurse. You could have had a life. But you gave it up, didn't you? DIDN'T YOU? You gave it up for this PIECE OF CRAP! YOU TREAT HER LIKE A SLAVE, YOU BASTARD. YOU THINK OF NO ONE APART FROM YOURSELF. YOU SHOULD BE IN PRISON FOR THE WAY YOU'VE TREATED US."

He pulled his forearm back and I stared at his fist.

"OK, COME ON, DO IT; TRY TO HIT ME AGAIN, YOU…"

Then I stopped shouting. I've no idea why. Possibly because this wasn't me. This was the reaction of someone I couldn't understand. So I just stopped.

For a few seconds I was so surprised, I couldn't speak; but, as I remembered to breathe, the calm person I recognised as myself returned.

"Why did you father me? Eh? Was I a mistake? Why father a child if you're going to hate him for the whole of his life? Did you? Did you hate me from the moment I was born? I would have asked you before, but you never talk to me. You don't even look at me. Today was the first time in years and that was just to make sure you knew where I was before you tried to break my jaw. You were a runner. I was proud of you. I told all my classmates about you. You could have stayed a runner and we could have been happy. We could have gone on holidays together, the three of us, could have built sandcastles. We could have had ice cream and you could have carried me on your shoulders, could have taken me to my first football match, framed my school certificate, told me about girls and bought me my first pint. You could have; but you didn't. You didn't because you hate. It's all you're good at. Hating. It's the only thing that justifies your life. I don't even think you love my mother. Possibly deep down. But you would never say it, even if you did. She's just there to organise your life; to give you the freedom to hate even more. For years I wanted you to love me. I would have given anything. You have no idea how much you upset me. I was a kid and my dad hated me. But now I don't care. You've given up your right to know me. If you asked how I felt about you, I would say 'with indifference'. Because you don't exist anymore. And now I'm going to walk out of this house and I will never see you again."

All the words in the world gushed through the pause that followed. None of them spoken, but all of them there.

Then the spell was broken.

I waited for the punch. It didn't come immediately. It was almost as if he knew I wasn't going to fight back, for he seemed to consider me for a few moments, before calmly taking hold of my shirt collar and throwing me against the wall.

I slid down it, paused for breath and then slowly got up, hoping this would be the end of it. Of course, I was wrong. He came at me again; paused again, as if trying to recognise me, then he punched me hard in the stomach. Even though I'd seen it coming and had tensed my abs, the thunderbolt was so hard that I went down on my knees, thereby being at the perfect height for him to punch me in the head. As I curled up, foetal, on the floor, there followed a seemingly endless storm of wordless rage as he kicked me; kicked me until it exhausted him.

When he stopped, nothing in the world moved. In the unbearable pain that catapulted around my body, I had a vague thought that everything had finished; the attack, my relationship with him, my family.

It took me several seconds to get up off the floor. I shook my head very slightly, which made it hurt even more and attempted to focus on the doorway.

'Just get yourself out of here', I said to myself.

But he came at me again.

I couldn't take being hit anymore.

"No!" I said, barely able to raise my fists.

"Don't you DARE hit your father," came a shriek from the bed.

I looked at her and I tried to take on board the ridiculousness of what she'd just said. In the second that this distracted me, he grabbed me by the throat; hard; fingers pushing in to my glottis like talons round a mouse.

'This is just to frighten me', I thought, 'he'd never do this'.

As he slowly pushed me to the ground, kneeling over me, forcing his fingers round my throat with ever-increasing power, I looked into his face and saw intense concentration, that of a potter throwing a prize vase; a slight tic in his left cheek pulsing the intent in his brain and I knew he wouldn't stop.

I began to choke and flail. I remember looking across at my mum, pleading with my eyes for her to help me. But she just sat there, curled up against the headboard, an expression somewhere between horror and bafflement.

Then I could no longer breathe. And, as the room began to leave me, I was only very dimly aware of the shadow in the doorway, only barely conscious of the swing of my cricket bat and, with the echo in my ears, could only just make out the cry of pain as the willow broke my father's nose.

I gasped for air.

"Slower breaths, my love," Lynda said, "long, slow breaths." And she held me with one hand whilst keeping a rigid grip on the bat with the other.

After a while my breathing began to return to normal and I was able to sit up. Then, with Lynda's help, I stood; very shakily at first, but then more steadily as the relief coursed through me.

When Lynda was sure I was OK, she turned to the man with the bloody nose, who had crawled onto the bed next to my mother.

"I will talk to Sam and we will decide whether to press charges. But, whatever the outcome, if you *ever* come near him again, I will report this to the police and have you locked up. You are the scum of the earth. You are not fit to share this boy's blood. What a pathetic specimen of a man you are that you prove your manhood by strangling your son."

Her eyes diverted to my mother.

"And, as for you. You are a disgrace to women. So subservient to this evil brute that you would watch him kill your son and do nothing to stop him. You gutless bitch."

Then she gently manoeuvred me out of the room and down the stairs.

As Lynda shut the front door behind us, I felt the weight of it closing; not physically, but the weight of the end of eighteen years.

"Lynda," I said, as we sat in the van, my voice straining to force an opening in my swollen throat, "thank you."

She stroked my hair as I leant on her shoulder for an awfully long time.

"How did you know?" I said.

"You'd been in there too long. And then I heard your mother scream 'don't hit your father' and I knew you must be having to defend yourself, so I grabbed the first thing I could find which, luckily, was your cricket bat and ran in."

"It was one hell of a strike," I said, "we could have done with you against Australia."

We laughed; a little harder than the joke warranted.

"Are you alright, love?"

"Yes."

"Really?"

"No, not really."

"We ought to get you to a hospital, you know; make sure you're OK."

"No, Lynda, then we would have to tell them what happened and then the police would be involved. I want this to be over; right now."

"I understand, my love, but if you feel ill, you promise you'll tell me?"

"I promise."

"Here, take this."

She took a pill out of a little bottle in her purse.

"What is it?"

"It's a Valium. It'll relax you."

"Um, do you really think I should?"

"Dr Lynda insists."

"Thank you, Dr Lynda," I said.

She started the engine and put the van into first. As we moved off down the street, I opened the window and looked back at the house. My mum was standing at the bedroom window looking out at me. I stared for a couple of seconds, then put my head back inside.

Thomas' house stands in a tree-lined street of Edwardian houses. There's a little front garden with azalea bushes and a red brick path. Lynda opened the black wrought iron gate and we walked up to the tiled porch and the black front door. Lynda gave me the key.

"Erm…"

"It's your house, my love."

"Yes. Yes it is. Thank you."

'Sanctuary', I thought, as I turned the key in the lock and pushed the door open.

Sometimes the house of someone who has recently died feels dead too. Like the fabric of the building and all their belongings have died with them.

But this wasn't like that. There was an energy, a life if you will. It felt as if the house was still being lived in. I expected Thomas to walk out of the kitchen and offer me a cup of Earl Grey.

I mentioned this to Lynda.

"Well, of course," she said, "positive people leave positive things. He's just a dimension away. It's like walking through an invisible wall."

The polished floorboards, the bevelled oak banister, the thick cream and terracotta rugs, the huge cream sofas, so large you felt you could swim in them, might just as well have had *Thomas* printed on them.

The kitchen, I was surprised to see, was modern; granite and beech ('he loves to cook', Lynda said), but the dining room was the real Thomas room; floor to ceiling bookshelves encompassing all four walls. An antique dining table stood at one end and two leather chairs and a small table at the other. 'Waugh or Forster could have sat here', I thought.

"There's so many books," I said.

"And you're surprised by this?" said Lynda, laughing. "They wouldn't all fit in here; the residue's in the third bedroom."

Like the downstairs rooms, the bedrooms had large fireplaces and cream walls.

"This was Thomas' room," Lynda said, breezily. "It's a new bed, which he asked me to buy. As this is the largest bedroom, he thought you might like to use it. Only if you like it, of course."

"I love it," I said.

We spent the next hour unloading the van and, when the final box and the famous cricket bat had been carried in, Lynda said:

"Right then, cup of tea."

She had stocked the fridge and cupboards with 'a few essentials'. A few essentials that would have fed a family of ten for a month.

"I must pay you for all this," I said.

"My treat," she said.

We sat on the huge sofas and chatted and chatted. After a while, we took our shoes off and put our feet up and I was suddenly aware of the effect the Valium was having on me as I seemed to be able to deal more easily with the trauma of the day, as though it had happened a long time ago.

We ordered pizza, grazed on pepperoni and mushrooms and, before we knew it, it was 10 o'clock.

"Do you know, you've been smiling for the last hour," she said.

"Have I?"

"Yes."

"I've escaped," I said.

And I felt the house engulf me in a walled embrace.

I yawned.

"Tired?"

"Yes." I said.

"Time you slept. I'll be in the third bedroom."

"No, Lynda, you mustn't. I don't want to put you out; you've been too kind to me already."

"Your father nearly killed you, my love; your mother sat and watched it; you've moved into a new house; you've had a very, *very* difficult day. And that's an understatement. I'll be here just for tonight, but I want to make sure you're alright."

"But Lynda-"

"Sam, let me give you a piece of advice: *Never* try to disagree with a woman who's made up her mind."

We laughed and I hugged her.

"Goodnight," I said, "and thank you for everything."

Upstairs I undressed and took out the Thomas the Tank Engine duvet cover and then the posh Stone and Mocha one. Then I put them both in a dustbin liner, for they belonged to an old me in an old situation; and I climbed into my new bed, between my new sheets and fell asleep in my new home.

16

I was rather sluggish in training the next day. My body was a mass of bruises and my mind appeared to be covered in mental ones. I'd worn a scarf to conceal those around my neck but, of course, could not hide them on the training ground. I told everyone I'd been attacked the previous evening but hadn't seen my assailants and so had not reported it. It took all my powers of persuasion to stop the boss ringing the police. 'Look at those finger marks, Sammy, they must have nearly killed you', the boss said. 'Yes', I said, 'but I just want to get on with my life, boss; I've had enough drama recently'. He let it go, but only just.

By Friday I had found some energy but was by no means myself and barely said a word on the coach to Wolverhampton. The team treated me with kid gloves, putting their arms round my shoulder and offering to help.

Joe was great to me in the hotel room that night. Making sure I was alright every five minutes and suggesting we just chilled out and watched a movie, most of which I slept through.

The game against Wolves the next day could best be described as unremarkable. We had the lion's share of both halves but Craig got injured early on and we just couldn't seem to fire properly. It was like having a speed restriction of 30 mph on a motorway; you want to go faster, but you can't. It ended 0-0 and is best consigned to the waste disposal of football history. Again, I was virtually silent on the journey back. Joe sat next to me and seemed to catch my mood. After half an hour, both of us fell asleep.

On Sunday morning Tara rang and asked if she could come round to see the house. I told her 'of course and to pop round at 2 o'clock if that was OK'. She said it was.

Then I rang Davey.

"What're you doing today?" I said.

"Not much. Possibly seeing Rachel later. Otherwise-"

"Good. Get your arse round here now."

I gave him the address.

"Now?" he said.

"Yes."

"But I'm only wearing my pants."

"OK, when you've put some trousers on."

"Alright, I'll just get dressed, have a shower and grab some breakfast."

"All at the same time?"

"Are you referring to the smallness of my living quarters, Hatchington?"

"Yes. And don't bother with breakfast, I'll cook you some."

"You? Cook?"

"Fuck you."

"I'll be there in an hour."

Almost to the minute, Davey walked through the gate.

"Wow," he said as I opened the door, "beautiful house."

"Come in, I'll show you around."

After a while, he said:

"It's a dichotomy."

"No, it's Edwardian," I said.

He raised his eyebrows at me.

"Alright, smart-arse, what's a dichotomy?"

"When something is made up of two opposing things. It's quite old fashioned yet it's got a young vibrancy to it."

We went into the dining room.

"Thomas' room," he said. "I can just imagine Evelyn Waugh or E.M. Forster sitting in one of those leather chairs planning their next novel."

We went upstairs.

"Third bedroom," I said.

"More books," he said.

"My room."

"Nice. No Thomas the Tank Engine duvet cover."

"And your room."

"Yes, this is a nice room too. The fireplaces are... Pardon?"

"This is *your* room."

"But-"

I had succeeded in that rare occurrence of causing Davey to be lost for words.

"I…"

"Yes?"

"Sam, I can't; I mean, it's your house."

"Yes it is, or will be officially very soon and I want you to live here. I'm fed up with you living in that cupboard and I want someone to share the house with and…well, who else would I ask? So, will you move in?"

"Yes", he said, "yes I will."

"Good," I said.

A smile curled the corner of his mouth and, like a contagious yawn, mine did the same. Then it spread to his cheeks and his eyes and mine followed suit. Suddenly we were laughing; silly, fun, hysterical, relief-laden laughing.

"We'd better book you a van," I said.

"No point; you could fit everything I own in the back of a cab."

"Let's book you a cab, then."

"OK, we'll work out when we're both free and-"

"No. *Now,* you idiot."

"What, straight away?"

"What other meanings do you know for the word 'now'?"

"But…"

"But what?"

"But nothing. I'll go and pack."

"I'll make us some dinner when you arrive."

"On second thoughts, I may just stay in the bedsit."

I pushed him out the front door.

He turned as he closed the gate.

"See you for dinner," he said, "and Sam?"

"Yes?"

"Thank you."

Tara arrived an hour later.

"It's a great house," she said. "Are you going to change the furnishings now or leave it for a while?"

"I'm not going to change them at all," I said, "I like them."

"Oh? But they belonged to Thomas."

"I know; that's why I like them."

"But don't you think you're maybe keeping them because you can't let go of Thomas?"

"Why should I let go of Thomas? He's only in the next dimension."

"Sam, please don't quote that religious crap at me," Tara said, ever the subtle atheist.

"It's not religion," I said.

"Well, what is it, then? You've been brainwashed"-

"I have *not* been brainwashed... Look, can you just be happy that I'm living in this terrific house and that I've escaped from my old home."

"How did your parents take you moving out?"

"Not well."

"Well, I think you're too young to own a place like this."

"I'm eighteen!"

"Exactly."

"So, you're saying I'm not mature."

"Der!"

"So, as you're eighteen, you're saying *you're* not mature as well?"

"Girls mature quicker than boys."

"Balls, do they," I said; in effect, losing the argument.

"But anyway," she purred, moving into me and running her hands over my chest and down my thighs, "at least we'll be able to have sex whenever we want to now."

"That is a definite point," I said.

Her hand undid my fly and slid inside my jeans.

"Like, *right* now," she said.

"No," I said, "not today."

The hand withdrew.

"Why?"

"It doesn't seem right yet. It still feels as though it's a transition between Thomas' and mine and..."

"Well, when *will* it be right?"

"I don't know. Give it a week."

"You're weird," she said. "And why are you wearing that scarf indoors?"

"Fashion."

"Don't be ridiculous. Take it off."

She grabbed hold of the end of the scarf and revealed the red and purple marks around my neck. In the next instant, I could see several scenarios flashing through her mind. She settled on the one that proved she didn't know me.

"Do you want to tell me her name, or do you want to make up some pathetic small-boy excuse that even the most gullible person in the world wouldn't believe?"

"My father tried to strangle me."

"Well, I've got to give you marks for originality."

"He beat me up and then he tried to strangle me. He would have succeeded as well if Lynda hadn't rushed in with my cricket bat and broken his nose."

"God you're good. Do they teach you improvisation at football training? No wonder you didn't want to have sex."

She picked up her bag and goose-stepped to the front door.

"One day when you've scored a goal in every vagina in London, look me up. I might be that desperate that I'd consider seeing you again."

She closed the door with enough force to show her feelings (as though I wouldn't be aware of them, anyway) but not so violently as to prove she was still in control (which I also knew, as she never really went deep enough to lose it).

I didn't bother even beginning to argue. I'd had enough of confrontation. My brain had temporarily retired from anything other than basic everyday tasks.

Half an hour later Davey's cab pulled up.

We took his things up to his room.

"I'll unpack later," he said.

"Look," I said, "I can't really be bothered to cook. Do you mind if we get a take-away? My treat."

"That's fine with me. I'm not wearing my cast-iron stomach lining at the moment anyway."

"How do you know what my cooking's like?"

"Well… I suppose, to be honest, I don't."

"Thank you."

"What is your cooking like?"

"It's shit."

We ate our sweet and sour chicken and beef with garlic on laptop trays with our legs crossed and talked for a couple of hours.

"Right, I'll make a cup of tea," I said, bending to pick up the plates.

"Hang on a minute," Davey said, his voice sudden and peppered with shock.

He lifted my T-shirt up.

"It's OK, I'm old enough to undress myself," I said.

"What the…?"

Then he took the scarf from around my neck.

"My God! I can't believe this, you're covered in them" he said, his fingers tracing the vulgar wounds on my neck, "someone tried to strangle you."

Then his voice changed. It deepened; hardened.

"Who did this to you?"

"Davey-"

"Who-did-this-to-you?"

"Promise me you won't go and do something stupid?"

"No."

But I told him anyway. The story of my father's attempt at infanticide and of Lynda scoring a six with the first ball of the over.

When I had calmed him down a little, he said:

"Why didn't you fight back?"

"I don't know; probably because, this way, I have a reason to never see him again."

"I understand."

"Good."

"If I ever see that bastard, I will-"

"No! Davey, don't; otherwise I won't have the reason anymore."

"I can't imagine how you must hate him."

"I don't hate him now," I said, "hate is pointless. Hating someone is like letting them live rent-free in your head. He doesn't exist for me anymore. That's worse than hating someone."

I put the kettle on to boil whilst Davey hovered around me, helping me; I think, belatedly trying to protect me.

We drank the tea and talked until an outbreak of yawning signalled the end of the day.

I took the cups into the kitchen. When I returned, Davey was standing, looking around the lounge, an expression somewhere between disbelief and contentment on his face; and, either the light was catching his eyes, causing them to appear crystalline, or something had happened that had breached the impregnable wall of his self-control.

"Are you alright?" I said.

"I have a home," he said.

"Yes."

"I've never had one before."

It wasn't the light. An eighteen year old tear broke the surface and christened his cheek. I went to hug him.

"No. No, you mustn't," he said, "you've been through hell recently."

"You always look after me," I said, "time for me to play the grown-up for once."

17

Davey saw Rachel the following day and, within a few minutes and four rushed texts, the gang knew all about 'the beating of my father'; which, phrased that way, sounds rather benign, like an Alan Bennett monologue.

They insisted on seeing me after college. We met in Thomas' and my cafe. When I walked in, they all rushed over. They, minus Tara.

Again, my scarf was removed and my T-shirt lifted up.

"Sam," said Seb, "you *have* to go to the police."

"I'm not going to, Seb. I want it to be over and, this way, I think I end up the bigger person."

"If he comes near you again, if you won't have him charged, I will," said New Tommy.

"Thanks, mate. Look, I'm fine and the bruises will go."

"Yes, but the memories won't," said Susie, her face, like Rachel's, struggling to deal with what she saw.

"No, but that's a good thing; it means I'll never forget what he's really like."

As I began to pull my T-shirt down, one of the baristas walked passed and said:

"Oh my God, they must be painful. Impressive abs, though."

'I *have* to keep my T-shirt on in cafes', I thought.

I told them all the details over assorted Americanos. It wasn't until I'd finished that the subject of my absent girlfriend came up.

"Does she know the truth?"

"Yes," Rachel said.

"Then why isn't she here?"

"She's too embarrassed."

"And rightly so," said Seb.

"Seb, darling, don't be nasty, she's devastated."

"Then why doesn't she apologise?"

"I'll ring her," I said.

"No mate, you shouldn't have to ring her; she should ring you. It's so bloody sexist. If she'd been the one who'd been attacked"-

"Seb," said Rachel, shoving half of his blueberry muffin in his face, "we all know Tara's been an idiot, but getting all male-righteous about it isn't going to help."

"I don't understand why she did it," I said, following the pause in which Seb tried not to choke on the unexpected muffin, New Tommy rearranged the three flowers in the vase four times and the two girls had one of those telepathic conversations with each other that seem unique to the female sex.

"Tara is crazy about you, Sammy," Susie said. We've never seen her act this way before. All her other boyfriends left her. She's sure she's going to lose you because you'll think she's too cold and distant."

"She *is* too cold and distant," said Seb, finally un-caking his vocal chords, "but, before you stick an entire Swiss Roll in my face, Rachel, we love her just the same. It's who she is, that's all."

"Little bit different when you're going out with her, though," said New Tommy.

"It's not as though I'm unapproachable," I said.

"That's just it," New Tommy replied, "you're not, she is. Tara's great most of the time but she prides herself on never losing this scary self-control that she has; her other-worldly mystique-"

"And because she's fallen for you, she's opened herself up to discovering deeply-buried feelings that she hasn't trained to be at her beck and call yet," finished Susie.

It felt so good to be with them. We talked about Tara, about my father's attack, about college. Then it seemed to dawn on all of us, almost simultaneously, that I hadn't celebrated my eighteenth.

Various suggestions were tossed into the air for us to catch or drop as we pleased. Abseiling, paintballing and white-water rafting being three. I dropped all of them.

"Guys, do you know what I'd really like to do? I'd like us all to have a meal at Thomas'... at mine and Thomas' house, on Sunday. It can be a double celebration for me and Davey. We can have a few drinks, play a few games; just chill out and have fun."

"Is that what you *really* want to do?" Susie asked.

"Yes."

"Then, let's do it. Rachel and I will bring the food and cook it."

"You don't have to," I said,

"Sammy, darling, we've heard about your cooking. I think it's safer this way. The local hospital can only deal with *so* many cases of E-Coli."

"This reputation I have of being a crap cook is a myth. I've never actually *cooked* anything."

"Yes, dear," said Rachel, "that's hardly a good CV for holding a dinner party."

I had to admit she was right.

"OK," I said, "I'll buy the food if you cook it."

This was heartily agreed upon.

"Oh and I might invite Joe from the team. He's my closest friend at Flitcham."

"Is he cute?" asked Susie.

"Yes, he's good-looking," I said.

"And what about Tara?" Seb added.

"I'll ring her this afternoon."

That Saturday we lost 3-0 at Liverpool, capping a decidedly unsuccessful week for me.

I did ring Tara. She was apologetic; but apologetic in the manner of a politician. That way they have of distancing themselves from whatever catastrophe has just occurred and that they are eminently responsible for ('So, Minister, this man died of a heart attack because his local hospital closed due to lack of funding'. 'Our thoughts are with his family on this tragic occasion but, was it the closure of the hospital or was it because he ate chips all the time'?). I told her that it was OK but that she had to trust me. She said she'd been two-timed by a previous boyfriend and didn't trust guys anymore. I said that was the same as thinking all Italians were like Mussolini.

So Davey and I celebrated our eighteenth birthdays a little late.

The Magnificent Seven and Joe sat round the dining table in Thomas' room. Joe had been an instant hit with his 'life is for screwing up and then laughing about' attitude and he permeated the, admittedly, friendly walls of our established mansion of camaraderie with ease.

Davey's very expensive champagne was used to toast our coming of age (and my being alive to join in) and then Rach and Susie brought in the starters. There was a pause of some considerable pregnancy. Almost a giving birth pause.

"Er... yeah, Rach, Suse, what exactly *is* this?" New Tommy said.

"It is mint, pea and spinach salad," replied Rachel.

"Right, good... didn't realise we were expecting the cast of *Watership Down*."

"Excuse me, Tom, but I had this when we celebrated mummy and daddy's silver wedding anniversary at the Savoy. It was a themed meal."

"Really?" Seb said, "What was the theme, Existentialism?"

Rachel's expression could have melted iron.

"It looks lovely," said Davey, ever the honourable boyfriend.

"Thank you, dear."

Davey took a mouthful, chewed for about four days, then said:

"Yum, the spinach is very…"

"Spinachy?" I offered.

"Yes, definitely spinachy," he said.

"And the mint peas are very…" Joe tailed off.

"Pea-like?" said New Tommy.

"Yes."

"Yes, definitely pea-like. And minty."

"Minty fresh," I said.

"Yes," Seb continued, "like mouthwash, only lumpier."

Rachel looked crestfallen, so we boys chewed in gastronomic penitence. Davey and Joe were brave and took a second mouthful.

"You don't *have* to eat it," Rachel said.

"Thank fuck for that," and five pairs of cutlery went down in unison.

Contrary to some worried expectations, the rest of the meal was superb. The joint of meat was the sort that has all those little chef's hats on the top, there was every vegetable you could possible pronounce (and some I patently couldn't) and a vat of gravy you could swim in.

And for dessert, an enormous chocolate cake, decorated with caramel icing and sporting two footballers and a goal on the top. One of the footballers was fashioned in the manner of scoring with a spectacular overhead kick, the other was unsuccessfully tackling him.

Davey immediately claimed the former and, when I protested, said:

"And exactly how many goals have you scored this season?"

"Er…"

"I'm guessing 'er' is some long lost Mayan word for zero."

"And how many have you scored?"

"Nine. In seven games."

"Well, *you* try breaking through Chelsea's defence."

"Oh, come on, Hatchington, you played Wolves last week; you could break through their defence with a Granny in a motorised wheelchair."

I realised what he was doing; making me laugh, making me rise to the bait, making me… well, *me* again.

There were thirty-six candles on the cake, their tiny flames becoming little doll beacons when Susie turned the lights off.

Rachel told us both to make a wish (I don't know what Davey wished for. I remember mine. It's funny how sometimes you can't work out whether they came true or not) and we blew out the candles, creating a huge cheer, followed by Susie saying, "Damn, where's the light switch, Sammy? Oh, I just kicked the table leg." "I don't have a wooden leg," Joe said. "Oh, Joe, I'm so sorry… Oh gosh, I hope that vase wasn't expensive."

When Susie finally reached the light switch, the rest of us, minus Tara, had surreptitiously crept to the other end of the room and were pretending to cower in the corner.

"No, don't hurt us, Chaos Woman," New Tommy pleaded.

"Chaos Woman," Seb said, in the style of those Basso Profundo American film announcers, "she destroys EVERYTHING in her path. Household furniture, footballers' careers. Nothing and no one is safe. See the mini dynamo of catastrophe at a cinema near you. In the dark, no one can hear your vases scream."

Six extraordinarily immature people collapsed in hysterics.

When we'd finally gained control, Susie looked down on us like a long-suffering mother with an uncontrollable brood.

"You do know how silly you all look."

"Er... well, yes, I suppose we do," said Rachel, grabbing hold of Davey's thigh to hoist herself into an upright position and so reclaim a modicum of dignity.

"Then get back to the table like good little kiddies and we'll have some more of the lovely wine that Sam has bought us."

"It is great wine, Hatch. What is it?"

"It's Chatow N..." I picked up a bottle and tried to read the label. "Chatow Noof d-"

"Chateauneuf du Pape," said New Tommy. "Typical footballer; *can* afford it, *can't* pronounce it."

I threw a pea at him.

"Oh my God, Sammy, we need some sausage rolls!"

And New Tommy relayed the story of the sausage roll-flinging picnic to Davey and Joe.

"You guys are really close," Joe said.

"Yes," said Rachel.

"It's really nice to watch you all," Joe continued, "the way you finish each other's sentences. I'm very envious; I've never had a group of friends like that."

"Then you must join ours," said Susie, "We're constantly on the lookout for new, rich, attractive people."

Joe laughed and said:

"But you've all known each other for ages."

"Not really," said New Tommy, "Tara, Rach, Susie, Seb and me have. Then Sam broke down our defences with his council house charm and Davey was given membership even though he's the world's best-looking bloke and we hate him for it."

"Isn't he just", said Rachel, kissing Davey's cheek, downing her glass of wine and beginning her slow descent into alcoholic oblivion.

"You're all gorgeous," said Susie, "look at you, five gorgeous men and I can't have any of you."

"Can't you?" said Joe.

"Do you like love poetry?" Susie said.

"Yes."

"Let's talk."

"More wine!" Davey announced. "Come on Sam, let's go down to your extensive wine cellar and bring back all three of the bottles in it."

"I don't do wine," I said.

"One doesn't 'do' wine, Sam, darling," Susie said, one 'experiences' it. A good wine is like good sex."

"Er, why's that, Suse?" Rachel asked.

"No idea, it just sounded profound in my head."

While Davey and I were opening the three bottles of unpronounceable wine in the kitchen, he said:

"Tara's barely spoken; is she OK?"

"I don't know; I'll probably find out later."

"You don't seem very concerned."

"I can't keep being concerned when I've no idea what I'm supposed to be concerned about."

"Good point. Maybe she's still feeling guilty. I mean, she didn't even hug you when she arrived."

"Tara doesn't really do hugging. She does sex instead. Not that I'm complaining. It's just that I'd like some of the cosy stuff too. Sometimes I think I'm just a giant human dildo to her."

"Giant?"

"OK, medium-sized."

Davey raised a quizzical eyebrow.

"Fuck you," I said.

The wine was despatched pretty quickly. Eight slightly drunk people can do that to three bottles. This was followed by lager and a bottle of Thomas' Peach Brandy.

So the evening began to descend into that happily drunken micro-world, where you can still recognise your individuality but that recognition is overridden by the acknowledgement that you are part of a malleable group, an ever-changing form of bodies, as the ether-cloud of friendship moulds itself to the moment and only the good things in life are of any significance. Finally I was able to throw off the last few tortured weeks.

That was until Tara, who had been completely silent for over an hour, suddenly got up and stormed out of the room.

"Toilet, probably," Seb said.

"I don't think so, Seb, darling. She had the look of a pyromaniac that can't find a box of matches."

"Do you want to go and talk to her, Sam?"

"No, I'm hosting a party and I won't leave my guests."

"But she's your girlfriend."

"Which doesn't take prece… prece ('precedence', Davey whispered)… presidents over you," I finished.

Coffee was unanimously agreed upon and, whilst I was firing up the percolator in the kitchen, Joe came in.

"Hatch, that was a terrific party, mate. Thanks for inviting me."

"It's my pleasure, mate, I wanted you here."

"Your friends are brilliant."

"Thanks. I thought you'd like them. I owe them so much. They helped me find myself."

Joe looked at me for a few seconds.

"I'm glad we're room-mates," he said.

"Me too. Well, until Steve gets back, anyway."

"Yeah. I'll miss you, mate, when he does."

As the night wound down and the coffee gained a small hand-hold on the alcohol, I again looked around the room at my wonderful friends and I realised the significance of all of us; extensions of each other, sitting here in mine and Thomas' house. 'If the world ended at these four walls', I thought, 'I would be happy'.

Rachel slept in Davey's room; Seb and New Tommy on the two sofas in the lounge; Susie had asked if she could share the third bedroom with Joe. She read him poetry - apparently she does this with every guy she sleeps with (I was suddenly less surprised that she was usually single) and, when I got to my room, Tara was asleep in my bed. She didn't move once during the night.

18

The last two years of my teens were ones of relative stability, for the first time in my life.

No, I had stability before; just unstable stability. I suppose you could say that I was finally in charge of my life. If I went down a dangerous path, it would be my decision to do it.

I know a lot of kids had it worse than I did. Davey never knew his parents; children are battered and abused, physically and psychologically, on a regular basis; some end up on the streets in their early teens. It's so very wrong. Society and government should be the foster parents of every abused child.

I hate it when people say 'be thankful for what you've got'. A platitude is an easy way out. It saves the need for thought or reason. We should have a Platitude Box in every town in the country; like a Swear Box only for mindless inanities. I guarantee, after a year, we would have collected enough money to build a thousand schools and hospitals.

Why should I be thankful for what I had? Thankful for a moronic father who didn't even acknowledge my existence, let alone love me? Thankful for a mother who I loved and wanted to spend more time with as I became an adult but who, ultimately, was prepared to let her husband murder her son?

No, I am *not* thankful for them. I am thankful for Thomas, for Gran and Gramps, for Davey, for the friends who helped me become a thinking person.

My blood parents were dead to me, though they were still alive. My adopted parent is very much alive to me, though he is dead.

That is all; before I confuse even myself.

I hadn't meant for Gran and Gramps to find out. I didn't want them to think any less of their only child. Of course, things like this don't remain secret for long.

They would visit my mother once a week; in the morning when 'he' was at work. She wasn't allowed to visit them.

Gran could tell there was something wrong immediately. She has scandal radar. However, unlike some women of her age, it doesn't come from a lifetime of over-the-fence gossiping or the twitching of net curtains. Gran has never been a gossip.

Within five minutes my mother had broken down and told them everything. As she leant on the table, buried her head in the crook of her arm and began to sob, my Grandparents tried to take it all in.

'I didn't know whether to comfort her or slap her', Gran told me later. Gramps, however, was more decisive.

He waited until my 'father' had returned from work. Then he walked into the lounge, startling him by his very presence, went up to him and punched him squarely in the face. My 'father' screamed as the blow landed perfectly on his broken nose.

"You evil bastard," Gramps said. "If you ever come near my grandson again, so help me God, I will kill you."

Game, set and match to Gramps, I think; and a pound to the Platitude Box.

They came to visit me, bringing with them a bottle of *Witch Hazel* and a huge tin of cream and jam scones. We drank so much tea in two hours that I had to go for a pee every twenty minutes for the rest of the day.

"She's still our daughter," Gramps said, "but she's no longer the person we knew."

Gran insisted on rubbing *Witch Hazel* onto every bruise, even the ones located in areas that eighteen year-olds don't really want their Grans to rub things on.

"Ooh, trendy underpants, our Sammy. *Kevin Kleins*, Herbert, they're a good make," she said, as she pulled them down beneath my bum.

My mother rang me once, six weeks after the incident. I didn't take the call.

Davey and I fell into a routine. A routine of hardly ever seeing each other. He worked long hours at the gym as well as training with Craytown. I worked less than him but trained at different times. As a consequence, the occasional half hour we would see each other became even more important and I would find myself leaving a social function early just to say hello before he went to bed.

We would sometimes meet over breakfast. Though, as neither of us (especially me) were morning people, the conversation wouldn't have turned either of its creators into Nobel Laureates.

"Toast?"

"Um."

"Butter?"

"Please."

"Alright?"

"Yeah. You?"

"Yes."

"Training?"

"Good. You?"

"OK."

"Goals?"

"Two. You?"

"None."

"No change there then."

(Pause while flying piece of toast misses Davey's head and hits kitchen cupboard)

"*Very* mature."

But, considering we were both in our late teens and had recently discovered freedom for the first time, our behaviour would have been acceptable even to the most fascist of teenage-haters. Our fridge didn't consist of half an Off Licence and one small, mouldy piece of cheese; we cleaned the entire house (apart from our bedrooms) every week; and we didn't play *Motorhead* at ear-splitting decibels until 3 o'clock in the morning. Mainly because neither of us liked *Motorhead*.

Of course, we didn't bake cakes, host coffee mornings and play Mah Jong every Sunday either.

We inhabited each other's lives totally but without ever encroaching on them.

If something went wrong, we fixed it. If one of us had a bad day, the other acted as counsellor. If we had success, the other shared in that; not with the subtly exaggerated overtures of the friend who needs to prove their loyalty, but with the ease that ties you inseparably and which has moved beyond the necessity to term it a friendship.

People say that you never really know someone until you live with them (and another pound in the Platitude Box, please), but I knew Davey before I lived with him and, when he moved in, nothing changed. He was my rock and nothing would ever come between us.

Or so I thought.

Tara re-appeared a few days later. I hadn't rung her; I'm not that nice a person that I would chase after someone who had been horrible to me. She arrived, unannounced, at the front door, holding a huge bunch of white roses (What they were supposed to signify, I don't know. Purity? If so, it was a bit late for both of us) and a book about the history of football.

"These are for you," she said, "though, in retrospect, I don't know why I bought the book as you already live in a library."

It's so much easier to forgive someone than to indulge in the whys, hows and wherefores of an argument; the legal jargon-speak of recrimination, apportioning blame until you both agree on a percentage; or kill each other.

So I invited her in and we had sex and she almost apologised, which was as much as I knew I was going to get. And, for the next nearly two years, we got along, at times remarkably well considering the polar opposites of our characters. I knew I didn't love her, but I liked her and she was a great teacher of the physicality of sex; the intimacy was lost on her but, at nineteen, was a sacrifice I was prepared to make. And, of course, she was a part of the gang: a gang that would have been broken up should *we* have broken up.

What Joe thought of Susie's love poetry, he never let on. In fact he never once spoke of their relationship, which lasted from Sunday to the following Thursday, the last two days of which, according to Susie, they didn't see each other. Susie, for once, was also reticent about their brief affair and it wasn't until several years later that I found out the reason why.

My career with Flitcham looked like one of those graphs of how the Share Index has performed. Steve recovered and was reinstated in the first team, while an imprint of my bottom gradually appeared on the substitute's bench.

Steve didn't exactly ingratiate himself with the team by referring to me as the 'young, upstart pretender' who he was determined to keep out of the side. Joe was pretty cold with him, occasionally to the point of hostility and, as a consequence, their relationship on the pitch suffered, as did our results. In my first season we escaped relegation merely on goal difference: minus 28 compared to West Brom's minus 30.

The second season began much as the previous one had ended. Our first ten games were either drawn or lost. Then the boss started to play me as a substitute a little more often. I began to replace Steve around the sixty-fifth minute, which gave Joe and me twenty-five minutes to rekindle the link we'd had originally.

And gradually that kindling caught fire and, two-thirds of the way through the season, the young, upstart pretender usurped the arrogant prince and, with a run of five wins and two draws, we avoided relegation by two whole points. Joe and I became roommates again and Steve put in a transfer request, which was accepted. Finally I could call myself a full time member of the first team. I hadn't scored a goal, but I'd scored a victory.

It was three months prior to my twentieth birthday that the cracks began to appear in my relationship with Tara. There had been cracks before, of course, but they had been papered over. It's rather difficult to paper over the Grand Canyon.

She would stay over three times a week. If Rachel was there too, everything was fine but, if it was just the three of us, she would become moody and then offensive, especially toward Davey.

"Why don't you go to bed, for God's sake? Can't you see we want to be on our own? You *can* leave him with me, you know; you don't have to guard him all the time."

"I'm not guarding him," Davey said, "I'm sitting in my lounge in my home."

"A – it's not *your* home, it's Sam's and B – there are other rooms, or do you want to watch while we do it?"

Davey, ever the gent, got up and began to leave the room.

"Davey, you don't have to go," I said.

"Oh, for fuck's sake, are you tethered at the hip or something."

"I'll go to Thomas' room," Davey said.

"Yes, make sure he knows where you are. Have you got some sort of fucking Sat Nav between you? Do you track each other's movements all day?"

Davey left the room.

"Do *not* speak to Davey like that. This is his home. He has more right to be in this room than you do."

"I've been your girlfriend for two years. Why the hell aren't I living here?"

"Because you've never asked."

"Did he ask?"

"No, but-"

"Point made."

"No! Not point made. Why do you *always* cut me off in mid-sentence when we're having an argument? Is it because you're scared I might say something which you have no answer to? When I started to live here, I asked Davey, not you, to move in because I wanted a housemate, not a marriage. Davey is my best friend-"

"And don't I fucking know it."

She ranted for another ten minutes. Eventually I got up and left the room.

When people who argue a lot get to the end of their lives and look back and count the total number of weeks/months/years that they've spent arguing, I wonder whether they think this has been a constructive use of their time?

I went into Thomas' room but Davey had gone to bed.

"You got a minute?" I said, tapping on his door.

"Yes, come in."

"Look, I'm really sorry, she's... God, I don't know *what* she is. Rachel's never like this, is she?"

"No. Never. I think she's insecure, Sam."

"Oh, I'm fucking insecure, am I?"

"Get out of my room, Tara," Davey said.

"No! I want to hear what's wrong with me."

"I said, get out."

"Don't threaten me."

"Tara," I said, "let's leave Davey's room."

"Oh, that's right, side with-"

"GET OUT OF DAVEY'S ROOM!!"

It was the first time I'd ever raised my voice to her and it was enough to shock her into doing what I'd asked. Only just; but enough.

"I'm so sorry," I mouthed, as I closed his door and her ridiculously strong arm pulled me in the direction of the stairs.

Arguments take *so* much energy; discussions take so little. I couldn't muster any further interest in her point of view, so merely listened to her expound on the cruelty of men in general and of her absolute self-martyrdom.

After she had finished, I ordered her a taxi and told her she had to go home. When it arrived and we stood at the front door, she grabbed my cock and pulled.

"I WANT THIS," she shouted in my face.

"You can't have it," I said, "You don't deserve it."

She let go, just before it started to react to her clenched fist and stormed off down the path.

The following morning I had the house to myself. Davey had his mad clients as I called them; people who thought going to the gym at 6 a.m. was fun. Nothing is fun at 6 am... apart from sleeping.

I had a lazy shower (what is a lazy shower? Do you just stand there and do nothing? Perhaps you can't even be bothered to turn the water on?) and an 'on your own' breakfast. This is the same as an ordinary breakfast except that, during its preparation, you sing Bruce Springsteen songs at the top of your voice because no one can hear; which, in my case, is a good thing. People might think my guttering was imploding.

I texted Davey:

Hey. Hope your mad lot enjoyed gaining half a millimetre of bicep at stupid o'clock. Have a good day at the gym and at Craytown. I'm training and then off to a charity gig for Charing Cross Hospital. News for you tonight. Xx

I had resolved to tell Tara that we were over. I'd always put up with the excesses of her rudeness and irrational behaviour because the good times usually outnumbered the bad. But no longer. When I was with her I had to act like a chess player, thinking three or four moves in advance in case I said something that offended her ego/feminism/rabid knee-jerk reaction gland. I decided to ring her after training and meet her in the hour and a half before the charity event. I would tell her to her face. Phone calls are for cowards and texting is for people who shouldn't be allowed to have relationships.

As it turned out, my call went straight to her voicemail and I left a message asking her to call me back.

Training was its usual mixture of high sociability and hard work (I *loved* it) and the charity bash turned out to be a corporate photo opportunity for the hospital managers. We smiled like schoolchildren posing for their end of year photograph, ate the canapés and indulged in conversation that would have struggled to excite a reluctant hermit.

I got home at seven, threw my bag down and yelled 'are you awake?' which, in retrospect, is one of the most stupid questions you can ask.

There was no answer, so I went into Thomas' room where he sometimes fell asleep, reading, after a long day. He wasn't there. What *was* there was a note. This was nothing unusual; we left notes all the time.

Dear Sam,

I am shaking so much I can hardly write this.

I have to leave. I am so, SO sorry. I don't want to do this but I have no option if I am to retain my sanity.

This is the hardest decision of my life. I have loved living here with you. More than loved. However, certain things have happened which mean that I can no longer stay.

The five years I have known you have been the best of my life. Firstly, because you introduced me to Thomas but, more than that, because of our friendship. You are the best friend I have ever had, or ever will have.

I will be leaving London. Please don't try to find me.

I know you won't be able to understand what I am doing and why I am doing it but, please believe me, it is the best thing for both of us.

I am so very sorry that I cannot say this to you in person but, please understand, it would be impossible.

I cannot write anymore. No words would make sense.

Just remember that friendship lasts forever; whether the other person is with you or not.

Love, Davey.

I sat in Thomas' chair, unable to move; unable to imagine life without him; unable…

19

Rachel, it turned out, also received a letter that evening. It had been pushed through her letterbox while she was at Uni He'd told her that he loved her but, because of circumstances that he was unable to explain, he had to leave her and London. Again, he apologised for not being able to tell her face to face and asked her not to hate him.

It was Rachel's call later that evening that ended my stupor. I was still clutching the letter. Neither of us could find many words but we agreed to meet the following lunchtime for coffee.

When we did it was obvious that we had both slept badly.

We hugged for an awfully long time; so long that the person behind us asked if we wouldn't mind ordering as they were in a rush.

Then we sat at a table by the window and, for a few minutes, were hypnotised by the traffic. It had been there when Davey was with us; it was still there now. Somehow it made things seem as if nothing was wrong.

It was Rachel who broke the self-induced spell.

"It's at times like this that I'm glad I'm a girl," she said, gently sweeping my fringe up and revealing two dull eyes; like two wasted sparklers at a firework display.

"Why?" I asked.

"Because we can at least grab a trowel and put on half a ton of foundation to pretend we look OK."

I tried to smile.

"I went out with the most beautiful boy in the world," she said.

"Yes," I said.

"Both physically and spiritually."

It was pointless me saying yes again.

"And you had a friendship that surpassed all others."

So to the traffic again.

"Rach, have you any…?"

"No," she said, "I've no idea."

"Do you think he'll get in touch?"

"No."

The brevity of her answer shocked us both. Eventually, through some unspoken agreement, we held each other's hands over the table, gradually letting our foreheads move together until they touched.

"Thought I'd find you both here."

We looked up. Tara.

"Gosh, it's so miserable, isn't it, this cloud. I wish it would just piss down and get it over with. Can I get you some coffees? Those look to have gone cold."

Again, it was Rachel who broke the stunned silence.

"No, thank you."

"Well, I'll just get a glass of water and join you."

Before either of us had time to decide how to react, she had returned to our table and sat down next to me.

For two years I'd been intimate with this girl. Now, her mere proximity appalled me. It was like those awful science fiction B movies when the beautiful woman suddenly peels her skin off to reveal a lizard underneath.

"I took the day off Uni," she continued, "there are some mornings when you wake up and think 'oh bugger it, I can't be bothered'. So I lay in bed till twelve – Heaven! – and then had my favourite breakfast – you know what that is, Sam; the one you tried and failed to make several times." She laughed. "Sausages with French toast and-"

"Tara," Rachel interrupted, "would you stop it please. Can't you see we're both upset?"

"Are you? Why, Sam? Tell your loving girlfriend and she'll wave her magic wand and make everything better." And she put her arm round my shoulder.

I threw it off.

"Davey has left," Rachel said, "left Sam, left me; left London for good."

"Yes, I know; Susie told me."

"Well then, you will understand how we feel."

"No, to be honest, I don't. OK, your boyfriend's cleared off, but it's not as though you ever slept together."

"What?" I said.

"Davey's strict Catholic," Rachel said, "he won't have sex before marriage."

"Catholic?" I said.

"So you obviously didn't know him as well as you thought," Tara interjected. "Did the two of you ever discuss sex?"

"Not very often," I said. "We... look, it's none of your business what we discussed."

"We did other things, Tara," Rachel responded.

"Yes, but not sex, Rachel."

"I can't believe you're behaving like this, Tara," Rachel said, "we know you didn't like Davey but you could at least respect our loss."

"Your loss? Loss of what? Someone who pretended to be a friend and then pissed off without ever explaining why?"

"You shut up!" I said, standing clumsily and slamming my chair into the woman behind me.

"I'm so sorry," I said to her, "are you alright?"

"Yes, thank you," she said.

I sat down and lowered my voice.

"Davey left because of you," I breathed, my slamming heartbeat forcing my tongue to have to think before forming the words, "you were a fucking bitch to him and all because-"

"Oh, don't be so overdramatic. I just asked him to leave the room-"

"And all because of your-"

"Because he should have had the grace to leave us alone and-"

"Your own insecurities," I said, finally getting the sentence out.

"I am not insecure and there is no need for rudeness."

"What! And what the f-"

"Honestly, let's just behave like adults and have a nice pleasant coffee."

"Don't fucking interrupt me," I said, my voice beginning to shake uncontrollably, "you are an egotistical, self-centred BITCH!"

"I will *not* be spoken to-"

"Yes, you will, you fucking psycho."

If she had been a guy, it would have been so much easier. I could have just beaten the shit out of him. But, instead, I had to find words that made sense in the storm that had enveloped my brain.

"You are only happy when you have everything on your terms. You won't accept anyone or any situation that you can't be in total control of; and you will go to any lengths to get your own way, even if it means destroying other people's lives. You are the reason that my best friend and Rachel's boyfriend left. You will leave this table and leave our lives. I can't begin to tell you how much I hate you. Now, get out."

"Well, coming from someone who always says it's pointless to hate-"

"GO!!!"

But she wouldn't. She actually sat there and continued to talk. I've no idea what she said.

Rachel and I got up and left the cafe.

When we parted at the end of the road, I wasn't sure which one of us was shaking the most.

"It's not been a good day, Sammy," Rachel said, "we've both lost Davey and, to a much lesser extent, Tara."

"I don't care about her," I said.

"Care just a little bit," she said.

Of course, I completely ignored Davey's request and made extensive attempts to find him. I rang his mobile, emailed him, went to the gym where he worked. He'd quit his job and left the same day; no one knew where he had gone. No response to the emails; no reply to my calls and, eventually, a dead line.

In the end I hired a private detective. After three weeks of fruitless attempts to locate him, I realised that I was beginning to act a little like Tara had been doing since the scene in the cafe; something approaching insanity and approaching at such a speed, it would be difficult to stop when I got there.

Tara had texted (sometimes fifty times a day), rang me repeatedly, thrown stones at my bedroom window at 2 o'clock in the morning and followed me home from training. Her first texts were breezy and chatty, telling me about things she'd done, things that made her laugh (?) and suggesting we meet up for a coffee or a trip to the cinema. I ignored all of them. After a few days she started saying that she couldn't understand why I wasn't replying. Eventually it reached a climax.

I was going to the supermarket. She was following at a distance. This was nothing unusual. I daren't look back, though the fact she was there made me ill at ease. I'd been in Sainsbury's for about two minutes when she suddenly appeared next to me.

"I WANT YOUR COCK INSIDE ME!" she yelled.

Not a lot of shopping was done in Sainsbury's in the next few minutes.

We were standing by the pasta shelf and most people seemed overwhelmed with a sudden desire to buy pasta.

"I WANT YOU TO FUCK ME NOW!!"

I was pretty sure Sainsbury's would run out of pasta within the hour.

Some bright spark piped up:

"If you don't want it, mate, I'll 'ave it."

"Go away, Tara," I said.

"No," she said and produced a courgette from behind her back.

If the first blow to my head hadn't actually hurt so much, I'd have laughed. It wasn't even a very big courgette.

The security staff were on her within seconds.

"Do you want us to call the police, sir?" one said.

"No. No, thank you. Just get her out, please."

"Oh, we'll certainly do that."

Suddenly I didn't fancy pasta anymore.

Someone said, 'can I have your autograph, please?'

It's the only time I've ever refused.

A few days later I asked the rest of the gang if she was insane or arrogant. "Arrogant," they all said.

Frankly, I believe that her arrogance was born out of insanity. 'Arrogance', as Thomas would say, 'is a thin layer of papier-mâché over a huge hole in someone's personality'.

So I stopped searching for Davey.

For a few weeks, I occasionally found myself holding imaginary conversations with him. When I got out of bed and staggered, bleary-eyed, downstairs, I would half expect him to emerge from the kitchen, black hair swept behind one ear, telling me that I had the IQ of an ironing board in the morning. That first night, I even slept in his bed.

Of course, none of this was going to bring him back.

In the end, I had a conversation with Thomas in his room. Our conversations consisted of me talking and then sitting silently, waiting for some, as yet undiscovered, part of my brain to suggest an answer that was already patently clear to me but that, until then, I had refused to acknowledge.

'Davey's gone', I said to Thomas and, as I talked and cried, I knew Thomas was there. 'When we leave this life, we're just a dimension away', he'd said to me. Everything he ever told me was right. Why would he be wrong now?

I sat in silence for an hour. Then I got up, decided that Davey had gone and I must get on with my life. So I closed the door, went upstairs and spent thirty minutes standing under the shower while it washed away all the bad things that had ever happened to me.

A month later I scored my first goal. And, wait for this, it was at Anfield. I scored at the home of the mighty Liverpool.

We'd had a bit of a good run in the preceding weeks, beating Stoke and Birmingham and managing a well-earned draw at Manchester City.

Funnily enough, in the hotel room the night before, I'd dreamt that I'd scored. I was still revelling in the congratulations when Joe woke me up by dripping water onto my forehead.

"Do you *have* to do that?" I said.

"Morning grumpy and where have you hidden the other six dwarves?"

"Up your arse."

"Was that an insult or the answer to my question?"

"Cock off."

"Well, that *must* be an insult because this little beauty is definitely still here," he said, grabbing his cock. Though, to be honest, Joe's hand rarely left that particular region of his body, even in front of the many different girls he brought to the Player's Lounge after the games.

"I'm asleep," I said.

"No, Hatch, you *were* asleep, you're now awake and, as usual in the morning, being a right moody bugger."

"Well, if you'd let me wake up to the alarm, rather than dumping half the Thames on my head, I might not be."

"Hatch, you slept through the alarm. Again."

"Oh," I said.

Nearly everyone in the team had a nickname. Mine had become Hatch. A name owing more to brevity than imagination. Joe's surname, being Stark, was a name you couldn't really do much with; so his name had remained Joe.

Rolling away, I put my head under the pillow.

I felt him sit on the bed. Then he pulled the duvet down to my waist.

"Hatchback," he said.

"What?" I said.

"Hatch – Back. Hatchback!"

"Hilarious," I said.

He was only wearing his pants. I leapt at him, pulling them down to the floor.

"Stark naked," I said.

He roared with laughter, which made me laugh too.

"Welcome back, my friend", he said.

I'd played twice at Anfield. Once as a sub and then in the first team. It wasn't a particularly happy hunting ground for us (it wasn't a particularly happy hunting ground for anyone). You needed luck and to play the game of your life to have a chance of coming away with a result.

That day, and to our great credit, we only needed the second of those.

We began the match with the Kop end behind us. That's the famous end of the ground that the diehard supporters treat as sacred. They make the most unbelievable noise. A torrent of singing, shouting and taunts of varying degrees of hostility. The amazing thing was that it was all in unison, like a well-rehearsed musical. I suppose, if you're there every week, year after year, decade after decade, you get to know the routine.

Oh, and it's as scary as hell.

Liverpool came at us like a bunch of Samurai warriors in the first fifteen minutes.

This is, of course, a huge exaggeration. They didn't have swords or man-skirts or those bizarre masks that look like the love child of Neanderthal Man and a particularly ugly Pekinese dog. However, the effect was much the same.

But we weren't overawed. We'd got some confidence from the recent results and we knew we were a match for other teams now. 'Confidence without complacency', the boss had said.

Our back four: Matt, Paulo, Kez and Andy, simply closed them down. Every attack was repelled with relative ease. The man to man marking was faultless and they pushed up whenever they could to play the offside trap. Joe and I played deeper than we normally would and gradually, as the boss said would happen, Liverpool began to get frustrated and mistakes crept into their game.

We'd been working on blistering counter attacks all week and that was the perfect time to put them into practice.

It was in the 33rd minute that Andy snatched the ball from the feet of the big Liverpool front man (six feet-five and more of a target for the long ball than a creator of elaborate patterns with his feet) and belted up the left wing, easily avoiding a sliding tackle that arrived at the place Andy had been about two seconds after he'd left it. As he approached the halfway line, Joe shot past him up the left touchline and I took off up the middle of the field a second later. Andy looked up, saw that Joe had drawn two Liverpool defenders and passed the ball to me with perfect accuracy, though at an alarmingly fast pace. I managed to control it on my second attempt, moving slightly clumsily to my right in the process. This then allowed me to break to the left, as the defender who had come out to block me thought I was making to begin a run to the right whereas, what I was actually doing, was trying not to fall over my own feet. I pelted toward their penalty area, looked up to find where I thought Craig might be, saw him in enough space to build a branch of *Ikea* and passed the ball just in front of him. I don't think Craig could believe how much time he had. Joe had drawn two defenders and me the other. He teed the ball up and cracked a thunderbolt at the Liverpool goal. I'll give the goalie his due, he did a fair impression of Superman, flinging himself to his left and covering so much distance, he was able to palm the ball back out to the right edge of the area and to exactly where I was standing. As my lost marker hurtled toward me and the keeper began to regain his feet and rush out, I brought the ball inside, to make it less of an acute angle and realised I had enough room to aim at the far left corner of the net, if I moved now. Of course, for the next second, my brain refused to acknowledge the existence of my feet but, the sudden deafening silence of the Liverpool fans, realising the sacrilegious fact that they could possibly go 1-0 down at home, jump-started me and, knowing that this was going to have to be a placed shot of precision accuracy as my left foot has about as much power as a broken elastic band, I put just a hint of curl on the ball and aimed at that six inches between the right post and where I knew the keeper could get his hand.

The ball crossed the line, hit the side-netting and slid, along with the rest of the world, to a temporary stop.

I was so stunned that I just stood there, looking like an eleven year-old who'd just escaped a beating by the headmaster.

My incredulity was broken by Joe jumping into my arms with such force that I fell over backwards. Seconds later I was at the bottom of a large mêlée of players, through which I could hear the three thousand travelling Flitcham fans making a noise that made the home fans' silence even more poignant.

Mine was the only goal of the game. When the final whistle went, we were ecstatic. We ran around like a bunch of kids, hugging each other and punching the air. We weren't in danger of relegation, we'd beaten Liverpool at Anfield and we'd deserved it, matching them for skill, possession and shots on target.

I was leaving the pitch, disappearing down the tunnel, under the influence of a major case of euphoria, when the boss appeared, grinning like a madman. He put his arm around me, congratulated me on my coming of age as a footballer and told me that the TV channel that had filmed the match wanted to interview me.

"Oh shit," I said.

"Yes, try to be a bit more eloquent on camera, Sammy."

I was placed in front of the TV channel's advertising hording and next to their interviewer, one that I'd seen many times on television. And back came that feeling of unreality; that I should be watching this rather than being watched. It was like those dreams you have, when you're watching a film and then suddenly you're in it as well. Two people within one person. One, knowing that there's nothing to be afraid of, that, ultimately, it's just a movie; the other, experiencing every feeling, every emotion and believing that, should he fail, there would be nothing beyond. Thomas believed that life is a mixture of both, but mostly the movie. He said that we shouldn't get too affected by things that happen in life; that we should try to laugh at them because, ultimately, they can't hurt us and that, when we leave this life and go back home, the massive dramas that we thought we'd experienced will just be a whisker-thin imprint on the sum of all things.

I thought we'd have several minutes before the interview began. What I was expecting, I don't know; Make-up to come and powder me down and Catering to dish me up a large portion of Chicken Arabiatta before we began? I'd had media-training; we all had; what to say, how to say it, the right inflections to use and the correct diplomacy. Having said that, I wasn't quite ready for:

'Rolling and... action!'

"So, Sammy, how does it feel to score your first Premiership goal?"

"Er, well, it feels amazing. I'm elated, to be honest. It's been a long time coming but they say the first is always the most difficult and now, hopefully, there'll be a few more."

"I saw your manager have a quick word before you came over. What did he say?"

"He congratulated me on my coming of age as a footballer and told me not to repeat what I said when he told me I was going to be interviewed."

The interviewer laughed.

"And how do you think your side performed overall?"

"Well, I think it was an excellent performance. The boss had obviously done his homework. We repelled their early attacks with some intelligent, organised defending. Then, as the game wore on, we grew in confidence and began playing some flowing, incisive football-"

I stopped at this point, due totally to Joe rushing in and upending half a bottle of champagne down the inside of my shorts.

"Down the Hatch!" he yelled, before charging off, laughing like a ten year-old who had just banged the Vicar's door-knocker and run away.

"Sorry about that," I said, "that was Joe Stark; he's on work experience with us from the 'Care in the Community' project. We'll give him his meds and take him back to his padded room soon. He'll be fine."

Even the cameraman laughed and I thanked God that I was still on an adrenaline wave and hadn't had time to panic before being flung in front of a camera for the first time in my life.

"So," he said, "you've had a good run of results. Any chance of Europe next season?"

"There's a definite chance," I said. "Sport is so psychological and we now go into games believing we can win which makes us better both as individuals and as a team because we can play with confidence and positivity."

"Thank you, Sammy," he said, possibly getting over the shock of conducting an interview with a footballer and not hearing any of the following lines:

It was a game of two halves.

We didn't really turn up.

It was a definite penalty.

It's not just about me.

The lads played well.

It's always a difficult place to get a result.

I made my happy, if somewhat soggy way, back to the changing room thinking 'today, even my penis drips champagne'. Though, later, I decided this probably wouldn't be a line that would appear in my memoirs, should I ever write them.

Later that evening, I met up with Susie, Rach, Seb and New Tommy and went to a particularly loud nightclub in Oxford Street. One where you have to use Nightclub Sign Language. This is not difficult to learn and consists of three things:

Holding your hand up to your mouth as though raising a glass, whilst wearing a questioning expression. This, of course, means, 'do you want a drink'? (Note: if you do, you have to have the same drink as before, which consists of pointing to the bottle/glass that you've just finished and nodding).

Pointing toward the dance floor whilst wearing a questioning expression. This, of course, means 'do you fancy dancing'? (Note: the female version of this is picking up your handbag before pointing to the dance floor).

(And this is just for the guys) Pointing to a really fit girl and cupping your hands under where your breasts would be if you were a girl, whilst wearing what you think is a particularly masculine expression. This, of course, means 'look at the tits on that'. (Note: don't do this if your girlfriend is in the same club. She'll know; it doesn't matter what part of the club she is in, she will know).

As you can see, Nightclub-speak doesn't have a large vocabulary, but it was one that suited me very well that day. It had been amazing and was fitting that, after the massive exposure of playing in front of thousands of fans and millions on the TV, I should relax and laugh and dance with the friends that I loved.

We finished eighth that season; outside the European places but our best finish for many years. I scored another six goals. They were right, it did become easier.

I also celebrated my twenty-first. Flitcham threw a big party for me. The whole team came, as well as all my friends. I also made sure Gran and Gramps were invited. Gran was the hit of the party; dancing with all the players and occasionally putting a crafty hand on their bottoms.

"I've never seen so many tight arses in one room before, our Sammy," she said, suddenly realising the double meaning and laughing uproariously as she swigged down her fifth glass of champagne. "Ooh, these canopies are really tasty, Herbert and they've got little jacket potatoes too," she added, picking up three.

"Erm, those are quails, Gran," I said.

"Oh, I'm sorry; do you think he wants them back?"

It was a terrific party. There was someone missing, of course, but he would always be missing and I would have to get used to that.

The following season we finished eighth again. I scored sixteen goals; eight from penalties (I'd become our regular penalty-taker). My social life became split equally between my closer friends from the team and the gang. And Joe became, not a substitute for Davey, no one could ever be that, but a best friend, albeit a zany, childlike one.

Tara disappeared. Who knows where? Who cares? Perhaps that's a little harsh. She was my first girlfriend and I have happy memories of some of the things we did together. And not just the sex.

Well, partially the sex.

OK, the sex.

20

Being a footballer gives you a mild case of schizophrenia.

Not to the levels of a medical condition (well, in most cases, anyway) but I suppose to the degree that, because you have two lives that are such opposites, your behaviour in each becomes polarised.

I was twenty-two. If I'd been working in an office, I'd still be near the start of the somewhat rutted road to management. No longer the tea-boy but still taking orders from 90% of the staff and only really able to hone my organisational skills on the cleaner and the tea-boy that had taken over from me. In ten years' time I'd be looking to become Head of Department, having qualified by rote of attaining the necessary levels of making arranging the holiday rota look as important as rewriting the Geneva Convention, causing more carnage than the final scene of Hamlet if I didn't get my own way, wearing pink braces even if they weren't in fashion, saying 'Ciao, I'm history' instead of 'See you tomorrow' and generally disappearing up my own rectum at the slightest opportunity. As the saying goes, 'Someone called me pretentious this morning; I nearly choked on my double shot gingerbread latte'.

But I didn't work in an office. I worked on a football pitch and the word 'anonymity' doesn't exist in a footballer's vocabulary.

I trained in front of hundreds of people, played in front of thousands; millions, if you count the televised games, though Flitcham were hardly a regular visitor to the nation's TV screens. The TV companies always made a point of saying 'we screen every single Premiership side during a season'; which was true; as long as you happened to be playing Man Utd, Chelsea or Arsenal.

I also occasionally gave interviews on behalf of the club; only if the boss or Craig (he'd been our captain for eighteen months) weren't available or didn't want to do them. Then you'd sign autographs and take part in corporate events with sponsors and other companies who wanted to become a part of the assumed glamour of a relatively famous football club.

You would pick up a newspaper, turn to the back page and see a picture of yourself bearing down on the opposition, expression locked in unconscious intent. And you'd stare at the photo and think 'he looks just like me'. And then you could be down for hours if some football critic had hurriedly plucked a number out of thin air and only given you five out of ten for your performance.

But I'd been playing for four years now (*surely* it couldn't have been that long?) and, if someone only gave me five out of ten, then it meant that I'd either deserved it or that it was just one person's blinkered opinion and they could go fornicate with themselves.

I tried to remain myself in my public persona. Being young and immature helped, as I hadn't yet learned how to pretend to be someone else. All that changed was that I smiled more often, got nervous more often and tried to remember not to say 'shit' in front of a TV camera.

Then I would go home and close the door to mine and Thomas' house and become the little boy who still inhabited the man in the photograph.

Please don't misunderstand me; I'm not complaining. It was more than I could ever have dreamed of. I drove a black Jeep Wrangler (could have afforded two more in different colours if I'd wanted), was on a salary most twenty-two year-olds would be hugely jealous of (actually, so would most sixty-two year-olds) and was treated like a film star by the football-loving public; and all because I happened to be quite adept at controlling a pig's bladder.

Of course, I was only really well known around Flitcham and West London. It wouldn't be until much later in my career that I would become vastly more famous. For two reasons. One of them for attaining the pinnacle of any footballer's career; the other for more controversial reasons.

But, at the time, I simply got on with my life. A life that I loved.

Although I remained childlike in a lot of my character traits, (I got ridiculously excited about going to Euro Disney, couldn't sleep on Christmas Eve and still had to have raspberry sauce on my ice-creams) I had grown up a little too. Some of the things that had happened in my life had given me no choice. My 'father's' attempted strangulation of me, my subsequent estrangement from my parents, my job, Thomas dying, Davey leaving; these all gave me extra layers to my adult skin. A hard, surface layer, getting harder each time; ending up, if I wasn't careful, like the skin of a crocodile; a crusted shell to stop any hurtful experience (and, as a consequence, any happy experience) from getting in. But also, of course, preventing the inner child, the real me, getting out. These adult layers need constant moisturising. We can't remove them, but we can stop them getting hard and stopping us from really living.

So I didn't bother looking for myself in the papers anymore. If I read a newspaper, it would be the front pages.

Gran and Gramps, however, kept every photo, every article and every statistic. They bought all the papers every Sunday and Gran kept everything meticulously in a scrapbook that was half the size of their bedroom. If I ever forget anything, I can just go and have a look at it.

I got them VIP seats for every home game. They attained something of celebrity status within the club and were on first name terms with all of the players and staff. Gran would bake a cake and bring it in to the Player's Lounge after the match. She became quite knowledgeable about football and would give little tips to the players:

"You're staying on the right touchline too much. They know you're going to go as near to the corner flag as you can. Cut in earlier like you used to. Keep them guessing."

"OK boys, now you know why they scored from that free kick this afternoon, don't you. You're not concentrating on the position of the wall because you're fiddling with your penises too much. Penises? Is that the plural of penis? I wouldn't know; I've only ever had one."

"I've only got your word for that," said Gramps, for which he got a smile, a slap round the ear and a 'not in front of the children, Herbert'.

I think she thought of us all as her children. The boys adored them.

Joe was their favourite though. They'd invited him for Christmas (his parents had moved to Canada when he was eighteen and he had no family in England) and the four of us had a ball. He lavished presents on them and they lavished food, drink and warmth on him. Present-opening took three hours, the Queen's Speech was banned ('she's lovely but she's crap with an autocue') and glasses of champagne and Irish Coffees were produced at extraordinarily regular intervals.

It was on a Tuesday afternoon, four weeks after my twenty-fourth birthday, when I'd popped round for a cup of tea and a Victoria Sponge Sandwich with enough cream to plaster a wall, when my agent rang.

"Sammy, mate, it's Ivan. I've got news. Taddersham want you. You and Joe. In exchange for some Croatian bloke who's apparently worth more than my yacht and my Merc put together... Sammy, you there?"

"Yes."

"This is big, mate."

"Yes", I said, "yes, it is."

21

The negotiations weren't protracted. Taddersham FC had been my team since I first kicked a ball (through a greenhouse window, unfortunately). The fact that they were prepared to pay me stupid money (stupid for a Deptford council house boy, not stupid for Christiano Ronaldo) and that I was part of a transfer package with my best friend made it, quite frankly, a no-brainer.

We passed the medicals with flying colours. Ivan secured the deals for both of us (he was Joe's agent too) and, within two weeks, we were meeting our new Taddersham teammates at our first training session.

Mixed emotions, of course. Amazement and happiness at becoming a Taddersham player and a large dollop of sadness at leaving Flitcham and everybody connected with it.

The boss even stopped smoking long enough to tell me that he felt the same way he did when one of his sons went to university. He told me to make him proud at Taddersham; within a year he wanted to see me on the fringes of the England team.

The boys were fantastic. They bought us each a series of flying lessons, an 'adopt a tiger' (Joe wanted it turned into a rug – I told him that was *not* the idea and, anyway, it wasn't the 1960s any more) and an all-expenses paid trip to Machu Pichu, which was a place I'd always wanted to see. I was so excited. I told Gran I was going to Machu Pichu. 'Oh', she said, do they open late, only I need some more coffee'.

I suppose a lot of people think of us footballers as being a bunch of pseudo-macho guys running around a field, drenched in testosterone and incapable of showing any feelings; until we get hurt, of course, when we suddenly turn into seven year-old girls until we get an ice-cream or the opposing player sent off. (I've only been booked twice; once at twenty-six, then again at twenty-nine. The first time for, admittedly, an ill-judged tackle; the second for taking my shirt off after scoring the winning goal in a vitally important match. Ridiculous law; it's not illegal on a beach or a building site, why should it be on a football field?). We're actually not like this though. As I hugged each player, there was no embarrassment, just an admittance, to varying degrees, of loss and friendship and, well, love, in a way; unspoken in most cases, but acknowledged with a look or the quick turning away of a head.

The boss at Devonshire Lane (Taddersham' ground since 1899) was new to the club as well as Joe and I. It's essential that he have a rapport with his players and this was immediately evident. The first thing he said to me was:

"Sammy, we'll obviously work on this in training, but I want you and Joe to continue this amazing partnership you have on the pitch and then we'll get you linking up with James and Scott up front. It's a real coup to have got you both; oh and the other two signings."

"Two, boss? I thought it was just me and Joe?"

"I believe your grandparents come as part of the deal. Tell them they're welcome whenever they would like to come."

So Gran and Gramps swapped allegiance at the drop of a hat (well, of a Flitcham scarf). I'd told my new teammates about them. To a man, they said I must bring them to the first home game. And come, they did; draped in Taddersham paraphernalia and carrying a cake that was the usual cardiac arrest between two pieces of sponge.

It's amazing how we adapt. Within a month, Flitcham had become a distant, though lovely, memory. I suppose this was helped by the fact that I was doing very much the same thing; just in a different place and with different people. I was still training, still playing matches, still the link between the midfield and the strikers. Gran and Gramps had become instant hits with my new teammates. Gran continued her tips (*Doris-coaching* as the boys called it) and continued to comment verbally and occasionally physically, on the guy's physiques. 'Ooh', she said, squeezing Andrius' pecs together, 'you could grind corn between these'.

On the pitch, things took off pretty quickly. The boss had brought with him a quick passing game and, with it, a rhythm to how we played. Add to that a large amount of time building an understanding between the players and consistency in team selection (none of this rotation crap) and we were rapidly becoming the most entertaining side in the Premiership.

Andrius and I had a particular understanding. He was Lithuanian but spoke perfect English with an accent that would have graced Winchester or Harrow. He was a great guy and we became good friends both on and off the pitch.

I didn't have a relationship for a year after Tara. I was perfectly happy about this – apart from the six weeks when I broke my right wrist. I'm right-handed and this makes life awfully difficult if you're single. People always say 'use the other hand, it feels like a stranger'. Well, the stranger needs to get some technique, that's all I can say.

There then followed:

SARAH: Brunette. Worked for a bank. Lovely. Warm and kind, but had no ambition to do anything; travel, expand her knowledge, get promoted. 'I just want to quit work and have kids, really', she said. Three months.

CAROLINE: Brunette. Ballet dancer. Knew her own mind. Great person. Amazing body. Graceful and beautiful. Drank pints and smoked like a steam engine. 'I want you to take me while I do an arabesque in attitude', she once said. 'Not on stage, I hope', I said. Got a world tour with the Rambert, so we decided to split. Four months.

KATY: Blonde. Marketing director. Nine years older than me. Sorted and in control. Ultra-organised. Everything was planned a month in advance. And I mean *everything*. Once, during sex, I asked her what time she'd like me to ejaculate. 'In forty minutes', she said. 'You've got a hope', I said, 'maybe second time round'. Three months. (Would have been two but I had to give a month's notice).

BECKY: No idea what colour. Something out of a bottle; not necessarily of hair dye. Sculptress. Loved 'colours and absolutism'. 'What exactly *is* absolutism', I said. 'Anything you want it to be', she said. 'Then why give it a title'? I said. 'You don't understand art', she said. Which was true. In the end I got fed up. Absolutely. Three months.

EMMA-JANE: Blonde. Hated football. Hated being disagreed with. Loved animals more than humans. Vegan. On our second date she took me home and introduced me to her pet Boa Constrictor; two metres long and called Archie. Two nights.

That was it really. There were a couple of one night stands. I've never really been into them. They were usually the result of me being slightly inebriated at a night club; something else I've never really been into.

Then, in the summer of my twenty-fifth year and seven years since I last saw her, I ran into my mum.

Gran and Gramps had been great; never mentioning her unless I did. Apparently, whenever she visited them, she would always take a look at the scrapbook. Since my 'father' had accidentally seen me on the back of his usual tabloid, newspapers had been banned in the house. She would ask after me and they would keep her up to date with my life. I did get a birthday card from her once. It said:

Happy Birthday, Sam
Love, Mum.
P.S. Please ring me. It would be lovely to see you.
I can sneak out when your dad's at work.

I kept the card on my bedside table for two days. Then I threw it away.

I was out shopping with the gang. New Tommy was going to Australia for a year, working for a law firm and wanted some smart clothes, 'so I look like a successful professional'.

"It's going to take more than clothes, mate," Seb said.

"Sebastian, that's very unfair," said Susie, "Tommy exudes a casual air of confidence with loose, carefree clothing that announces its own personality and distinct style."

"He wears Led Zeppelin T-shirts, ten year old trainers and jeans that are so low-slung, you can almost see his hamstrings."

"That is another way of looking at it, yes."

"You should feel comfortable in your clothes," New Tommy said.

"Not to the extent that people give you money in the street, Tom," I said.

"I'm grungy."

"Then you should take a shower," Susie replied.

"Ooh look, Selfridges," blurted Rachel, "let's go in; the new Lagerfeld range is out. We're bound to find a nice suit for you there."

"Fabulous," said New Tommy, "I'll just pop home, sell my car, my Mum's Lalique vase and most of the furniture and then I'd only have the trousers to buy."

We finally kitted him out in a new grey suit, some chinos, a couple of slim-fit shirts and a pair of black shoes that he described as 'uncomfortable, constricting and weird to walk in'.

"That's because the sole's still attached to the upper shoe," Rachel said.

We adjourned to our cafe for a mocha-break.

"So, Suse, how's James?"

"Oh Seb, he's just so yummy."

"How long is it now?"

"Two months," she said, beaming.

"My God, that's like a lifelong marriage in Susie years," said New Tommy.

"He's so lovely. He laughs at my jokes."

"Well, that's hardly a full-time occupation."

"Shut up Sebastian. He cooks for me, he hates sport and he loves poetry."

"Well, let's face it dear," said Rach, "it's the only way he's going to get sex."

"Sounds gay if you ask me," said Seb.

"We weren't," said Susie.

"And what about Quentin, Rachel?" continued Seb, "is he still making a personal fortune out of palming off a few Van Gogh's for more than the Gross Domestic Product of New Zealand?"

"His name is Jonathan and, yes, he's still an art dealer."

"It's sort of like your life was planned out when you were born, Rach."

"Why?"

"Rich parents, horses, a degree, mummy and daddy buying you a flat and then a fiancé who's an art dealer."

"I'd like to point out that it's a small one bedroom flat."

"In Chelsea."

"Admittedly in Chelsea."

"Actually, I'm just joshing, I'm chuffed for you, Rach."

"Thank you, Seb."

"And Quentin's quite a nice bloke, actually."

"Jonathan."

"And what about you, Sammy?"

"Oh, happily single," I said, "I just don't seem to be able to meet the right person."

"Well," said Seb, "Tara set the bar so high."

After an 'ouch' second, we all laughed. Time heals everything, as the song goes. Well, most things, anyway.

"Oh, Tommy, love, I'm so sorry; we shouldn't be talking about this subject in front of you."

Susie, still the diplomat and slightly off the wall mother earth figure, had remembered that New Tommy had ended a seven year relationship with the girl from Bananarama only three weeks earlier.

"No problem, guys. Really. It had been on its last legs for two years. It's rather a relief actually. And, of course, it frees me up for all that hot Aussie totty!"

We didn't bother asking Seb. He was a serial one-night-stander. The word 'relationship' was on a page that had been torn out of the hymn book of his life.

A little later we got up to leave. As New Tommy stood, he revealed his bottom to the entire cafe.

"Tom, we have to go back to the shop," Susie said.

"Why?"

"You have Mickey Mouse on your underwear, it's not cool."

New Tommy laughed, blew that blond lock out of his eye and hitched his jeans up about seven millimetres.

I was the last to leave the cafe and, as the others cleared the way, someone was standing outside the door. My mother.

We stared at each other for a while, unable to move this unexpected plotline along.

After a minute, I vaguely heard Susie say:

"Sammy, are you OK?"

"Yes," I said. "I'm fine."

"Sam, please can I talk to you?" my mother said.

"Er, yes, I suppose so."

"Sam, mate, you sure?"

"Yeah, Tom. You lot go on. Ring me when you're going for lunch."

"OK mate. Look, take care, yeah?"

"Thanks, mate."

"Bye, Sammy."

We went into the cafe. There was an awkward fumble as I held the door open at a weird angle with my suddenly sweaty hand and it almost slipped.

"Would you like a coffee?" I said.

"Yes. Yes, please."

"What sort would you like?"

"Just a coffee."

"Er, an Americano and a skinny mocha, please. Look, why don't you sit at that table in the window and I'll bring them over when I've paid for them."

"OK," she said, "I thought it was table service."

"Er, no, not in most coffee bars."

"Oh."

As I sat down and set her coffee in front of her, no one would have guessed that we were anything but a mother and son having our regular coffee and chat. Though, if they'd looked at our faces, they would have seen the strain of resistance. Me, resisting any form of relationship between us; her, resisting the overwhelming maternal desire to take me in her arms like a child again.

"You've grown up a bit," she said.

"Just a bit?"

"Well, you still look young for your age and you've still got the floppy fringe."

"Yes, I like it. I suppose it's a sort of trademark."

"Yes, but don't let it cover your beautiful eyes."

"You haven't changed at all," I said.

She hadn't really. She was still pretty, though the grey patches under her eyes detracted from this.

"I'm sure I have," she said.

"No, really."

We shifted in our chairs and changed our line of sight.

"Sam…"

"Yes?"

Then she started to cry.

"I'm so sorry. I told myself I wouldn't do this if I ever saw you."

I wanted to hug her; to tell her that it was alright, that we all make mistakes and that we could go back to the way it was before.

But I couldn't, because it wasn't true.

"It's alright," I said, handing her my napkin, "just take your time."

If she'd thrown me out of the house, burnt my toys, barred my girlfriends from coming round, stopped speaking to me because of an argument over money, I'd have forgiven her, if she'd apologised.

I suppose most of us have our levels beyond which we cannot forgive. And, as I've admitted before, maybe I'd be a better person if I did. But she would have watched me die and done nothing about it; and *that* was beyond my personal level.

"I wanted to stop him."

"Yes."

"Really."

"Yes, I believe you… But you didn't."

"No."

She began to cry again.

"I don't expect you to forgive me."

"OK."

"I told him I was going to try and meet you. I told him I didn't care whether he agreed or not."

"Good, it's time you lived your own life."

"Your grandparents have shown me all your photographs and the interviews you've done on television."

"Yes, I'm thinking of hiring Gran as my publicity agent. She'd scare the pants off the media."

We laughed. A strange, normal laugh; as if the past seven years had been wiped away.

"I'm awfully proud of you. Look at you, a famous footballer. Successful and handsome."

"Well, not really succ-"

"No, you are. And I no longer have any right to call you my son, so I shan't. But deep down, you will always be. I love you so much."

My mobile rang.

"I'm sorry, I'll ring them back."

"No, take it. I must go, anyway."

"I'll call you back in a minute, Suse… Look, we can stay longer."

"No, you must go and meet your friends. I *will* tell him, you know, that I've seen you."

"OK."

"It's been so lovely. Goodbye."

"Hang on. Look, this is my mobile number. I'm not promising anything, but give me a ring sometime and maybe we can do a proper coffee."

She took the card, nodded and walked away. I could see that she was still crying, even when she was just a hazy dot at the far end of the street.

New Tommy flew to Australia the following Wednesday.

"And then there were four," Susie said.

22

I don't think any of us expect to grow up. I know I didn't. Don't.

But, in footballing years, I was now positively middle-aged. Of course, I still thought of myself as a young kid, but there were young kids coming into the squad who were nine years younger than me.

However, this was to be the period that made me as a player.

At the age of twenty-seven and in my third season with Taddersham, we finished fourth in the Premiership and so qualified for the Champions League. This is the league where all the best teams in Europe play each other. I suppose you might say it's the ultimate club competition.

We were, as you will have guessed, playing very well. Joe Andrius and myself had built up a pretty formidable midfield partnership, we had a strong defence and James, Scott and, to a certain extent, myself, were scoring freely and regularly. We were pretty much unbeatable at home.

Of course, I was used to all the razzmatazz and publicity that came as a side salad to my job. I actually didn't mind the magazine interviews (as long as the questions weren't *just* about football), the fashion shoots and the being noticed nearly everywhere I went. I didn't want it all the time but I also didn't crave solitude. I was a very, *very* lucky guy. I had an amazing salary, no mortgage and a considerable amount of savings and, if signing the occasional autograph at a restaurant or spending a couple of hours in front of a camera was a direct consequence of this, I was more than happy to oblige.

Having said this, I *still* went home, closed the door and talked to Thomas in his room.

I *still* automatically thought twice about whether I could afford a new pair of shoes or download a few albums. It's the old, over-used adage, isn't it? 'You can take the boy out of (stereotypically deprived area - in my case, Deptford), but you can't take the (stereotypically deprived area - in my case, Deptford) out of the boy'.

I tried to spend a lot of it, but that proved fruitless too. I thought about buying a top of the range Merc; the all-singing, all-dancing model that does 0-60 in minus three seconds, has a top speed of 600 mph, voice command, makes coffee for you while you're driving and turns into a helicopter at the flick of a button, but I was happy with my black Jeep. It was getting on a bit, but it had character and I loved driving it. I didn't give it a name; that's more of a girl thing and, frankly, I find it a tad annoying. The only time I've ever liked the idea was when I briefly went out with a girl called Polly. She called her car 'Catshit'. When I asked her why, she said, 'because it's the colour of cat shit and, in the winter, it smells like it too'.

When I had saved enough money, I told Gran and Gramps that I wanted to buy them another bungalow, but *not* one in Deptford.

"That's so sweet of you, Sammy," Gran said, "but Gramps and I have been living here for nearly fifty years. We wouldn't want to move. It's our palace, isn't it, Herbert?"

"It's a pig-hole, Doris."

"But it's *our* pig-hole," they said in unison.

So I insisted on paying their fuel bills for them, paid for them to go to France (they'd always wanted to visit Paris, but had never actually been out of the country) and bought Gran a computer.

'I've only got the players' mobile numbers. I want to be able to e mail them tips as well', she'd told me.

Gran had, inadvertently, started on-line football coaching.

I had a website built for her – www.doriscoaching.com. There was a photograph of her with all the Taddersham team on the Home page and another for people to e mail their questions to her. Within a few weeks it was getting thousands of hits a month.

I also bought her a book to teach her how to use it. A couple of weeks later, while she shovelled cake into my mouth, she showed me what she'd learnt.

"Look, Sammy, I can 'cut and paint' and, if I don't know where to look for something, I just Goggle it. The only bit I didn't like was, when I was writing a letter, this little man shaped like a paper-clip appeared and said 'looks like you're writing a letter, can I help'? So I typed 'yes I am, you moron and I've been writing letters for sixty years and I don't need any help from you, thank you, so piss off'. And it worked coz he's never come back."

I would meet my mum for a coffee, once every three or four months. It had to be at a time when 'he' was not around (i.e. the couple of hours he actually worked in the morning) as she had lost the tiny candle-spit of confidence she'd temporarily achieved when she told him she was going to see me.

I could have said no. I wanted to. But I forgave her a few small percentage points; enough to meet up occasionally and conduct a conversation. It was rather like one of the magazine interviews. We asked questions; we answered them; we drank our coffees, making them last until we departed in order to have something to do with our hands or fill an awkward silence. I didn't want her to be unhappy, but she had chosen to be and it was a road from which she was unable to reverse back down.

Maybe I felt sorry for her. Maybe I still loved her (I still loved her), but I met her mostly because I didn't want her to suffer more than she did already; and to have never seen her only child again would have been too much pain.

New Tommy, as we suspected might happen, fell in lust with Australia and decided to stay. Seb also finally fell in love; with a Canadian ex-punk rock singer called Gwendolin (no matter how many times I re-read that line, it doesn't sound right). I think she must have rebelled against her name. Anyway, in her late twenties she had left punk and moved into Real Estate; not exactly the most predictable of career moves. He met her whilst on holiday and, within two months, she had persuaded him to move to Toronto.

I missed both of them, awfully. Funnily enough, Seb a little more than New Tommy. He was so dependably straight-forward; defined within the narrow perimeters of his thoughts and opinions. And, of course, there was that irrepressible memory, in Susie's car, of our penises magnetised to Rachel's bottom.

Suse, Rach and myself still met up regularly, still laughed, still threw sausage rolls when they were in season; but it's difficult to make three people into six.

So Taddersham FC entered Europe for the first time in a couple of decades. Just before our first match – away to Borussia Dortmund, who had finished second in the German Bundesliga the previous season – Joe and I had a joint interview with one of the Saturday morning football programmes. It was to take place in the Player's Lounge at Devonshire Lane.

"Do you know what we're going to be asked?" Joe said to me, as the make-up girl dabbed powder on his forehead, "only I've never been on TV before."

"Don't worry; you'll be fine. It'll probably be the usual thing: football, girlfriends, what are our chances in Europe. Oh and it's the female presenter that's going to be asking the questions; Susannah someone; you know, huge hair and boobs like a sideways view of the Himalayas."

"Result."

"So, no grabbing your cock during the interview."

"Spoilsport."

"So, ladies and gentlemen, welcome to Devonshire Lane," said Susannah someone, blazing ice-white teeth at the camera, "and two of the stars of this hugely successful Taddersham team; Joe Stark and Sammy Hatchington. Hello, gentlemen."

"Hello, Susannah."

"The two of you have forged an incredible rapport on the pitch. Is this through years of playing together or do you have extra-sensitive perception?"

"Never had a medical complaint in my life, actually," Joe replied.

Susannah laughed at this perceived joke so early on; though, of course, Joe had no idea what extra-sensitive perception was and was actually being deadly serious.

"Well, we've always had a connection between us, even when we first met. We have the same style of play, which helps and over the years we've got to know each other's games so well that, I suppose, there *is* a sort of telepathic understanding on the pitch," I said.

"And, of course, you're both very close off the pitch."

"Yes," I said, "though we're not planning on a family just yet."

We talked about how exciting it was for Taddersham to be in Europe again, how far we thought we could go, the entertaining way the team was playing; and then Susannah brought us back to personal things.

"So, Joe, I hear you're a bit of a Lothario."

"No, I'm British."

"You're a blast. Isn't he a blast?! He must be so entertaining to be with," she said to me.

"When it happens, I'll let you know," I said.

She smiled and looked down at her notes. Joe continued to look awkward and I quickly removed his hand from his cock.

The interview went on for another ten minutes, at which point, she wrapped it up.

"That's it. Thanks so much, guys. It'll be heavily edited, but you were both great."

We said our goodbyes to Susannah and left the ground. Joe had volunteered to drive me home as the Jeep had decided it didn't like its current radiator and wanted a new one.

"How do you think it went?" he asked.

"Pretty good. You were really funny."

"Thanks, mate."

"Without intending to be, of course."

"Fuck you. What is 'extra-serial'…"

"It sort of means knowing what's going to happen before it happens."

"Oh."

Joe was silent for a while, appearing to be in deep thought; which was an entirely new state of mind for him.

One hand on the wheel and only half concentrating on the road ahead is not the safest method of driving and when I yelled 'LIGHTS!' and Joe brought us to an emergency stop, centimetres from the car in front, I said:

"Mate, are you OK?"

"Yeah, just a bit… you know. I'm fine, really."

In the hotel near Dortmund's ground, the team was a mixture of anticipation and nerves.

Later, Joe and I sat on our beds, facing each other and chatting. He had stripped naked to have a shower and was, as usual, unconsciously playing with his cock which, as usual, had started to get aroused.

"Erm, hello," I said, pointing at it, "bit of a Tim Henman going on there."

"What?" he said, looking down.

"An unexpected semi."

Joe smiled and tugged even harder, thereby creating what could be referred to as a 'Double Tim Henman'.

"Put it down," I laughed.

"Don't want to," he said.

The hotel had given us a few boxes of complimentary doughnuts; the ones smothered in icing and with a hole in the middle. A quick text to the other lads and, a minute later, they burst into our room, doughnuts at the ready.

I held Joe's arms behind his back.

"OK," said Andrius, "first person to land a doughnut on Joe's penis wins a prize."

"Really depends what the prize is," said Scott.

"Do you think the holes are going to be big enough?" said James.

"Easily," said Andrius.

"Fuck you," said Joe.

For five minutes, the boys laughed, fought for the best throwing position, whooped when a doughnut bounced off and generally shared in some half-remembered schoolboy merriment. All of us, including Joe, were pretty much in hysterics by the time that Scott landed his twenty-second attempt over Joe's still erect penis. He had cheated, admittedly, by doubling the size of the doughnut's hole. As the hysteria died down and the last of the guys went back to their rooms, I let go of Joe and sat back down on my bed. As I did so I noticed that look of mischievous revenge creeping across his face and tried to get away but to no avail. He would always be stronger than me.

He pinned me to the bed.

"Have you got anything to say before the punishment starts?" he said.

"Your erection is in my belly button."

"You lucky bastard. There's many a woman who would kill to be in your position."

"But not me," I said, in a fake falsetto, sounding more like a character from *Toy Story* than a woman, "I'm saving myself for my wedding night."

"Then I shall take your navel virginity," he said.

"Shouldn't we be on a ship?" I said.

"Take that," he said, rubbing his cock up and down my tummy.

"If I get pregnant, I want the child named Prunella Poppysox," I said.

"Alright," he said, "but what if it's a girl?"

"Stop having sex with my navel, will you!"

"You love it," he said, climbing off.

"Go and have shower," I said, "and no wanking. You know the rules; no sex the day before the match."

"Spoilsport," he said.

We won 2-1. Joe scored. Cracking volley from just inside the penalty area and on his weak foot too. They equalised late in the first half. We had been caught out by how easy it was to play our normal passing game and had forgotten to defend in numbers. They counter-attacked, slicing through our defence with worrying ease.

In the changing room at half time, the boss told us to continue playing our normal game but to do it a little deeper so as not to get caught out again.

It worked. We were the better team. And, when Andrius passed to me about twenty yards out, I cut inside their right back and scythed the ball through the gap between their central defenders to where Scott, unmarked, had timed his run to perfection. Their keeper had no chance; Scotty never missed from there.

We celebrated afterwards. Even the boss, who doesn't drink, had a glass of champagne. Halfway down it, he started putting his arms round all of us and telling us we were the best team he'd ever managed.

"This is why I don't drink!" he said.

Two days later my father died.

Mum rang one afternoon. I'd just got home from training.

"Hi, mum," I said.

"Oh, Sam…"

"Mum, are you alright?"

"It's your dad."

"What's he done now?"

"He's died, Sammy."

I could hear a stream of tears descending her girl's cheeks.

"I'm so sorry for you, mum," I said.

"He had a brain haemorrhage about two hours ago. I called an ambulance but he died before they got him to hospital."

I know it's wrong, but the first thought I had was, 'well, at least it proved he had a brain'. Obviously I didn't say this.

"Look, mum, do you want me to come over?"

"I'm at your grandparents. I can't be in the house."

"Of course you can't. I'll come straight over."

I arrived to find Gran cradling her daughter in her arms.

"Would you mind helping Gramps make a pot of tea, Sammy," Gran said, rocking my mum like a child, "and we'll each have a slice of cake. Cake makes everything better."

We had some cake. It didn't make it better, but it gave our mouths something to do, other than form carefully pre thought-out phrases that we hoped would help my mum. It's very difficult when only one person in the room is grieving.

In the days that followed, mum moved back into her old room at Gran and Gramps' bungalow whilst they arranged the funeral. After five days, she had recovered enough to move home and help. She did that little flip thing that your brain does when it needs to go into survival mode and became hugely practical about the whole situation.

"Sam, I want you to choose the coffin," she said, during one of the many phone calls we had that week. I'd continued to train and hadn't mentioned anything to the team as a whole; just Joe and Andrius.

"Mum, look I don't want you to be upset, but I don't want to choose a coffin."

"But you were his son and you haven't chosen anything yet."

"No."

"So you must."

"I don't want to, mum."

"But it will be nice for you when you see it at the funeral."

"I'm not coming to the funeral, mum."

"What?"

"I'm not coming to the funeral. My feelings haven't changed about him just because he's died. I'm not coming. I'm sorry."

"Well, I'm *very* disappointed. You're his son, for God's sake. You went to the funeral of that Thomas person."

"That Thomas person didn't try to kill me."

"Oh, that's right, use your clever rhetoric at a time like this. He makes one mistake and you can't find it in your heart to forgive him now he's no longer with us."

"Mum, I -"

"*One* mistake! Are you not man enough to turn the other cheek?"

"Why? To have made it easier for him to strangle me?! He made my life a total misery. He was rude to me and, apart from a few sentences, he didn't even speak to me for twenty-three years. Then he tried to kill me. And I'm supposed to write that off? I'm not glad he's dead, but I wasn't glad when he was alive either."

"He was your father!"

"NO! No, he wasn't. And as for the way he treated you! You should view this as an escape. Start your life all over again. *Have* a life. He took it from you. He stopped everyone from living so he could continue his pathetic little existence. I know you loved him. I don't know why, but I know you did. You're an intelligent woman; you *know* he imprisoned you. Why do you still defend him?"

"He was a good man underneath."

"He wasn't a good man anywhere! Grieve for him, then get over it and start living. You're still young and pretty enough. *Have* that life he stopped you from having."

"I had hoped my son would have turned out better than this."

On that discordant note, she ended the phone call.

I called back but it went to voicemail. I did manage to see her the day before the funeral. I told her that I was sorry she was sad and that I hoped she would be happy in the future. I said I would try to help her enjoy life again. She said nothing and refused to let me kiss her.

I didn't ask how the funeral went.

We reached the quarter finals of the Champions League. We lost to Real Madrid. *Everyone* loses to Real Madrid.

23

I met Julie when I had just turned twenty-eight (a man's prime, apparently; we'll see). Australian. Very English accent, though. Just the occasional twang of an Aussie vowel, like someone tuning a guitar. She'd been here for three months of a two-year placement as a lawyer.

We met on the Tube. I was going to say it was love at first sight, but it was more like similar literary tastes at first sight. We were both reading John Irving's *A Prayer for Owen Meany*. We had acknowledged each other with a smile and a nod to our books. She was pretty; dark brown hair and that natural beauty that just needs a hint of autumnal make-up.

We both got off at Leicester Square and I found myself behind her on the escalator. She looked round.

"Have you got to the bit where he goes in the army?"

"No," I said.

"Ah," she said.

I faked annoyance.

"Well, I'll probably just throw the book away, now I know the whole story."

"OK, so I'd better not tell you that he has a sex change."

"What?!"

"Kidding."

My brain formulated a hundred and one things to say about the warm coincidence of us both being in the same carriage with the same novel. All of these things, unfortunately, were blasted out of the way by my mouth forming the sentence 'Can I buy you a coffee'?

"Yes, you can," she said.

"Erm, surely it's not supposed to be this easy?"

"Why not?"

"True," I said, "but if this was a TV drama, nobody would believe the script. There'd have to be another twenty-five minutes, two more chance meetings and a commercial break before anything happened."

She smiled.

We went to a cafe on Haymarket. She had a double-thick chocolate with whipped cream.

"I'm not dieting," she said.

She didn't need to. Her pencil skirt and tapered blazer showed off what were obviously the same gorgeous curves underneath.

"So then, 'Mr Lover of John Irving'," she said, "what do you do when you're not reading?"

"Actually, I'm more a lover of his books than the man himself." I don't wish to denigrate him, I'm sure he's very attractive, but I read *The Cider House Rules* about six months ago and have had to read everything he's written since. Oh and I work in sport."

"You 'work in sport'?"

"Yes. And what do you do? Please don't tell me you're married to John Irving."

She smiled that lovely smile again. Wider this time.

"I'm a lawyer."

"That's interesting. Do you specialise in any particular aspect of law?"

"Oh my God," she said, "you're the first man I've met who hasn't said 'oh yeah, better stay on the right side of *you* then'! I *hate* that sort of man."

"In that case, I'm not going to say 'well, I'm not that sort of man' either."

The full smile happened.

"Do you often go straight in with an invitation to coffee?"

"Never. To be honest, I'm surprised I said it. Must have forgotten I was British."

"Well, that's highly laudable and I'm glad you did."

"Oh, sorry, I'm Sam."

"Julie."

We went to shake hands, then stopped and laughed.

"Too British," we both said together.

"So, how long have you been lawyering?"

"Great verb. To lawyer. I lawyer, you lawyer, he lawyers, nous lawyerons, vous lawyerez, ils law... no, that's impossible to pronounce. Two years now. Twenty one months in Australia and three over here. I'm over from Oz, obviously, on a two-year placement. I'm working for a lovely firm. *Very* English. Bowler hats and tea-breaks every twenty minutes."

"Sounds great. I've never really understood the law."

"Nobody *understands* the law. In some ways it's easy. Murder is bad, rape is bad and embezzlement is bad. It's just a case of *how* bad they are; and that, of course, comes down to one person's opinion in the end."

"You're not selling it very well."

"It doesn't need selling. It just is."

"Yes, I suppose so."

As the hum of the cafe's conversation and the fizz of the coffee machine faded into the background, we discussed bits of our life histories; the socially acceptable bits you can tell someone the first time you meet them, without some level of bum-squirming.

"Look, I'm really sorry," she said, "but I've got to be at the office in twenty minutes. That isn't a brush off, by the way, I've really enjoyed talking to you. Maybe we could-"

"No, let me do this bit. It'll make me feel like a man."

"OK."

"I'd love to meet you again and maybe-"

"I don't go as far as 'maybe' on a first date."

"Ah, well *I* always make a point of not getting to 'maybe' until, at least, the third. That way you get to know the person."

"Look," she said, "why don't we spend the first six months drinking lemonade and holding hands?"

"I'm not comfortable with holding hands that early."

We exchanged numbers, kissed each other on the cheek and began heading off in our separate directions.

About ten metres away, she turned and said:

"That was a great goal you scored against Arsenal last Saturday."

"How did you know?" I said.

"I'm a Taddersham fan."

We didn't reach 'maybe' on the first date, but we did on the second; and 'maybe' turned into 'definitely' on the third.

I think I was a little bit intoxicated. I'd found a girl who fitted all the different compartments of romance. Funny, beautiful, drank pints occasionally, followed sport, was feminine without being girlie and was - the most important thing - a really good friend.

Within two months she was spending most nights at my house and, a couple of weeks later, I officially asked her to move in.

"I thought I had," she laughed.

"That's because you're pushy," I said.

She slapped my bottom.

"Guilty," she said.

"So?"

"Look, Sammy…"

"Yes?"

"I *know* how much this house means to you and I know how much you love Thomas…

but I think it's time you moved on and lived somewhere else. I want to live with you; very much. I love this house, but I want to live somewhere that's *ours*, not yours and Thomas'. I don't mean sell it. Just rent it or leave it empty. Have a cleaner come in every week. And you can always still pop in and talk to Thomas. We could spend the occasional night here… I'm blabbering, aren't I?"

"Yes," I said.

"Look, I don't want to hurt your feelings."

"You haven't. You're right, let's get a place of our own. I won't rent it. I don't want anyone else living here; but I think we should start looking tomorrow."

I had agreed so readily that I knew Thomas must have been guiding me.

She kissed me and told me I was a gorgeous boy.

So we began to hunt for a flat to rent. We decided on Highgate. As it turned out, we had completely opposite tastes. I liked fireplaces, exposed wooden beams and floorboards; she liked oblongs, built in wardrobes and double-ovens.

"This is gorgeous," she said, while we were looking round a penthouse flat in a relatively new building.

"Oh, come on," I said, "It's just a box. Admittedly a bloody *big* box. And look at the kitchen; it's so Eighties. *Don't you want me baby?* No, I don't! Even the cupboards have got shoulder pads."

Eventually we settled on a flat high up on a hill. You could see St Paul's Cathedral from our kitchen window. It had a fireplace in an oblong room; the perfect compromise.

We put down a deposit and moved in two weeks later.

"You can see St Paul's Cathedral from our kitchen window," she said every morning, grinning at me.

And I would throw a piece of toast at her.

It was our game, our flat, our life together. It was my first proper grown-up relationship and I could see no reason for it ever to end… apart from her work visa, of course. But I wasn't prepared to admit that and so pretended it didn't exist.

24

Gran and Gramps adored Julie. Everyone adored Julie. She had a battalion of friends, even though she'd only been in the country a short while.

"Have you ever lost a friend?" I asked.

"Yes, once," she said, "in a department store in Adelaide. No idea where she'd gone. Had to ask them to put out a message over the tannoy."

I slapped her bottom.

She was more mature than I was (she's a woman, she had a head start) and more intelligent too; but the thirst for knowledge and education that had partially fuelled my one way journey from Deptford had left us able to converse at the same level in most subjects.

And I found out that sex means more when it's with someone you love. Before, it had always been separate. I loved some people but had sex with others.

There was no longer the thrill of the chase or the heightened naughtiness of it being with a temporary stranger whom you would never see again after two months. But it was better in every other way and, when I exploded inside her, I felt for the first time that it confirmed our 'oneness'. Like when you're in a restaurant and you put a spoonful of your dessert into your partner's mouth so that they can taste it, but what you're really doing is underlining to the rest of the diners how much you belong to each other. Well, it's like that; only messier.

Of course, I missed mine and Thomas' house dreadfully. I would often find myself popping in on my way home from training. I'd sit in his room, tell him my news, watch a DVD, wander around upstairs, open my wardrobe, take a nap on my bed as if I still lived there, go into Davey's room as if…

But, because I knew I was never going to sell it and that it would always be there and because I genuinely loved this wonderful new life with Julie, I soon didn't need to visit so often.

After a while I realised that I wasn't having to try with this relationship. 'If you have to *try*, Sammy, there's something wrong', she said to me. I liked nearly all her friends. There were a couple of pompous ones who considered themselves more intelligent than everyone else (probably because they *were* more intelligent than everyone else). The sort of people who suddenly start speaking in a foreign language simply because they can. I remember one particular time during a dinner party, they started speaking French in the middle of a discussion on film and the psychological thriller genre. So, mainly due to boredom and the five glasses of wine I'd thrown down my throat to counteract said boredom, I decided to resurrect my schoolboy French and tell everyone how much I liked *The Silence of the Lambs*.

"J'adore Le Silence Des Lanneaux," I said. Except I didn't. What I actually said was, "J'adore Le Silence De Les Oignons." I was met with blank stares as everyone tried to remember where they'd seen a film about a bunch of silent onions.

Julie also loved Susie and Rachel. In fact, Rachel asked her to be one of the bridesmaids at her wedding to Quentin. It was a real society wedding. The newspapers and upmarket magazines were all over it like a rash. As usual I was amazed to see my name appear in the list of attending celebs as I had spent most of the time looking round the room to see who they were.

It was a great day. New Tommy and Seb came back for it with their respective girlfriends. New Tommy had met someone who was a dead ringer for a younger Olivia Newton-John and so continued his love affair with pop star look-a-likes.

I'd been expecting Rachel's parents to be really snooty, but they weren't at all. In fact, they were extremely friendly and rather down to earth, albeit with an accent you could ferment champagne with.

Rachel's dad also had a great sense of humour. He began his speech with:

'Rachel didn't do very well when she first started school. Her mother and I were rather worried. Somebody once asked me what I thought she would be when she left. I said, twenty-eight'.

After the wedding breakfast we all played cricket. Bride's family and friends against the groom's. It was a very competitive affair with a lot at stake. Well, alcohol-inflated macho pride, to be honest, but a lot if you happened to be a proud, semi-drunken male at the time.

In the end, the bride's team won by three runs and Seb, New Tommy and myself returned with the rest of the victorious team to the dining room.

"Erm, tough game was it, dear?" Julie said, as I slumped, breathless, into the chair next to her.

"Yes, very close. Good fun, though."

"Yes, thought it might have been."

"Why?"

"Oh, nothing much; just the scuff marks on your shoes and the mud stains on your trousers."

"Well, you know, the England team fling themselves all over the place when they're fielding."

"Yes, dear, but they're not usually wearing Pierre Cardin suits while they're doing it."

"You look gorgeous," Susie told Rachel.

"Thank you, darling."

"And Quentin's actually quite a decent bloke," added Seb.

"He's called Jonathan, Sebastian," replied Rachel, "and if you call him Quentin again, I shall throw one of the sausage rolls we ordered especially for Sam, at you."

The remaining members of the gang fell into private and uproarious homage to that glorious picnic ten years earlier.

Later, during the disco, the five of us had a communal slow dance; arms wrapped around each other's shoulders; a circle so tightly bound, it was barely possible to move. We swayed, all of us, looking at the floor, breathing and touching, taking a beyond-human delight in the closeness of each other; in its physicality, its history, its love. And, when the song ended (*Eternal Flame* has always been special to me since) and we slowly, reluctantly parted, there were tears in all of our eyes; tears that, in the ever-changing multi-hued lights, glistened with the various colours of our characters but shone out in their rainbow unity.

I know that, although we loved our respective partners, a small part of ourselves would have given anything to go back for even a short while, those ten years, to the innocence and the tranquillity and the grass and the trees and the idleness and the boisterousness and the talk and the silence and the food and the champagne and the delight and the expectancy and the breeze and the sun and the slumber and the cigarettes and the charm and the energy and the wit and the inconsequentiality and the magnitude and the sausage rolls and the togetherness of that most beautiful of summer days.

I have a photograph of it in my head and I look at it often.

Two weeks after the wedding, Julie and I were having our usual breakfast conversation. Hers, a busy, energised communication of wit and plans for the day; mine, mostly throwing toast.

As she headed to the front door, hair and scarf tied back, huge leather folder under one arm, she said:

"Oh, Sammy, don't forget I've invited Alex and Karen for dinner tonight to thank Alex for all the help he's given me at work recently."

"Oh great, another solicitor's dinner party; I'll do a handstand."

"You'll like Alex, he's got appalling taste in music as well."

"Terrific. Well, you and Karen can discuss world politics while we dance round our briefcases to *Le Freak C'est Chic*."

"And Karen's a fitness trainer with an amazing body, apparently."

"I've always felt it's good to entertain."

She slapped my bottom.

That evening as I was getting ready in our bedroom, I could hear her scurrying around the lounge, arranging things that didn't need arranging.

"Can you tell me the time?" she yelled.

"Yes, but only with help from an adult. It's the small hand I have trouble with."

I could see her pretend patronising expression through two walls.

"What *is* the time, Samuel?"

"It's 8.30; they're half an hour late."

I went into the lounge.

"Does this dress make my hips look big?" she said.

"Enormous."

"Well, fuck you *very* much."

Then the intercom buzzed.

"That's them. Check on the lamb for me, would you. It's in the kitchen. You know, that room where I prepare all your meals."

"Oh, *that's* what it's for."

As I opened the oven door and inspected the lamb, which just looked like lamb, really, with some weird twigs on it which, I presumed, were rosemary, I could hear Julie bringing them into the lounge and Karen apologising that it was all her fault they were late.

I prodded the joint inexpertly with my finger, which burnt it to the point of me yelping. Then I took a deep breath and prepared for another evening of food, law-talk and remembering not to speak French.

"Alex, Karen, this is Sam," Julie said, as I entered the lounge, sucking my finger. "What's the matter with your finger?"

"The lamb was hot," I said.

"Astounding. That's never happened before when a joint of meat has been in the oven for two hours."

Julie and Karen laughed. Alex smiled; the way the Lord of the Manor would smile at an errant footman.

"Sammy, this is my boss, Alex and this is Karen."

I went to shake hands with them, then realised I'd just had my finger in my mouth and so tried to adjust my footing and half extended my left hand instead, before deciding this was not appropriate and so switched back to my right whilst trying to curl the guilty finger into my palm so it wouldn't touch *their* hands, then establishing that this would also be ludicrous. All of this made me look like I was doing some sort of Country and Western dance designed for people with mobility problems.

Finally and with great confidence, I just shook hands normally with them, which would have been fine, had I not said 'sorry about the sucked finger' at the same time.

A couple of angels of embarrassment backed out of the room, then Alex said:

"I'll divert the attention away from this unfortunate situation by saying something remarkably cool and pretending that the mentally-challenged footballer hasn't just made a complete arse of himself."

Actually, he didn't. He said:

"Darling, you were going to tell Julie and Sam why we were late."

But that's what he meant.

So Karen began telling us the story whilst I poured four gin and tonics.

"Be careful," Julie warned them, "Sam's gins are potent; there's barely any room left in the glass for the tonic."

"Ah, a man after my own heart," Karen said, smiling at me and making me warm to her a little. "OK, it was 6 o'clock and I was just about to knock off, when this guy walks in the gym wearing no top, so I asked him if he would go to the changing rooms and come back properly dressed. Anyway, he returned about five minutes later wearing – absolutely nothing!"

"No way!" said Julie.

"Way," said Karen, "stark-bollock naked. Sorry, Alex, darling. He then proceeded to assist one of our middle-aged ladies with her ab crunches."

"Well, that was very nice of him."

"By lying on top of her, Julie."

"Oh my God! So, did you have him thrown out?"

"We had him arrested. Then I had to try and placate the woman on the ball. Except she wasn't on the ball now, in any sense. I tried to make light of it at first. I told her there'd been a mistake and that sort of thing only happened to our gold card members and we'd have to charge her an extra twenty pounds a month from now on."

"Did she see the funny side?"

"I don't think so."

"How do you know?"

"It was the hysterical crying, mostly. We quietened her down in the end and got her a cab home. Apparently he was making a stand against women only sections in gyms."

"Well, he does have a point," said Julie, "we've spent centuries tearing down the barriers only to build them back up again from the other side."

All the while Karen was telling the story, Alex kept patting her hand, looking at her lovingly, smiling in that dual way people have; devoted and patronising at the same time; 'I own you but I'm nice enough to give you a long leash'.

'I wonder if you've ever slipped over on your own smarm', I thought.

The conversation began to trickle in and out of the various inanities that these evenings always begin with, before the drink kicks in and everyone goes from barely disguised ennui to promises to go skiing together the following spring. 'Where do you live'? 'What sort of flat do you have'? 'What are the schools like in your area'? Even though no one actually has any children.

My social automatic pilot joined the conversation occasionally, but usually to back up a point that Julie had made or to smile at something Karen had said.

"Right!" said Julie, suddenly getting up, "I'll go and check on the ashes that were once dinner."

"Oh, I'll come and help; if you don't mind, Julie."

"Gosh, no, always glad of a hand."

They left the room, chatting like they'd known each other all their lives and making the subsequent aeon of silence between Alex and myself even more pertinent.

Women seem to be able to talk about anything from the moment they meet; music, cooking, lipstick, pushchairs, politics, Pilates; they call each other 'my girlfriend' and can be intimately tactile; or they just despise each other on sight. Men are so different. We either have to know each other for two years, or drink seven pints of lager before we can say 'I fucking love you, mate'.

So it was that the 'unbearable silence of being' continued until neither of us could take it any longer.

"So, you're a footballer?" he said.

"Yes." I said, not wanting to risk any further faux-pas.

"I'm afraid I don't know much about football."

(No, you wouldn't. And I bet you're about to say you're more of a rugby man, yourself).

"Actually I'm more of a rugby man, myself."

"Really?"

"Yes, always preferred it; even at school."

(And which toffee-nosed, stuck up, fee-paying British institution dating back to the Stone Age did you grace with your all-knowing presence).

"Which school did you go to?"

"Charterhouse."

(Bullseye).

"Oh, well, I suppose all those schools prefer rugby."

"Well, actually, mine didn't."

"Oh?"

"You do know that modern football was invented at Charterhouse?"

"No," I said, genuinely surprised.

"Yes, in 1862. The first matches were"-

I was saved from a lecture about *my* sport by Julie popping her head round the door and announcing that the lamb was almost salvageable and would we like to come to the table to drink and chew for a while.

Of course, there was a part of me that was intrigued by the fact that he knew about the origins of football.

When we all came back to the lounge, three bottles of Merlot later, things were a tad more convivial.

We slumped down on our respective sofas; Julie and Alex on one, Karen and myself on the other and congratulated Julie on what had been a terrific meal, prompting her to make the speech she'd been itching to make all evening.

"I'm so glad, I wanted it to be just right because this evening is a vastly understated thank you to Alex for all the help he's given me at work."

Alex actually looked slightly humble, or was it the wine.

"Julie, you're more than welcome. You know what an incredibly difficult man my father is to please but he thinks that you're a 'damn fine lawyer'."

"To Julie," Karen said, raising her glass.

"Julie," we echoed, downing glasses of brandy that, judging by how much we'd already had to drink, should probably have stayed in the bottle.

"Gosh," said Julie, "I hate being the centre of attention."

I pretended to choke on my drink.

"Ice," I said.

"There isn't any ice in your drink, Sam."

"Bugger."

Karen said, "I do admire you, Julie; I mean, how long did you have to study for?"

"Five years," Julie and Alex said in unison.

"Five years! No, I couldn't do that. Could I, darling?"

"No," said Alex.

I actually found myself laughing at something he'd said.

"It's Alex's one failing," Karen said, "honesty."

"But, Karen," said Julie, "you do get to see naked men in your line of work, which must be a perk; so to speak."

"I wouldn't call today's over-exposed chipolata and cherry tomatoes a perk. Brad Pitt would be a perk."

"Is that the ultimate female fantasy, then," I said, "sex with a good-looking film star?"

"Oh God, yes," Karen replied, "as long as we could kick him out whenever we wanted. Isn't that right, Julie?"

"Never a truer word slurred."

"So," Alex joined in, "your ultimate fantasy is to be single but have Brad Pitt on the end of a fishing line that you can reel in at your whim?"

"I'm amazed at how easily you've broken in to the woman's psyche," said Julie.

"It wasn't a difficult lock," replied Alex.

"So, Sam, you're saying you wouldn't be happy being single but having Sienna Miller on call whenever you wanted?" said Karen.

I tried to be neutral; and failed, of course.

"I think guys tend to miss their freedom more than girls, anyway. I think we're just more suited to a single life," I said.

"So, you'd have no qualms about washing up, cooking and cleaning?" Julie said.

"Suited to a single life that included hiring a maid."

Alex said, "I think it's all to do with the old adage of 'Man the Hunter' and Woman, the-"

"Everything Elser?" said Karen

"Certainly, woman is the more social creature. I'm not saying men aren't, but we tend to retain our caveman instincts. It's as if, when we're single, our bedroom is our territory; a sort of sanctuary to be defended against all comers."

"That's right, Alex," I said, suddenly forgetting I disliked him, "posters on your cupboards, three week-old socks stuck to the carpet and porno mags stuck to the mattress."

"That's exactly it, Sam. Posters are the symbol of being single."

"Yes," I said, getting very excited about the point we were making, "like, when you're single, you can have whatever God-awful posters you want blue-tacked to the wall. Then, when you get into a relationship, you have to give up those posters and your cricket bat and the love-letters from Helen who was studying sexual science at Uni... and elsewhere and your *Brut 33* after shave and exchange them for fitted valance sheets, his and hers bedside lamps and Laura sodding Ashley mix and match quilt and curtain sets."

"That was almost poetry," said Alex.

"Yeah, so's rap music," replied Karen. "Anyway, it's not just boys who buy posters you know. You'd be surprised, but us girls aren't as different from you as you think."

"You used to wear *Brut 33*?" I said

"Only when I'd run out of *Old Spice*."

Then their cab arrived.

We were doing the 'nice to meet you's' and the 'yes, we really musts', when Alex suddenly turned to me and asked:

"Do you play tennis, Sam?"

"Er, occasionally," I stammered.

"Do you fancy a game sometime?"

Here it was, the skiing moment.

"Yes, why not."

"I'll ring you."

When they'd left and Julie and I were snuggling on the sofa, she said:

"Thanks for putting up with yet another lawyer's dinner."

"That's OK," I said, as she kissed my neck and gently bit my ear, "wasn't too bad. Karen's great; calls a lump of shit a lump of shit."

"Yes, dear, we know what she calls it."

"Just saying she was friendly and straight forward."

"Which is obviously what you're not saying about Alex. Did you really not like him at all?"

"Didn't get to know him; mostly due to his not coming out of his arse long enough for me to do so."

"But you're going to play tennis with him?"

"No, that was just drink-talk. One decent thing, though, football actually started at his school."

"So, you did learn something tonight, then."

"No, I learnt two things. To use a knife when I'm checking the lamb."

25

Alex did call and, because I can never think of an excuse to say no on the spur of the moment, I agreed to play the following Wednesday after training. This just happened to coincide with the next stage of my football career.

We had almost finished the training session when Jed, one of our juniors, came to tell me that my agent was with the boss in his office and wanted to see me as soon as I'd showered.

Joe turned to me with a smack of worry stinging his face.

"Mate, tell them you don't want a transfer."

"I *don't* want a transfer."

"Even to Man U?"

"*Especially* to Man U."

"OK, just make sure they know."

"I'm not going anywhere, mate."

An hour later, I was in the boss's office at Devonshire Lane, trying to discern a message from the downcast expressions that he and Ivan were wearing.

They didn't speak. I couldn't.

'Someone's died', I thought. 'I'm being fired'.

"Sammy," the boss said so suddenly, it made me jump, "there's no easy way to tell you this… We're just waiting for a phone call."

On cue, it rang.

"Answer it, Sammy, it's for you."

It was a routine call, really. Just the England manager telling me that he'd been watching me recently, was extremely impressed with my performances, that I was in the squad for the upcoming match against Portugal, was to report for training on the Monday and that he was very pleased to have me in the England set-up. That's all.

I needed two hands to put the phone down as it had suddenly appeared to have tripled in weight.

"That was very childish of us and we're very sorry, aren't we, Ivan."

"Definitely. *Very* sorry."

Their grinning faces didn't exactly back that up.

"Congratulations, Sammy."

They shook my hand and told me that a news conference would be held for me and the other two new players the following Monday.

When I was a child, I lay awake in the evening because I'd been sent to bed early and it was summer and warm and I was very angry at this state of affairs. But, when that anger began to abate, I needed to fill my head with happy thoughts to pass the time. So I pretended I was an adult, doing adult things; driving a car, getting married, going to the moon, playing football for England. And, as that beautiful lulling slide into sleep began, for those few seconds, I really believed it was true. This was the opposite. For a few seconds I was lulled into a heightened state of awareness and I couldn't believe it *was* true.

There had been murmurings about me in the England establishment. I knew that the scouts had watched me in various games since I joined Taddersham. But that's all there ever was; murmurings. And, at twenty-nine and heading rapidly toward football's mid-life crisis, I really thought my chance had passed. I wasn't disappointed; I'd achieved more than I ever thought possible and was happy in that knowledge. But this was... well, let's just say that Gran was going to have to turn a new page in the scrapbook. Maybe even get a *new* scrapbook.

I was ten minutes late arriving at the tennis club.

"Sorry," I said, "I was called into an impromptu meeting."

"That's perfectly alright," Alex said, managing to convey nonchalance and annoyance at the same time.

It was a surprisingly good match. I had more power; he, more finesse. We rallied to the point of exhaustion (not difficult after three hours training). In the end, he won it on a third set tie-break.

Fortunately the game gave us something to talk about as we changed after showering. Then, my duty done and, as I was about to take my leave and not see him again until the next force-fed dinner party, he asked me if I fancied a quick juice at the bar.

I had rehearsed so many excuses to say no. They all crowded together in my head, trying to be the one I would use. Maybe they got jammed in the entrance to my mouth but, as usual, I heard myself saying 'yeah, why not'.

We sat opposite each other in a pair of armchairs while he sipped his juice and I gulped mine.

"So," I said, dispensing with any pretence at small-talk, "if you know somebody's guilty of a crime, how can you defend them?"

"Well, it depends on the individual case. Obviously one has to go through the testimony of the plaintiff with a fine toothcomb, trying to find any small irregularity or contradiction in their evidence-"

"No, that's not what I mean."

"I know what you mean."

"What I'm saying is, how can you find it inside you to bend the truth?"

"Well, thank you for putting it so diplomatically."

"Diplomacy is 'lying for people in power'."

"That's an unusual interpretation. What exactly are you getting at?"

"Well, look at some of the big trials that hit the press. In some cases the person is *obviously* guilty but, because they're obscenely rich, they can hire a lawyer who wouldn't recognise morals if they kicked him in the nuts and who's slimy enough to twist the facts because it'll get him a couple of million dollars in his bank account. I don't know why we don't just use lie detectors; it would save money and be a darn sight fairer."

"Certainly. In an Enid Blyton novel. There has to be a structure to the law otherwise the public's faith in it would fall apart. Everyone has to be entitled to a defence. If this weren't so, there would be more innocent people convicted than the other way round. And, for the record, I've never defended anyone who I knew to be guilty. Does that make me a better person?"

"I wouldn't know. I've got to be going."

"How about arranging a date to play again?"

"I don't think either of us actually *wants* that. Let's not just go through the motions."

"I wasn't."

"Right."

"You have strong principles, Sam and I admire that. In fact, I agree with a lot of what you said. Just think of a lawyer's relationship with his client as being like that of a Priest taking confession. No situation in life is perfect."

"Maybe, but I'm not the sort of person who can pretend just for the sake of a few social graces."

"I wouldn't want you to."

"I don't really think I fit into your social group."

"Who gives a fuck about social groups?"

"My God, you swear."

"Yes, I've also been known to go a whole day without a shower and occasionally cheat at Monopoly. Look, I know we haven't exactly hit it off straight away and I know I can seem a bit aloof at times; it's just that... well, I tend to do that when I'm nervous."

"Nervous? About what?"

"You're a famous footballer. I'm just a lawyer."

"No, *you're* a lawyer. I'm just a footballer."

"Look, Sam, I think you're a really nice guy. How about we start again?"

"Why not?" I said and we clinked glasses.

"Thank you," he said, "so, tell me something good about yourself."

"I've just been called up to the England squad," I said.

26

I'd said goodbye to the guys at Devonshire Lane after the match, a 2-0 victory over Newcastle, on the Saturday evening.

On the Monday morning I was at St. George's Park, training with the England team.

It sounds so glib to just write that line. My favourite diaries are the ones that tell you all the minute, inconsequential details and gloss over the major events.

I'm not saying that I wasn't daunted, because I was. However, I knew these guys. Not well; but I played against them every season. They weren't gods anymore; well, maybe demi-gods; demi-semi quaver gods.

At the press conference afterwards, we answered the usual stock questions. Twenty slightly differently worded variations of 'what does it mean to be picked for England', followed by twenty variations of 'everything'. Then we were photographed holding our England shirts, grinning like the cat that got the cream or the footballer that got into the England squad.

As the week wore on, I made myself realise that I should be enjoying this: to not be scared that I wouldn't be good enough or that I would become over-awed with the situation. This is what I had always wanted. This was an opportunity that swings by maybe once or twice in a lifetime; something that runs alongside you, but only for a short distance, before it goes away forever. And how many of us pretend we can't see it. Our peripheral vision knows it's there, but we don't look because it's easier not too; and, when it's gone, we convince ourselves that it was never there in the first place. Except we don't convince ourselves, do we; not really. What was it Mandela said? 'It is not our weaknesses that frighten us, it's our strengths'. Something like that, anyway.

So I told myself to ditch the fear and to begin to shape a memory that would be framed in gilt and hung on the galleried wall of my old age, to look at as the sun set and a breeze, blowing through the open window, brought with it the phrases and actions of that eternal time.

Joe came to dinner on the Thursday and he, Julie and I made each other laugh all evening. Julie cooked chicken Kievs with so much garlic in them we should have had a two-mile exclusion zone round us for the next forty-eight hours. Afterwards, we joked and talked and played games. Julie and Joe had become rather like brother and sister.

"Can't tell you how much good luck I wish you, mate," Joe said as he was leaving. "Hope you get in the team, but just get the match over and come back to us; I'm going to miss you."

"He really loves you," Julie said, after Joe had gone.

"Of course he does," I said, "I'm an awesome person."

"Hang on, dear," she said, "you've dropped something. Oh, it's OK, it's just your modesty." I slapped her bottom and she slapped mine; and then other things happened.

The following day we trained as usual and were then driven to our hotel, ready for the short trip to Wembley.

In the evening the team was announced. I was on the subs bench.

That night I shared a room with Graham, a damn nice guy and a stalwart of the England team for eight years.

"It's just the same as playing club football," he said; "after all, most of the world's top players play in the Premiership."

"Yes, I suppose you're right," I said, not entirely convinced but appreciating the gesture.

That night I lay in bed, staring at the fuzzy darkness of the ceiling.

"I'm on the subs bench for England tomorrow, Thomas", I said in my head. "I may even get to play. I'm a bit scared, to be honest. I want to go back fourteen years to the boy that hung around your bookstall. Adulthood can be a bit frightening sometimes; but you know that."

Portugal went 1-0 up in the 23rd minute. Their passing was just out of this world. It was like they had magnets attached to the ball and their feet.

They came at us from all angles. We couldn't establish any rhythm. The boss was on the touchline, barking orders, encouraging the team to relax and keep possession.

You'd honestly think the match was being played in Lisbon. You could see their players thinking 'I know when I pass this ball it's going to go exactly where I want it'. Football is a state of mind, not a state of feet, or a state of the pitch.

Even with only one recognised forward, they went two up just before half time. The worst psychological blow you can take (apart from losing 10 - 0, I suppose); and, if it wasn't for Jonny in our goal, they could have had another four.

The boss's half time pep talk concentrated on the one thing he'd been shouting to us for most of the first half: "Keep possession and you break their rhythm. Then we can start playing."

As the whistle blew for the second half, that's exactly what we set out to do. It wasn't pretty, it wasn't even plain, but it began to work.

Then, in the 65th minute, the boss turned to myself and Danny and said, "Start warming up, boys."

As I stretched and ran up and down the touchline, I locked myself into forward-thinking mentality and repeated to myself that the ball would go wherever I wanted it to.

In the 70th minute I watched my number go up on the board and, a few seconds later, Jamie came off, high-fived me and I was on.

I'd been on the turf before in the warm-up, but the grass had been sedentary then. Now it was charged with a million chemical experiments; sparks of energy combining together to create some surrealist's idea of a lightning rod, blasting the touch-paper of a new life. The only question: whether that new life would be a child prodigy or Frankenstein.

"Play just behind Nicky and Stewart," the boss said; "get the ball and run at them; split their defence open, Sammy; ruffle their buggery over-confident feathers."

"Right you are, boss," I said, as though I played against Portugal every day.

It was five minutes before I touched the ball. We'd been playing a midfield holding game, waiting for the through pass to our strikers. Unfortunately, you had to *get* the ball in order to hold it. If we'd been kids, our parents would have come out and told them to stop being so clever and let us have a turn.

Finally, Glen slid in to tackle their right-winger deep into our half, won the ball brilliantly and leapt to his feet like he hadn't been flat on his back two nanoseconds earlier, looked up and floated a perfect ball to Steve in the centre circle. Steve and Rob kept short-passing the ball to each other in some weird rain-dance as they tried to shield it from the advancing army of Portuguese midfielders.

Then I saw their two centre halves moving up but leaving just enough of a gap to squeeze through.

"Steve," I yelled, letting most of Northern Europe know what I was about to do.

Steve glanced my way as I started a run up the centre of the park. It needed the perfect pass to reach me; he had the acutest angle to play with. But Steve is a master craftsman; the pass was perfectly weighted, perfectly aimed at my right foot and, as Jack belted up the left touchline on one of his now famous dummy runs, I slipped between the two centre-halves. Rob had drawn their right-back and their left-back was marking Stewart. I had two options; one- a floated pass wide to Jack on the left; two- to run at them.

I ran at them.

As the spare central-defender came out to me, I feigned a move to my left, then shot right and, as he spread his legs to gain balance and alter his direction, I slipped the ball through them. At the edge of the penalty area I looked up, saw that Stewart had cut inside their right-back and was thundering in on goal. I got the pass spot on but, as he hurtled in from the right, their goalkeeper had cut his angle right down. Stewart's pass threaded the goalie's lunge and the defender's flailing left boot and reached me, unmarked, about two metres out. All I had to do was side-foot it with my left foot. Gran couldn't have missed from there. I didn't either.

From my first goal for Flitcham to my first for England, I'd still not developed a specific style of celebration. Some guys do somersaults, some dive, spread-eagled, to the ground, some take up a bizarre gladiatorial stance. I tend to be very English about the whole thing and look rather apologetic. 'Terribly sorry to score against you, old chap; wouldn't have even considered it had you not left the goal rather wide open for me'.

At this precise moment, I really felt I should have cultivated one.

Devonshire Lane holds about 42,000; I'd played at Old Trafford (75,000); but almost 90,000 raising a victory cry as one is beyond sensibility; especially when you're the reason for it.

I ran a few steps, then stopped. Jack piled into me first, then Danny, followed closely by the rest of the team. Even Jonny ran from his goal to join the celebrations.

To say I was overwhelmed is an understatement. But, even though my 'whelm' was over its stated limit, it could only be temporary and I was experienced and professional enough to remember that we were still 2-1 down.

But our heads were up, our inner belief somewhat restored and we began playing the ball around the pitch, not only with more confidence, but with a modicum of panache.

Portugal, of course, continued to play in their languid, flowing style but, whilst their game was a Matisse or a Rembrandt, ours was a Picasso; unexpected, angular, bold, in your face. And sometimes, as in a fight, the artistic, martial arts moves may look impressive, but a good punch on the nose often wins.

As the clock ticked over into injury time, Jamie hoofed the ball up field from the edge of our penalty area. Danny happened to be the closest to where it landed, brought it down impeccably, turned and passed to me about ten yards short of their area. The newspapers wrote that I had a great footballing brain in having the vision to send a heavily-weighted pass within inches of Stewart, from which he headed in a bullet of a goal; but, to be honest, I'd had no choice as they'd cut off every other option for me.

Two minutes later the ref blew the final whistle and, as we congratulated each other on a pretty good comeback and shook hands with the Portuguese team, I looked around at this vast stadium and I breathed in the grass and the mud and the sweat. As I left the pitch, I turned back and waved to the crowd in case I never came back again.

One final thing. I exchanged shirts with a certain Portuguese player. *The* certain Portuguese player. Mr Ronaldo had asked for mine and I, shocked more than scoring my goal, took his. It's framed on my wall. Always will be.

27

Three weeks later, Alex, Karen and Julie took the day off work and we drove to the coast.

It was the end of May. We'd played our final match the previous week, a 2-1 defeat at Man City, consigning us to fifth place in the Premiership and putting us just outside the Champions League placings for the second consecutive year. 'Disappointing', the boss said, 'but the foundations to go on to greater things next season'.

We'd all said our goodbyes. Some I would see socially; Joe and Andrius, especially, of course, but it's good to have a break from your work colleagues occasionally. It's a long season; August to almost June; training beginning again in July and a small, pre-season tour thrown in for good measure; so this little six week window becomes almost sacred.

We found a relatively deserted part of the beach (weekday, no school holidays, no kids; Heaven) and set down our gigantic beach towels on the soft sand.

Five minutes later we were all prostrate on our towels, the girls in bikinis - Karen's so small it was hardly worth wearing it - Alex and I in Speedos; the prospect of several hours of sunbathing ahead of us.

The warmth and the breeze and the sound of ripples falling over each other on the sand was instantly soporific and, within ten minutes, we were all fast asleep.

It was Julie who stirred first which, as ever, woke me next to her; and so it passed down the towel-line to Alex and Karen.

"Hurrah for whoever invented sunbathing," I said.

"God invented sunbathing," Julie said, "He only invents things that please Him,"

"So, God likes everything, does he?" said Alex.

"Yes."

"So, how about nuclear bombs and the *X Factor*?"

"God invented all the components parts of life which, in their original form, were perfect. He then gave them to us to use in whichever way we desired. To make Michelangelo's David or a plasticine ashtray."

"You don't think that's rather passing the buck?"

"No."

"So, mass starvation, global warming and heart disease; you're saying, Julie, that, if we put all these component parts together in a happy, smiley way, we'd get something wonderful, like a huge Banoffee Pie."

"If you go back to the Creation, Alex."

"The Big Bang."

"God creating the Big Bang."

"The Big bang caused by the build-up of gasses to the point where the pressure was so great that-"

"Do you think you could have this conversation somewhere else?" Karen piped up, rising slightly from her towel.

"Do you want us to move further down the beach, darling?" said Alex.

"I was thinking of Sri Lanka, actually."

"But it's an interesting question, isn't it. Who did create the very first thing that created the very first thing?" I said.

"I think I'm going to create a coma and slip into it," said Karen.

"Nobody *created* it, Sam."

"So, Alex, what was there to begin with because, if it was anything other than a vacuum, someone or some*thing* must have created it?"

"Everything in the Universe vibrates-"

"Oh *finally* something interesting," said Karen, sitting up.

"And it was these vibrations that started the ball rolling in the first place."

"But Alex," I said, "how can *nothing* vibrate?"

"Can we open the wine?" Karen asked.

"If you're brave enough," Julie answered, "Sam chose it."

"Alright. My taste in wine isn't that bad. I'll open the red, let it breathe."

"It's cheap Bulgarian, Sammy", Julie said, "It won't breathe, it'll just wheeze a bit, then expire."

"'Toilet Duck Surprise'. The latest in a large range of asthmatic wines from Samuel Hatchington," said Alex.

"Actually, I'd rather have an ice cream," Julie said, "anyone else?"

"God, yes, brilliant idea," said Karen, "I'll come with you. Alex?"

"Can I have one with a flake in it?"

"Come on fitness freak," Julie said to Karen, "race you to the ice cream shop!"

"OK, er, doesn't Sam want one?"

"Yes, but he always has the same."

The girls departed, giggling like... well, girls, really as they ran, stubbing their feet in miniature dunes and trying to push each other over."

After a few seconds, Alex said:

"So, what is this famous ice cream that you always have, then?"

"Well, it's not exactly famous; it's just an ordinary ice cream, but with raspberry sauce on it."

"Raspberry sauce?"

"Yes."

"Raspberry sauce?!"

"No, only once."

"That's a bit..."

"Yes?"

"Young, isn't it?"

"So you're saying there's an upper age limit to raspberry sauce? Like the reverse of alcohol. You can't buy alcohol until you're eighteen but, at the same age, you can't buy raspberry sauce anymore."

Alex smoothed his blond hair back from his forehead, smiled and turned over onto his front.

"Put some sunblock on my back will you, Raspberry."

"Er, yeah, OK. Where is it?"

"In Karen's bag. In a bottle marked 'Sunblock'."

I retrieved the bottle from the bag, squirted a large amount into the palm of my left hand and suddenly and for no rational reason, felt embarrassed about rubbing it on his back. I couldn't work out why. The tactility between my teammates was vastly more intimate than this; Joe had pretended to shag my navel, for goodness sake. But it seemed acceptable there. Davey aside, take the same set of circumstances out of the football situation and it seemed suddenly awkward with anyone else.

"Hatchington, I'll be burned to a cinder if you don't start soon."

"Yeah, sorry, right."

I began smoothing the cream onto his shoulders.

"Ooooooh!"

"What?!"

"Cold."

"Oh."

As I worked my way down his back, past the contours of his shoulder blades, down over the rhomboid muscles to the small of his back, I properly took notice of a man's body for only the second time in my life; the first being when Davey and I had been showering, some eleven years ago. I had been so used to a woman's body; the curves, the smoothness, the silk of the back and legs, the hillocks and dales of feminine territory, waiting for exploration.

Now I was subtracting that ever-changing art-form and replacing it with muscle pads that barely gave to my touch, to a strength of body that resisted me, that challenged my hands to alter its patterns, that was my equal and therefore either threatening or completely understood.

As I massaged the final bit of cream inwards from his hips, I saw that his Speedos, which were already skimpy, had slipped ever so slightly and left the faintest crack of his bottom visible.

I stared for two or three seconds, then looked away.

Alex, like Davey, seemed to sense something.

"You OK?"

"Er, yeah; yeah fine."

"Finished?"

"Yes."

He cocked his head to one side, while I sought for something casual to say.

"I meant to bring *Trivial Pursuit*."

"I'm glad you didn't. I hate it. I always think the game reflects real life. Some people go straight for the cheeses but the vast majority constantly aim for the grey squares so they don't have to answer any questions."

"You know Alex, there are occasions when I find it very difficult to believe that you've never touched drugs. But there is another way of looking at it. There are some people who get all the cheeses and go straight to the centre without even trying and others who have difficulty getting the board open."

"Then they should try harder," said Alex.

"But some people don't have the chance."

"Everyone has the chance."

The girls returned with the ice creams.

"You're going to burn, Alex," Karen said, "I'll put some sunblock on."

"It's OK, darling, Sam's just done it."

"But we always put each other's sunblock on."

"Well, you weren't here."

"Well, I wasn't exactly emigrating. Couldn't you have waited?"

As she noticed Julie and I staring at her, she laughed and said that her stroppy gland was working overtime and to ignore her. Then she gave me my ice cream.

"Enjoy your raspberry sauce, Sam," she said.

"Thanks, Karen."

"Raspberry sauce," Alex said.

"Fuck off, Alex," I said.

28

In September, England played another qualifier for the World Cup Finals. Once again I made it into the squad and onto the subs bench.

It was a home game against San Marino. Comparing the two teams was like comparing Lake Superior to a puddle. England were a team of highly paid, highly trained full-time professionals; San Marino were a bunch of accountants, mechanics and firemen who got together occasionally to knock a ball about. *But* they had guts and fight and determination and, although I didn't even know where San Marino was, we weren't going to treat them with any less respect than we would Germany or Brazil.

We won. 8-0.

I was brought on in the 60th minute. Their fitness levels were obviously going to be inferior to ours and my job was to run them into the ground. We scored five goals in that final half hour. Mine came in the 86th minute. We'd won a free kick about twenty yards out on the right side of the pitch. Steve thundered it against their wall and it bounced out to me just inside their penalty area. Unfortunately it came toward me at a really awkward angle and I was forced to flip the ball over my head with my left foot before twisting and cracking a volley past their keeper.

It was, according to the press, the pick of the goals, though, to be honest, it was far less spectacular than it actually looked and, if it had gone another few centimetres to the right, would have been just another speculative effort on goal.

We had, of course, been expected to win comfortably, but eight goals were still worth celebrating.

So we did. I'd invited a small army to the Player's Lounge afterwards. Julie, Joe, Alex, Karen, Gran and Gramps. Andrius, Susie and Rachel were all deeply ensconced in after-match analysis when I arrived; Gran, the self-appointed guru of the game, leading the way with her extensive knowledge, correcting even Gramps if she disagreed. Gramps knew four times as much about football but was, of course, too much of a gentleman to say so.

Alex and Karen met Gran and Gramps and Joe and Andrius for the first time. As with everyone I know, the whole bunch seemed to get on really easily without any of the usual social stuttering of the first meeting.

That is, with the exception of Joe and Alex. I couldn't hear what they were saying but it wasn't exactly an epic conversation and their expressions ranged between guardedness to a barely concealed disinterest.

This was confirmed a bit later when I was chatting to Joe.

"That Alex is a stuck up twat, isn't he?"

"Not really. Once you get to know him, he's actually a nice guy."

"Hmph," said Joe which, I presumed, meant he didn't agree.

Later, Gran was regaling Alex and Karen.

"So, you're another lawyer," she said, making it sound like there had been an infestation of them; I don't know how our Sammy does it, mixing with so many posh people. But it's nice to get to know people from outside your own social circles. I mean, *I* always thought you lot were right up your own arses but, now I've met some of you, you're actually lovely people."

Alex was diplomacy personified, saying that a person's accent didn't make him any better or worse than anyone else and congratulated her for speaking her mind.

"Oooh, aren't you nice. You ought to think about becoming a footballer," she said, slapping his bottom, "you've got the legs for it."

The celebrations went on well into the evening. Gramps had to take Gran home at 9 o'clock as she'd reached the 'what do you mean we've got to go, Herbert; I've only had ten gins' stage.

I realised toward the end that I'd barely spoken to Julie all evening; just the occasional passing comment or smile from the opposite side of the room. This always seemed to happen. There was no need to be constantly at each other's sides; no need to prove that we were together. I remember a teacher at my school putting down an unruly classmate who said, 'I can say what I like coz I'm confident'. 'If you were *that* confident', she'd said, 'you wouldn't need to say it, you'd just *be* confident'.

So Susie went home to her poetry, Rachel to Quentin, Andrius to Rachmaninov and Joe to his right hand, whilst Alex, Karen, Julie and myself fell asleep on each other in a cab.

29

We'd been at the pub for three hours. To say we were not sober would be an inadequate description.

At around 10 o'clock and, after Julie had beaten Alex at pool for the second time that evening and I, lager-fuelled, had relentlessly taken the piss out of him, a bunch of Taddersham fans came in. Nice guys, all in their late teens.

We were sitting in a far corner and, as they were ordering drinks and looking around for a spare table, one of them spotted me.

There then followed some finger-pointing and taps on shoulders before all six of them walked very sedately over to our table. They stood for a few seconds before one was pushed unceremoniously to the front.

"Erm… we're like *really* sorry to interrupt, but we were wondering if we could have your autograph."

"Of *course* you can," said Karen, grabbing the proffered beer mat and pen, "what's your name?"

"Er..."

The four of us began to laugh and then the lads caught on as well and I signed eight beer mats and shook hands and chatted with them and, twenty minutes later, when they were still there, Julie announced that we had to leave as I had training in the morning (which I didn't) and so we got up, shook hands all over again and walked back to our flat.

"Do you mind that happening all the time?" Karen asked.

"No," I said, "without them, I wouldn't have a job."

"What does it feel like, though, to have that much adulation?"

"It's not adulation; I just score goals for the team we love. It's like bonding."

"Bollocks."

"You need to learn to speak your mind, Karen."

"They were totally in awe of you. You're like some sort of god to them."

"I'm lucky in that the thing that I'm good at happens to be the nation's favourite sport."

"Do you like it?"

"I can't say I don't like it but, if it didn't happen, it wouldn't bother me."

"I only live with him because he's sort of famous," said Julie.

We fell in the front door.

I was ordered to pour gin whilst the other three arranged themselves in varying degrees of slumping, slouching or, in Alex's case, falling on the floor.

"Oh, I didn't tell you," said Karen, "our flasher came back today, wanting to renew his membership."

"Did you tell him you'd seen enough of his member for one year", said Alex, collapsing in hysterics at his own joke.

"They should bring back hanging for flashers," said Julie, "there could be two types; 'Hung' and 'Well Hung'."

"It's very much a gender thing though, isn't it? I mean, if women started flashing, how many men would you see running to fetch a policeman?" I said.

"Just gay ones," Karen said. "You know what I think? I think we should have stickers, like they have on cars, but for men and women."

"Right," said Alex, "so on women's, instead of *My other car's a Rolls Royce* we could have *My other mood's bloody awful as well.* Or *Baby on board – no sex for two years.*"

"And on men's," said Julie, not missing a beat, "we could have *I went to Orgasm – but I didn't take my girlfriend with me.*"

"Or *Clitoris is not a Greek island.*"

"I think it's simply a lot easier to understand your own gender," said Alex.

"Then maybe we should live as the opposite sex for a week; find out what it's like," suggested Julie.

"I'd want to be a rugby player," Karen said, "they're just so... so strong and muscle-bound."

"What I want to know," Julie asked, "is what do they say to each other when they go down in the scrum?"

"'Your turn to eat the biscuit'," I said.

"What?"

"Alex will explain; he went to public school."

"You bastard. OK, there's a game that adolescents and men with no girlfriends and too much spare time play, called *Soggy Biscuit.* Basically, you put a biscuit on the floor and all the men stand round it and... well, they all..."

"Wank," I said.

"Masturbate over it until they've all..."

"Come."

"Ejaculated; and the last person to..."

"Ejaculate."

"Come, has to eat the biscuit."

"No, that's revolting!" Julie said.

"Well, not always; sometimes it's a *Hobnob*."

"I think the two sexes are becoming more alike," said Karen.

"Definitely," Julie agreed. "It's like with Sam, I can talk to him about anything. There's no macho crap."

"Exactly," said Karen, "same with Alex. He's not at all butch."

"Still in the room," said Alex.

"But it's true, darling. It's so good to find a guy you can talk to about your deepest fears, books, art and then shag senseless."

"I didn't realise that your ultimate fantasy was to shred the headboard with your fingernails whilst discussing the latest Modigliana exhibition, darling."

"Oh absolutely."

And then Karen went into that *When Harry Met Sally* scene.

"Oh God, yes; yes, *there*... oh, oh... but do you think Modigliani was heavily influenced by Picasso, or that his work... oh yes, more MORE, Henry Moore... yes, just there... there, next to the Monet... what an ENORMOUS... contrast between Monet's florid, subtle brushwork and Van Gogh's almost naïve representation of his own room... oh, oh... NOW, NOW! YES, YES... MY GALLERY IS OPEN!!!!!"

We all applauded. It was a very good performance.

"Twister!!!" Shouted Julie, making Alex fall off the sofa again.

"I hate that game," I said, but a drunken guy is never a match for a drunken girl and, within a minute, the mat was laid out and Julie was spinning the dial, giving it something in common with my head.

Alex, who was having difficulty negotiating gravity, was first up.

"Right hand on red," Julie announced.

Alex just about managed it, in slightly less time than it took Nostradamus to write his prophecies.

Karen started across the other side of the mat, leaving me to put my right leg on a green spot close to Alex's hand.

Within a couple of minutes we looked like a modern art installation. *Three drunk people on a Twister mat*, someone with no talent whatsoever would have proudly called it.

I had somehow ended up partially underneath Alex and with my arms wrapped around

Karen, so that when Alex finally gave in, I was trapped underneath.

Julie helped the situation hugely by collapsing in fits of giggles while Karen extricated herself from me and joined her on the sofa.

"I'm lying on you," Alex announced.

"Really? I hadn't noticed. Do you intend staying there all night?" I asked, when he'd made no attempt to get up.

"… Intend… staying… there," he slurred, making me start to laugh and, as a consequence, him too.

So a winding-up order was put on the gin bottle and a request for caffeine and Paracetamol placed with the hostess.

30

Why do the best times of your life go so quickly and yet time shifts into stationary mode when everything is wrong?

Julie and I were together for another year; but, looking back, it seemed like a couple of months. It was as if Concord had flown by and whisked our time together on board, flying us to our destination at the speed of sound. I didn't want that. I wanted some cranky old plane; the next version up from that motorised clothes airer that the Wright brothers flew; something that had to land every three minutes; something that would make Julie's return to Australia seem like it was a hundred years away.

Neither of us ever mentioned her leaving, but as the time drew closer, it was inevitable that something would have to be said and that the someone to say that something would have to be Julie.

We were in our favourite restaurant when she announced that she'd had a brainwave.

I think I must have looked sceptical because she said:

"Sammy, don't look sceptical."

"So, what *is* this brainwave then? Have you sorted out the world's energy problems?"

"Yes. Use less."

"Um, very good. And how many years and special committees did it take to come to that conclusion?"

"None. We're not politicians; we don't need a decade to state the bloody obvious and then ignore the conclusions."

"So, what is it really?"

"Why don't you come back to Australia with me?"

"Well, I…"

"OK, that's probably not the most direct answer I've ever been given."

"I just wasn't expecting the question, that's all. Look, why don't we talk about it nearer the time?"

"Sammy," she said, taking my hand, "it *is* nearer the time. I leave in a month."

"Then ask for an extension."

"I did. You know that."

"Then ask again."

"There's no point. It was only ever going to be for two years."

"But Alex's dad loves you."

"Yes, but they don't need me and I have to go back to my old company in Adelaide. I have no choice. We both knew from the outset that we had a limited time together."

"Yes."

"So, what do you think?"

"I don't know."

"Just imagine. A fabulous new lifestyle, amazing weather, wall to wall sunshine. And you could easily get a transfer to an Aussie team. They'd be falling over themselves to sign you. You said yourself it's what players do toward the end of their careers."

"I'm thirty, Julie, I've still got another five or six years."

"Yes, sorry."

"Julie, I… I don't want to lose you; I don't want you to go; but I need to be here because of England. I love you; Can't you… I mean, I could…"

"Darling, you're not making any sense."

"I know. It's something I'm very good at."

"Look, it's just a suggestion. I have to go back. We *have* to deal with this."

"So, the choice is that I come over there or we…"

"Say it, Sammy. It has to be said, because," her voice cracked, "it's probably what's going to happen."

A tear began to pool in her eye and I took her hand to comfort her, but I knew, as my own eyes began to fill, that it would be an impossibility for me to do so.

"No." she said, "we're not doing this, Samuel, OK? We're not going to cry. We're going to spend the next month having a blast and, at the end of it, you're going to take me to the airport, I'm going to fly home to Oz and you're going to go to training. After that, we'll both weep a lot for a couple of weeks and then we'll begin to adjust. And, whatever happens in the future, promise we'll always be friends and always stay in touch. Come on, football star, you can do it."

I retracted the tears, blew my fringe out of my eyes and gave her my best smile.

"And your hair needs cutting; you won't be able to see to score soon."

"At least I'll have an excuse when I miss."

She laughed. And then she cried while I held her and the waiter waited twenty minutes before asking us for our dessert order.

The month passed in the space of an eye-blink. We stretched each day as much as we could, staying up till we could no longer keep awake. We filled every moment. Every second became a tiny particle of gold dust, not to be spilled.

We spent several evenings with Alex and Karen, all of us feigning normality; indulging in our private sayings, our private sarcasms, as though they would continue for years.

Our sex life became even more meaningful, more frantic, at times almost frenzied with this need to fuse ourselves as hard as possible so that we may be held forever in some permanent orgasm.

Julie said her goodbyes to Gran and Gramps and to Joe, Susie and Rachel. She had two Bon Voyage parties; one for the company, the other for friends.

We did the little things we loved about each other as often as we could. She bought me ice cream smothered in raspberry sauce every day, I would throw toast every morning, she would curl up in my arms and sip her coffee from the wrong side of the mug and she would tell me we could see St Paul's Cathedral from our kitchen window.

And when she began to pack her things, I pretended it was for a holiday. When she removed her books from mine, her CDs from mine and finally her body from mine, we kept smiling, kept encouraging each other, kept reinforcing this special reality as she called it. And, although we both knew it was make-believe, we continued with it because it was easier that way.

At 5 o'clock on a particularly cold early October morning, we put her things in the Jeep and I drove her to Heathrow. We talked as if we would only be apart for a few hours and would be meeting up for lunch later.

We sat in the concourse, munching croissants, drinking coffee, commenting on a woman's ghastly orange and purple boots.

At the departure gate she pushed my fringe out of my eyes and we looked at each other and said 'I love you' which is a phrase that either makes you smile or cry. So we cried until someone told Julie she really had to board. We looked at each other for one final time and could not say goodbye; so we turned and walked away, neither of us able look back.

I cried as I drove to work, I cried during training, I cried when Andrius took me for lunch. And when I got home, I shut the front door and cried for the rest of the day.

31

She Skyped me when she got home. She said she could see St Paul's from her kitchen window. I laughed and then she showed me the tiny model of the cathedral that she'd taken with her.

We chatted for an hour; then I had to go to training. Half of me felt like I'd lost her all over again and the other half felt happy because I'd seen her.

We Skyped every day for the first week and then every other day during the second. By the end of the month it was down to a couple of times a week and both of us realised, by mutual consent, that we were beginning to withdraw from each other.

I got used to having the bed to myself, got used to singing badly as I burned my breakfast, got used to my singledom again and took some comfort in the fact that I had survived it many times before; on several occasions, actually enjoying it.

I missed her terribly. A loss that eventually fell by a couple of percentage points each day until the practical, survival mode kicked in and I could see that there would be a new chapter now that the old one had ended. I just needed to have the balls to turn the page.

My friends were amazing. I barely cooked one meal for myself in the first month. Andrius treated me to just about every expensive restaurant in London, Joe took me to a couple of concerts and fed me lager and burgers, Gran and Gramps wouldn't let me leave their bungalow until I'd put on twenty pounds in saturated fat and, of course, Alex and Karen had me over to their flat on every evening that I wasn't doing any of the above.

Eight weeks after Julie had gone back, I got a call from Alex. 'Was I doing anything that evening'? 'No'. 'Could he come round? Nothing to worry about'.

"What is it?" I said.

"Doesn't matter," he said.

"It mattered enough to ring me."

"No, it's not fair on you."

"Don't make me say it again, Alexander."

"I've broken up with Karen."

"Mate, I'm so sorry. What happened?"

"Lots of things, Sam. We've never really been right for each other. She kept saying she wasn't upper class enough for me. Naturally, I said that it didn't matter, which it didn't. I know I'm a snob, but not when it comes to personal relationships. And she was getting so controlling. I couldn't go out on my own without handing her my itinerary before I went."

"Look, Alex, I've got to go; I'm doing an interview with a newspaper in five minutes. It'll hurt now, but it's the right thing to do. Come round about 8 o'clock and I'll have the gin bottle ready."

"Thanks, Sam and good luck with the interview."

Apparently Karen had thrown a final fit because he and I had played tennis four days ago without giving her enough warning and she'd threatened to leave. So he told her to go, which she did. Then she tried to come back the next day but he'd said no.

"So, this happened four days ago?"

"Yes."

"Then why didn't you tell me straight away?"

"Because of you and Julie."

"Alex, that's really nice of you and very typical if I may say, but you *have* to tell me these things. I'm fine with Julie being back in Oz now. We'll stay friends but, of course, the relationship is over. We've both emotionally moved on, because we have to."

He told me how guilty he felt about finishing it but also how relieved he was (which he was also guilty about). I told him that he was brave to do it and that I was going to anaesthetise the wound by pouring him the largest gin he'd ever had. There wasn't much resistance.

He was very unhappy. I tried to say the right things, but mostly, just listened.

"Another gin?"

"Sam, we've had four already; that's about twelve in real terms."

"Small one?"

"What are the chances of you pouring a small one?"

"About the same as me becoming an astronaut."

He smiled for the first time that evening and said:

"OK, as long as you've got something large enough to put it in; like a Greek urn or a claw-foot bathtub. Can you remember the first time you broke up with a girl?"

"God, yes. Messy. But it's something you have to learn. A rite of passage, if you like."

"Yes, like losing your virginity."

"Yes", I said, "that's certainly a rite of passage. Or a wrong of passage in my case."

"Why was that?" he asked and I told him the bus stop story.

"I remember mine," he said, "doesn't seem like eleven years."

"Eleven?" Hang on, but you're thirty-one!"

"Yes."

"Which made you twenty."

"Congratulations, Pythagorus."

"But..."

"Yes?"

"Nothing."

"Erm, was the word 'late' going to figure in your next sentence?"

"... Possibly."

"Don't worry, I have no problem with losing my virginity in my twenties. It's not a race and I hadn't met the person I wanted to lose it to."

"But, didn't you, like, experiment at school?"

"I went to an all-boys school and, contrary to popular opinion, buggery is not a compulsory subject on the public school syllabus. Look, thanks for listening."

"Anytime; it's my job."

"I'm glad we became friends, Sam."

"Me too."

"Gosh, I'm drunk. What a piss-awful day. Lost a case as well."

"Didn't you ever want to do something else, Alex? You know, become a hip-hop star or a breeder of rare goldfish? Just seems so Victorian, your dad moulding you to tow the family line."

"I was very lucky, Sam. I had everything I ever wanted when I was growing up."

"Did your dad hug you?"

"No."

"Then you didn't have everything you wanted, did you."

"In comparison to the majority of children I was extraordinarily lucky."

"It's just that, from what you've told me, your dad makes Attila the Hun sound like Bob the Builder."

"That's just his way."

"Yeah, but you could say that about the Yorkshire Ripper, couldn't you? 'Oh yeah, he murdered lots of people, but that's just his way'."

"He can be a bit stand-offish and somewhat dictatorial, but he's very fond of us and very protective. He just... isn't emotional, that's all."

"You're not like him."

"Aren't I?"

"No."

"What about your parents? What's your dad like? Sam?"

"Don't ask me, Alex. Ask me when I'm sober."

"Sam, what's…"

I must have looked hopeless or something. I was too drunk to know what my face was doing. Alex staggered over to my sofa and sat next to me.

"Sam, what happened?"

"It doesn't matter."

He put his arm round my shoulder and lifted my head.

"Sam, please tell me."

"He didn't speak to me for most of my life. Then he tried to strangle me."

"Oh my God. Do you ever see him now?"

"He's dead."

"Oh Sam, I'm so sorry."

The memory of the next bit is blurred; like trying to watch a scene through a frosted window. I remember suddenly missing Julie again. I remember my 'father' with his hands round my neck. Then I saw Alex, with such genuine pity in his eyes. I remember looking at his face, at how close his was to mine. I remember our lips meeting. I remember considering pulling away; and then I remember not wanting to.

32

I don't remember how long the kiss lasted, though.

Alex stood up with a start, as if a Colonel had walked into the room and he was standing to attention.

"I'm sorry," he said, "I don't know why I did that."

Any analytical powers that may have been left had been washed away on a tide of gin.

"Don't worry," I said.

"I was completely out of order. Look, nobody must know about this."

"Well, I wasn't going to make a poster and stick it in the window."

"I'm going."

"Alex, don't be… don't be ridiculous. You're pissed."

"Going anyway."

"Don't be stupid," I said, barring his way.

"We didn't kiss!" he said.

"OK," I said.

"Let me through."

"No. No, you stay in the spare room; s'too late for you to go."

"I'll get a cab."

"No."

"Let me THROUGH!"

Not being able to judge the strength needed to push me, he threw me against the wall. As my head cannoned off it, I was nearly parted from my senses.

"I'm sorry. I didn't mean to... I just meant to move you..."

I think he left at that point. I'm not sure.

I woke up at 4 a.m. and managed to stagger to my bed. When I awoke properly at around midday, it took me a few moments to remember what had happened. I also tried to rate my hangover on a scale of one to a hundred but gave up when I realised I would have to add extra numbers.

For a while I tried to work out why we did what we did. A couple of ideas washed around my head for a while but the hangover soon drove them away.

The only thing I did for the rest of the day was to ring Alex's mobile. It went straight to voicemail, so I called his office and was informed that 'Mr Harewood had called in sick'. At least I knew then that he was alright and had got home. The rest could wait until I felt better.

The following day, all that remained of the hangover were the remnants; that annoying background element that induces comments like 'never again – *really*, this time'.

I rang Alex. Voicemail again. I rang later. Same thing. I rang about a dozen times during the next few days. He didn't answer once. I got the message.

At first it worried me. I wanted to talk about what had happened between us. Strangely, I wasn't embarrassed by it. I wasn't shocked or particularly bothered either. I was, however, slightly bothered by the fact that I *wasn't* bothered.

I wanted to ask him why he had done it; what he felt. Did he think it was just the alcohol? Had he ever done anything like that before?

But, after four days of no communication, I began to get really annoyed. If he was such a good friend, why was he hiding from me? Was he breaking off our friendship?

And, anyway, I wanted to see him.

Joe came round during the week to cheer me up because 'I know you're still missing your gorgeous girl' and we spent a night chatting and watching films. He had a couple of beers but I still couldn't face alcohol. When he asked why, I told him about getting absolutely drunk with Alex. Obviously I left out the bit about the kiss.

"Oh right," he said, "Julie's toffee-nosed boss."

"Well, he's not really toffee-nosed. He's actually become a good friend."

"How are you, Hatch? You seem distracted."

"I'm good. Just..."

"Still missing her, then."

"Yeah. Not as bad now, of course, but sometimes it still hurts."

"She was a lovely girl," he said, frowning.

"She's still *alive*, Joe."

"Yeah, I know, but she's not here. Sorry, mate."

"Thanks. You know, it would be really great to see you settle down. You have a different girl every week."

"Yeah, I change them as often as I change my underwear."

"Then you need to get more girlfriends, you dirty sod! In all the years I've known you, you've never actually had a relationship."

"No."

"Why?"

"For God's sake, Hatch, you're beginning to sound like my mother. Because I'm a walking sex machine. I like sex and I like my mates and I don't want to be tied down."

The next day Andrius and I took in an exhibition at the Portrait Gallery. Then we went for a very expensive meal and had one of those conversations where we discuss a single subject for hours. I *would* say it allowed my intellectual self to come to the fore, but I don't have one. However, it always made me feel like getting a second-hand one from somewhere. I loved my time with him. We were great friends but without the emotional attachments that I had with Alex and Joe. He was just a damn good friend that I could trust implicitly.

Eight days after Alex had thrown me against the wall, he rang.

"Yes?" I said.

"Sam, I need to talk to you."

"Yeah, I needed to talk to you, but you weren't around and I'm not entirely sure I want to now."

"Please. Can I come round to yours?"

"No", I said, "I'll come to yours."

'That way, I can leave when I want to', I thought.

33

I was still angry. Very angry. I don't like losing friends when the situation can be resolved by talking.

But I was also confused. Confused about *why* I was so angry with him.

"Thank you for coming over," he said, "I have some things I need to say."

"Yeah, well we could have done that during the week you ignored me."

"I thought it was best."

"What, to finish our friendship?"

"What?"

"Well, that's what you've effectively done."

"You don't mean that?"

"Yes. Yes I do. A *friend* would have talked it through."

"I couldn't deal with the situation. That was all, Sam."

"You're a lawyer. You're *supposed* to deal with situations."

"I thought we shouldn't see each other. You... you made me look at myself in a different light; and it scared me."

"What do you mean?"

"When we grow up and start dating, we lose our innocence. Not so much sexual innocence, but innocence of thought and purpose. We have to become a different person. We begin playing a role; protector, provider, socialite, two-dimensional cardboard cut-out. We have to conform to all the blinkered regulations and unnecessary moralities. We lose the ability to think freely, as adolescents do; to find the world an exciting and challenging place.

You make me forget all this silly convention; convention that I epitomise. I don't have to vet my thoughts so they will sound acceptable to the so-called rule-makers, whose thoughts are probably far worse than most of ours. How much more dangerous is a hidden thought than an expressed one? No one should stop being a child, Sam. Tasting a drop of your dad's wine for the first time and pretending to be drunk; running through grass that's almost as tall as you; wanting to touch things - the bark of a tree, a cow's nose and being completely satisfied with that experience should the moment never happen again. Please don't end our friendship, Sam, please. You're my best friend."

The speech, beautiful as it was, sounded just a little too rehearsed.

"Then you should treat me as one."

"I'm sorry, I was wrong."

"You really upset me, Alex."

"I didn't mean to. I'm a fuckwit. I'm sorry"

'Fuckwit' wasn't rehearsed, though.

"Alright, you're forgiven, you fuckwit."

He smiled.

"Not exactly Elizabeth Barrett-Browning, but it'll do."

"Elizabeth Barrett-Browning? Didn't she make biscuits?"

"Oh God and we have to something about your culture level."

"I was joking. I know who she is. 'How do I love thee? Let me count the ways'. And there's nothing wrong with my culture level. Andrius even took me to an opera last year."

"Oh? Which one?"

"Erm… the one with lots of singing and costumes and shit."

"Singing and costumes and shit?"

"Yes."

"Well, that narrows it down."

"Shut up."

I sat next to him on the sofa.

"I nearly passed out when you threw me against the wall."

"I'm sorry. I was scared and drunk," he said.

"You actually cut my head."

"Oh God, where?"

"Just here."

We knelt, facing each other, whilst he searched through my hair for the cut.

"There's nothing there," he said.

"Well, there was."

He was holding my face again. We both knew what was going to happen, so neither of us tried to stop it.

I closed my eyes and waited for the impact. The thrill of something new and the comfort of something known surged down my spine and, as his tongue sought mine, I gave in to a force more powerful than me.

We kissed and I slowly undid the buttons on his jeans. As I slid his pants down, I explored his cock in my hand; familiar movement, only someone else's. And, as he took mine and a whisper of oyster breath told me that this was OK, I relaxed and we moved for each other, mouths and hands in unison, until we were spent.

That's all we did that night. I imagine this is what it must be like for public schoolboys who, giving in to uncomplicated love for their friend, take them in their hand for the first time.

34

I didn't question what was happening between us. Looking back I wonder why I didn't.

I've always been easily led, but I'm not entirely sure he was always leading. If he was, I acquiesced without any disagreement.

I didn't even consider what we were doing. I didn't judge it; I didn't search for reasons or excuses.

There can only really be two explanations for this. Maybe I was in denial and not to analyse the situation was the easiest option. Or maybe there were no problems to solve because there were no questions to answer.

Whatever it was, I had accepted this new addition to my life as if I'd known all along that I would end up having a relationship with a man.

I'd always been happy with girlfriends. Until Julie, though, my closest friends, my confidantes if you will, were guys. Looking back, I suppose you could say that my relationships with my girlfriends had not been a series of colossal successes. 'Failures' would also be too strong a description. 'Varying degrees of non-event' possibly?

Until Julie.

Of course, I'd always been tactile with my close male friends. Seb, New Tommy; Davey especially. And this was evident, too, in my footballing life. In the changing rooms, on the playing field, within the bubble of our own environment, there was no embarrassment at the touch of physicality. It was a weird mixture of masculinity and the innocence of boys at play. If Freud had still been around, he would, no doubt, have refereed the game; black shorts and shirt, blowing the whistle at every point where the aggression of physical contact, the feigned machismo of the play fight, the touch of crotch on crotch at the scoring of a goal, could be construed as a muslin-veiled substitute for sex.

I don't know.

I had never considered why. If you constantly analyse life, there's no time left to live it. This is just what we did and I accepted it. Perhaps some of the guys got some sexual pleasure throwing doughnuts at Joe's erection; perhaps it was just a game. We all have erections. We all eat doughnuts. Who knows?

There was one occasion when Joe and I were just in our pants in a hotel room. For some reason he hugged me and I could feel his cock pressing up against me. After a few seconds, I began to get aroused. I pulled away but I think he noticed as he glanced down there. I don't know why this happened. The closeness of touch of someone you love? The fact that I hadn't had sex for several months?

Prisoners use each other. Soldiers at war use each other. Perhaps because there are no women. Perhaps because there is some comfort in it, some escape from their situation.

And many of them fall in love with each other. Maybe then, the brute physicality of the sexual act brings down the masculine barriers, the pre-set extents of male behaviour and allows real feelings to surface.

Perhaps sometimes people fall in love and then have sex. Perhaps, at other times, people need to have sex to fall in love.

I don't know.

All I know is that, when I awoke the next morning, Alex's breathing falling rhythmically on my back, I felt no embarrassment, no shame, no downgrading of my manhood. I felt happy, I felt normal. As sunlight engulfed his bedroom, I rolled onto my side and smiled at somebody I loved.

That day he drove us to the Lake District. We paddled in ice-cold brooks, yelping at the freezing water; we re-enacted *Chariots of Fire*, running in slow motion down remote roads, singing the theme tune and being grinned at by passing families in their cars; we raced each other to the top of impossibly steep hillsides, falling over grass-hidden rocks, stumbling into rabbit warrens, reaching the pinnacle together, gasping for breath and then me holding on to Alex's arm as, in the midst of this frenzied visitation of our early years, I temporarily forgot my fear of heights.

We lay on the grass halfway up a mountain, the sun trapping us to the earth and we talked and laughed and threw clumps of grass at each other.

Then we stopped. And I looked at this man, this boy, this person whom I had decided so quickly, so irrationally, so decisively to love; looked at that blond fringe mirroring my own darker version, those perfect blue eyes shining forth the breeding of his family; an ocular coat of arms of centuries of 'have' opposite my brown almond eyes still trying to find their way in the grand scheme of things. I leant across and kissed those lips; the lips of a woman, of a man; just lips. I think the only difference I felt, was consciously aware of, was that I was not, as with a girl, necessarily the stronger.

That night in our hotel bed we tried new, alien things. We laughed when we got it wrong, were surprised, delighted when we got it right. The movements were the same as always. The feelings, the same catalytic blend of animalistic and emotional. I can still picture the first night now; an ice-melting frieze that fed the eternal roll of honour.

In the weeks that followed, our friendship deepened, overtook, though did not alter my closeness to Joe; never reaching the untouchable link with Davey, but a friendship that I would have thought insurmountable had I not known him. And Davey had been gone for what? Ten years now. Surely not that long? Surely?

35

We told no one. Neither of us could.

His father would have disowned him. He'd fathered him so that he could continue the family line, continue the family firm; not even daring to nudge the privileged status quo. The unspeakable vice of the Greeks is fine if you're fifteen and at public school. As long as it's just a passing phase and matron doesn't catch you, then you can leave it all behind and move into adulthood having thrown away childish things. Another boy's penis in this case.

I couldn't tell anyone because footballers couldn't be gay. You have a girlfriend, then a wife, then kids. All pretty early to prove that you're straight. Then your club buys you a house and pays for your kids to go to a fee-paying school. Sort of an Old Gentlemen's club, only for young gentlemen.

The footballing world had never accepted a gay player. It would have accepted an adulterer, a thief, a violent thug, but not a homosexual. There was no place on football's closeted heterosexual planet.

Anyway, was I gay, or was I just having my fifteen year-old dormitory fumble a little later on in life?

Whatever the answer, this new variant of my love-life wasn't due to some sordid, latent desire to have sex with a man, nor to a sudden need to flaunt my feminine side. I'd never wanted violent sex with anyone and had always, I hoped, been in touch with my feminine side.

Alex would come to my flat a couple of nights a week; I would go to his occasionally. We were friends; there was nothing unusual in this. The fact that we didn't leave till the morning was nobody's business.

I felt like a kid with new toy; a child building a hidden fort at the bottom of the garden to house his pretend world.

There were, however, occasions when the reality of this was brought home to me.

The first was an evening I'd spent at Alex's flat.

We'd been out for dinner with Susie and Rachel. Rachel had been regaling Alex with some stories of Quentin's success in the art world (she'd originally been regaling all of us but Susie and I have a very low regaling threshold when it comes to art dealing).

"How's Julie?" Susie asked.

"She's fine," I said, "she's currently prosecuting a fat-cat financier for embezzlement and deciding whether to have her hair cut short."

"Gosh, tell her 'no'!"

"The financier or the hair?"

"The hair, you silly; it's beautiful the way it is."

"I know, but her boyfriend likes girls with short hair."

"Oh... ah... right. How long?"

"About twelve centimetres."

"No, the relationship."

"A month."

"How long since she went back?"

"Four months."

"Oh."

"I'm fine. We both agreed to move on."

"But you haven't."

"Well, I have, really."

"But not *with* anyone."

"Well…"

"Sammy?"

"Susie, I-"

Then Rachel cut in and told me that Quentin was buying them a five-bedroom house in Surrey with ten acres and a paddock.

"That's fab, Rach."

"For my horses," she said.

"Yes, well I didn't think you were going to use it for bear-baiting."

She threw a bread roll at me.

Alex looked startled.

"It's a ritual," I said; "it's supposed to be a sausage roll. It's from when I used to be common."

"*Used* to be?" he said.

I threw the roll at him.

"Have you heard from Seb and Tommy?" Rachel asked.

"Yes", I said, "I got an e mail from Seb yesterday. He seems OK."

"And they're both still in love," Susie added, "so it's just you and me who need to find someone, Sammy."

"Yes," I said, after the minutest pause which, naturally, failed to evade Susie's radar.

She looked at me. One blonde eyebrow almost imperceptibly raised.

Then Susie, Rachel and I talked about general gang things for a while.

"Sorry," we all said to Alex after we'd realised, "it's like a massive reunion every time we get together."

"Which, as it happens once a month, is a bit over the top," said Susie.

"That's fine," said Alex, "it's fun hearing about your adventures and what Sam used to be like before I met him."

I could feel us both tense ever so slightly at that innocent line which now bore two meanings.

"Then you must consider yourself an honorary member of the gang," said Susie.

"Thank you, that's very kind," said Alex. "Has it always just been the five of you?"

"No," said Rach, "it was originally six, then Davey joined so it went up to seven, then Tara went mad, so down to six again. And then Davey left, so it's now five."

"And Davey was...?"

"My best friend and Rachel's boyfriend," I said.

"Oh."

When we left the restaurant, Alex said:

"Your place or mine?"

"Yours. My bedroom's chaos."

"That's hardly news."

"Bog off."

That evening we watched a movie in the position we'd adopted over our weeks together. I would lie on the sofa with my head propped up on cushions; he would lie between my legs with his head resting on my chest. It had been his turn to pick the film. The previous week, I had chosen *Alien* because it still spooked the hell out of me. Alex had decided on a Hungarian film about a psychiatric patient who pretends to be a lawyer.

"How could they tell the difference?" I asked, for which I got a slapped thigh.

The film had subtitles and a score written by a tone-deaf butcher who had never heard of a major key, so was guaranteed to send me to sleep within five minutes, which is precisely what happened.

Fortunately, Alex was still completely engrossed in it when his front door opened and someone walked down the hallway toward the lounge.

Alex jumped so high that I woke up. He was halfway across the room and I was sitting upright, if a little groggy, when Karen entered.

Nothing was said for about ten years. Then Alex found his voice.

"What the hell are you doing here, Karen?"

"I had a duplicate key cut before I gave mine back to you."

"You have no right to barge into my flat like this."

"Hello, Karen," I said.

"I've been having therapy for my control issues, Alex and I think I've pretty much got it sorted now."

'And storming into someone's flat unannounced with a key that you've had illegally cut is proof of that'? I thought.

"What's that got to do with me?" Alex said.

"Because it means we could get back together again."

'And dictating what Alex is going to do with his future? Yep, really got it sorted'.

"Karen, I'm really pleased you've dealt with it but I'm seeing someone else now."

My heartbeat slammed into overdrive.

"Well, you didn't waste any time, did you," she snapped. "Who is it?"

Hyperdrive.

"Someone I know, that's all."

And back down to overdrive.

"Well," she said, "I'm so sorry to have disturbed you. I took the therapy for *you,* you know."

"I don't know what to say, Karen. Thank you. Look, I would like us to be friends again. I love you but I'm not *in* love with you anymore. I'm sorry."

"Goodbye, Sam," she said, "nice to see you again."

Alex made to go after her, but I stopped him.

"Let her go. It's a big enough mess already. Talking more will only make it messier."

"You're right," he said.

"Oh and get your locks changed."

"Why?"

"She took the key with her."

That night we just slept. It was enough just to be in the same bed. It often was.

As I lay there, I tried to work out how I would have felt if Alex had told Karen about us. This was the first reality check. The second happened two weeks later.

We were walking out of a shop on Carnaby Street. I'd finally persuaded him to buy some trendy jeans and a couple of fashionable T-shirts. He was always impeccably dressed, but always just a little too 'proper'. Too many cashmere cardigans.

We had turned left, heading for Carluccio's and a spot of lunch, when my mother did her aspirating trick again and appeared right in front of us.

We hadn't spoken since just before the funeral.

The shock was so acute that I stopped immediately. It wasn't so much that she was there, more the expression on her face; it was as if a sculptor had created 'extreme dislike' in stone.

"Mum," I said.

She stared at me.

"How are you?"

"As fine as a woman who's just lost her husband and whose son doesn't care, can be."

"That's not true, or fair. You haven't spoken to me. And he died over two years ago."

"Which makes it OK?"

"No, but-"

"No, you're right, it doesn't."

"This is my friend, Alex."

"Pleased to meet you, Mrs Hatchington."

"Look, mum, we need to talk."

"No we don't. You stopped being my son when you didn't come to your father's funeral. I'm sure *Alex* would have gone to his."

"To be frank, if my father had tried to kill me, not only would I not have gone to his funeral, I would have made sure he spent the rest of his life behind bars."

I don't which of us was the most shocked. She looked stunned for a fleeting moment, then a hard hate resumed the stranglehold on her face. She shot a look of disgust equally between us and, as she strode away, I had the feeling that, in order to cope with the loss of her husband, she had become him.

Alex put his arm around me, walked me to the restaurant and bought me lunch.

It was bizarre, feeling protected. Not protection from my mother but protection from her attitude and the fact that I had, in effect, lost both of my parents.

But I knew Julie would have done the same thing.

Verbal and emotional support from- go on, say it- my partner, who just happened to be male and who I couldn't tell anyone about.

36

Alex began to come to all our home games.

"I thought you didn't like football," I said to him in bed one Sunday morning after he'd stayed over.

"I don't come to see the football," he said, "I come to see you in shorts."

"Erm, hello," I said, lifting up the duvet, "this is me *without* shorts. Surely that's better?"

"Not always. Sometimes it's the anticipation of what's underneath."

"That's my point, you *know* what's underneath."

"Yes, but I can't see it and that makes it even more exciting. And I can just picture those tight glutes gyrating."

"Gyrating?"

"OK, probably not the right word."

"Probably not."

"I'm just saying that you can see how cute your arse is even through baggy shorts."

"Well, aren't you the smooth talker," I said, rolling onto him.

"Make me an omelette," he said.

"I can't," I said.

"Because I'm holding you too tight?"

"No, I just can't make omelettes."

"In that case, I'm not going to let you go – ever!"

"OK," I said.

We stayed in that position for a short while until I fell asleep. When I awoke, I was my usual muddled self.

"Er... how... what am I...?"

"You fell asleep."

"You should have pushed me off."

"I didn't want to wake you. And, anyway, I like you sleeping on me."

"Yes, I can feel that you do."

"Yes, sorry about that. It's your fault."

"Erm, how?"

"For lying on top of me."

"The jury finds in favour of the footballer. That's a worse defence than Stoke City."

While he had a shower, I attempted an omelette. The result was something that had the same shape and texture as a melted Frisbee.

"Yum," he said.

"Is it OK?" I asked.

"Exquisite."

"What's it really like?"

"Hideous. This has to be the worst omelette in the world. It looks like something discovered in Pompeii."

I must have looked a little crestfallen because he grinned at me and took another bite.

"I'm joking, it's not that bad... Actually, it *is* that bad. It's appalling."

So he showed me how to make an omelette and I can honestly say that, since then, my omelettes have improved enormously and now taste as though I actually use eggs in their preparation.

"So, what plans for today?" he asked.

"Meeting Joe at eight this evening, otherwise I'm free."

"Um, that's nice."

"Why don't you like Joe?"

"I don't *dis*like him, but I can't feel friendship for someone who obviously cannot bear me."

"Do you know, you're the only two friends I've ever had who haven't got on? Apart from Tara and Davey, of course, but then, Tara was mad."

"Did you ever search for Davey?"

"Yes, but I couldn't find him."

"Do you miss him?"

"Every day."

"Look, why don't we go to the South Bank for some lunch and look around the bookstalls," he said. "We can spend the afternoon just relaxing; maybe walk up to the *Globe*. What do you think? Then you can go and meet Joe and I'll have some time to work on the case I've got tomorrow."

"I think that's a great idea."

The relaxing wasn't quite as relaxed as we'd have liked. There seemed to be a plethora of Taddersham fans around the river that day. It happened this way. Some days, no one would take any notice of me (I loved these days) and others I would have a crazy time signing shirts, envelopes, arms and shaking enough hands to give me RSI. This was one of those days.

Alex took it all in good part and smiled and introduced himself as 'a mate of Sam's', though the word 'mate' in his accent sounded like a foreign language.

As our food was served, the fans withdrew, leaving Alex to ask:

"I wonder if they think it's weird that you're dining with another guy."

"Why should they think that?"

"Well, it's unusual for a football player."

"No it's not."

"You don't think that they might guess that we're together?"

"Not a chance, especially after the really butch way you said you were my mate."

"Are you taking the piss?"

"Alex, footballers aren't allowed to be gay. We're exempt. There's a blind spot with the fans where homosexuality is concerned. We could go down on each other right here and they'd just laugh and say, 'look at them just arsing about'."

"So to speak."

"So, what's the case you're prepping for?"

"A man's suing a supermarket because he dropped a can of tomatoes on his foot."

"What?! Who's he going to sue? God, for inventing gravity, or his mother for not teaching him the ability to grip things? Wanker."

"An accurate description," Alex said.

After the meal, we walked back along the South Bank. At one point our hands brushed each other and I automatically took his in mine.

A few metres later I realised what I'd done. Removing it, I said:

"I'm sorry."

"Don't be sorry for holding my hand."

"No, for dropping it."

"Don't be sorry for that, either."

We were silent for a while.

"Sam…"

"I know. We've been in a bubble. We have to talk about this."

"Yes."

"Just not now, Alex. Let me get the season finished first. It's the final match next Saturday. Let's talk about it after that."

"OK, Flitcham at home, isn't it?"

"Hark at you, Mr Football Pundit."

We won 4-0. It didn't matter anyway as we'd already secured third place in the Premiership and the prospect of the Champions League the following season.

The party afterwards in the Player's Lounge was the usual happy, convivial get-together. Gran had printed out general notes for each player about their overall performance throughout the season and things to work on during the summer. The guys sat, rapt with attention, treating her almost like a goddess. 'Cleopatra in her dotage', I thought.

A few days later, Alex and I had our discussion.

We'd met up with Andrius in the afternoon and gone to the remembrance exhibition of Eve Arnold's photography. Alex and Andrius were huge fans and were locked in conversation about Eve and her life and cameras and techniques and how much more of a story a black and white photograph told as opposed to a colour one. Alex said that it was partially because you still had to use your imagination when you looked at it. I joined in occasionally but generally felt rather like a kid on a school trip trying to cram everything into my head for a test the next day.

Later, Alex and I were on my sofa. Usual positions.

"So," he said.

'Bugger', I thought

"We need to talk and you need to not use humour to divert attention from the point I'm about to raise."

"Well, I'm certainly looking forward to seeing you raise your point," I said.

"Er, case proven." he said.

"Alex, do we-"

"Yes. Yes, Sam, we do. We have to decide where we're going with this. We know where we've been and where we are, but what's our future?"

"I hate this," I said, "I hate asking 'why' all the time. Why can't we just carry on as we are?"

"We can, but for how long? Six months? Five years? Ten? At some point people are going to notice. No girlfriends; always with each other. It would only take one slip, one surreptitious kiss that wasn't surreptitious enough."

"We could tell our close friends."

"Who would then tell their close friends, who would then tell *their* close friends until the social media of conversation brought it to the attention of someone who could do us damage."

"Do you want us to finish, Alex?"

"No. Do you?"

"No. This shouldn't be difficult, Alex. Not nowadays."

"And if you were not a famous footballer and I didn't have a father whose homophobia makes the Nazis look open-minded, it wouldn't be. But pa would fire me as soon as he knew and I would be ostracised both from my family and my inheritance."

"You're kidding?"

"I'm not. And you, Sam, you're a public figure. How do you imagine people will react? You couldn't just come out to your friends, you'd have to announce it to the media and the fans as well."

"I dread to think. It's bad enough when any sportsman comes out. I *hate* that phrase; what is there to come out *of*? It makes it look as though we've been hiding in the first place."

"Which is exactly what we're doing."

"It's ludicrous. Most sportsmen can't admit to being gay until they retire."

"Are there any gay footballers?"

"There must be; but they can't admit to it, like I can't now. It's the last taboo."

"Do you still fancy women, Sam?"

"Yes, I think so. I haven't given it any thought since we got together. No, I must do. I was with Julie less than a year ago. You can't just change that quickly. Alex?"

"Sorry, it's just that the blasé way you spoke about it made me feel suddenly jealous."

"Well, it shouldn't. Do *you* still fancy women?"

"Yes."

"OK."

"And how does it make you feel?"

"I don't know."

"Sam, do you think it might be better if we just finished it?"

"No! No, why should we be made to"?

"So, what we have then is this. Do I love you more than my family and my job and do you love me more than your career?"

"I can't answer that, Alex, because they're different kinds of love. And, anyway, I shouldn't be forced to choose."

"No, you shouldn't. But you are. That's the reality, Sam. There's no 'what should be', there's just 'what is'."

I suppose I was a little annoyed at Alex for raising these issues; though he was absolutely right to.

"Look," I said, "there is no solution; well, not one that is clear at the moment. I want to be with you. If it turns out to be for life, then that is a situation we will have to face in the future. Right now, let's not change anything, even if this means it remains a secret."

"What if we each just tell one friend?" Alex said.

"What's the point in that?"

"It would make our relationship seem real. But only someone we could completely trust, of course."

I walked to the window. I could see his face straining to ask a question.

"Do you love me, Sam?"

"It's suddenly difficult to say the words," I said.

"Because you've gone a little bit macho-straight on me. Because you've finally had to admit what's going on between us."

"What does 'a little bit macho-straight' mean?"

"Come on, Sam, admit it. If I was a girl, you would have no hesitation. I'm sorry. I'll leave you for a while," he said, getting up, "I shouldn't force you."

"I love you, Alex."

"I'm so pleased, I'd hate it to be a one-way thing and I couldn't bear to lose you. I don't know what happened to me that night in your flat. I'm never normally that forward. I have no idea what came over me."

"I shouldn't worry, it's supposed to be good for the skin."

My cheap Christmas cracker joke blew away the tension and, as my hand sought his fly, my body gave in to un-judged feelings, whilst an invisible angel of fear never left my shoulder throughout.

37

That summer I played my third match for England.

This time I made the starting line-up against Serbia and this must have given me the extra confidence I needed to finally feel at home playing for my country.

I laid on a goal for Steve and scored one myself. A header from a corner that stunned Serbia, as it put us 3-0 up and stunned me as well as I'm about as good at heading as I am at training elephants.

The 3-1 final score in Zagreb ensured that we made it through to the World Cup Finals, finishing second in our group. The boss was ecstatic. We were ecstatic. The country was pretty pleased too.

Now it was just a 'wait and see' as to who made it into the squad for the actual competition itself.

The season began on a great note for Taddersham too. It was pretty much the same team who had been together for the past four seasons and that knowledge of each other's games was paying dividends. Five victories in the first six games, including two over Man Utd and Arsenal, saw us top of the Premiership, albeit on goal difference from Man City and a feeling amongst us and the fans that this could be our season.

After a 4-0 home defeat of Stoke, I reluctantly agreed to go to a nightclub with five of the lads. In the Player's Lounge I'd asked Alex if he'd wanted to join us but he'd said that he'd 'rather stick his penis in a jar of jam and stand in a swarm of bees', which I presumed meant 'no'.

We'd reserved a booth for six people at the club, which would have been a reasonable size if we'd been Hobbits.

Consequently, two hours and six cocktails that looked like strawberry juice, tasted like strawberry juice but could have knocked out a hippopotamus, later, the six of us were sitting on a banquette that held four and Joe was virtually in my lap.

"What is this song?" he shouted in my ear.

"I don't know; it sounds exactly like the last four."

"Listen to you, Sammy; you sound like an old man."

"I'd like to point out that you're two years older than me, Starkers and *you* have no idea what we're being deafened by, because *no one* knows nowadays, not even the seventeen year-olds."

"And this needs to get some action soon," he yelled, sticking his hand between my legs.

"It's fine," I yelled back, removing it, "just because I don't have a permanent periscope in my trousers doesn't mean I'm not getting any."

"So you *are* getting some, then!" He shouted.

As the dregs of the sixth strawberry-flavoured potential coma slipped down my throat, I realised my mistake.

"Come on then, you sly old fox, who is she and why haven't you told me?"

I can't lie when I'm sober, let alone when I'm finding foot to floor co-ordination somewhat difficult, but I knew that I had to now.

"Come on; do I know her?"

Which, of course, would have to precipitate another lie.

"I have to go, Joe," I said, "I'll ring you tomorrow."

"Oh, come on mate, it can't be that bad, surely? What's up? Have you caught something from her? Oh God, she's not pregnant, is she?"

"No. None of those things."

I stood up and realised I shouldn't have had the last three cocktails.

"You're drunk, mate; you can't go on your own."

I suddenly felt very tired; felt like the over-amplified pulse of the music and the carouselling lights had stolen all of my energy, that I had used up a lifetime's brain in thirty years and that this secret that I had kept for six months had eaten away everything inside me.

"I'm going," I shouted, holding on to our table and trying to plan the route I would take through the throng to the nearest exit door.

"Bye guys," I yelled, "going home; not well."

I couldn't hear what they said so I just smiled and walked away.

Then there were people dancing all around me. A couple of guys slapped me on the back. I think I acknowledged them. I think I shook hands with a girl who said something about me being her favourite player. I hope my face fell into the appropriate expressions of 'thank you', 'excuse me' and 'sorry, not now' as I angled, sometimes intentionally, sometimes involuntarily, toward the door.

When I reached it, there was such relief in my body, that it fortified me for the next stage of my escape.

I looked at the stairs as a climber would look down from the summit of Everest and, knowing that I would need the handrail, had the last-gasp awareness to wait for a kissing couple ascending the final steps to pass, their mouths locked in a superglue moment of passion. Then, like Einstein working out his Theory of Relativity, I planned the difficult task of which foot should go on which step.

With great purpose I reached the bottom with only one minor adjustment when I decided that my left foot would be the next one to move even though all my weight was on it.

I managed a 'goodnight' to the bouncers, heard a garbled sentence which I thought contained the words 'leaving early', over-enunciated an answer that I had a migraine, waited a few lengthy seconds whilst one of them (bless his heart) hailed a cab and was spirited through the London streets by a thankfully, silent cabbie.

When I got home I threw up for about an hour and answered a text from Joe:

What the hell was all that about, Hatch? X

I love you mate, but I can't talk tonight. Speak tomorrow. X

The following day was my day off, which was fortunate as I didn't wake till late morning. I showered, changed and returned one of the five missed calls I'd had from Joe.

We agreed to meet in a cafe in the centre of Highgate village, overlooking Pond Square.

I felt hugely better. Arriving early, I ordered a grande mocha and sat outside, watching the polite hubbub of a Highgate Sunday lunchtime.

When Joe arrived I hugged him like I hadn't seen him for five years.

"I was worried sick, mate," he said as we sat down and he ordered a hot chocolate. "First you wouldn't answer my question and then you just got up and walked out. It just wasn't like you."

"I know and I'm really sorry. I was drunk and I suddenly didn't feel well and…"

"Look, mate, I love you. You can tell me anything. I've been round the block a few times, you know. There's not much I haven't seen, or tried."

"You haven't tried *this*."

"It doesn't matter, OK? Don't worry; there's nothing that can't be sorted out."

I watched a couple of little kids across the road, posturing with Star Wars light sabres.

"I've been having a relationship with a guy for the last six months."

I was still staring at the kids. One of them was dressed as Darth Vader.

It was the thirty seconds of silence that made me turn to look at Joe. I studied his face for a while and still couldn't work out what I saw.

"Mate, please say something," I said.

"Who?" he said.

"This is the awkward part," I said, "not that the first bit was easy. It's Alex. I don't know why it started, Joe. I can't explain anything. I don't even know if this makes me gay. I just had to tell someone… and you're my best mate. I'm just sorry that I've waited so long. Look, Starskie, this won't-"

He got up and walked away, his shoulders hunched into his neck; hands dug deep into his pockets.

I rang him four times during the rest of the day. No answer. Eventually I texted him:

Joe, please ring me. I hope I haven't offended you. Please talk to me, mate. I need you right now. Xxx

No reply.

The following morning I went in for training, as usual.

Andrius was waiting at the gates of the training ground, as were a posse of media, taking hundreds of photographs as I drove through.

"Hey Andrius," I said, "How come all the reporters? We've been top for two weeks now."

"Sam, the boss wants to see you."

"OK, thanks."

"Look, Sammy…"

"Yes?"

"If you need to talk afterwards, I'll be here."

"Er, right; will do."

What the hell? Was I being reprimanded for being drunk at the nightclub? The look on the boss's face did nothing to dispel my worry.

"Sit down, Sammy," he said, barely able to look me in the eye.

I sat.

"Do you know why I've asked to see you?"

"No. No idea, boss."

"Do you read the papers?"

"Only on Sundays."

"OK."

"Boss?"

"Look at these."

He slid the back pages of three of the tabloids across the table to me.

'HATCHINGTON OUTED'.

'TADDERSHAM TO SUSPEND HATCHINGTON. WHAT A BUMMER'!

'HATCHINGTON IS GAY'!

Taddersham and England sensation, Sammy Hatchington has been outed as being in a gay relationship with another man. The news has shocked the football world, especially as Hatchington has been known to have had several girlfriends, including his recent long-term Australian beauty. This startling revelation comes from none other than his teammate, Joe Stark. In an interview with this paper, Stark said, 'I can't believe it. I thought he was my mate, but he's hidden this secret from me for ages. There's no way I can trust him or play with him now. He's let himself down'.

I was stopped from reading any more by the boss taking the papers away.

"Sammy, is this true?"

I could see the end of this conversation, the end of this day, the end of my contract with Taddersham, the end of my career.

"Yes, boss, I've been seeing a guy. Julie's boss. Don't know why it happened. Don't understand the reasons. Don't understand anything right now. Apart from the fact that it's nobody else's business. I just… WHY THE FUCK DID STARK DO THIS?!! I TOLD HIM IN FUCKING CONFIDENCE. WHERE IS HE? I'LL CUT HIS FUCKING BOLLOCKS OFF!!"

"Sammy. SAM! CALM DOWN!! This won't help. I will be dealing with him later. Before I do, I need you to tell me everything. You understand? Everything."

When I'd finished, he said:

"Sammy, are you gay?"

"I don't know, boss," I said, feeling a bizarre mixture of relief that the secret was finally out and abject terror at the consequences of it. "I suppose the label would be 'bisexual'. Maybe I'm just experimenting. I don't know. I wish I did."

"OK, Sammy, this is what we're going to do. I have to talk to the chairman and the board. In the meantime I will hold a short press conference and explain that you have been absolutely frank with me, that you will make a statement at some point soon and that I have excused you from training for the next week. Then we'll-"

"No, boss, I don't want to be excused training."

"Sam-"

"I have to face this. Fuck them. Why is this such a big deal, anyway?"

"Because this is football, Sammy. *You* know that. And you *will* take the rest of the week off. I would advise you not to talk to the press until we sort this out. Go straight home and ring Ivan. I'll be calling him when I've dealt with Joe. Straight home, Sammy. I'll ring you later. I *promise* you that you will get all the support you need. And try not to worry."

"Yeah, right."

I floored the Jeep as I drove out of the gates, through the clamouring press; *at* a couple of them. When I reached my flat, there were another twenty outside my building. They flooded toward me in one centipedal pincer movement and partially blocked my path. 'If anyone so much as touches me', I thought, 'I will kill them'.

Fortunately for me (and them) no one did. Decking a reporter wouldn't exactly have helped my cause; though, perversely, may have helped to prove my manhood to the unthinking fraternity.

Instead, microphones were thrust in front of me, flashes went off like a meteorite shower and a barrage of blatant, provoking questions were shouted in my ear.

"So, Sammy, are you gay?"

"Did you try to have sex with Joe Stark?"

"How long have you been gay?"

"Do you think Taddersham will sack you?"

"Did you fancy any of your teammates?"

I strode through them, looking resolutely ahead. When I reached the door, I tried hard not to fumble my keys; any physical sign of weakness or them getting to me would have been fatal. I opened the door to the building and climbed the stairs to my flat. I went into my lounge, sat on the sofa and waited for this one hundred and eighty degree reversal of my life to sink in.

Soon I could feel myself beginning to shake and, as anger crammed the last vestiges of my consciousness, I turned the TV on to drown out the voices in the street and lay for hours without moving.

38

When the shaking stopped and the anger had relented a little, I got off the sofa, glanced out of the window, they were still there and checked my voicemails. Surprisingly there were just two. One from the boss, the other from Ivan.

I rang Ivan first.

"This is the end of my career, isn't it?"

"There's no reason for it to be… but, possibly, Sammy."

At least I could rely on him to be honest with me.

Then I rang the boss.

"I'm making a statement on behalf of the club at 6 o'clock," he said. I've suspended Joe for a week until the furore dies down."

"It's not going to die down in a week, boss."

"The worst of it will. I'm going to play this down; pretend it's insignificant."

"How is it insignificant? There's a horde of press outside my front door."

"Listen, Sammy. I'm going to say that it's your private life and people should respect that."

"Like, *that's* going to happen."

"The more we make it seem un-newsworthy, the less of a storm it will become."

"But it *is* a storm. Footballers aren't allowed to be gay. The first 'out' footballer ended up hanging himself, the poor guy."

"Times are different now, Sammy."

"Are they? Are they *really*, boss? And what are the club going to do?"

"The board…"

"What, boss?"

"They're considering the situation."

"Like the bad publicity of having a poof on the team?"

"Sammy, please."

"I'm sorry. I'm just a bit… you know."

"I know. Look, I meant it when I said that you *will* be supported."

"By whom?"

"The club, Sam. The players support you, you know that, but they've been asked not to contact you for a couple of days. I'm sure Andrius will flout that rule-"

"Why can't they contact me? I haven't got fucking leprosy."

"It's just easier this way. Then there can't be any conspiracy. They will make their feelings known in a while. In the meantime, everything comes through me."

My strength was still there but the will to use it had ebbed.

"OK."

"Try not to leave the flat for a bit, Sammy."

"I don't have any food."

"Order it online. Get a friend to bring it round."

"I feel like a prisoner."

"I know. Just ride these few days, Sammy. I'll be in touch."

"OK. Thanks, boss."

"You'll get through this."

"Yeah."

You'll get through this, not *we'll* get through this. I know he meant 'we' but I was vulnerable and that syllable took away my mental safety net.

The boss did make a statement saying exactly what he told me he would. He refused to field any questions but managed to keep smiling all the way through; as he said, as though this was hardly even newsworthy.

The truth was that, not only was this newsworthy, it was the biggest scandal for English football in years. There was going to be a massive fallout. Footballers are *not* gay.

That evening, I closed the blinds, turned on the lights in every room (there was enough darkness inside of me) and tried to steady myself. I also attempted to watch a film, but could feel my concentration slipping after only a few minutes. Later, I tried to eat something but, having made some soup and a sandwich, could only sit and look at it as if it were raw sewage.

Then I rang Alex.

Voicemail.

'*Alex, it's me. Please call me back. I don't know if you've seen the tabloids – probably not – but I think it's in the broadsheets as well and it's all over the news. Joe has outed me. I told him about us yesterday. I'm sorry. You mentioned both of us telling someone to make it real, so I did... and now it is real. He was my best mate. I never thought he'd do this to me. I don't know whether you've been named; I don't think so. Look, I just need to talk to you right now. I need to see you, but you mustn't come round; half the country's press are outside. Alex, I... God, I wish you were here. Call me back...Please'.*

He didn't.

So in the fortress of my flat, my life had become one big contradiction; gay and straight, exhausted but unable to sleep, unashamed and guilty, resolute and uncertain.

I slept for maybe an hour that night.

The following morning I lay in bed, hoping that some delayed sleep would come, but to no avail. Eventually I got up, couldn't be bothered to shower, threw on a T-shirt and trackie bottoms and checked the window, knowing what the answer would be. There were even more of them there.

Like an idiot I went online and checked the back page headlines:

HATCHINGTON GAY SCANDAL. TADDERSHAM BOSS SAYS 'FAIRY NOUGH'

'GAY FOOTBALLER – 'IT'S HIS BUSINESS' SAYS TADDERSHAM BOSS'

The Taddersham manager yesterday spoke about the gay relationship of Taddersham and England star, Sammy Hatchington.

'Sammy has had a lot of girlfriends in the past. However, he has recently been involved in a relationship with another man. He has been completely frank with me and hidden nothing. It is his life and his decision and everybody should respect that'.

Before I turned off this depressing barrage of overblown, headline-grabbing hysteria, I read the entire piece of yesterday's article that the boss had shown me.

'-has been having a gay relationship with another man'.

I mean, would moronic, illiterate twat would write that line? Of course it would be with another man. What did the prick think I'd be having a gay relationship with; a fridge freezer?

'Stark says, I can't play with him now'.

Was that deliberate? If it was, how puerile can you get? And I notice Stark didn't mention the time he stuck his cock in my navel and rubbed himself up and down me for two minutes.

The urge to hit something, to break something, to rid myself of this massive aggression that had taken hold of me, became too much. I wanted to go downstairs and take out every fucking reporter, break every bone in their stupid bodies so they couldn't sit like hyenas waiting on the kill, manipulating people's words, spreading the evil started by one man, like plague-bearers rejoicing in their devastation. I wanted to visit the homes of those fans who, forty-eight hours ago, were clamouring for my autograph, but who were now posting statements like:

'Fuck off, poo-puncher. We don't want you no more'.

'Poofs out! Go play with your own lot'.

'There's no place for people like you in the game'.

'Hatchington – you've brought shame to this club. We're the laughing stock of the world because of you. We wish you were dead'.

I wanted to tell these people to get a life and that we don't live in Victorian Britain anymore; to maybe think for themselves instead of joining the brainless, egocentric mob who spend their life in the gutter constantly looking down in case the rest of us, who tell them that there *are* stars above them, are actually right. As Thomas said, these people sit in the shadows, terrified to do anything in their lifetimes because they might fail, because they might get noticed, because it's easier not to try to become an individual. But these are the same people who have enough energy to rush to the front of the queue in order to criticise anyone who *is* brave enough to try and make something of their lives. What small-minded, nasty, two-faced, pathetic fuckwits are these people? What if everybody had the same negative mentality? What if no one took a chance and did something out of the ordinary to better themselves? Would they like that, I wonder? No one to be actors in their soap-operas, no one with the brains to invent the mobile phone, the notepad, the iPod; no one with the ability to perform life-saving surgery; no one to be their favourite footballer. Morons! All of them. FUCKING MORONS!!

My fist tore itself from the rest of my body and, as the impact with the wall recoiled through me, I roared with relief, screaming as the control left me. Twice more my fist shattered the plasterwork.

Then a voice said, 'this is not you'. And the voice was mine.

The anger drained from me like the final rush of bathwater and I lay down on my bed, picked up my book and read for maybe half a page, before sleep took me.

I awoke to my phone ringing.

"Gran?"

"Sammy, my love, we've just heard. Are you alright?"

"Yes, Gran, I'm OK."

"Well, you're not. I can tell from your voice. Of course you're not, my lovely boy, you're being treated like a criminal."

"Gran, it's true. I'm having a relationship with Alex."

"I don't care if you're having a relationship with the Prime Minister, you've done nothing wrong. Where are you?"

"At home."

"Thomas' or the flat?"

"The flat."

"We'll be there in an hour."

"Gran, you don't-"

"We'll be there in an hour. Put the kettle on."

True to her word, as she has always been true to her word, she and Gramps arrived an

242

hour later. I went down to let them in the main door as it was pouring with rain.

As I opened it, I could see them marching through the press pack.

"Out of my way, thank you, I'm not getting any wetter because you haven't got any homes to go to."

When she reached the front, Gran turned and waved her umbrella at them.

"Now you lot, listen up. If any of you writes so much as one nasty word about my grandson, I will personally stick this umbrella right up your arse... and then I will *open* it. Is that clear? Now, sod off before I beat the crap out of yer. Go on!"

She closed her umbrella and swung it at the guy closest to her.

"Here love, that was my camera!"

"Just be thankful it wasn't your testicles. Now, piss off."

They did. It was amazing. They just picked up their kit and shuffled off down the road.

Once we were all inside the flat, Gramps went into the kitchen and Gran produced, from the smallest bag in the world, some *Witch Hazel*, teabags, paper plates, cutlery and an enormous cake. I don't know how Grans do this, but I'm glad they do.

"I should have told you both before," I said, as Gramps brought in the tea and Gran administered to my damaged knuckles with the *Witch Hazel* and some gauze.

"Of course you should," she said, "but it was easier not to. It was a shock for you that you were in love with a man and you had to get used to it before you could tell anyone. And you probably wondered whether people of our generation would approve. Well, we had gays when we were young, you know; they're not an invention of your generation. You're our beautiful, famous grandson and we love you whatever you are – and we would love you even if you weren't beautiful and famous. Have some cake."

"Gran, I don't really-"

"Eat!"

And she all but forced it into my mouth.

"Now some tea."

I drank.

"Now, have you cried yet?"

"No."

"Then it's about time you did."

But it's impossible to turn on tears on demand... unless, of course, your upright, conventional grandfather puts his arm round you and says:

"We love you, kid."

Then it's possible.

Long after I had purged the last, hot, desperate tear, I ordered them a cab. As they were leaving, Gran said:

"And it doesn't matter what the club say, you should go out. You're not a convicted criminal, for buggery's sake. You've got to face this, our Sammy and the sooner the better;

otherwise these homophobians win."

I smiled and waved them off; and I thanked God for grandparents and the warmth and non-judgemental love that they represent.

That night I slept deeply for nearly ten hours; the *Witch Hazel*, the tea and the cake being the lullaby that carried me there.

39

The next morning I showered, shaved, made an omelette, put on some jeans and a white 'T' and began to make plans for the day; plans that included leaving the flat.

As it happened, just as I was deciding where I would go and with what purpose, Susie rang.

"Sammy, darling, I simply can't imagine what hell you're going through. Rachel and I found out this morning. We insist that you drop everything and come and meet us for coffee at 1 o'clock."

"Well, Suse, there's not exactly much to drop at the moment. Certainly as far as football is concerned, I'm persona non grata."

"Darling, with that face and that body, that's an impossibility. Sammy, how are you coping?"

"Not brilliantly, Suse."

"My poor boy. Don't worry, Rachel and I will sort it all out."

At 12 o'clock I left the flat. About half the previous press had returned. These were obviously the ones brave enough to chance the wrath of Gran, or who maybe liked having an umbrella opened up their arse.

But they were just doing their job; and I understood. However, I threw them by pre-empting their next move.

"I will not answer any questions at this moment as I'm already late to meet friends for coffee. However, I will make a statement later this week."

I went back inside where I'd left a tray with ten mugs of steaming hot chocolate.

"These are for you," I said, "it's freezing out here. Just leave the mugs by the front door when you've finished."

And I walked off to the tube.

I'd nearly got there when my text alert beeped at me.

Andrius.

Sammy. As you will know, we're not supposed to contact you. But, screw that. I want to say that I'm so sorry that you're being treated like this. It is totally unfair. You are a fantastic person and I know that your depth and warmth will win the day. I'm thinking of you and will see you ASAP. Oh and there's a new exhibition at the Tate Modern; it's a must see. Next week? Take all care of yourself. Your friend always. X

Rachel and Susie lavished huge mochas with extra whipped cream on me until I began to feel positively nauseous.

They didn't ask me if I considered myself to be gay, or how long I'd had these feelings, or whether I still loved Alex. All they said was:

"Well, it's about time you had another relationship."

"So, have you spoken to Alex?" Rachel asked.

"He won't answer my calls," I said.

"Selfish bastard," Rach said, surprising me somewhat. "Too worried about his own reputation. Well, at least you now know what he's really like."

Towards the end of the girls' lunch break, two guys who were walking down the street, looked in the window of our cafe. They saw me and immediately doubled back toward the door.

'Oh God', I thought, 'please want an autograph'.

They didn't, of course.

"Look, it's the poofter," said the slightly less ugly one, "the poof's having a drink with the girls."

"All girls together," said the very ugly one.

"So, gay boy, here's a warning. Don't you fucking come back to Devonshire Lane. EVER. Got it? We don't want your sort in our team."

"Backs to the wall, lads," said the very ugly one.

"Are you hearing me, Hatchington?"

Of course, the entire cafe was hearing them.

But, before I could tell them that it was none of their business, Susie stood up.

"I'm just trying to work out what your problem is," she said.

"What?" said the less ugly one.

"Well, the need to be so aggressive in public. It's as though you were trying to make up for some inadequacy in yourself."

I could see the two of them struggling with the word 'inadequacy'.

"Perhaps it's because you've got a small penis," she said. "Shall we see?"

Susie grabbed his cock.

"Yes, I thought so. Ladies and gentlemen, this man has a small penis."

Then she tugged it, just once. You could have cooked a joint of meat on his face in about twenty minutes.

"And doesn't get much bigger when erect either. I'm presuming you're erect. Anyone got a ruler?"

"Here you go, dear," said a guy at the back, loving every second of the show.

"Thank you, sir. Oh dear, six centimetres; *very* disappointing. You ought to get an extension, like they have on snooker cues. Make you a real man."

She returned the ruler ("you may want to wash this, sir") and sat down.

Laughter and applause rang loudly around the cafe. The apes were mortified and backed up to the door where, of course, they suddenly found the courage to have the last word.

"If we ever see you again, faggot, you're dead."

I wanted to smash their nasty little faces into the nearest concrete pillar, but there was no point. I *would* be guilty of something then and it would show that this sort of low-life was getting to me – which, of course, it was. So, instead, I just said:

"Thanks, Suse. You're amazing."

"It was nothing, darling. Literally."

"I'm just worried that this is what it's always going to be like now," I said.

"No," said Rachel, "two morons against you, us and everyone else in this cafe. The odds are very much in our favour."

They went back to work, whilst I went back to making bad decisions.

They buzzed me straight in to Alex's office. Of course they would; I'd been there many times before.

"There's no one with him at the moment," Adrienne, his secretary, said, "just go straight in."

I didn't quite accomplish that as my breathing took several seconds to bring under control.

"Come in," he said and I half melted at the sound of his voice, half froze at what he might say.

He was looking intently at some papers on his desk.

"Two ticks," he said, without looking up.

I sat down.

"Sorry about that, just going through some awfully boring… what the hell are you doing here?"

"Nice. Nice welcome."

"Get out of my office."

"Don't worry, I wasn't followed; and, to my knowledge, you haven't been implicated in this yet. I'm surprised, considering how much Joe dislikes you."

"No I haven't. And I don't want to be. It would be the end of my career if anyone found out."

"Like it is for me? You didn't return any of my calls."

"Of course I didn't."

"Of course?"

"I *will* deny everything if you tell anybody."

"Alex, cut the superficial lawyer shit for a minute. Do you seriously think I'm that sort of person? Well, do you?"

"No."

"I get it, Alex. I just wanted to make sure that your phone wasn't broken. I shan't come here or see you again. I just needed to find out whether you were really so self-absorbed that you would pretend to forget our relationship."

"It wasn't a relationship... as such."

"Oh, Alex, it was. We laughed together, we watched movies curled up on the sofa together, we fell asleep and woke up together. We had *sex*, Alex. It was a relationship."

"Please go," he said.

Later I decided to take a walk through Regents Park and clear my head. As I went past the lake, my mobile rang. I was a little surprised when I saw 'Karen' on the screen. We'd not been in touch. In fact she'd deliberately ignored me when we'd passed on the street once.

"Hello?" I said.

"So, I *do* have you to blame for my relationship break up."

"Actually, you don't. Alex and I happened purely by chance sometime after you broke up."

"It might have been chance for you, but it certainly wasn't for him."

"I beg your pardon?"

"He had designs on you even when you were with Julie."

"Bollocks."

"Is it? You don't know him."

"I think I do, actually."

"Really? He told you about his other two boyfriends, did he?"

I stopped walking.

"Thought so," and I could hear the perverse enjoyment in her voice. "Andrew, 19, the love of his life at Cambridge. Simon, 24, another lawyer; left his then girlfriend, Sarah, for him. Of course, he can't possibly come out. I do think he is genuinely bisexual though; he was certainly pretty hot in the sack. And now he's finished with you and you're suffering instead of me. I can't say I'm sorry."

"Fuck you, Karen."

"Well, I'm the only one of the four of us you didn't."

"How did you know, anyway? His name hasn't been released."

"I've been following all your… adverse publicity and I put two and two together. Oh, don't worry, I'm not going to out him to the papers, but it *will* cost him."

"You ought to get together with Joe Stark," I said, "you could write a modern day 'Mein Kampf'."

I hit the *end call* button and turned off the phone.

As I was walking past one of the football pitches in the park, there was a game being played and I realised just how much I missed it. Lost in my own thoughts, I stupidly stopped to watch it for a few minutes.

A couple of the guys saw me.

"Fucking hell, lads," one of them said, "it's the gay footballer."

A few others turned to look.

"You having a look at my arse, mate? Eh? Faggot? Look, it's a cute arse. Do you want a bit of it?"

He dropped his shorts.

"Mine's nicer," his mate said and followed suit.

"Come on, fag, I'm offering you my arse. Don't insult me by not even looking at it."

A short mental battle with my instincts ensued. I walked away; I had no choice.

"Oy, poofter! Don't walk off when I'm talking to you."

"Bum-fucker, you scared or something? You disgusting faggot."

I could hear five of them, maybe six, running up behind me.

"Do you get off on rubbing yourself up against other players when you score? Eh? You get a hard-on in the showers, looking at all that cock? Your sort make me fucking sick. They should kill the lot of you. What use are you? Keep the game clean. I wish you were fucking dead, mate."

They were right behind me. I turned. I was right, there were six of them.

"Kill all the poofs!"

"Yeah!!!!"

They were so close now. I could feel their breath on me.

The leader put his face within an inch of mine.

"You should have your cocks cut off so you can't rape little boys."

I was expecting a punch, not a head butt.

It knocked me backwards onto the ground. Then there were three on me.

"I bet you like this; bunch of guys on top of you, you fucking poof."

The blows rained down. One of them landed squarely in my crotch and I cried out and tried to put one leg over the other to stop them doing it again.

They wouldn't stop. So I lay there and gave up; on everything; even on life, I think. And through the obliterating pain, I felt some sort of ease come over me; as though, if I died now, I'd achieved more than I'd ever thought possible.

Then the kicking began. All of them. In my ribs, my crotch, my head, my ears. Through some barely-held semi-consciousness, I thought I could hear a siren. And then the last boot-studded kick landed and I was free of pain.

40

I was unconscious for two hours apparently.

The thugs thought they'd killed me and ran off. Not before two people had filmed it on their mobiles, however. I wonder what used to happen before mobiles. Maybe people helped then. However, because of the filmed evidence, they were all caught. Two of them belonged to one of the teams who were playing and the rest were their mates.

As I came round, the room seemed to be shrouded in mist; people moving as if disconnected from the floor; their voices, an entwining echo that bounced closer, then moved away. One echo moved close to my ear.

"Are you in pain?" It said.

"Yes," I said.

"Where?"

"Everywhere."

I was dimly aware of the word morphine, felt a sudden surge of comfort and then decided it would be much nicer to sleep, so that's what I did.

When I awoke again I was able to see and speak properly. The nurse, a lovely Australian guy, said 'good afternoon' and introduced himself as John.

"Hi John", I said, "I'm Sam."

"Upsy daisy," he said, lifting me into a sitting position and plumping up the pillows.

"John, how am I?" I said

"You're doing great, Sam," he said, as if I'd just stubbed my toe rather than having nearly been killed. "If you've got any beauty contests lined up in the next week, I'd probably pull out, but I can see you're a good-looking guy and you'll be back to having the ladies falling at your feet in no time."

"Um," I said, "that's debatable. So, is there any permanent damage?"

"I'm going to let the doctor tell you everything; he'll be round in a minute."

"Meaning that there is."

He bent down and whispered in my ear:

"I'm not allowed to say anything, Sam, but you'll probably have some loss of hearing. If you're lucky, that's it. You're a very fit guy, mate and that's what pulled you through."

I took his hand.

"Thank you," I said.

He squeezed mine.

"I didn't say anything, remember."

"Well, I probably wouldn't have been able to hear you anyway," I said.

True to John's word, the doctor arrived three minutes later.

"Well, I *am* pleased to see you awake," he said, "You gave us a bit of a scare."

Doctor Fitzgerald was the doctor equivalent of John. Late thirties and with that bright, happy demeanour that does away with the need for drugs and operations because you immediately feel fifty percent better as soon as you speak to him.

"So, I have major congratulations to give to you, Sam. You are one of the fittest people I've ever known."

He sat down on the bed and gestured to John to sit on the other side.

"You endured one of the worst beatings I've ever seen. You should, by rights, have several broken bones, head trauma, plus all sorts of other major problems that come with this sort of action - by morons who should be locked away for the rest of their lives - but that is, of course, just my opinion; collapsed lungs, permanently damaged testicles, internal bleeding, brain damage even, but (and, at this point, he took my hand), you don't have *any* of them. What you *do* have, however, are some very bruised bones, especially your ribs, some nasty cuts, which will heal and leave no visible scars, so those rather famous good looks of yours are intact. However and this is *the* only bad bit (he said it in a sort of sing-song, children's TV presenter voice), you've got some damage to your right ear-drum; it's not totally perforated but you'll probably find that you've lost some hearing in that ear and, it will be permanent, I'm afraid. Having said that, considering what could have happened, you're in amazing shape. Now, how do you feel?"

"Incredible, after that," I said and I shook both of their hands, "thank you both so much."

"I'll come and see you again tomorrow," Dr Fitzgerald said, "and we'll see about letting you go home."

"Thank you. Really," I said again.

He smiled; genuine; not a rehearsed 'on to the next patient' smile, but real and designed specifically for that moment. Then he nodded to John, who moved to a position on the bed right next to me, took my hand and said:

"It's going to be OK, Sam. They've got the bastards and you're going to be back to normal before you know it. You've just got to relax, sleep and heal. But take your time, alright? The next England match isn't for ages."

"Oh, John," I said, "I won't be in the England team again after all this."

"Who says?"

"I just won't. I won't be in anybody's team."

"Well, come and live in Oz, mate, we'd have you in our team any day."

"Thanks," I said.

I slept for most of the rest of the day and said 'yes' almost before they asked me if I wanted a sedative that night.

The following morning I was feeling considerably better and was officially allowed visitors.

Gran and Gramps, it turned out, had been at the hospital since just after I was admitted. They'd seen me a couple of times whilst I was asleep and Gran, in her own inimitable style, had actually talked the hospital into letting them have a spare room further down the corridor.

They came in smiling – everyone smiles in hospitals – and pulled up a chair.

Gran deposited a cake on my bedside table. "Shop bought," she said, in the tone of voice she reserved for people who had trodden dog poo into her carpet, "didn't have time to go home and bake."

"How are you, our Sammy?" Gramps said.

"I'm OK, Gramps," I said, "a bit shaken up, but just some damage to my hearing. I'm a very lucky guy."

"I'm so glad," he said, "we thought we were going to lose…"

His voice trembled so much, he couldn't finish the sentence.

"But we didn't, Herbert, did we?" said Gran, holding Gramps' face in her hands.

"No, Doris, love, we didn't."

"Because he's here, isn't he; our lovely boy. He's sitting right here, admittedly looking like he's just gone ten rounds with Muhammad Ali; but that'll clear up and, in a couple of weeks, no one will ever know it had happened."

"It's all over the news," Gramps said, needing to change the subject.

"I bet it is," I said. "I don't think it will ever end."

"Of course it will, my love," Gran said, "but the main thing is that you're OK. Forget about everything else. *You're* OK. That's all that matters, isn't it, Herbert?"

"Yes, Doris… We love you, lad."

He got up and kissed me on the cheek and my own tears were triggered by his.

"Now, stop it, you two," said Gran, reaching for the tissues, "you've got me all weepy; and you *know* I don't do weepy; that's for women who wear petticoats."

At that moment, John brought some tea for us.

"I'll leave you guys alone."

"Now, come on," said Gran, wiping her eyes and picking up a knife, "let's have some tea and cake."

We did.

"What do you think to the cake, Sam?" Gramps said, winking at me.

"It's really nice, Gramps," I said.

"It's shit," Gran said.

Andrius turned up a little later. It was great to see him but, from the moment he saw me, I knew he was wrestling with the desire to find the perpetrators and do the same to them.

He also told me that Arsenal had made a bid for him, almost doubling his wages.

"I'm thirty-one, Sammy, I think I ought to take it."

He was almost apologetic.

"I think you should, too." I said.

"Really?"

"Yes."

"I wanted to know what you thought. I wouldn't have gone if you'd said no."

"Andrius, you'll be moving a few miles away and, let's face it, the chances of me continuing with Taddersham after this, are remote. And we'll still see each other regularly; we have to; you're the only person who can save me from a cultural abyss."

"Sammy, you put yourself down too much."

He kissed my cheek ('everyone's kissing my cheek', I thought) and hugged me.

Just as he was going, Susie and Rachel arrived.

As soon as Susie saw me, she burst into tears.

"Suse, you said you wouldn't," Rach said.

"Yes. Yes, of course," Susie said, regaining control, "and I shan't. I shall be strong for Sammy,"

And promptly burst into tears again.

They stayed for an hour and talked of the future and the things they had planned for the rest of the day and what we would do when I got out and, when they went, I felt the energy leave the room with them.

I snoozed for a while and then had the two visitors I'd been dreading.

Ivan and the boss brought enough flowers to open a chain of florists.

But the flowers and their overly-cheery demeanours could not disguise the word 'agenda' which loomed like some monster waiting for the right moment to attack.

"I'm so sorry, Sammy." the boss said, "I can't believe people would do this to you just because…"

"Just because I had a gay relationship?"

"Yes."

"Can't you really, boss? *You* know how football works. Close ranks, avoid the subject; never speak against it, but never speak *for* it, either."

"I don't care, Sammy, it's a disgrace. How are you?"

"I'm OK. Bit of hearing loss, that's all. They say I'll be ready to train again in a couple of weeks."

The pause was a second too long.

"That's great, mate," Ivan said.

"Bit of a disappointing result against Swansea, boss. What went wrong?"

"They didn't allow us to play, Sammy. Scott was injured, you and Joe weren't in the side and, with Andrius' imminent transfer to Arsenal I think the team were all badly affected, psychologically."

"Better get back to full fitness, then, hadn't I," I said, testing what I was pretty sure were only tepid waters.

"You feel up to talking, Sport?" Ivan said.

"Yes. Totally."

"OK," said the boss, "how do you see yourself coping in the future?"

"Coping with what, boss?"

"The fallout, Sammy. It doesn't matter what I write in the programme notes about the club and the FA supporting you and tolerance and equality, there are still going to be some morons who will chant obscenities at you."

"Forever?"

"I don't know the answer to that."

"What does the chairman say?"

"I've spoken to him and the board and…"

"Tell me, boss. I'm a big boy. I can take it."

"I know you are, Sammy. I've never doubted that. The club, of course, totally supports you. And a lot of the fans will want you to stay, but there will be others who… well, we've discussed this. In normal circumstances there would be no problem."

"But these aren't normal circumstances."

"No. Look, you're one of our star players; an England international and our playmaker. One of our most popular players, too."

"*Was* one of our most popular."

"We're trying to weigh everything up, Sammy. For a start, how will your relationship with Joe be, both on and off the pitch?"

"Off the pitch, it won't exist. On it, I'd continue to play the same game and be as professional as, indeed, I hope he would."

"Of course. But it's also going to affect the rest of the team.

"So, are you saying it's him or me?"

"No."

"Players haven't got on before, boss."

"I know and teams have suffered as a result."

"So, it *is* him or me?"

"No, Sammy, but I won't lie and say that it would be easier if one of you weren't in the team."

"And it would be easier if that player was me?"

"Not necessarily. You're one of the best players I've ever managed. You're an incredible asset to this team and what you do in your personal life has absolutely zero to do with your professional life."

"But?"

"The FA have made an official statement saying that they support you totally, whatever your decision.

"My decision?"

"Whether you want to continue in the game."

"Why would I not want to continue in the game?"

"Look, Sammy, we all want to eradicate homophobia from the sport."

"Well, it's not working, is it boss."

"How do you mean?"

"Well, look at me! It's not exactly easy to 'come out', is it? Do you seriously think I'm the only current footballer who's had a gay experience? Really? The law of averages would say no for a start. It's supposed to be one in ten men who have 'dabbled'; that's one per team, let alone the rest of the squad. And what about the fans? How many hundreds of thousands watch the games every week? And they're all straight, are they?"

"What we're suggesting, Sam," Ivan said, "is that it might be worth considering a move to another club. You know, fresh start; leave the baggage behind."

"What?! You seriously think the baggage isn't going to come with me?"

"It's just a suggestion, Sammy," said the boss, "it's *your* interests that are paramount."

"*My* interests? *Really?* Everybody else's interests, more like. Clean up the crap and move it somewhere else."

"No, Sammy. I've said, the club *will* support you; are supporting you. We don't want to lose you but we're trying to do what's best for you in the long term. Look, what do *you* want to do?"

"I don't think I really have much choice, do I? There isn't really a place for a 'gay' footballer, is there; apart from in a hospital bed or on the end of some thug's boot."

"We're just saying, if you did decide on a move, I'm sure there would be huge interest and-"

"Don't bother, Ivan."

"And we could get you a great severance package. I mean, you won't-"

"I couldn't give a fuck, Ivan. Got it? I don't care what the severance is. I didn't go into football to be severed."

"I'm sorry, Sammy."

"I know you are, boss."

"Look, the decision is still yours."

"No it's not. The decision has been made and worded to sound like it's mine. I'm still the same player, boss. Nothing's changed. I haven't lost a foot. I haven't lost my ability and yet suddenly I'm not wanted anymore. It's not right."

I was discharged from hospital that afternoon.

When the cab turned into my road, I was amazed to see that the reporters were no longer there.

The hospital had insisted that there was someone to look after me when I got home. I told them there would be, knowing that I didn't want to be with anyone. Gran and Gramps had insisted that I spend a couple of days with them but I'd said I just wanted to sleep and would spend the night at the flat and visit them the next day.

It was 7 o'clock in the evening when I arrived home. Although it was dark, I only turned the hall lamp on, leaving the streetlamp to cast its phantomesque glow in the lounge.

I fell onto the sofa with the heaviness that comes with the final drip of adrenalin leaving your body and that sudden realisation that that's all you've existed on for the past few days; that all fun, hope and life-lust have abandoned you; silently creeping out of the back door of your consciousness.

I looked around the room and all I could see was austerity; nothing that bore the stamp of my personality. Julie had taken her things when she went, leaving just some temporary items I'd bought for a period of my life which I knew would end but hoped so much would continue forever.

Who knows what would have happened if it had? I probably wouldn't be sitting here, searching for an identity, trying to fit myself into a place whose dimensions and space cut jagged edges into my life.

I could deal with the physical beatings; from my father, from the thugs. They were senseless, but I could partially understand them. They were tangible, physical, something that made a definite imprint on my life. What I couldn't understand was the pattern of events that had changed me from the person I had been so happy to discover as I grew up, to the person whose connection to his existence had become tenuous, to say the least.

What had I done? I hadn't two-timed anyone, hadn't broken anyone's heart, hadn't suddenly become a bad footballer, hadn't murdered a child and hadn't turned against humanity. I'd just finished one relationship, left a healthy gap before starting another, scored a goal for England, helped my team to the top of the Premiership and confided in my best friend.

So I sat, adrift on the sofa; my mind, very occasionally, trying to revert to default mode and spark a happy thought or a plan to re-invent my fortunes.

But the sparks never caught and, as the darkness began to consume me, I wondered what the point of... anything was.

Fear stared me in the face. Not fear of what might happen to me, but fear because I didn't care about anything anymore. My past had destroyed my future.

If I couldn't play football, what could I do? Be a dustman, like my father? Become the person I would have been? Throw away everything I'd fought to become?

And for what reason?

Because I happened to fall in love with a man.

I was under the impression that the Nazi's didn't win the war, that we lived in a free country, that homosexuality was no longer a criminal offence. Maybe my rose-coloured spectacles had shut out the fringes of reality. The most vocal of opinions always seem to be the radical 5% at either end of the spectrum. The bigots, the racists, the homophobes, the anti-everything brigade. I wondered what it would be like if the fair-minded 90% in the middle were the loudest for once. Maybe there would be a more tolerant world. Who knows?

I'd been so lucky to have become a footballer. It had given me so much. I had done a job that I loved; I'd been paid too much money for doing it, been lauded for weaving a ball around people and kicking it between two upright sticks of wood.

And now the profession that had helped transform my life was the reason it was being unfairly taken from me.

I remembered the footage of the Gay Pride march that I'd watched on the news. Gay accountants, gay policemen, gay archaeologists, gay soldiers. No gay footballers.

No gay footballers.

As the evening wore on, so the darkness solidified and I mentally began to lose touch with everything and everyone I loved. I didn't need them anymore. I felt the fight leave me and, behind it, all the emotions, like a line of toy soldier deserters leaving base camp at the mercy of some unengageable enemy. I wanted simply to escape from this vacuum, this senseless purgatory.

Yet, from some deeply-buried place, I could hear a tiny, fragmented voice that was still me; but, hard as I sought to find it, it was swallowed and I looked up to see a shroud of hell approaching.

I didn't want to cry, to scream, to thunder in anger. I just wanted to...

I stared into the dead darkness and the world ceased to exist.

41

My phone rang.

The noise must have startled me so much that, on impulse, I picked it up. A mobile number I didn't recognise. The noise seemed to mesmerise me, the vibration sensitising my palm. To this day, I have no idea why I answered it.

"Hello?"

"Sam."

"Yes?"

"It's Davey… It's so good to hear your voice. Look, I know this is a shock. I know I've been gone a long time… Sam? Sam, please don't hate me. I had to go. I couldn't tell you the reasons then; but I want to tell you now… if you would let me. Please."

"WHY THE FUCK HAVE YOU HIDDEN FROM ME FOR TEN YEARS!!"

"I know, I know. Please let me explain."

"NO! NO, YOU LISTEN TO *ME* EXPLAIN. YOU WALKED OUT OF MY LIFE WITHOUT GIVING ME ANY REASON. ANY *FUCKING* REASON. YOU WERE THE CLOSEST FRIEND I'VE *EVER* HAD. I WOULD HAVE DONE ANYTHING FOR YOU. YOU HAVE NO IDEA HOW MUCH I CRIED WHEN YOU LEFT. WHAT SORT OF A FRIEND DOES THAT? EH? WHAT MADE ME SO FUCKING AWFUL THAT YOU LEFT…? AND… AND HID FROM ME SO I COULD NEVER FIND YOU!!"

"Sam, please don't cry (and through this uncontrollable anger, I could hear his voice break, picture his own tears). If could change it all, I would. I didn't want to go. I had no choice. I understand how angry you are, but can I see you and tell you everything? I owe you that much."

"No! No you can't."

"Sam, please. Just one meeting. Then, if you don't want to see me again, I promise I'll walk out of your life for good."

"Again."

"I'm sorry. Please, Sam… Please."

Sometimes we just need a tiny percentage change to angle our view of a situation differently.

"OK, but not for a couple of days. Things are not good right now."

"I know," he said, "I'm so sorry."

"I'll ring you... when I'm ready."

"Thank you."

After I had hung up, I got undressed and climbed into bed. Although I was enveloped by darkness, it no longer threatened me.

When I awoke the following morning, I rang Ivan.

"Ivan, organise a press conference for me, would you."

"Er, yeah, OK. When?"

"This afternoon."

"Bit short notice, isn't it?"

"If I don't do it now, I never will. And it's not as though nobody's going to turn up."

Taddersham allowed me to use their press room.

I'd been in there so many times; usually for happy reasons. I'd always had a joke with the reporters; we'd had our own banter; we understood each other. Now I was walking in for the last time. Happy memories mixed with an uncertain present.

As I entered, the usual crew, the flashes, the rolling TV cameras, were all there. The same, yet not the same.

"Good afternoon everyone," I said. "I just want to thank you for coming. I've got a statement prepared and then I'll take a few questions."

"*Ladies and gentlemen. As you will know, the past few days have not been quite as successful as I would have liked. Last week, Taddersham were top of the Premiership and I was still excited and proud at having scored for England. What higher pinnacle can you achieve than helping your country qualify for the World Cup Finals? Then, one of my closest friends in the Taddersham team decided to out me. I'd confided in him about a relationship I'd been having with a male friend of mine; a relationship whose beginnings I cannot explain, whose meaning I cannot explain, but a relationship I am not embarrassed to say that I had. I fell in love with a person, not with their gender and to deny this would be to lie to myself as well as to my friends and to the legions of fans who, apart from the neo-Nazi minority, I have the utmost respect for. Why didn't I say anything about this gay relationship before? Because of these. These injuries caused by six thugs who, two weeks ago, cheered me on and asked for my autograph and then suddenly felt the need to kill me. Why? I don't know. Possibly because football is so steeped in tradition and so slow to change that we have not caught up with the fact that it's acceptable to be gay nowadays; that we are all equal. Possibly because some people don't have the ability to look beyond the camp stereotype. Well, the world's most successful soldier, Alexander the Great, conquered the entire known world and he was gay. The Emperor Hadrian conquered a few countries and built a rather large wall; he was gay too. Perhaps it's just the pack mentality. Maybe it's a vicious circle; the fans hold us up as icons, therefore we feel that we must be straight in order to live up to that level of reverence. There are a very few homophobic players. To these I say 'that's fine; you are perfectly entitled to your opinion'; but to the overwhelming, fair-minded majority of players, I say 'please speak up and let your feelings be known'. Maybe this minority of fans are scared of something they don't understand. I have not changed. I'm still the same football player, whether you rate me or not. I love football; I have had a gay relationship. The two are not related. However, because of this current lack of tolerance within the game and with huge reluctance, I have decided to leave this club that I love so much. I would like to thank everyone connected with the team; the boss, the players, the backroom staff and the fans, for everything that they have ever done for me and to wish them every success for the future. To sum up; I don't know if I am gay. To be honest, I don't care. But, we have done our best to eradicate all inequalities in football. It is still the beautiful game and it must be enjoyed by everyone, regardless of their colour, class or sexuality. 'Different' means 'different', not 'enemy'. Thank you all very much."*

I thought the world had stopped, it was so quiet. Then a couple of reporters began to ask questions:

"How do you see your future, Sammy?"

"I don't know."

"Is your relationship completely over?"

"Yes."

"Do you still want to remain a player?"

"Definitely."

"Does it feel awkward to be the only gay footballer?"

"That would depend on whether I *was* the only gay footballer."

As I left the press room, the boss was standing outside.

"Beautiful speech, Sammy. Would you come and see the players? They want to say goodbye."

I went to the Player's Lounge where they were waiting. As I walked in, they, to a man, applauded. We spent half an hour chatting, saying our farewells, wishing each other good luck. Some I would see socially; Andrius certainly. We hugged and then, as I began to leave, I asked the boss where Joe was.

"In the changing room last time I saw him, Sammy."

I headed for the changing rooms.

I could hear nothing as I listened outside.

He was alone, sitting on one of the benches, just wearing his pants and staring at the floor. After a few seconds, he looked up. His face betrayed everything; guilt, love, defensiveness.

"Why did you do it, Joe?"

No reply.

"You were my best mate. Why did you ruin my career?"

I stood right in front of him. He was still looking up at me like a small boy awaiting his punishment.

"Get up," I said. "GET UP!"

He did.

And suddenly it all made sense. Suddenly I understood.

I flexed my fists and moved half a step toward him. I grabbed his pants and pulled them down. Then I took his cock in my hand. He made no move to stop me but hardened immediately.

"A different girl every week? No relationship in the twelve years I've known you?"

I started to pull him, slowly at first.

"Pretending you were after Susie at the party, that you were desperate to have her. But you didn't, did you. Susie told me you just slept in the same bed; that nothing happened.

I pulled faster.

"You didn't drop all these girls because you were a sex machine. You dropped them because you don't like girls."

He came in my hand, spurting twelve years of hidden love into my palm and across the floor. As he did so, he gasped and cried out.

"I hope it was worth waiting for," I said and left the room.

42

The headlines the following morning were in complete contrast to the previous days. No hurtful double entendres, no pandering to thinly-disguised homophobia. It seemed that my press conference had been a success.

Gran had rung to tell me that I'd 'knocked the nasty little sods off their perches', that it was 'the best speech she'd ever heard' and that I could 'teach them buggery politicians a thing or two'.

One back page headline even said:

'*SO WHAT IS WRONG WITH BEING A GAY FOOTBALLER, ANYWAY*?'

I wasn't pleased as such, but I was relieved. Relieved that prejudice didn't blind everybody; that, maybe, the majority of people didn't have to follow whichever direction the current hysteria took.

Later on, I Skyped Julie.

"Well," she said, "good choice, Sammy. I'd have certainly gone for Alex if I hadn't been with you. Of course, you have to allow for his total self-absorption. I bet he dropped you like a hot stone when the excreta hit the air-extractor."

"Aren't you shocked?" I asked.

"Yes and no," she said. Yes, because you were obviously straight as far as we were concerned. No, because you are very much in touch with all aspects of yourself. You're always open to new things."

"Well, 'new things' certainly covers it. And, you're right, he refused to answer my calls and then threw me out of his office when I went to see him."

"Yes, that's Alex. Doesn't mean to say he doesn't love you though."

"Doesn't matter one way or the other," I said.

"Good for you," she said.

"Davey rang," I said.

"Really?"

"Yep."

"And?"

"I shouted at him."

"Rightly so. And then?"

"I said I might agree to meet him."

"'Might' meaning 'yes, but I'm going to make you wait because I still hurt like hell'?"

"How do you know me so well?"

"We dated, remember?"

"Um, were you the blonde hairdresser or the redhead accountant"?

She wafted her hand at the camera.

"This is me slapping you," she said.

I laughed.

"How's your new other half?"

"Fine. Working stupid hours, as always. See him about twice a week if I'm lucky. Still, at least we can't get bored with each other."

"Thanks for not being surprised at what I've done."

"Darling, we dated, we had sex and we became very close friends. We don't do the first two anymore, but we're still the last. And anyway, I had sex with two girls when I was at Uni."

"Fuck me!"

"A little difficult from twelve thousand miles away, dear."

"It's been hell, Julie."

"I know, baby; but you've come through it and, from the news over here, your press conference certainly made people re-evaluate."

"Really?"

"God, yes. Look, I know how much you've suffered. 'Sammy contra football mundum' (I looked it up later). You must have felt that the world was collapsing in on you and that there was nothing worth living for. Follow your heart, Sammy. And, whoever your heart follows, bring him or her to Australia. I want to see you again."

"That's a date," I said.

Taddersham were at home to Newcastle that evening. I decided, as part of the healing process that I should watch the game on the TV.

As the players stood in a line before the start of the match, the most bizarre thing happened. I could see James was holding something. It looked like a rolled-up rug. Then he began to unfurl it and pass it to Scott, who passed it down the line until it was fully open. At which point the boss joined the end and revealed the last part of it and everyone could finally see what was written.

WE MISS YOU, SAMMY. GOOD LUCK.

Not only that, but there was applause from around the ground. Not everyone, but the vast majority.

At half-time, with Joe still on the subs bench and Taddersham 1-0 up, my mobile rang.

"Hi Ivan."

"Hey Samuel Hatchington. So, did you see?"

"Er, yes."

"Feel better?"

"Yes. A bit."

"OK. Good. Anyway, have a listen to these and tell me what they have in common."

"Ivan, I'm not really in the mood for quizzes."

"Just listen, OK?"

"OK."

"QPR, Liverpool, Westington Utd, Aston Villa, Stoke, Everton, Sunderland."

"Erm…"

"Any idea?"

"None of them have fielded a player from Bangladesh?"

"That is, indeed, something they all have in common. But, funnily enough, it's not the answer I'm looking for."

"Look, mate, I don't know."

"They are all teams that are desperate to sign you… Hello, caller?"

"Yeah, Ivan, I'm still here."

"So, shall we meet for lunch and discuss each club's terms and decide where you'll be playing in a couple of weeks."

"Ivan, mate, this isn't a wind-up, is it?"

"I don't wind people up, Sammy. I do my job. Which is why I'm so damn rich."

"Why?" I said, a little ambiguously in retrospect.

"Because you're a bloody good player with a great pedigree and three England caps to your name."

"And the gay thing?"

"Where you put your penis appears to be of secondary importance. It's how good you are at football that seems to have won the day."

"Thank God for that," I said.

"Yes", he said, "maybe we've saved the game's reputation, after all."

We agreed to meet three days later. Hopefully my head would be a little clearer by then. I celebrated this unexpected and, until this morning, unbelievable piece of news by making myself a cup of tea which, for the first time in my life, was actually drinkable and cleaning the flat.

As I hoovered, I realised that I was actually singing (not good for the music world, but good for my spirits) and, for the first time in what had begun to seem like a year, I was smiling. I really *had* thought that my career was over and that no team would ever hire me again; that I would end up back at the Deptford Cross Sports Centre as Nibbsy's assistant. I wasn't stupid enough to think there wasn't going to be *some* prejudice, but there *was* hope now. Seven teams wanted me, despite the baggage I may bring. Of course, I was still worried about the fans' reactions of whatever team I joined; but there was absolutely no hope before; and now there was, against all the odds and my hoovering had never been so good. Not that it had a lot of competition.

I rang Davey later that afternoon.

"You free now?" I said

"Yes. Where?"

"The old coffee shop. In an hour."

"I'll be there. And, Sam?"

"Yes?"

"Thank you."

As usual I was early. Jani, the barista, had my mocha virtually made by the time I reached the counter, such was the frequency of my visits and the predictability of my orders.

I stared out of the window, rearranged the flowers in the little vase, made a paper aeroplane out of my napkin, stared out the window again, decided the flowers weren't quite as I'd wanted them after all and eventually sat on my hands to stop the onset of flora-induced Obsessive Compulsive Disorder.

Each time the door opened, I looked up; obviously with so much startled anticipation that one person actually waved to me. I waved back and subsequently decided to just stare at the table and so didn't see him come in.

He sat down and placed his coffee in front of him.

So we faced each other across the tiny table. Not the slightest muscle movement; no words; just examining each other's faces. For what? Change? Age? Familiarity? To prove that the past actually happened? To marry our histories to now?

I don't know. I just know that I needed to look at him; that I wanted so much to reach out and touch him, but couldn't in case my fingers passed through him and none of this was real.

"You still look seventeen," he said.

"You look a couple of years older," I said.

"I'm so proud of you," he said, "I-"

"Don't, Davey."

"Why?"

"Because you could have told me, whatever you are about to tell me, at any time in the past ten years."

"I know, but I don't know how else to begin."

The anger began to claw at me again. What the hell was the matter with me?

"Try beginning with why you got the fuck out of my life and haven't seen me for ten years. Then explain why our friendship meant so little to you that you couldn't even be bothered to give me an explanation."

My right hand was on the table. He made as if to take it in his, but I snatched it away.

"Yes, you deserve to know everything."

"Yes I do."

"Sam, you are the closest person to me in the world"-

"Funny, I see no evidence of that."

"Please, let me say this… Sam, when we were living in Thomas' house, I was beyond happy. I could have stayed there for the rest of my life, living with you. I had two jobs that I loved and I was sharing the house of a man I admired enormously with the most valuable person in my life. Then Tara made me realise the practicality of this situation; what the future held. I knew she hated me. I knew the set-up wouldn't work with her; wouldn't work with any other girlfriend that you had in the future; certainly wouldn't work when you got married."

"But you were going out with Rachel."

"… Yes."

"Why did you hesitate? Didn't you love her?"

"Oh, I loved her; but I wasn't *in* love with her."

"I wasn't *in* love with Tara."

"No, but for different reasons."

"Yes. Tara was a bitch. Rachel is lovely."

"True. But that wasn't the reason I wasn't in love with her."

"Oh?"

"I was already in love with someone."

"I don't understand."

"I know you don't, Sam; that's why I left."

For once, I didn't need anyone to spell it out for me.

"Rachel said you never slept with her because you were Catholic."

"Yes, that's what I told her."

"The most beautiful man on the planet and yet you turned all the women down."

"Yes."

"When did you know that you were in love with me, Davey?"

"When we were fifteen. It was just teenage love then. Doesn't make it any less meaningful, but it wasn't fully formed. It was, though, by the time we were eighteen; and, by twenty,

I knew that I could never love anyone else as much as I loved you. Of course, I knew you were straight, but I would have been happy just living in the same house as you, just seeing you every day; texting you, having toast thrown at me every morning, hugging you every evening. I wouldn't have needed the sex part; just being with you would have been enough. Then, through Tara, I saw what was going to happen; that, at some point, I would have to move out; would see you with your wife, your kids; would have to spend the rest of my life pretending to my best friend that I wasn't in love with him; spending the rest of my life single because nobody could ever match what I felt for you. That's why I had to go; to try to make a life for myself. That's why I couldn't tell you, because you may have thought that all I wanted from you was sex. And that was never the case. All I wanted from you, that I didn't already have, was for you to be in love with me. And, as I knew that couldn't happen, I began selfishly to want you never to fall in love with anybody else. And that was ridiculous of me and not fair on you. I cried as I wrote that note for you. I cried as I closed the front door for the last time. I cried in the cab to the station; on the train. I cried for three weeks afterwards. I thought I would never stop. I'm so very, *very* sorry."

"I thought you were dead," I choked.

"No, Sam," and he tried to smile, "I was living in Birmingham,"

"Nearly dead, then."

We laughed. A brave, unexpected gulp of a laugh; and a tear ran into my mouth.

"I don't expect you to totally understand," he said, his voice wavering as he fought against the rekindled memories, "neither do I expect you to forgive me. And I certainly don't expect you to allow me back into your life."

"You were never *out* of my life."

"Really?"

"I thought about you every day, you bloody idiot."

"Same here."

"Look," I said, "we've got to get out of here; this is turning into *Brief-fucking-Encounter.*" For a while we walked in silence.

"Did you get back in touch because of the revelations in the press?"

"No," he said, "well, not for the reasons you're thinking. I'd been considering getting back in touch for some time, especially during the last year. I thought I may be strong enough to see you again. Then, when I read about you, I knew you were going through hell. I wanted to tell you that it would be alright, that the fascists were in the minority. But I thought you would have had enough without the drama of me reappearing on the scene. Then, when I heard about the attack…"

He put his hand on my shoulder. This time I didn't remove it; just felt that oh so familiar weight.

"And I wished I could have been with you so-"

"There were six of them. Even *with* you there, we would have lost."

"No permanent damage?" he asked.

"Not really. Lost some hearing in one ear, that's all."

"And the cuts and bruises on your face are clearing up."

"Yes, nothing permanent there, either. I looked like a bit of a battleground just after it happened."

"They caught them?"

"Yes."

"If ever I get my hands on-"

"Davey, no. If anything, they did me a favour. Only the hardliners could agree with what they did and they will *never* change."

"Yes, I suppose you're right. And you're OK, so that's all that matters."

We'd reached the end of the street where it met with a main arterial route south of the river. On the corner there was a bench and some fuchsia bushes, set just off the pavement in some small show of defence against the onslaught of Urbania.

"So," I said, "how long are you staying in London?"

"Next forty years, with a bit of luck."

My head requested a time out, so I didn't say anything.

"I'm teaching Sports Science at Goldsmiths College," he said, "and doing some private fitness training and, you won't believe this, Craytown have taken me on again."

"Of course I believe it; you're a great player. So, what made you quit Birmingham?"

"The need to stop running."

"Right. So, what were you doing up there for the last ten years?"

"Mostly, being a fitness coach for a couple of corporations. I enjoyed it and, of course, they pay ridiculously high wages."

"And... did you fall in love?"

"Yes."

"Oh."

"His name was Andrew. He was a lawyer. Lovely guy. Worked for one of the companies I was employed by. I started out as his personal trainer and then he became mine."

"Sorry?"

"I was a late starter, remember? He'd been gay for a lot longer than me."

"Yes. Yes, of course. And how long were you together?"

"Six years."

"Oh... that's a long time."

"Yes."

"Why did you... um...?"

"I wanted to move back here. He didn't. And he'd begun to take the relationship for granted. I told him the spark we'd had was diminishing. He told me to stop trying to be a poet and that this is what happened after six years. I said the spark should still be there after sixty years. He said that it's impossible to retain that level of love for a lifetime; that, once you knew everything about each other, it plateaued and then fell as you got older. I told him that you could never know everything about someone. He told me to ditch the rose-coloured spectacles and be honest."

"And?"

"I bought him a pair of rose-coloured spectacles and moved out."

"Good. I mean good for you."

"Sam?"

"Yeah?"

"It's been wonderful seeing you again."

"Davey, I'm in a very mixed up state at the moment. I can't think straight; unfortunate choice of words. I need some time to get my head round things."

"I know. Look, when you're ready, ring me and maybe we can meet for lunch. And, if you ever need to talk... well, I have ten years to make up for."

He lifted his hand in a half wave and walked off down the road.

43

I chose Westington Utd.

Not because they were offering the most money or the longest contract, but because they were a London club, the new boss told me he wanted to play me in my usual position and I knew and liked several of the team.

Ivan got the deal completed in über-quick time. I think he realised the necessity of some sort of closure for me and, of course, the devastation of leaving my beloved Taddersham was somewhat offset by the fact that I still had a career in football and would still have the continuity of living in London.

I rang Gran as soon as I left Granby Park (Westington Utd's ground).

"Gran, it's Westington Utd," I said.

"It's Westington Utd, Herbert. Claret and blue; lovely colours. Get online and order some scarves and hats, would you? Sammy, I'm so pleased. You deserve this. You see, God *is* a football fan. So, when do you start there?"

"Monday."

"Fantastic. I'll bake an extra-large cake for Saturday."

"Thanks. I met Davey the other day, Gran."

"Our Davey?"

"Yes."

"And where has the world's most beautiful man been for the last ten years?"

"Birmingham."

"God, he *must* have been depressed. So, why *did* he move away?"

"He… he was in love with someone and couldn't tell them."

"And how long had he been in love with you?"

"How do you do this, Gran?"

"Do what?"

"Just… I don't know; work things out without any clues."

"I'm a Gran. We're omni… omni… we know buggery everything, alright? And, when we don't, we're such busybodies, we just wear people down until they give in and tell us."

"I love you," I said.

"We love you too; very much."

"Love to Gramps."

"Bye, our Sammy… and well done."

If the world was run by Grans, there wouldn't be any wars; just a lot of practical, down-to-earth advice. And cake.

The next week I trained with my new teammates. The players went out of their way to welcome me. The days flew by; familiar, yet new. I threw myself back into training, blasting the remaining (and there was still a small amount of it) anger and fear in the process.

I was roomed with Owen in the hotel on Friday night. As we shut the door of our room, I was suddenly aware of this new scenario; this worry about how my behaviour would be read.

It turned out to be unnecessary. Owen and I chatted for an hour before we both stripped down to our underwear and climbed into our respective beds. I'd averted my eyes as he let his jeans drop to the floor. Whether I was trying to convince him or myself, I'm not sure.

The next lunchtime we arrived at Granby Park for the visit of Everton.

Outwardly I attempted to pretend that this was just another game but, as my head spiralled with the enormity of what was about to happen, I found this charade increasingly difficult.

During the pre-match rub down, I lay there as one of the physios, coincidentally named Sam, began to knead my muscles and prepare my body for the upcoming ninety minutes. Suddenly, even this ritual became tinged with different thoughts and meanings. I began looking at the situation through his eyes as he started on the tops of my thighs.

'My hands are just millimetres from a gay man's crotch', he must be thinking. But, of course, he wasn't. He was simply massaging a football player. End of. And, even when he moved to my right inner thigh and the back of his fingers accidentally brushed the part of my body deemed private, he just carried on chatting, without even a hint of a reaction.

So I stood in the tunnel; the torture of a million fallibilities inhabiting my body. 'This is it', I thought, 'in the next minute I find out whether I will be accepted; whether I still have a career'. Most players had publicly supported me; as had the managers and the Football Association. But would the fans? Because, if they didn't… well, no man could face 40,000 dissenting voices week in, week out.

The announcement was made and we ran onto the pitch to cheers and applause.

Then the teams were called. Theirs first; then ours, starting with Felipe, our goalie and, seven players later:

'Number 9, please welcome Sammy Hatchington!!!!'

The cheer, if anything, was slightly louder than the others. A welcome cheer, if you will. I smiled and waved to the crowd.

The whistle blew and, within seconds, the ball was skimming along the grass toward me. And, for two agonising seconds, I forgot how to play football. So I looked at my legs and inwardly screamed 'RUN! JUST BLOODY RUN!'

I did. And, after a trademark side-step of one of their central defenders, I passed the ball through the inviting gap between their right back and their inside right and Tim crashed the ball into the corner of their net.

A goal inside thirty seconds.

We ran them ragged. Tim scored a penalty in the 25th minute when I was brought down and, two minutes before half-time, I floated a cross into their area which David chipped over their keeper for number three.

Everton pulled one back ten minutes into the second half but, in the 70th minute, I passed the ball to Ben on the left wing just inside our own half and, after an eleven-pass move, I jinked inside their right-back again, knew I had an angle to shoot, knew also that Ryan had a much better chance, so slipped the ball to him and, when he scored, was the first to celebrate with him.

The boss took me off in the 80th minute. I knew why. I hadn't scored but I'd laid on three goals and played well. The ovation would have brought down the most reinforced roof.

I applauded all four sides of the ground, accepted congratulations from the boss and took my seat in the dugout.

In the Player's Lounge after the game, I walked in with Gran and Gramps and the cake.

I needed it to be normal; another day at the office. I willed myself to stop analysing every sentence, expression, movement, reaction. And I did. And it *was* normal; wonderfully, excitingly normal.

"Hello everyone," said Gran, "I'm Doris and this is Herbert. We're Sammy's back-up team. 'Medical'," she said, producing a bottle of *Witch Hazel*, "'Dietary'," as Gramps placed the usual gargantuan cake on the table, "and 'psychological', as this one's the shoulder he cries on. The other one's got arthritis and the damp doesn't help."

There were laughs all round and Gran and Gramps began to circulate.

I was standing with Ben, Tim, Owen and Luke.

"She's a gem," Ben said.

"She's got more bollocks than most guys I know", I said, "I don't know what I would have done without them both."

Owen put his hand on my shoulder and said:

"Sammy, I think I speak for the whole team when I say that, with you in the side, we have a real chance of getting near the European places this season."

Later that evening, as I was walking to my car, a sharp movement caught my attention across the other side of the road.

"Mr Hatchington!" a voice said and a huge guy stepped out into the beam of a headlight and began moving toward me. Early forties, I guessed, slightly gone to seed; skinhead, face you could use as a road map.

'Oh God', I thought, 'not now'.

I knew that, to have any chance, I had to hit him first.

"May I shake your hand, Sammy?"

"Er, yeah; yeah, sure," I said, taking his huge hand in mine.

"I just want to say, you were very impressive today. I personally think you're the best signing we've made in years."

"Thanks," I said, "thanks very much. Er, what's your name?"

"Stewart," he said.

"Well, Stewart, it's great to meet you."

"Would you sign my autograph book?"

"Yes, of course I will."

He stared at it for a while, then began to walk away. When he'd gone a few yards and I began to breathe again, he turned:

"And it don't matter that you shagged a bloke; you're a bloody good player."

I got in the Jeep and finally had time to check my mobile.

Amongst the texts from various members of the Taddersham team, was one from Davey: *Sam, you played the perfect match. I know what you were going through; what absolute hell it must have been in the build-up, especially in the tunnel. I'm very proud of you. I hope you don't mind me saying this. Davey.*

Two days later I met Susie and Rachel for lunch.

As we tore our salads and sipped on mineral water, I made the announcement that I knew would make Rachel's heart jump. I wasn't quite sure how to word it subtly, so I didn't bother.

"Davey's back," I said.

Two sets of cutlery froze in mid-air, leaving Caesar sauce dripping off poised lettuce leaves.

"He's been living in Birmingham," I said.

"Oh God," they said in unison.

I told them the story that Davey had related to me, including the gay part.

"In a way, I'm glad he's gay," she said, "because... well, you know why."

"So," Susie said, "the gang's going to be back together again."

"Sorry?" I said.

"We're all going to be back in England. Gosh, we must plan a celebration. Rachel, do you think we could use your garden. We could have a"-

274

"Hang on!" I said, "What are you talking about?"

"Well, you got Seb and Tommy's emails, surely?"

"Erm..."

And I realised that I hadn't checked my emails for three weeks, having received a few of the most vile, threatening messages during the first days of my revelation.

"I haven't actually read my emails for a while."

"Of *course* you haven't, darling. There must have been some very nasty ones. Well, the news is that Seb is sick of Canada. The usual succinct Seb reasons: 'Too bloody cold, fed up with job, bored with relationship'. And Tommy has been offered a fantastic promotion to the London office of his company and, together with missing the old country, he's moving back at the end of March. He arrives two days after Seb. It's wonderful news, isn't it!"

"Yes, it is," I said and we dripped Caesar sauce for a few more seconds.

Later that evening, I went to mine and Thomas' house and lay on my tummy on the rug by the fireplace, legs up in some clumsy ballet pose, reading in the warmly-tinted glow of the art nouveau lamp. And I ruminated at how I'd spent the last weeks desperate for dull, monotonous normality and how happy I was to now have it. Because life doesn't just piss on you occasionally, it can sometimes be incontinent.

The evening wore on and the logs became embers. My legs dropped from their upright arabesque and my head slowly lowered onto the book.

44

In the following midweek game we drew 2-2 at Manchester City; an amazing result against the Premiership leaders. Then, on the Saturday, a 1-0 home victory against Stoke took us to the dizzying heights of ninth place.

I'd met Davey once during the week. Another coffee, another melting of the ice that I had so fervently kept frozen in my hurt at him leaving. We told each other a little more about our time apart. He'd bought a flat, learnt to play the piano, got a first in Sports Science, travelled to Israel, Australia (where he saw the New Year in by Sydney Harbour Bridge) and Nepal, which he briefly considered moving to.

"Why did you decide against it?" I asked.

"It was very tempting, but I think I'd have missed civilisation."

"So, no different from Birmingham, then."

He went to playfully slap me round the head but stopped when he realised that we hadn't yet returned to that stage in our friendship. When we parted, much as a chunk of me willed all the ice to disappear, I couldn't make it. We shook hands and he told me he would come to see me play in the match on Saturday.

The match on Saturday. Westington Utd away to Taddersham.

But it wasn't for several days and I had things to do before then. One of which was to meet Lynda for coffee.

Lynda had been living in a tiny village in the Lake District for the last six years. She'd got demoralised with Deptford (not difficult) and then, in a good place financially, had upped sticks and moved to an area where it's not the end of the world if you just miss a tube and

276

have to wait three minutes until the next one.

"I'm going to write poetry." she'd said, "I want to be known as Mrs Wordsworth."

"Don't write about daffodils," I said, "it's been done."

We'd corresponded regularly by letter ('emails are for business', she'd said) and I was really looking forward to seeing her for the first time since she'd moved.

She looked no different. Younger, if anything; and certainly more relaxed.

We drank several coffees and caught up on each other's news.

"How are you?" I said.

"Blissfully happy," she said.

"Well, it's not often you hear that!"

She told me about her writing (a book of short stories published), the amateur drama society she'd set up, the view from her lounge window (a mountain and a bit of a lake, if it's not cloudy) and her morning walk across a six hundred year-old bridge to a three hundred year-old corner shop for fresh bread and coffee.

I asked if she'd heard about my revelations.

"Yes, my love, we do have newspapers up north! No electricity, obviously, just newspapers."

She asked me how the house was and I told her that I lived most of the time in the flat that Julie and I had rented.

"Why?" she asked.

"Erm... I don't know," I said.

"Move home," she said. Two words that said more than a grand speech ever could.

"OK," I said.

And so to Saturday.

Of course, fate has a very over-developed sense of the dramatic and, as we lined up side by side in the tunnel with my old friends from Taddersham, I just knew that Joe and I would end up next to each other.

So it proved. I'd dealt with the feelings of being back in this wonderful ground and adjusted to being in the visitor's changing room. Just before we ran out on to the pitch, Jorge, who was standing behind me, put his arms around my shoulders, pulled me slightly backwards and asked me if I was alright. As he did so, my hand brushed Joe's and, in my peripheral vision I could see the pained look on his face and then him stare at his hand.

On the pitch, I walked down the line, shaking hands with my former teammates. I had spent several hours considering what I would do when I got to Joe. The decision I came to was part superficial, part emotional. I would shake his hand. Superficially, it made me look good; made it seem as though I was a decent person for behaving with civility. Emotionally... well, he'd been a close friend for twelve years; he'd ended that with his actions, but they were happy times and I didn't want to deny the memories. And, to be honest, a little part of me felt sorry for him for having had to live a lie for so long. I shook his hand and looked at his face. He stared just over my left shoulder.

We lost 2-1. Joe scored the opener. I equalised in the 30th minute with a half volley from just outside their area, but Craig cracked in a wonder goal from thirty yards, ten minutes from the end.

It didn't matter though. I'd scored for my new club and had been accepted back by my old one. My past had joined with my present and my future.

At the final whistle I hugged my former teammates, then my new ones.

Owen put his arm round me:

"Well done, Sammy, the score went against you but the situation went for you."

'Another burgeoning friendship', I thought.

Joe had left the field immediately the match finished, so any further embarrassing bodily contact was averted and, later that evening, I went out with several of my Taddersham friends for a curry and some 'vivant' that was most certainly 'bon'.

The following Wednesday I took Gran, Gramps, Andrius and Davey to the Ritz for afternoon tea.

"My goodness," Gran said, as we were shown to our table, "I feel like Cleopatra."

"If only I had an asp," Gramps said.

Gran absolutely loved it.

"These are my boys," she said to our waiter. This is Sammy, our grandson, the famous footballer; this is Andrius, who plays for Arsenal and has more culture than... well, even this place; and this is Davey, who's come back to us after a long time away, plays for Craytown and is the most beautiful man in the world."

"Isn't he?" Said our waiter, placing a perfect china plate of sandwiches in front of us and raising an eyebrow at Davey.

"This is posh," she said, "no crusts, Herbert. Will we be having some of those Volubles later?"

Gramps, as usual, pretended to cough to cover his laughter and Davey and Andrius, as always, were utter gentlemen, though Davey's leg did twitch in his attempt to keep control.

"No Gran," I said, "they don't do Vol-au-vents here."

"Probably a good thing," she said, "the pastry gets right down my cleavage."

We talked for ages and, when I was satisfied that the conversation was in full swing, I withdrew for a few minutes and took in these people who I loved so much. I watched their mannerisms, their laughter, their ease with each other, as if I were watching it from the future on an old cine-film.

I re-joined the proceedings as Gran said:

"Oh Herbert, look at this place; it's just like Breakfast at Tiffany's."

"Yes, my dear," said Gramps, "except it's not breakfast and it's not Tiffany's."

Gran laughed again and stuffed a tiny apricot and walnut cake in his mouth.

"You wouldn't exactly get fat on these," she said. "And now, young man, it's time we talked about you."

Davey looked down at the table.

"What the buggery bollocks were you doing running away like that? You don't have to tell me because I know. Well, you ran away from lots of people who loved you, you silly boy. But now you're back and," she put her hand on his knee, "*nothing* has changed, alright? We still love you as much. But I'll tell you this; if you ever do it again, I will take your trousers down and spank your bottom so hard, you'll be sitting on a rubber ring for a week."

"And she'd enjoy every minute of it," said Gramps.

"Herbert"! Gran said, turning the colour of the strawberry slice she was holding, "don't be so naughty."

Then she grinned and popped it into her mouth.

Seb and New Tommy arrived back at the beginning of April, devoid of partners but delighted to be back in the bosom of… Susie, as Seb so perfectly put it.

The reunion was one of the happiest moments of my life. We met in the National Theatre cafe and spent five hours catching up on each other's news. Rachel suggested another picnic to properly celebrate our being back together. It turned out that we had all been thinking along the same lines.

"We must invite Davey," said New Tommy.

There was general agreement.

"Oh and that other gorgeous friend of yours, Sammy; Andrius. I mean, he's just yummy."

"You can't seduce *all* my friends, Suse," I said.

"Show me the commandment that says I can't and I won't."

And, indeed, I couldn't.

We met the following Sunday. It was mid-April and unseasonably warm. We pitched up a few picnic blankets on a high clearing on Hampstead Heath and sat in sweaters and jeans in the beam of a water colour sun amidst Constable's trees and grass.

"I still think it would have been nice to go back to the same place," Susie said.

"No, darling," Rachel answered, "it would be wrong to recreate that day. This will be different. A different perfection."

"Besides," added Seb, "if you were driving, Suse, we'd probably all be killed on the way there."

Automatically, Susie went to pick up something to throw at him.

"Where are the sausage rolls?!" she yelled.

"We don't have any," said New Tommy. "Sam got culture."

"Don't blame me," I said, "blame Andrius; he keeps taking me to exhibitions and stuff."

"And do you understand the art?" Seb said.

"Of course," I said, "I'm amazed at how they can colour in between the lines so well."

Rachel hugged Davey.

"It's so good to see you again."

"And you too, Rachel. Look, I-"

She put a finger on his lips.

"No," she said, "you were the best shag I never had."

"Oh my God," said Seb, "Rach said 'shag'!"

"I do say words like shag, Sebastian, I'm not some prissy posh girl."

"Who are you and what have you done with the real Rachel?" shouted Seb.

"Problem is, Rach," New Tommy said, "every time you say 'shag', a little girl's pony dies."

"Damn," said Rach, "where *are* those sausage rolls?"

And we explained to Andrius about our adolescent picnic.

"I'm really sorry, guys," he said, "I didn't think he would take to culture. I wasn't going to bother at first- lost causes and all that- but I've always wanted to work for a charity and this seemed like good practice," and he patted me on the head.

"You cheeky little f-"

I leapt on him.

"Oh gosh, here we go," said Rachel.

While I was attacking Andrius, Davey turned to Seb:

"So, what are your plans, Seb?"

"Slob, drink quite a lot, slob a bit more, catch up on all the wanks I missed during the last year of my loveless marriage-"

"Sebastian!" Choked Rachel.

"Slob for another week, wank a bit more, run out of money, then grab the first job I can get."

"Seb," said Davey, "I love your mentality."

"He doesn't *have* a mentality," said Suse.

"So, Tom," I said, emerging, defeated from the battle with Andrius, "are you happy to be home?"

"Mate, I'm ecstatic. Don't misunderstand, I had a ball in Oz; loved the country and the people; but it never became home. And there's no point living somewhere just to prove you had the bollocks to move there. So, when I was offered this managerial role in London, it wasn't exactly a difficult decision. I said goodbye to the other half who, to be honest, had become more of a roommate and got my arse on a plane-"

"An arse still almost entirely uncovered by your jeans, Thomas," said Rach.

We bantered for a few more minutes until Rach suddenly said:

"Champagne! How could I forget!?"

"Probably because you had half a bottle for breakfast. I should imagine Quentin insists on it. Do you have it with every meal?" asked Seb.

"Of course they do," I said, "and, if there's any left over at the end of the week, they use it as bubble bath."

"His name is-"

"JONATHAN!" we chorused.

"Samuel, open this please," Rach said, proffering a bottle to me, "the cork's at the narrow end."

We laughed because Rachel had, for once, not gone into a posh sulk.

"And Thomas, open the other one. Perhaps you can stick it between your bum cheeks that we can see so clearly and open it up there."

"I'll have mine from Sam's bottle," Andrius said.

I sought Seb's eyes. The old telepathy was still there. We rolled New Tommy on to his front, pulled down what was left of his pants and pretended to shove the bottle up his bottom.

"Bloody hell," said Seb, covering the bottle with a tea towel, "it's completely disappeared."

"I think I can see the cork coming out of his mouth," I said.

"You're both bastards!" laughed New Tommy.

The champagne (both bottles) was drunk but, before we took our first sip, Rachel said:

"Guys, I just want to make a toast, if you don't mind. To true friends, old and new."

"True friends, old and new," we echoed.

Then, after we had downed our first mouthful, we came, unspoken, together and knelt in a communal hug.

"Welcome Andrius," Susie said, "and welcome back to Seb, Tommy and Davey. Please never leave again."

"We won't," they said.

Then Rachel unwrapped a black forest gateau.

"For Sam," she said, "the dessert equivalent of sausage rolls."

I tickled her until she screamed.

"So, no little Quentins planned yet then, Rach?" asked Seb

"No," she said, "Jonathan's been working in Italy for ages. I haven't even had a shag in two months."

At that precise moment, there was a loud bang from close by.

"What was that?" Susie said.

"A child's pony dying in the next field," Davey said.

But it wasn't. It was thunder. We had failed to notice our sun disappear and some of Constable's clouds join the rest of his landscape.

"Bugger," Susie said, "we haven't finished the food. Let's pack it up quickly."

"No," said Seb, "screw the weather. Put the food on the ground and we'll all sit under the blankets."

"That's madness," said Rachel.

"Total madness," said Seb.

So we threw the blankets over ourselves and made one big, increasingly soggy, tent, whilst we continued to talk, laugh, eat, drink and drown in the unpredictable spring weather.

When it was too wet for even us to continue, we flushed the rainwater from our eyes just long enough to be able to look at each other.

"Drinks next Sunday evening?" Susie shouted as we headed for our respective cabs."

"Yes!" We shouted back.

I'd intended getting a cab back to the flat but, at the last minute and remembering Lynda's comment, changed my mind and decided to go back to mine and Thomas'. So, Davey and I shared it.

"You're dripping on me," he said.

"*You're* dripping on *me*," I said.

When we were nearing the house, I suggested he come in for a cup of tea and then we could both grab showers.

"Well, if it's no trouble?"

"Oh, I'll charge you for the hot water and the tea bag," I said.

I made us tea, which Davey said was just as undrinkable as it was ten years ago.

An hour later we were sitting in Thomas' room and I was talking about the match at Taddersham and the feelings that had wracked my body that day, when I realised that Davey had hardly spoken.

"You OK?" I asked.

"Yes," he said.

"You're a little quiet."

"I never thought I'd be able to come back here."

"No," I said, "of course not. Well, you *are* here."

He got up and walked around the room, touching the occasional book, Thomas' chair, all the old familiar things that had been as big a part of his life as they had mine. I told him that I was going to get rid of the flat and move back here.

It was 11 o'clock when I said:

"Gosh, it's really late."

"Yes. I'd better go."

"Look, why don't you stay here tonight and I'll drive you round to your place tomorrow before we both go to work."

"Well, if it's not too much trouble."

"If you say that again, I'm going to punch you."

We went upstairs.

"Your old room," I said, letting him go in front of me.

"Yes," he said, looking around. I tried to read his face.

"Everything as it was," I said, "apart from the fact that there's no bedding on the bed and I don't have any spare here. Bugger, I'd forgotten."

"Don't worry," he said, "I'll ring for a cab."

"Look, just share with me."

"No, Sam, I-"

"It's not as though we haven't shared before."

"OK, thank you," he said.

We stripped to our underwear and climbed into my bed. Maybe an awkward silence as we did so. Maybe just a silence.

The rain continued to beat down at the window.

"I love being in bed when it's raining outside," I said.

"Sam"?

"Yes? ... For God's sake, Davey, the suspense is killing me."

"I..."

At that second, I moved. One of those funny little moves we do that are half stretch, half involuntary twitch. It took me a centimetre toward him so that we were just touching. So many impulses were triggered as the heat surged through me, so many recently buried feelings, so many newly- discovered ones, I thought I might catch fire. I tried to understand this new part of Davey that I had previously failed to recognise or maybe, just pretended, wasn't there. Perhaps I had just been too young...

"I love you, Sam." he said.

"Well, I love you too."

"I want to be with you."

"Well, you will be as long as you don't piss me off again."

"No, I don't mean that. I mean *with* you."

"*With* me?"

"Together; in this house."

"That's a great idea. You can have your old room."

"No Sam, I don't want my old room. I want this room to be *our* room. Look, I know this scares you, but I lost you before when I kept quiet; I *can't* lose you again. I'm sorry that I'm being so blunt, but I *have* to say this and I have to say it before we slip back into our old routine."

He raised himself onto his elbow and, with his free hand, touched my face.

"I think it's time you grew up, Sam. I'm not saying we have to change the love we had for each other as kids. I'm just saying we need to keep that and add to it."

He leant into me and rested his forehead on mine.

"I want us to be together for the rest of our lives."

"I don't know, Davey. I mean, I want... I just don't know. You've felt like this for fifteen years, but for me... well, you were everything to me; everything apart from... I don't know what I am. I'm not sure what's happened to me. I love you, God knows, but..."

"Sssh," he said, "it's alright. Get your life back together again, then think about it. Take as long as you like. And, Sam, don't worry if the answer is no."

We slept.

In the morning my frog vomited and, as per our eighteen year-old selves, we woke wrapped up in each other.

Throwing back the covers, I leapt out of bed.

"Right, shower, then something to eat," I said.

Davey made us breakfast in order, he said, to 'save us both food poisoning later in the day'. I threw toast at him.

As we pulled up outside his flat, he said:

"Thanks for the lift, Sam. Have a good training session."

"Davey," I said.

"Yes?"

"I'm going to think about this quickly, you know."

"You don't have to."

"No, I want to. You're right, I need to grow up. I'm going to spend the whole day thinking about it. Just... well, don't hate me if the answer is..."

"I will never hate you, Sam."

"How about we meet tomorrow afternoon?"

"OK."

"Coffee?"

"No. There's a travelling fair on Clapham Common. I'll meet you at the entrance at 3 o'clock. It will be less dramatic than a face-off in a cafe."

After training and lunch with Andrius, who was meeting Susie that evening for dinner, ('Thank God you like poetry', I'd said. 'Why'? He'd asked. 'You'll find out', I said) I went back to mine and Thomas', rang the management company of the flat in Highgate and gave a month's notice, then sat myself in Thomas' chair to think.

The thinking had lasted all of two minutes when my phone rang.

"Bugger," I said. "Hello?"

"Sammy, how are you?"

It was the England boss.

"Very well thanks, boss. And you?"

"Terrific, thank you. As you know, we've got a friendly against Nigeria in two weeks. You're in the squad. I'd like you to report for training a week on Monday. You know the drill."

"But, boss... you mean... even after..."

"Even after your impressive display against Serbia? Yes, even after that."

After the call, I ran around the room twice and jumped up and down like an idiot. Then, when I had remembered that I was actually an adult, I turned my phone off, resumed Thomas' seat and promptly couldn't concentrate for the life of me.

"Thomas, help me," I said.

But after half an hour of attempting to work out who I was and how that fitted in with Davey, my brain had turned to soup.

So I picked up one of the books from the shelves. One of mine amongst the thousands of Thomas'.

I held it on my lap, aimlessly turning the pages in an attempt to prevent a complete shutdown of my mental faculties. And there, halfway through the book, was a piece of paper hidden between two pages, with a quotation in Thomas' immaculate hand. A quotation I knew so well because I had used it so often:

If you spend too much time analysing life, there's no time left to live it.

DECISION (Epilogue)

So here I am; half an hour early, as usual; waiting at the entrance to the fair for Davey to arrive. Still unsure; still deliberating; still hopeless, but hoping not to be.

I can hear the squeals of the children. The innocent, uninhibited shrieks of fear and excitement drenching the fairground. And I'm telling them in my head never to lose that feeling.

Because I'm experiencing that same fear and excitement; that fight or flight dichotomy that makes life what it is. How dull it would be if we knew the ending.

I have come to the conclusion that there are another two categories of people. Those who take the book of their life and live each page, experience each line and learn from the good chapters as well as the bad. And there are those who immediately turn to the last page to find out the outcome so that the rest of the book becomes meaningless.

Now I can see him, walking up the South Common road, early for once. His body absorbing the sun of this warm spring afternoon. And I see that we have both opted for 501's and grey T-shirts, though his buttoned sweater is blue to my black.

"Hi," he says.

"Hey," I say.

We pay our £5 entrance fee and become children again.

"Let's go on the waltzers," he says.

"No!" I say.

"Why?"

"They scare me."

"What?! You've played football in front of ninety thousand people. How can you be scared by waltzers?"

"It's the round and round motion. It makes me go wobbly."

"Gosh, you're such a girl sometimes."

We go on them anyway. And I scream; like a girl.

"Candy Floss?" he says.

"Sam Hatchington," I say, offering my hand, "nice to meet you, Miss Floss."

He grabs me in a headlock and pretends to punch me. Some little children are watching and scream delightedly at the naughty adults mucking about.

"So, is that your porn name?" I ask.

"No, your porn name is an amalgamation of your first pet's name and the street you were born on."

"So, what *is* your porn name?" I ask.

"I never had a pet," he says.

I put my arm on his shoulder.

"And yours?" he asks.

"Er... Kenny Baxter. Kenny the hamster and Baxter Road."

"How awfully neutral. Not much of a porn star. Sounds like he has a bit of a beer belly and a two-inch penis."

I wrestle him to the ground.

We have a go at shooting ducks and I'm pretty good at it, as it turns out and I win a big, beige teddy bear.

"Just don't give it to me," Davey says, "it'll be like a scene from *Grease*."

"No way," I say, "I'm not playing Olivia Newton-John."

"Again," he says. "So, what are you going to call him?"

"Thomas," I say, "and he's half yours."

Then, for some unknown reason, I burst into the chorus, complete with dance routine:

'Go, Greased Lightning, you're burning up the heat lap trials, Greased lightning, uh-oh, Greased lightning'.

"Please stop," Davey says.

"Am I embarrassing you?"

"No, you've just got an awful singing voice."

I make Thomas punch him in the arm

We walk around this fairground, the remnant of more innocent times and I'm happy, energised, buzzing like a mad-arsed bumble bee at a summer window.

We win at the coconut shy and give our coconut to a little girl who is crying. We lose at quoits, badly; we go on the big wheel, because it doesn't scare me... until we get to the top.

As we are getting off, two guys are coming up to me.

"Hi, Sam... it *is* Sam, isn't it?"

"Yes," I say and we shake hands. "Oh, this is Davey." And they shake hands.

"I'm Craig and this is my boyfriend, Luke. We just wanted to say thank you. You're an amazingly brave guy to do what you've done."

"Erm, well, it's my pleasure," I say and they smile and move off before I can go into full stuttering mode.

We end up on the dodgems, crashing into each other, into everyone; laughing, exchanging one-liners with eight year-old kids, with eighty year-old grandmothers.

"That was such fun," I say.

"It was OK," he says.

"OK?! Stop trying to be cool."

"I *am* cool. I is well street, innit," he says, mimicking the hand movements that the teenagers do.

"More like cul-de-sac," I say.

He grabs the teddy and pretends to storm off.

"Thomas and I are not speaking to you," he says.

I laugh and a waft of breeze simultaneously blows our fringes up into the air.

"Would you like an ice-cream?" he says.

Suddenly the world has stopped; all movement frozen in time. And I know what the ice cream signifies. I know that I have to make the decision now.

The moment runs through me like an electric shock and a thousand *maybe's* spark another thousand *what if's*.

Because I know that if I accept the ice cream, I accept Davey. That I admit this total love. Not just the spiritual, unbreakable, wordless love that has always existed between us, but a sexual love as well. And I know that this will mean an admittance of a sexuality, until recently, unknown to me. That Alex was not just a dalliance, but a precursor to the real thing. Until a year ago I'd never positively wanted to have sex with another man (though, if someone had asked me, who knows what I would have said?). But this would mean changing me. Or would it? Maybe it would just mean using a piece of me I'd never used before; not turning to the last page. I know that I love Davey *ultimately* because, how do we know what degree of love we feel unless we have something to compare it to. And the thought of lying in bed with him, throwing toast at him, texting him my daily thoughts when we weren't together, lying in his arms when we were, letting this absolute love flood over me as mine flooded over him, is making me faint, making me happy, making me almost strong enough to leave the fear behind.

And if I don't accept it? What then? I continue to live, to move forward. I find happiness somewhere else; with someone else, some*ones* else. I keep Davey as my friend, he said that; but in a different capacity; because we have come all this way only to go back a step. But I could have a girlfriend, a wife, children, happy convention. And I *would* be happy. I would make it happen.

But would I be happi*est*?

In fifty years' time, sitting in my old chair, watching some ravaged autumn evening turn into night, reliving the smiles and falls of my footballing youth, would Davey appear to me in some wind-blown dream, standing tall and beautiful, like the perfect statue of what could have been.

So I look at him, falling mentally into those apprehensive, expectant eyes, and thoughts that have smashed around my body like a pinball machine suddenly stop; and the answer becomes clear; as, I believe, it has always been clear.

"It had better have raspberry sauce on it," I say.

And those eyes open wider, tear-glazed and smiling, and all the suffering of the previous weeks is swallowed up and disappears forever.

"One thing before you buy it, though."

We're a little way from the fair now. There is a tree just behind him. I take Thomas from his arms and gently sit him on the grass; then I cradle Davey's shoulders and lean him against the tree. And, as his arms envelop me, bringing me against him and so completing the final two centimetres of my journey, all need for self-analysis ends, and my fifteen year-old self joins with the Me of now.

The kiss that follows lasts for twenty-three eternal seconds, and this tiny, colossal moment takes me to a new page in my life; one that is printed, not sketched in pencil.

"Look," I say, "forget the ice-cream; let's just go home."

Davey picks up Thomas and the three of us begin to meander our way through the fairground. He takes my hand, and the sun blazes the path of our future.

ABOUT THE AUTHOR

David began writing in 2007 whilst on a break from acting. He has written five plays: *The Moon Is Halfway To Heaven, 20:40, Save Your Kisses For Me, Gay Pride And No Prejudice,* and *Murder on the terrace.* He has also adapted several novels for the theatre, including: *Billionaire Boy, Mr Stink, Ratburger, Pride and Prejudice, The Secret Garden, Dracula* and *Peter Pan.* This is his first novel. Originally from Leicester, David now lives in Muswell Hill with a washing machine that looks like Darth Vader.

Lightning Source UK Ltd.
Milton Keynes UK
UKOW06f2007220817

307774UK00010B/744/P